Legends and Lore

*To Brian,
I literally don't know what to write here. I hope you enjoy it!
♡ Alyson Grauer*

An Anthology of Mythic Proportions

LEGENDS AND LORE

R. M. Ridley • Alyson Grauer • Sarah Hunter Hyatt
Lance Schonberg • M. K. Wiseman • Danielle E. Shipley
Sarah E. Seeley • A. F. Stewart • Emma Michaels

The Brother-Sister Fable, © 2014 Alyson Grauer
Faelad, © 2014 Sarah Hunter Hyatt
By Skyfall, © 2014 Emma Michaels
Charon's Obol, © 2014 R. M. Ridley
Peradventure, © 2014 Sarah E. Seeley
Natural Order, © 2014 Lance Schonberg
Two Spoons, © 2014 Danielle E. Shipley
Grail Days, © 2014 A. F. Stewart
Downward Mobility, © 2014 M. K. Wiseman

No part of this publication may be reproduced, stored in a retrieval system or transmitted in any form or by any means, electronic or mechanical, including photocopying, recording, or otherwise, without written permission from the publisher. For information visit www.xchylerpublishing.com

This is a work of fiction. Names, descriptions, entities, and incidents included in this story are products of the authors' imaginations. Any resemblance to actual persons, events, and entities is entirely coincidental.

Xchyler Publishing
an imprint of Hamilton Springs Press, LLC
Penny Freeman, Editor-in-chief
www.xchylerpublishing.com

1st Edition: October, 2014

Cover and Interior Design by D. Robert Pease, walkingstickbooks.com
Edited by Penny Freeman and Kristina Harris

Published in the United States of America
Xchyler Publishing

TABLE OF CONTENTS

FOREWORD	i
THE BROTHER-SISTER FABLE by Alyson Grauer	1
CHARON'S OBOL by R. M. Ridley	33
GRAIL DAYS by A. F. Stewart	77
NATURAL ORDER by Lance Schonberg	116
PERADVENTURE by Sarah E. Seeley	143
DOWNWARD MOBILITY by M. K. Wiseman	190
BY SKYFALL by Emma Michaels	219
FAELAD by Sarah Hunter Hyatt	262
TWO SPOONS by Danielle E. Shipley	317

FOREWORD

The Post-modern Man has long since abandoned the notion of supernatural forces influencing our day-to-day lives; of omnipotent beings with power to determine our destinies. We are far too intelligent to embrace the superstitions of the past. We are independent, free-willed creatures, forging our own paths, making our own choices. Our victories are our own, as are our mistakes.

However, for some, their persistent faith in the ancient wisdoms remains undaunted. They assure us this world—and others—contain far more wonders than mere human eyes see or modern minds comprehend. In this anthology, our authors explore the consequences should the reality of myth and legend confront today's mortal.

When we are forced to admit that powers beyond our comprehension surround and affect us, we experience a paradigm shift, and nothing will ever be the same.

THE BROTHER SISTER FABLE

by Alyson Grauer

Once upon a time, there was a family that lived in a white house on the edge of a great and winding wood. There was a mother and a father, of course, and a daughter and a son. The trees behind their house blended into a forest uneven from the rocky ground it grew upon. The little mountain that rose even higher beyond the wood confounded bicycles and cars alike, allowing only for travelers on foot to pass over its peak.

When the summer's bright green canopy began to fade, the trees gained their true dress of fall as only trees in New England can, transforming into a vast mural of aging gold and crimson, flame-bright orange, and pale butter yellow. Their ordinary, leafy, verdant uniform was just a placeholder for the luxurious garb of autumn. It was this time of year that the light breezes of summer's end changed, too, growing cooler against the warmth of dying days, and as the leaves changed, the mystery winds began to blow.

Every year, when the mystery winds began to blow, the children felt their hearts turn toward the mountain, though they never knew why. It was the way springtime inspires some folks to travel or try new things, or the way New Year's instructs adults to rewrite their goals and begin new challenges. That was the way of it, but there was no challenge, no inspiration, just a cool, dark, strange need to look up at the mountain at night, and to listen to the mystery winds in the trees.

Every Hallow's Eve, the children of the neighborhood would spend the evening in elaborate costumes, going from house to house as children do on that holiday, asking for candy. Then they would turn homeward again, parading proudly back to their beds to count their stash like greedy little dragons with their hoards. This ceremonial begging and masquerading marked the ending of the mystery winds' time to blow. Soon after that, the frost of winter wound its way down from the mountain, stripping the leaves and putting the trees to silence.

Each year, everything would repeat again: the leaves would turn their colors, the mystery winds would blow, and after the harvest moon and All Hallow's Eve, the frosts came and erased the world away.

Now, this brother and sister who lived with their parents in the white house at the foot of the mountain were much like any other children in the neighborhood. They often ventured into the woods of their backyard and found the deer trails to wander. They knew which berries were good and which were poison, and they knew that chewing on twigs from a mint bush was far better than stealing gum from the store. They knew that sitting still in the crux of a birch tree was the best place for you to actually see the birds that were singing, and hear the trees talking.

For many years, the brother—who was younger than his sister—was silent. He was a somber child, reluctant to speak aloud. Where the brother chose to observe and follow, his sister chose to step forward and lead. The sister was much occupied by her own imagination and did not often step down from her intellectual heights to play with her own brother. Even though they weren't close, she usually kept an eye on him and defended him from bullies if needed. The sister had friends that she would run the deer paths with, or build things from sticks and stones in the sandy patches of dirt, and the brother found other boys to play with in the area, although none of them were as quiet as he was.

One day, the brother went off with some neighbor boys into the woods, simply to take a walk. It soon became a lengthy and lonely hike, however, and they wandered all afternoon on the lower parts of the mountain until one of the boys finally acknowledged that they were probably quite lost.

"I think we've lost the path," said Jake.

"No, we haven't lost it," replied Kyle, the elder of the two. "We just left it back there." He pointed into the woods.

The quiet brother stayed quiet.

The boys stood looking around and around, as though at any minute a sign would appear to point them homeward.

"We should stay here until someone comes to get us," said Jake.

"There's no one looking for us, stupid. No, we have to find our own way home." Kyle shook his head firmly. "I'm going this way."

"No, don't!" Jake cried. "Mom said if we ever got lost to just stay in one place!" The brother nodded his own head in agreement, and Jake pointed at him. "See? He agrees with me."

Kyle rolled his eyes. "She meant that in the city, dummy. Like at the mall or on a field trip or something. Not in the woods."

The brother thought he saw something in the trees—a dark shape far off on the hill above them. He did not say anything, but stared at it, waiting for it to move again.

"Mom said stay put," whined Jake.

"Stay here, then! Be a baby. See if I care." Kyle stomped off into the woods, winding his way back toward where he thought the houses were. Jake called his name several more times before Kyle vanished completely, and it was just Jake and the brother standing on the crunchy dead leaves.

They walked on until they found a rock to sit on, and sat there for what felt like hours, until at last Jake stood up.

"We should have gone with Kyle," he said angrily. "You should have said something!"

The brother stared past Jake into the trees. The afternoon light was beginning to cast longer shadows now, and the warmth of the day was fading. The dark shape up on the hill was still there. Jake followed the brother's gaze.

"What are you looking at?" he demanded. "There's nothing there."

The brother pointed toward the thing on the hill, but Jake crossed his arms angrily and turned his back to the trees.

"You're a dummy. And a scaredy cat. I'm going home now."

The brother furrowed his brow, worried at this.

"Don't you ever talk? Stupid!" Jake began to walk away.

Something big crunched in the woods behind them, like a large branch being snapped from a tree. Both boys looked at each other and froze, the unspoken question written on their faces: *What in the world was that?*

"I can't just sit here anymore," Jake stammered. "I gotta find Kyle." He bolted away without looking back, and the little brother was left alone on the boulder, wondering how long until dark, or until the black shadow on the hill came for him. He fell asleep on the rock, like Rip Van Winkle, and let the trees whisper around him in the slanting sunlight.

In this version of the tale, both Jake and Kyle found their way home after more walking through the woods, arriving with scraped knees and messy tears staining their frightened faces. The little brother did not return. Hours had gone by when the sister came into the house and her mother asked where her brother was.

"I don't know," said the sister, with a shrug. "I was climbing trees with Sarah."

The father came into the house, and the mother asked him where the brother was.

"I don't know," said the father, with a frown. "I was in town at the bookshop."

The mother put a hand to her head and thought very hard about where the brother could be, and then she and the father went out of the house to ask the neighbors if they had seen the brother. The sister sat on the front porch, waiting, certain that her quiet little brother would turn up any minute covered in dirt and grass stains. She watched as her parents and the other adults in the neighborhood searched the backyards, walking back and forth from house to house. She watched the fathers running their hands over their heads worriedly and the mothers pressing their palms to their mouths in soundless distress.

The sister waited at the door of their white house for many hours, unable to comprehend what had happened. She saw her parents panicking and crying, and watched the policemen come and go, asking questions and going out into the woods with dogs to look. The sister was deeply unnerved by this disappearance, and knew that something was amiss. Something was wrong. He must still be out there. He must be coming home. But the brother did not return that night, and the police did not find him with their dogs and searchlights.

That night, as the sister lay awake in bed wondering where her brother was, she heard the wolves come down from the hill, their howls and yips growing louder and louder. She got up and went to the window, peeping through the sheer curtains, and saw the lean, shaggy canines tumbling and chasing each other in the street outside the house.

They sound like they're making fun of someone, the sister thought. *Like a gang of bullies on the playground. Neener, neener, neener.* The sister had a disturbing idea then. *What if they know what happened to my brother? What if they were there?*

One of the wolves snapped its head up and stared at her in the dark, the dim light from the streetlamp reflecting eerily in its eyes. It parted its lips, baring sharp teeth, and panted in an unsettling smile. Several other wolves looked over at her, too, their eyes gleaming, their grins amused.

The sister shut the curtains again and went back to bed, hot tears of confusion spilling down her cheeks. *What if he never comes back?* She dreamed that night about the mountain, saw it stretching higher and farther away from her, and in her dream she could not remember her brother's face.

Years passed, and the leaves changed and fell away again. The mystery winds blew, the harvest moon rose like an enormous will-o'-the-wisp over the mountain, and the snows came. The bears lumbered through the backyards, the deer passed by, and the wolves played in the street at night, laughing at the fear of the neighbors.

The parents were never quite the same after the brother disappeared. The mother was stricken with grief and threw herself into her work, and the father grew somber and stoic, rarely laughing or smiling. The sister grew older, and the world became more complicated, but as she grew, she held the truth in her heart.

He's still out there, she thought. *I have to wait for him to come home again.*

The neighbors frowned as autumn came each year, warning their children against wandering too far out of sight. It wasn't just the animals that came down from the mountain at night, but it was a fear of something bigger and darker that led hikers astray and never let them go.

The sister grew older still, and she was not afraid of the mystery winds or the great harvest moon. When the wolves yipped and howled at night, she would spring from her bed and run to the window to catch a glimpse of them. She would meet their gleaming stares with her own hard gaze, and she would scowl until they were out of sight. More than once, she found a bear in the backyard, simply sitting and passing the time, and each time the bear saw her, it would gather itself off and lumber away to the woods again in silence. She would often spot a doe or a buck on the hillside, in the trees, and she would stare back at it until it bounded away in the blink of an eye.

When the shimmering colors of autumn had at last overtaken the final sprig of jade in the trees, the sister stood in the backyard one evening listening to the birds. There had been a rainstorm, and they shrieked and chattered and sang so noisily that she could bear it no longer. The words bubbled out of her before she could stop them: "I am not afraid. I'm going to find him. I will find my brother." The birds stopped singing at the words, but did not fly away, and the sister went inside again, feeling the birds' eyes watching as she went. Even though she had said it aloud, uncertainty brewed in her mind. Where would she go? Where would she look? How could she possibly find him, after others had tried and failed?

Just before she closed the back door behind her, the sister drew a deep breath of the still-warm night air. There was a faintly familiar smell on the wind, and she paused to dredge her memory for it. She stepped outside and inhaled again. The birds erupted from the trees and took to the sky, the only sounds the beating of their wings and the breeze through the leaves of the trees. The scent of the air and the peculiar feeling that she should look up to the mountain were equally familiar and unsettling: it was the first mystery wind of the season, ten years after her brother had vanished.

The wind blew around her, growing in strength and speed, and the leaves above her rattled like broken toys, fluttering and flapping. The sister turned her eyes up to the mountain, watching the trees bend and shift. The mystery winds had to come from somewhere on the mountain. That was what the kids always said to each other: *it's up there*. The sister was older now, but remembered the shrewdness of her childhood, and felt that the moment was suddenly right. Instead of turning toward home, she began to walk up the hill, into the woods, and to the mountain where the mystery winds blew.

It was darker and darker the higher and farther she went, but she did not stop and did not question. She climbed over rocks and ducked under low branches, moved through thickets and around streams. She did not step within fairy circles of little mushrooms and did not touch the trees with shining bark, avoiding their sap. She moved without faltering, pushing onward without burden, and soon she knew she was surely lost, deep within the forest. It would have been impossible to say where precisely she was, but she knew that the mystery winds were blowing, and it was the time to find out where they came from and where her brother had gone.

Hours and hours she walked and never stopped to rest or consider her direction. She was like an arrow, fired sure and straight, and she never stumbled. At last, she reached a very narrow tall place, where there was a rock too large to walk around or past. She would have to climb it, and climb it she did, finding footholds and handholds in the dark, like an animal herself.

She pulled herself up, her limbs aching in protest, and finally reached the top of the great point, covered in moss and lichen. She stood up, slowly, and found that she was above the trees now, where the moon shone down through the clouds. She stretched her arms above her head, wanting to relieve the soreness from the climb, and looked out across the forest and the mountainside beyond the rock.

It was peaceful in the dark, and she drew a deep breath of the night air. The mystery winds shivered through her, whispering and calling and pulling at her heart to go, to move forward. She could almost feel someone watching her, and a warm breath on the back of her neck . . . or was that part real? The sister flinched and turned to look, and she was face to face with an enormous black bear, silent and staring.

The sister nearly screamed, but her voice caught in her throat. She was paralyzed with fear. She knew that being this close to a bear was perhaps the most dangerous proximity she could have to any wild beast on the mountain. Her mind raced as she tried to remember what one was supposed to do when surprised by a bear. All she could remember was that if you ran in a zig-zag shape, bears had a hard time following and would probably get confused and fall behind.

Run in a zig-zag, the sister thought. *Or is that a myth?*

Her legs turned to jelly as the bear opened its mouth and she saw the gleam of huge teeth in the moonlight. A faint noise began to rumble out of the bear's mouth. She staggered back and spun away, running as fast as she could. She swerved this way and that, thinking of the zig-zag shape, but then there was no more space to run on the hilltop.

She stumbled, trying to stop before she reached the steep edge on the far side. She toppled sideways and slid like a baseball player, and then stopped quite short. One foot dangled just over the side of the cliff—at least a fifty-foot drop below. She looked back sharply. The bear was standing over her, one gigantic paw pressed down, pinning her jacket to the ground as firmly as stone.

The sister panted, trembling all over, and the black bear grunted as though it might laugh at her. Then it leaned closer and pulled its other paw across her body, rolling her back from the edge of the cliff.

When she was at last lying on her back a safe distance away from the sudden drop, the sister breathed hard to catch up with her racing heart.

"Thank you," she stammered aloud. She did not know if the bear would understand. She looked at her scraped palms and saw her hands tremble. "Thank you for saving me."

The bear sat down on its hind legs like a dog and stared down at her. It did not seem interested in attacking, or even inspecting her further. It seemed calm, almost as if it had been expecting to meet her here.

"I'm sorry I got startled," the sister said, and then felt silly for saying it aloud to a huge bear. But the bear gave a little huff of air through its nostrils, and the sister felt as though it was telling her not to worry about it.

"Were you waiting for me?" she asked. Her heart still pounded in her chest.

The bear nodded its big head. The sister felt both exhilarated and terrified. *What kind of bear can understand English?* She was surprised, but hope welled inside of her. She had to try.

"I'm looking for someone, my—"

The bear nodded again before she had even formed the rest of the question.

"You already know why I'm here." She swallowed back her nerves and drew a deep breath. "Are you my brother?" asked the sister. "Brother bear?"

The bear blinked at her, then lowered its head in apology. It was not her brother.

"No? All right. It was worth asking, anyway." The sister let out a shaky breath, both disappointed and relieved that her brother had not become a bear. "Do you know where he is?" she asked, determined, but not frightened.

The bear turned and looked over its shoulder down the mountainside. The trees were tall and full of shadows, but the sister did not see anything there, no immediate signs of life or civilization.

"That way?"

The bear got to its feet slowly and gave a low grunt that ended in a huffing sigh, then began to walk away. The sister got to her feet and followed without hesitating. They walked together for some time, the bear and the girl. The woods were lit dimly by the moon, and the air was quiet, except for the occasional ripple of the mystery winds through the trees. Gradually, it grew darker, as the moon rose higher and the trees grew thicker and fuller.

At last the bear stopped, and the sister nearly collided with it in the dark. The bear looked back at her, eyes shining, and then looked ahead, pointing with its nose. The sister looked past the bear and saw that some hundred yards away was a magnificent stag. His antlers were newly sharpened, gleaming ivory in a patch of moonlight, and he stood staring at them like a statue in the dark.

The bear nudged her with its big dark snout, and she jumped a little.

"Another guide?" she asked. The bear nodded. "Thank you for helping me," she said, and the bear sat down to wait and watch.

The sister looked at the stag and hesitated. *This is not what I expected,* she thought as she moved beyond the bear. She slowly made her way across to the deer, who watched her, his ears swiveling as she came nearer. The stag did not seem upset by the bear's presence, nor by the sister's closeness. He simply stood still and looked at her with deep dark eyes, his nostrils flaring. His fur grew thick like a mane about his neck and chest, tangled with burrs and leaves and little tendrils from the forest.

"You know who I am?" the sister asked the stag. He dipped his nose down once in a nod. "Then you know what I seek. Are you my brother?" The stag scythed his strong antlers in a curve over his head, then looked down at her again, and the sister knew it was not her brother. "Please," she whispered. "It's been so many years. I have to know. Where is my brother?"

The deer turned away from her and looked further down the path, into the darker part of the forest. The sister did not see anyone waiting for her there, but she looked carefully, peering into the darkness. She could feel herself being watched, and felt the breaths of things unseen in the trees and underbrush. She walked cautiously forward, but she was not afraid. The deer came with her, walking patiently by her side in the dark.

The sister glanced back, wondering if the bear would come, too, but they had already gone too far; the bear was out of sight. As she turned to look ahead, she caught a glimpse of glowing eyes in the dark. She stopped to look, but the eyes vanished. The sister almost asked the stag if he'd seen the eyes, but as the stag did not seem to be able speak, she did not bother.

They walked on in silence, but a feeling of unease grew within her with each step they took. She glanced up at the tall stag in the dark and, once, she thought she saw the ivory bone of his slender skull gleam in the moonlight, crowned with his mighty antlers curving toward the sky. She blinked in surprise and saw once more the shaggy dark fur about his neck and the flicker of his slender ears.

Calm down, she told herself. *You're imagining things.*

They traveled in quiet, the stag and the girl. She kept her gaze forward, stealing glances out of the corners of her vision, fretting about the eyes she thought she'd seen, but there was nothing there. Nothing but trees and darkness.

Something heavy shifted in the trees behind them, and the stag stopped walking.

"What is it?" the sister whispered. The stag's ears swiveled in the dark, his eyes darting back and forth. The sister listened, but heard nothing. Not even the mystery winds disrupted the silence, and the sister felt that even her own heartbeat was suddenly hushed.

The stag tentatively lifted a hoof to take a single step onward. A branch snapped, and the stag nearly jumped out of his own skin, whirling about and nearly knocking the sister to the ground.

Three pairs of those glowing eyes were moving through the trees behind them, yellow and perfectly round and pupilless. They moved swiftly, racing toward them as though they did not need to navigate the rocky terrain or dodge the trees. As they swept nearer, the wind picked up again, rattling and shuffling the leaves on the ground.

The inky, bulbous shadows attached to the eyes were massive, bigger even than the bear had been. The sister could not make out what precisely they were, or whether they even had legs or faces, but those lightbulb-yellow eyes were empty and fixed on her.

"What are they?" the sister cried. The stag made an angry, frightened sound. He scythed his antlers again, kicking his legs at the leaves as the wind began to whine past them. "What do they want?"

The stag turned and bowed low, dipping his head, and the sister did not hesitate: she grasped the base of one of the ivory antlers and swung herself up onto the stag's shaggy, forest-tangled shoulders. Then he broke into a run, faster than she had imagined, and she held tight to his thick mane, squeezing her legs against his sides.

The stag ran hard, leaping over stones and fallen trees, never looking back, and whatever trail they had been following before was lost now. The hulking shadows howled with voices like the wind, giving chase and reaching with dark tendrils to try and catch them. The stag's powerful legs carried the sister forward, and the wind whipped at them as fiercely as if they had been flying instead of fleeing. The sister clung to the stag's neck, breathless and white-knuckled.

What happens if they catch us? she thought, and shut her eyes tightly against the wind.

Then, another voice joined the howling shadow-creatures. Sharp, hearty yips and snarls filled the air, and the sister looked back. Wolves came hurtling out of the woods, tongues lolling from open grins of sharp, white teeth. They raced toward the black shadows, lunging and snapping, tails held high. One inky creature turned its yellow eyes on the wolves and swiped a thick, paw-like limb at them. The wolves dodged and danced out of reach. The mocking voices began to multiply as more and more of the wild canines came streaming out of the dark.

The sister almost laughed in relief as one of the giant dark shadows toppled over, disoriented by the wolves running circles around it. The stag's quick legs carried them farther and farther away, and the sister saw the hollow eyes blink shut into darkness as the wolves swarmed over the shadows.

The stag began to slow once they were out of sight, his sides heaving and his nostrils flaring.

"Thank you," the sister told him. Her hands shook as she stroked the wiry fur. "Thank you for saving me."

The stag huffed a breath of relief and flicked his ears back and forth, walking more slowly to catch his breath.

"Are we very far off from where you were taking me?" The sister looked around and saw how tall the trees had become, how thick the smaller bushes and bracken grew in this part of the wood. "It would have taken us a long time to get this far if we'd only been walking," she observed.

The stag flicked his ears again and shook his head.

"Is my brother an animal now?" She hoped not, but at least if she knew that much, she could maybe find a way to bring him home, and cope.

The stag gazed at her with what she thought might be sadness, but before the sister could ask another question, a branch above her rustled in the dark. She looked up, and swallowed back a cry of amazement.

There were large, predatory birds perched all around her—owls and small kites and large hawks alike. They gazed down at her with their intelligent eyes, and she stood still.

"Where is my brother?" she asked them. A red-tailed hawk, the largest of the lot, moved to another branch, flashing his red tail feathers at her. He tilted his head and flew farther along, leading the way.

The sister hesitated, looking back at the stag. The great deer was still panting from their run, but he lowered his head in acknowledgement. She nodded in return. "Thank you," she said again, then turned to follow the hawk.

She felt the eyes of the other birds watching her and, although their numbers were intimidating, their presence was somehow comforting. They remained where they were in the canopy as she left them behind and let the hawk lead her. She imagined they were having some sort of meeting or conference, so stoic had their gazes been. Wondering what they could be discussing, this council of birds, she walked on in silence. Gradually, her pulse slowed to normal and her breathing became regular again.

"Thank you for guiding me," the sister called softly to the hawk somewhere above her. "I'm looking for my brother."

The hawk did not respond. She went on silently for a time, and tried again.

"I know it probably isn't so," she said, "but I have to ask. Are you my brother?"

There was no answer. She felt a little worried by this and squinted up into the trees.

"Hawk?" She stopped walking and looked around in concern. "Are you there?"

The sister was completely alone except for the mystery winds that blew from time to time. She hoped that nothing bad had befallen the hawk, and hoped even more that it would return to guide her if she lingered long enough. The wind was soft, coaxing, and cold. She pulled her jacket around her, shivering, and listened to the darkness.

There was a tiny sound from a few feet behind her, something like a polite cough. It startled her, but the sister held her ground.

"Where is my brother?" the sister asked, without turning around.

"I can take you to him." The voice was like the quiet darkness of a hiding place in a closed closet, or under a bed. There were soft footsteps, and leaves rustled on the ground as the owner of the voice came quietly around to face the sister. She found it difficult to see him, as in a dream, where the moment you look directly at something, it vanishes.

"Who are you?" she asked, curious.

"I belong to him," said the voice, as if it was a stupid question.

"What are you?" asked the sister.

"I don't know," replied the voice honestly. "But I'm his. And if you want to find him, I can bring you there."

Uncertainty shivered through the sister. The animals had guided her, kept her safe, and they had not spoken a single word.

This speaker didn't know what he was, and she couldn't even see him clearly enough to guess at it herself. She was alone in the place where the mystery winds came from. She worried what might happen if she tried to turn back now.

The sister did not voice her doubts. Instead, she said, "Please bring me to my brother."

"Come this way," said the voice kindly, and something that felt like a hand took hold of hers and led her forward in the dark. She could no longer see by the moon, but she felt the eyes of hundreds of animals around her in the dark; at least, she suspected they were animals. They may not have been.

She walked for some time, led by the unseen voice with an unseen hand, through the dark that got deeper and darker with every step on the hard ground carpeted with the crackling leaves. The sister began to wonder if this were a dream, and if she had never climbed the mountain at all.

Then she saw light.

The light up ahead was orange-yellow, warm and promising, and so she felt relieved to see it at last. They reached a clearing, and the light was not a fire as she had thought it to be, but a tall lantern on a lamppost in the woods. It was ornate and black iron, and the light inside was not a candle or light bulb or a gas fire: it was simply light, glowing and unyielding. There were trees lit all around by this light, and the sister looked around.

"Where are we?" she asked her guide, who could sort of be seen now and looked kind of like a person's shadow, rather than an actual person. He was tall and thin, with prominent ears and a somber tilt to his head.

"The front gate," he said, as if it was the only logical answer.

Then something truly wonderful happened, and the sister did not know how to understand exactly what it was. The shadowy guide led her toward a gap between two trees, off to one side, where the light did not shine, and they stepped into the darkness itself. When they emerged on the other side (though the other side of what, she did not know), they were in what looked like a small town. The trees were infinitely tall, winding cobblestone streets spread out before her, and there were people everywhere.

The sister stared for a moment in disbelief. The road was normal cobblestone, and the people were normal-looking and real and well-dressed. Everyone about the place paused what they were doing to raise their hands in greeting as she was led forward by her guide, who looked less like a shadow and more like a skinny man in dark clothing now.

The sister was amazed, and she was certainly a little nervous, but still she was not afraid. "Where are we?" she asked, but he did not answer.

The guide led her through the meandering streets of this strange town, and people everywhere smiled genuinely and looked amazed and joyful to see her. It was not the eerie false joy of a nightmare, she thought, but genuine curiosity and pleasure to observe her presence. It was very strange.

At last, the guide found their way to a fountain in the town square, and people were bustling into the streets to see whatever was about to happen. Her guide let go of her hand, and the sister felt suddenly quite anxious.

"Here," said her dark guide, stepping back from her as though to make room. "Here is where your brother is."

"I don't see him," said the sister, looking around at the other faces.

"He's here," answered the guide, with certainty.

"What's all this?" asked a bristly man nearby, gesturing to the sister. "Brought us another one?"

The guide shook his head politely. "Not exactly. This is his sister."

A ripple of concern and acknowledgement rushed through the crowds of people around her. The sister craned her neck, searching for her brother anywhere in the mass of people.

"His sister?" The man's jaw dropped. "How did she—"

"How did I find this place?" interrupted the sister, with her eyebrows raised. "I felt the mystery winds begin to blow, and I followed them here."

"You could not have made it this far without help," pressed a woman to her right, her smile bright, but a little forced. "Surely you had help?"

"The animals showed me the way, and this . . . guide brought me the last leg of the journey. I have come to find my brother." This was met with more murmuring and wide-eyed shaking of heads.

"Your brother died," declared a voice in the crowd.

The sister turned, shocked by the words, and for a moment, she faltered.

"No, he didn't," she replied. Her hands balled into fists as she tried to stay calm.

"Your brother got eaten by bears," insisted another voice.

"Wolves," suggested a third.

"Mistaken for a deer and shot by hunters," added a fourth.

"No," insisted the sister firmly. "He lived, and he was taken somewhere. He was taken here; now bring me to him." Her heart pounded. Something strange was going on. The faces of the people around her were blurring, changing.

"Your brother is not a little boy anymore," said someone.

"Your brother is not a little human anymore," said someone else.

An eager, anxious giggle rippled through the people. The crowd was nodding with wide, serious eyes, and pressing in closer and closer to her.

"I don't care!" she cried, turning and turning, looking for him among the faces. "Let me see him. I want to find him."

"Gone, gone, gone," some of the ghoulish people chanted happily.

"When the winds begin to blow, children climb the mountain," a sing-song voice cheered; "then the darkness takes its hold, when they reach the fountain!"

"He's here, I know he's here!" The sister felt dizzy, unable to focus clearly on any one face in particular; the people were like smoke, like shadows twining around her. Then, all at once, her vision cleared and she gasped, recoiling from the crowd.

LEGENDS AND LORE

The people had changed, and the sight was both horrible and captivating. There were creatures that looked like goblins, with wrinkled, dark skin and hooked noses. Some looked like pixies, slender and sweet-faced despite the dark holes they wore for eyes. There were things that looked part bird or part wolf, and some that were more like toothy monsters than real animals. There were some that seemed to only be pieces of things, like a pair of legs or simply an arm and a head.

The sister's heart beat faster, and she tried to find her guide in the sea of shadowy faces and limbs that reached for her.

"Let me see my brother!" she demanded, her voice strong despite her trembling hands.

"Why should we allow this?" said a new voice from behind her, and she turned to look up at the fountain.

There was a man seated on the top of the fountain, seemingly without care for the water that gushed up and around it. It was not really a man, though, for all he appeared to be was bones: long, thin, impossible bones, housed in a very old-looking, black tailored suit. When the bones moved, the suit shimmered like the night sky, like shadows moving within shadows, and the sister felt cold all over.

The bones looked at her, the way a king might look at a peasant. Everyone around the sister was quiet now, gazing up at the bones. Everything around them had changed, too: the streets were not cobblestones but bones, and the buildings leaned at strange angles, like rough illustrations drawn by children's hands. The sister looked up at the man of bones, the skeleton sitting on the fountain.

"Who are you?" she asked, her voice small.

The skeleton made no answer.

"Please, I'm his sister," she said, softly. Her heart was pounding, though she told herself she was not afraid. "I need to bring him home."

The skeleton did not move. If it had been a man, maybe it would have blinked or breathed, but it was not a living man, so it did neither. The sister was running out of ideas.

"I came all this way to find him. Tell me what you've done with him. What has he become? What is this place? And who are you?"

"I am the king," said the skeleton, lifting his hand in a regal but still eerily comical way. "I am the king of the shadows, and I am the king of the dark. I am the one in the nightmares and the one in the dreams, and it is I who sends the animals walking. I am the fear and the nerves and the gasp of air, and I am the *don't-look-behind-you*. I am the mystery winds, and I am the harvest moon. I am the *it's-just-a-story*, and the *don't-be-a-scaredy-cat*, and the *you're-just-a-baby*, and the *stay-here-till-I-come-back*. I am the *don't-move-or-they'll-see-you*, and the *don't-blink-or-you're-dead*. I am the holding your breath and the shutting your eyes and the *where-did-he-go*? I am the all-hallows! I am the midnight and the black and the creaking floorboards. I am the lost. I am the searching. I am the lost!"

"You said lost twice," said the sister, shivering in spite of herself.

"I am the lost," declared the skeleton fiercely. "I am the lost little boy; I am the dark woods at night; I am the bears hunting for their supper; and I am the ghost of the thing you lost!"

The sister stared up at him. He was trying to frighten her, but his words were beginning to get twisted up, and she felt a deep pang of familiarity.

"You're repeating yourself," she told him.

"Gone, gone, gone!" the ghouls cried all around her.

"The darkness takes its hold," declared the skeleton, "when they reach the fountain. And I reached it long ago."

"If you're lost, you should stay in one place until someone finds you," the sister said, remembering what her mother always said.

"I tried!" the skeleton snarled. "I tried to stay put as long as I could, but it got dark, and the winds began to blow, and they left me there, alone . . ."

Hope soared through her. "I know you now," the sister told him. The skeleton stood up in anger, his bones quivering with fury.

"I am the king!" he cried. "I am the king of all this!" He stepped down from the fountain in a tantrum and stood towering over the sister, impossibly taller than she was.

"You are my brother," she insisted, with certainty. "And you were never meant to be the king of all this."

She reached out and took the enormous bony hand in both of hers. Like a match being struck, he was no longer just bones, but had muscles and skin to go with it, and he was a tall, thin man with strange hair and dark, deep-feeling eyes and a boy's face. He was tense with anger, but he did not pull his hand away. He looked down at the sister, and she saw the cold rage subside.

"I am the king," he said, uncertainly. "I have been the king." He raised his eyebrows, and his forehead wrinkled so many times that the sister had to smile.

"Maybe," said the sister, squeezing his hand. "But you are my brother, and you were my brother first. You weren't meant to be king of all this. Come home."

"But he is the king!" one of the strange, misshapen ghouls cried in terror. "You can't just take him!"

"You'll have another king," she said firmly. She gave the ghoul a stern look. "Don't worry about it."

"But!" someone else cried, sputtering in disbelief. "But! But you can't!"

"No 'buts,' " commanded the sister, looking round at everyone. She and the brother began to walk away from the fountain.

"No!" roared several voices at once, and the shadows bloomed and swarmed like birds unfurling their wings. The wind kicked up, cold and fierce, and the shades and spectres opened their wide mouths and howled, advancing on her.

"Stop!" The brother put out his free hand, long fingers spread wide. The ghouls paused, suspicion on their eyeless faces. "I am going home now. Stay here. I mean it."

The sister squeezed her brother's hand. "The next time you find a king," she said in her most serious voice, "it must be a volunteer, not someone you pluck out of the woods for no reason. Now, all of you, go to bed."

For a long moment, nobody moved. Then the brother frowned at the ghouls, and suddenly there was a great ruckus. There was moaning and grumbling and wailing and grousing, but the ghouls and monsters and shades and imps shuffled off into the dark, leaving the sister by the fountain with her very tall, very thin, very bewildered brother, who was so much older than he had been when he was lost in the woods.

She looked up at him. "Now. We're going home."

He looked tired and uncertain, as if he were about to say something, but he could not think of the words. She waited for a moment to see if he would figure it out. He seemed dumbstruck, however, and so she squeezed his hand again reassuringly.

The sister led him back the way her shadowy guide had brought her, through the town, over the streets made of bones, through the front gate of blackness, and past the infinitely glowing lantern. They walked through the woods in silence, past the owls and the hawks and the kites, past the wolves and foxes and deer, past the bears at the top of the hill, and together they climbed the rock and back down the other side.

They walked down the mountain, and the air was as still as summertime, without a hint of the mystery winds, without even a ruffle of leaves in the night. They walked and walked and walked, and at last they stepped out of the trees into the backyard of their white house from when they were children, and the moon was above them in the night, and the touches of colorful dawn were coming over the horizon.

"Welcome home," said the sister, and the brother looked very surprised to see their house. The sister found that her brother was now small again, as young as he'd been when he vanished, and his blue eyes looked up at her from under a serious brow.

"Thank you," said the little brother, and together, they went into the house.

In one version of the story, the little brother did not return, and the sister could not understand what had happened to her brother.

In another version of the story, both of the first two boys made it home in one piece, and the police were called to search for the little brother, who—although the sister recalled it differently—was found just after dark and brought home to his family in their little white house at the foot of the mountain.

The parents were overwhelmed with relief that he made it home in one piece. His sister asked him if he was all right. The little brother nodded and said that he was tired, and cold, and a little bit hungry, but that he had just fallen asleep in the woods and waited to be found.

The sister asked then if he had been scared of the woods in the dark. The little brother shook his head and told her that he saw a bear once, but it just looked at him and walked on by. Other animals had passed him by as well, without even stopping to look at him. All in all, he seemed quite unharmed by the experience, and the family was happy to have him back again.

Years went by and the brother grew out of his childhood silences and somber expressions, and he and the sister were very close and had many adventures together as they got older. Occasionally, the sister would have dreams about yellow eyes in the dark, or a deer running through the woods under a full moon, but she didn't let them bother her, and the dreams faded over time.

One year, when they were both nearly teenagers, the sister was looking all over the house for her brother. He wasn't in his room, or the basement, or the front yard. She looked everywhere, and finally came to the back door. She looked out the screen door into the evening twilight of late summer and saw him standing in the grass, looking out at the woods. She opened her mouth to call to him, but her voice stuck in her throat.

There was a shadow moving slowly through the trees toward him, and it had yellow eyes that glowed without pupils.

The brother stood motionless, watching it, his back to the house. The sister gripped the doorknob tightly and willed herself to move, to call out a warning, but she could not. She was paralyzed with fear.

The shadow moved closer and closer, with the lopsided slow gait of an ape moving to inspect a zoo visitor on the other side of the glass. It paused out of reach of the brother, staring with blank yellow eyes, and tipped its head. The sister felt the air shift through the screen door, and the mystery winds began to blow, ruffling the leaves on the trees and the wild grasses on the ground.

It's too soon, the sister thought, her throat closing up even further. *It's still summer. It's too soon for the wind and the harvest moon!*

The shadowy creature reached out one of its limbs, slowly, tentatively, and the brother slowly raised his own hand as though to meet it. The sister tried with all her might to throw open the door, but as hard as she pressed, she could not move, and the door did not budge. Her heart pounded in her chest as she strained against whatever was holding her there, but to no avail. The shadow was almost touching her brother's hand, and she was helpless to stop it.

She shut her eyes, and remembered the yellow eyes in the dark, and the moon, and the bear, the stag, the wolves, and the hawk.

The wind flared up with a howling sound, and her eyes flew open.

The shadow had recoiled and was wailing and hissing, backing away into the trees. One of the wolves was on the hill beyond the yard, baring its teeth and growling at the shadow. Each step the shadow took backward, the wolf took one forward, driving it back to the woods. When the shadow vanished, the wolf gave a few mocking yips of laughter and loped off after it, chasing it with tail held high.

"Are you all right?" she called to her brother, breathless and dizzy. She threw the screen door open, her hands trembling.

The brother turned to look at her as though surprised to see her, and his eyes were as yellow as the shadow's had been. Then he blinked, and his eyes were their normal color once more.

"I'm alright," he said simply, and went inside the house.

When the mystery winds at last began to blow that year, the young brother and sister did not look up toward the mountain as the other children did, but they lowered their heads and kept walking. A few years later, their family moved to the Midwest, and for the brother and the sister, that was the end of the mystery winds.

CHARON'S OBOL

By R. M. Ridley

Jonathan Alvey put down his battered copy of *Ovid*, leaned forward in his chair, and grabbed his coffee mug off the cluttered desk. He took a long drink of the cold, bourbon-flavored coffee and hoped it would wash away the taste of self-reproach.

He almost wished for a client—even an infidelity case—to distract him. Something to let him channel his personal seething guilt into disgust at the self-absorbed idiots that walked the dirty streets of New Hades. He was in a morose mood—he wasn't even enjoying his own company.

His office had always been his sanctuary, but lately he needed a reason to get out of it. He wanted an excuse to curse the ignorant populace, unaware of what life really was, instead of reflecting on his failure to save a client who had needed him.

He sighed and lit a cigarette. It would be cliché for him to say he was getting too old for this job, but it didn't stop him from thinking it. He picked up his book again and held it in front of his eyes.

"Excuse me."

There was a quality to the voice Jonathan couldn't place, and he looked up from pretending to read. He had, in truth, already returned to his brooding, and the voice had thrown him.

On seeing the person at his doorway, he understood his problem: he wasn't used to children talking to him. As a private investigator, there wasn't much call for dealing with kids. There wasn't much call for him dealing with kids in any part of his life.

The girl standing in his office doorway couldn't have been more than twelve. A cute kid, with dark eyes and an olive complexion, yet long straight hair the color of wheat in the sun.

She wore oversized jeans rolled at the cuff, and a New Jersey Devils sweatshirt. Jonathan wondered where her coat was. It was cold as hell out there, despite being April.

And why is she here?

He crushed out the cigarette he had just lit. "Are you lost?" he asked, getting up to come around his desk.

"I don't think so." The girl glanced behind her at the door with his name on it. "Are you Mr. Alvey?"

Jonathan stopped.

He was used to the question; it seemed every client who came through his door wanted to hear him say his own name. However, to hear it from a kid's mouth rattled him.

"Uh—yeah. I'm Jonathan Alvey."

"Then I'm not lost," she replied with a shy smile.

"What's your name, kid?"

She looked down for a moment and then, with a grin, said, "Just call me Des."

"All right, Des. Look, I don't know why you're here, but—"

"I want you to find my parents."

Jonathan nearly severed the tip of his tongue biting back a curse.

"I don't do pro-bono work."

This wasn't strictly true, but he didn't want to get involved with a kid's adoption issues. When he'd thought about getting a case, this had not been what he meant. He hadn't meant it at all, actually, and he should have known better than to tempt fate.

He looked at the dead cigarette in the ashtray with longing, and then brought his eyes back to the girl.

She pursed her lips.

"It means I don't work for free."

"I know," she said. "I watch TV. But I can pay you. Well, a little, but once you find my parents they can pay you the rest."

"Yeah." He ran his hand through his hair. "I'm sure they can."

She came further into the room and stood beside the chair on the other side of his desk.

"I just want to be with my mom and dad. Please, Mr. Alvey?"

"Why did you come to me, kid?"

"Because you're my best hope of finding them."

He leaned against the side of his desk.

"And why's that?"

"Because you're a magician," she stated as calmly as one might when talking about the weather.

"Magicians pull rabbits out of their hats. I don't own a hat."

"Then, a sorcerer, wizard, conjurer—you're a *Magos*, Mr. Alvey."

He wondered how she knew the ancient Greek term. The accepted term for the past few centuries was *practitioner*, but what did names matter?

"There's no such thing, kid," he lied to her.

"Sure there is," she chirped.

"What makes you so sure?"

"Because you are one. It's obvious to anyone who looks."

Jonathan thought about all the books on his shelves. He supposed a clever kid could put it together, but only after arriving here, which did nothing to explain how she came to be in his office in the first place.

"How did you find me, Des? Phone book?"

She shook her head. "No, silly. Dike told me."

Jonathan had to admit it: this kid knew her Greek pantheon. It didn't get much more obscure than Dike.

"I see. And she said I'd help you find your parents, did she?"

"Uh-huh."

"What's your last name, Des?"

"Pater."

Jonathan sighed.

"What's your mother's name?" he asked, taking a fortifying sip from his mug.

He didn't really give two hoots what the woman's name might be, but he figured if he could get the kid talking, he might find out where she belonged. He wanted to get her out of his office but, for some reason, he felt reluctant to call the fine people over at the New Hades precinct and let them deal with it.

"Persephone."

"Pardon?" Jonathan asked, putting down the mug.

"My mother's name is Persephone."

"Uh-huh."

If he didn't think the kid had come to yank his chain before, he did now.

So why haven't I picked up the phone?

"And your father?" He set himself up for the punch line.

"Plouton."

"Look, kid. I don't know what you think you're up to, but it isn't really funny, and I got work to do."

"It's not supposed to be funny." She scrunched up her cute face. "I miss my parents, and I want you to find them." She had tears in her eyes now.

She dug her hand into her jeans pocket, and when she pulled it out, she had a fistful of coins. She dropped them on the desk, where they clattered and rolled.

Jonathan looked at the small, scattered pile of silver and copper and almost wanted to laugh; it wasn't hard to hold back the urge.

"My parents will pay more, I promise."

Jonathan heaved a sigh. "How did you lose your parents, kid?"

"My mother got taken away by cops, and then I wasn't allowed back to the apartment."

"Why?"

"They said I couldn't live on my own."

"What about your father?"

She looked at her feet. "He already went ahead."

"Ahead to where?"

"He goes first to make sure everything's ready."

"Ready?"

"Yeah. He's not really supposed to go, but if he gets everything ready before, then we can 'take to the road'." She said the term like she didn't really understand, but had often heard it.

"So, your mom was arrested and your dad is missing?"

She nodded.

"So where do you live now?"

"At a group home," she said sullenly.

That only made Jonathan more certain he didn't want anything to do with this. However, he had no idea how to get rid of the kid unless he bodily picked her up and hauled her down to the street.

"Which one?"

"If I tell you, will you promise to find my parents?"

Jonathan didn't answer. He didn't know what to answer.

Just lie.

"Sure. Yeah, why not, Des?"

It hadn't felt like a lie.

⁂

Completely unsure how he had found himself in this position, Jonathan walked Des up the sidewalk and through the front doors of the Gaia House for Children.

At first, as the occasional small form darted by, no one took notice of their presence.

To their right, a tall woman stood in a doorway, from which emanated the sounds of young voices.

A man sat talking rapidly on the phone behind a small front counter positioned in the center of two halls that ran down toward the back of the building. On seeing Des, he covered the mouthpiece and called out for someone named Althea.

The tall woman crouched down. "Honey, are you okay?" she asked Des, while shooting Alvey a suspicious glance. "Where were you?"

Before Jonathan could speak, a shorter, more round woman emerged from a door to the left and said, "Take her in with the others."

Biting her bottom lip, Des looked up at him. When the tall woman guided her toward the right side door, Des' chin dropped against her chest.

As soon as Des had disappeared from sight, the woman Jonathan assumed was Althea spoke. "And who are you, may I ask?"

He held out his hand. "Jonathan Alvey. I'm a private detective."

It could have been a dead fish from the way the woman looked at it. She did, however, grasp it lightly, shaking it once.

"Why don't you come in my office?"

"All right." Jonathan threw a glance at the doorway Des had disappeared through.

Althea closed the door behind him, then stood beside a desk heaped with papers and file folders. If she had sat behind it, Jonathan doubted he'd have been able to see her.

"So, Mr. Alvey, care to tell me how you came to be in the company of that little girl?"

He could hear all the unspoken accusations and innuendoes, and he couldn't blame her.

"I can tell you my side of it, which starts with me looking up to find a small child in the doorway of my office. As to how she got from here to there . . . " He shrugged.

He saw some of the unease drain from the woman and decided to tell her a refined version of the events that had led him there.

"Not knowing the situation, I figured I'd simply bring her back here instead of calling the cops about a twelve-year-old."

"I see." Althea nodded.

She seemed to believe him, to Jonathan's relief. He didn't need to be facing false accusations from a couple of cops.

"So, what is her real name?"

Althea sighed and leaned her hip against the desk.

"Well, first off, she's eleven—or so she says. As for her real name, I'm not sure what it is. She told *us* it was Ina."

Jonathan raised an eyebrow.

"We assumed it was short for Regina," she said with a shrug.

"What's her story? Why *is* she here?"

"She's here because her mother was admitted about a month ago to St. Dymphna's; it's a—"

"I know what St. Dyms is. What about the father?"

"Father seems to be out of the picture," Althea sighed. "Not uncommon, I'm afraid to say."

"But if her mother gets released, will Des—Ina be able to go back to living with her?"

Althea paused. She looked at him with eyes practiced to see past lies and then rubbed her forehead. "She disappeared a week ago. No sign of her."

"There is no other family?"

Althea shook her head. "Asking Ina's mother that question was part of what resulted in her ending up in St. Dym's"

"I don't understand."

"Listen, I really can't tell you more, Mr. Alvey. I mean, I'm grateful for you returning Ina—really I am—but I can't divulge..."

"No, you're right. Forget I asked."

"Thank you for understanding." Althea opened the office door.

He saw Des lingering at the doorway to the far room. He waved to her. She gave him a smile, empty of hope, and lifted her hand in return.

◈

Jonathan sat in his car, watching kids of all ages playing in the yard. A few enjoyed themselves with abandonment, but many only went through the motions. Worse, some sat hunched over their knees, staring at nothing.

He started the Lincoln and pulled out of the parking lot. "There's nothing I could do. It isn't my problem."

He made it two blocks, with the heater running full-bore, before he hung a right and started in the direction of St. Dymphna's Institute of Mental Health.

※

Jonathan didn't just know what St. Dyms was; he knew how it worked—from personal experience. He'd been sent there once by the law, and had checked in voluntarily other times.

He liked to use the place as a means to get away from it all. He found no one looked for you in a mental institute. Even cults and big corporate operations gunning for him had failed to think of it.

Due to his times inside, Jonathan had developed some tentative relationships with a lot of the staff. Most of the time, this just got him extra Jell-O, but sometimes it got him something more substantial.

He pulled his old Lincoln into the staff parking lot. He had twenty minutes until next break. Jonathan left the engine running to keep warm, and thought about Des.

Logic told him this was just a confused kid, although a smart one; a girl who liked Greek myths, with no sense of reality boundaries. However, logic also dictated there were no such things as magic practitioners, and so far he had failed to vanish in a puff of reason. The very fact she had come to him because he used magic troubled him.

"Of course, opening the phone book, reading my name and then, in her fantasy world, making me the friendly wizard isn't out of the equation."

Jonathan took a long swig from his flask and then, because coincidence didn't sit well with his gut, he took another.

He didn't like the alternative to the logical story, however. He wasn't against the concept of gods, per se, but not as things still walking the earth.

Worship meant giving over energy. Collected and molded around a spirit or other such insubstantial, this energy gave power to affect the material world. This, in turn, led to more worship and the cycle went on.

Jonathan knew gods' names and symbols had power; it was part and parcel of his own spell work. The thought of them actually walking the earth, though, distressed him—maybe because he called on their names so often. It might also simply be the way it violated his concept of reality.

The client he'd failed—the way it had happened—had also violated that concept and left him off-kilter.

His examination of his psyche would have to wait; the staff entrance had opened.

Only one person had emerged, but Jonathan didn't mind. Nurse Alice Keso had been just the woman he hoped for. With no one else around, his odds of getting her to talk went up significantly.

He got out of the warm of the car with regret and walked briskly to the smoking shelter ten feet from the door.

Nurse Keso looked up as he approached.

"Jonathan." She smiled automatically, but it faltered. "What are you doing here?" She expelled a plume of blue-grey breath.

"What, I can't visit my favorite nurse?"

"Usually when you visit me, you come carrying an overnight bag."

He sat down and pulled out a cigarette of his own. "I had an interesting morning, Alice."

"You need to talk through it?"

"No, I need some information."

"So, you're not here as a patient." She took a long drag off her already half-done cigarette.

"Sorry, this visit is professional." He cocked his head. "Well, semi-professional."

"And how can I help?"

"Tell me about the patient who went missing last week."

Her mouth fell open. She blinked twice, then, crushing out her smoke, asked how he knew.

"From the mouths of babes."

She took a deep breath.

"You know I can't talk to you about patients, Alvey."

"I could commit myself and talk to the other patients about her."

She groaned. "No. I'm not putting up with you on the ward causing trouble."

"At least I *eat* my Jell-O."

"All right, all right. But you didn't hear it from me." She lit another smoke. "Stephanie Cour."

"Kore?"

"Cour. C-o-u-r. She's a schizophrenic, came in about six weeks ago, believed herself to be some sort of goddess."

"Persephone."

Nurse Keso nodded. "Yeah, that was the name. The meds did nothing for her. She made more and more of a fuss as the weeks went by."

"She violent?"

"No, never even had to restrain her. When she arrived, she calmly explained that she didn't belong here, had a child to go home to, the usual stuff. But instead of growing more resigned to the situation, she grew worse."

"And then she was gone."

"Yeah." She colored. "I thank my lucky stars it wasn't on my watch. Administration is blowing steam because no one seems to know how she managed it."

"What *do* you know?"

"A careless nurse let her slip out of the ward, security camera caught her going down into the basement, and an intern arrived one minute later." She took another long pull from the cigarette and shook her head. "She wasn't *in* the basement—anywhere. And she'd never come up the staircase."

"Do you happen to know where she worked?"

Nurse Keso looked around, but no one had come out. "Yeah, she was a *dancer* at the Pomegranate Room."

He knew the place. The front awning proclaimed it a 'gentleman's club', but the inside screamed 'strip joint'.

"All right, thanks, Alice."

"Remember, Alvey. You didn't hear any of this from me."

"Do I know you?"

She shook her head and stubbed out her smoke.

※

Jonathan had crossed town with the windows up and the heat on. He still had no idea why he wasn't back at his office already. He had returned the kid to where she belonged. He had no further obligations.

He parked across the street from the Pomegranate Room, smoking his second cigarette since he'd left St. Dyms.

Motorcycles occupied all the spaces in front of the club. This hadn't surprised him. It was a well-known fact that the biker group 'Acheron Pilots' owned the Pomegranate.

Jonathan got out and pulled his coat closed as he dashed across the street.

The sound of music thumped through a thick wood door on which was painted a snake wrapped around a red fruit.

He pulled open the door and stepped into the smothering noise and darkness. His eyes slid past the bright circle of light in which a pale figure writhed, and toward the bar.

"Highway to Hell" faded out, and then Mick was asking to be allowed to introduce himself, as a man of wealth and taste.

Soon, Jonathan's vision adjusted enough for him to cross

to the bar, where he took an empty seat between two other men.

To his left sat an old guy whose nose looked more like the fruit the place was named after than a breathing orifice. To his right, a burly man slouched. Letters tattooed on his knuckles spelled S-T-Y-X on the right, and S-T-O-N on the left.

Jonathan wondered if there was an 'E' on the guy's thumb.

A bored woman in short shorts and a shirt that would be better used as a baby's bib asked his poison. Jonathan said bourbon, and wondered just what he thought he was doing here.

When his drink was set before him, and his five dollars disappeared from the counter, Jonathan asked the woman if her manager was around. Asking the question in this place felt like putting a gun muzzle to his own head.

She stiffened only a little and managed to keep her eyes on him.

"You a cop?"

"Do I smell like bacon?"

The old guy beside him snorted.

"Manager's not in," she informed him curtly.

"Who can I talk to about one of your dancers?"

"If you're interested in our dancers, pal, why aren't you looking the other way? Just drink your drink and move on."

She turned away and went to talk to a waitress in a similar outfit at the end of the bar. He caught the bartender tilting her head in his direction, and then the waitress glanced his way.

Jonathan acted like his only interest lay in his glass. When a sleazy voice announced the newest performer to take the stage,

LEGENDS AND LORE

Jonathan spun around on his seat. He wasn't interested in the dancer; he *was* interested in where the waitress went.

She delivered the drinks to a table, and headed for a door on the other side of the bar.

Jonathan figured he'd better get the drink in him. He might need it to dull the pain he expected was headed his way.

"Should have left well enough alone," he muttered to himself and downed the watery bourbon.

The question: which way did he want to leave? If he moved quickly, he could go by the front door, but without any information. Or he could take prize number two—get escorted out the back and hope to get answers by listening carefully to the questions put to him one punch at a time.

He hadn't had a good knuckle massage in a number of weeks.

If simply asking after a dancer, without a name, got this much attention, Jonathan's perverse sense of curiosity was piqued.

The waitress came back out and went about her business. Jonathan swung around on his seat again and waited.

He didn't wait long.

A moment later, he saw the old drunk swivel his head and pull his beer closer to his body. A heavy hand landed on Jonathan's right shoulder, but before he could look, another man leaned onto the bar to his left.

He had a square jaw, thin lips, and a nose with a flat front—on the whole, the face looked more animal than human. This guy looked at Jonathan, tilted his head as though trying to puzzle something out, then huffed.

Curling his lip, he snarled, "Let's go for a walk."

The hand on his shoulder half lifted, half pulled Jonathan off the stool. He offered no resistance, especially when he saw the guy holding his shoulder: a giant of a man at six-five, if he was an inch, and three hundred pounds. Though not bulging in muscle, the ease with which he moved Jonathan across the floor spoke of steel sheathed in soft leather.

They didn't take him out back, or even to the washroom. He got propelled across the bar and through the very door where the waitress had disappeared.

He found himself in a small, plywood-paneled office that smelt oddly of extinguished matches. Sitting on the edge of a desk, a third man waited. This one was under six feet but had hard, sculpted muscles. His face bristled with whiskers and his eyes had the texture of flint.

Jonathan got forced into a seat and the pug-nosed of the trio said, "This is the guy—he looks familiar, Cur."

"He a regular?" asked the one called Cur, ignoring Jonathan for the moment.

"No."

Cur nodded and then looked at Jonathan. "Who are you?"

Jonathan decided to play it silent.

"All right, mystery man, wanna tell me why you're nosing about?"

When Jonathan didn't answer a second time, Cur nodded his head.

The big guy stepped around in front of Jonathan and drove a sledgehammer of flesh and bone into his gut. Jonathan doubled over and coughed. He looked at the ground and found a measure of delight in discovering there was no blood there. He tried to straighten up and was aided by a hand in his hair.

"You here to harass one of the girls?"

Again, though his abused stomach begged him not to, Jonathan held his tongue.

The second punch hurt more, especially since the pug-nosed one kept his grip on Jonathan's hair, pulling his head back.

"Think you're tough, huh? Let me tell you something, buddy. You won't be feeling so tough if I let him hit you much more."

The guy waited, and when Jonathan still didn't say anything, he shook his head. "Give him another."

Cur was right: he didn't like the third punch.

Jonathan desperately tried to suck air into his lungs, but his diaphragm just wasn't cooperating. He coughed and gasped for a breath that just wasn't coming.

Pug-nose's face, looking down at him, blurred and distorted as tears streamed out of Jonathan's eyes. "We protect our own, pal. You think we'd tell you where to find one of our girls?"

They were starting to get somewhere now.

"You hear him?" demanded Pug-nose. "We don't rat out our own."

Bingo!

"Maybe I was just upset about my missing wallet."

The guy's eyes narrowed as he let go of Jonathan's hair.

Jonathan gave Cur a lopsided grin. "Or maybe, I was hoping for a lap dance from someone who hadn't been around for a month."

Cur pulled back his lips. "You want to dick around, tough guy? Fine, have it your way."

He motioned to the mountain of a man, but even as he eclipsed the light, Pug-nose spoke.

"Hey, wait. I know who this dude is—he's a private dick. John Alley or something."

"Alvey. Jonathan Alvey."

"Yeah, that's right." Pug-nose came to stand beside Jonathan.

"All right, Alvey, who are you working for then?" growled Cur.

"The daughter of one of your dancers, maybe ex-dancers. I don't quite know."

"A daughter, you say?"

He had kept the snarl on his face and the skepticism in his voice, but the other two in the room betrayed their interest.

"Look, some girl shows up at my office this morning asking me to help her find her folks. Don't ask me why, but after I brought her back to the group home, I decided to do some follow up. It led me here."

"What this kid's name?" Cur barked

"Des. Her mother is—"

Pug-nose got out one syllable—'Per'—before Cur bit him off. "Stephanie. Yeah, all right. So, what are you going to do about it?"

"Guess I'm going to try to find this kid's mother . . . and her father."

"Yeah, good luck with that," Cur growled.

"Hey, I'm just interested in this for the kid's sake. Anything else isn't my concern."

"Cur, I think we should help him out. I mean, if Des went to him . . ."

"Shut up, Berus. Let me think."

After a moment, Cur said, "You tell me your story, dick. If it rings true, maybe you leave here on your own two legs."

Jonathan figured he already had one of them on his side, and maybe a second. He also figured he had nothing to lose now by being straightforward—except the chance for internal hemorrhaging.

He told his story for the second time, editing it only a little to keep the worst of the crazy out. Before he finished talking, he knew even Cur believed him.

"And now I've found myself here. I guess you have to decide if you're going to help me, help this kid, or toss me out like yesterday's trash."

Cur looked him in the eye without blinking, then suddenly he slouched and sighed.

"All right, Alvey. Stephanie dances here three months a year, sometimes four."

"Only three?"

"Yeah, that's right. It's in her—contract."

"But she's not here now?"

"Haven't seen her since the cops did the raid."

"You know she was at St. Dyms?"

"Bastards," spat Berus.

"No, we didn't," Cur said, "but since you seem to, why'd you come around here asking questions?"

"Because the key word in that question happened to be 'was'. She slipped out last week."

He grinned. "Good for her." Then the grin slid off his face like dirty grease.

"But since she hasn't come back here, something's wrong, I'm taking it?"

"She couldn't. Contract says she's free. Crap!"

"Okay, so would she have taken off after Des' dad? Des said he leaves early to make sure everything is arranged. Whatever that means."

"I don't know if even *she* could find him. Once that man hits the open road, it's like he becomes invisible. But he had to know."

"Because he didn't come back here when the contract was up," Jonathan filled in.

Cur flicked his eyes to the side. "Yeah."

Clearly, they weren't telling him everything.

"So, her father . . ." Jonathan prodded.

"Peter," supplied Berus.

"Right. So Peter, I take it, is a member?"

"Yeah." Cur nodded. "You could say that."

Jonathan thought he understood. Peter held a high position in the gang, so the connection to Stephanie, or Des, remained in-house only because no one wanted the authorities to connect the dots.

"So, Peter's on the road already. He can't come back because he might get pulled in about Stephanie, who can't come in because she slipped a mental hospital, and Des is left alone because neither of them can risk showing their faces."

"It's not like . . . They love that kid, man," Cur snarled. "Do anything to protect her. We shouldn't even be talking to you about her, but since Des herself came to you . . ."

"But, Des' mother—she really the best person to take care of the kid?"

"Her mom don't do drugs," Berus snapped.

Cur nodded. "She's a good mom. She likes her wine, but she don't do anything serious."

"That's not what I asked."

"Yeah, she is. She'd die for that girl."

"This Perseph—"

"It's her stage name," Cur snapped.

"Why does St. Dyms think she believes she is—"

"Sometimes, you know when her contract's up, she gets a bit full of herself. Taking the show on the road, she's an important headliner. They probably just, you know, misunderstood."

"Yeah, and then I bet they forced meds on her which, I mean, wouldn't help, would it?" added Berus.

The third guy still hadn't uttered a single word. Jonathan wondered if he could.

"Look," Jonathan said, trying to ignore the rusty bear trap gripping his abdomen. "I don't give a rat's ass what her mother does, or her father for that matter." He took out his flask and took a drink to dull the pain. "Maybe I should, but I'm not one to throw stones. What I *am* worried about is the kid."

"Des belongs with her folks," Cur said levelly. "That's just the truth of it."

Jonathan put away his flask and decided to play a hunch it wasn't just the parents who loved this kid.

"Fine. I can walk away from this, makes no difference to me. Kid didn't look too happy to be back at the group home, but then, maybe that's where she belongs."

Cur looked to the other two bikers, then back at Jonathan. He clenched and relaxed his hand a few times before finally coming to a decision.

"Listen, it's not like we're in a position to help her. How about you take a look at their place? See for yourself the way they care for that girl."

Jonathan thought about it. No doubt, Social Services already had, but so what? Even if the place turned out to be a shrine to the perfect family, with the father unreachable and the mother in St. Dyms, they were left with few options.

"All right, sure. Why not?"

Cur nodded, and Berus actually gave a sloppy grin.

Cur turned to the big guy. "Hound, bring him up. Let him poke around."

Hound led him out the back door of the club. On the side of the building, behind a chain-link fence, a small patch of dull green stood out against the asphalt of the alley. Against the wall of the club, a raised flower bed grew clumps of dirty snow.

Hound brought him up an enclosed staircase on the side of the building and unlocked the door at the top. Jonathan brushed past him into the apartment.

It was clean, bright, and quiet. None of the noise from the club below escaped into this sanctuary. Potted plants grew on windowsills, and pictures of the family hung on the walls.

Jonathan saw where Des got her good looks from. She had her mother's hair and her father's eyes. He could see both of them in her face. He could also see the ease and joy each photo captured.

Brightly colored drawings decorated the fridge with cheery flower magnets. Des' room belonged to a fairytale princess: a canopied bed with stuffed animals obscuring the pillows, dolls on shelves, and an open chest at the foot of the bed out of which escaped toys of every type.

Still, it could have been a sham. The toys and dolls: bribes for bruises. Jonathan wandered back to the pictures and didn't believe it.

"Okay," he said to the large man. "I've seen enough."

He had seen and heard enough to think Des' current situation far more screwed-up than her home-life would be. What he still didn't have enough of was answers. He was no closer to actually being able to help the kid—if he actually planned to do so.

He decided to come clean with the girl. Tell her the truth and explain he simply had nothing to move forward on.

Althea saw him coming up the front walk and met him at the door.

"Is there something I can help you with Mr. . . . . Alvey?"

"I was just wondering if I could talk to D—Ina?"

Althea pulled at her earlobe. She glanced across the lobby to the doorway from which the sound of children's voices carried.

She gave him a wavering smile but finally nodded. "Sure, why not."

She led him to the large open room, dotted with low tables and chairs, where children played.

"There she is." She pointed.

She caught the attention of a tall woman, and gestured to him and then Des.

"I'll be in my office." She turned away.

Des sat at a low table, drawing with colored pencils. Jonathan saw a page divided top from bottom. Above, bright flowers, vines with purple dots and green trees filled the paper. Below, a big bed and many toys dominated the page.

"Hello, Mr. Alvey," Des said, looking up.

"Hi, Des." He crouched down.

"Did you find my mother yet?"

Jonathan looked to the floor for a moment and sighed. "Des, your mother was in a mental ward."

Des nodded and pressed her lips together. "I know." She looked away briefly. "Because no one believed her. But you were in there once, too. What's the difference?"

Jonathan jerked his head back and felt his heart beat double time. "How . . . how did you know that, Des?"

She giggled. "A girl can't tell all her mysteries to a man, now can she, Mr. Alvey?"

All he could do was blink.

A contradiction to herself, from one moment to another, Des oscillated between oracle and young girl.

He finally found his voice. "Des . . ." But he wasn't sure what exactly to say. There were questions he should ask, but couldn't find the words for. Part of him thought he should just say goodbye, but he didn't seem to have the guts.

"Des, I talked to friends of your father. They say he's gone, and they don't know where."

"He'll come." She gave him a patient smile.

Jonathan sighed.

"And no one knows where your mom went. She didn't go back to—to her work."

Des shook her head. "No silly, she doesn't have to be there anymore."

"Okay, so why don't you tell me, Des. Where would your mom go?"

"I don't know. This never happened before. This isn't the way it's supposed to be." She stuck out her bottom lip and her eyes grew wet.

"Why do you think she hasn't come to get you herself?" he asked, hating himself for doing so.

Des sniffed and wiped her eyes with the back of her hand. "I think . . . I think she's afraid they might lock her up again. That can't happen, because she's got to be free now."

Jonathan ran his hand through his hair. He didn't know where to go with this. It seemed the child could differentiate between the myth of Persephone and the reality of the situation no more than her own mother could.

Yet, something nagged at him. Too much lined up, or, perhaps, too much didn't. The shroud draped across this whole situation made it hard to see the truth, and Des herself held too much unknown.

Suddenly, the little girl before him drew herself up, gave one last sniffle and said, "You lost your faith, Mr. Alvey. You used to know your way, but you spent the winter lost. You don't want to be a lost boy, and I don't want to be a lost girl."

"Lost my faith a very long time ago, Des. Probably when I was your age."

"Not your father's faith. Your faith in yourself."

Jonathan tried to find something to say, but realized he was just moving his jaw—his tongue frozen.

"This is *kairos*. Do you know the word?"

It rang a bell. "It's Greek, I believe . . . for 'weather?' " he said in confusion.

"Yes." She smiled. "There's another meaning, though."

She held him with her gaze. "*Kairos* is a passing moment when an opening appears that must be driven through with force to succeed."

This girl left him dizzy with the way she moved from hopeful child to knowing sage.

She took his hand between her two small ones. "This is your *kairos*, Mr. Alvey. What you do now is up to you. I can't do anything else."

She let go of his hand. Somewhere in the room, the sound of laughter erupted, and Des looked over her shoulder. When she turned back, a laugh transformed her face.

"I'm going to go play now." Then she got up and skipped over to a cluster of children.

Jonathan watched her among the other kids. She could have been any eleven-year-old then. She probably was, but there remained a chance she wasn't.

Jonathan knew he needed to decide which he believed.

Getting up stiffly, he turned away from the young faces and turned his gaze inward.

Des wasn't wrong. He had lost his faith—his way. Since that case had ended horribly a few months ago, he'd been off balance. Not knowing what to think of anything. He blamed himself for the outcome of that case every day.

The moment he stepped out the front door of the group home, the cold clung to him like death, and he pulled his coat around him, tight as a shroud.

Jonathan sat at his desk. The bourbon had dulled the ache in his gut but hadn't given his head the nice buoyancy it usually did. The cigarette between his lips just tasted bitter and spread ashes about. He really didn't know what to do—or believe.

The book before him, *Balance and Bounty,* lay open to the ritual of *Nestis' Tears.* He'd never done the ritual himself—he'd had no reason to—but it purported to lead one to the place where the greatest harvest would be sown—an allusion to where the goddess Persephone would rise from the Underworld and bring forth spring.

He took another unhealthy portion of the contents of his mug, and debated closing the book and trying to get drunk. The alternative was to do the ritual based on the advice of a child who believed she was the offspring of gods.

"In which case, why does she need me?"

Jonathan chided himself for asking after the workings of the gods. Then he admonished himself for thinking of her that way.

"Damn it."

He threw back the rest of the bourbon in his mug and pulled the book closer.

⁂

Jonathan pulled the old Lincoln onto the shoulder of the road. The ritual had led him to a small ghetto on the west side of the city.

This place, according to the function of the ritual, would be where spring would rise from the ground.

He got out of the warmth of the car, and, pulling his coat tight about him, looked around.

An old tenement building loomed over an empty lot, covered in dead grass and desiccated weeds. On the other side of the lot, a cement block building squatted; it had been cored by fire so long ago, the char looked like old stone.

The half-burned sign wedged among the dried tansy blooms decided it for him. He didn't know what the burned-out building might once have been, but now the sign read 'lethe'.

Inside, he found little of interest. Barren, save for a few twisted metal shelves rusting away in penitence for some forgotten crime, the place appeared to hold no secrets. A doorway near the back led to another room—more grim than the first.

The fire had burned the hottest here, the cement crumbling and pitted from the heat. The smell of smoke still lingered, trapped in the cenotaph of a space. Jonathan was turning to leave when his eyes fell on the door set in the far wall.

He had missed it at first, for the blackened metal blended with the walls. He grabbed the doorknob and twisted. The piece came away in his hand without effort. He dropped it and threw a hip against the door. It didn't budge, no doubt rusted in place for years.

He turned away, but paused as a whiff of perfumed air caressed his senses.

A floral scent.

It had come from the door beside him, not through the doorway in front of him—there was nothing out there to create such an aroma.

You're crazy. There's no way . . .

"It was crazy right from the start. Crazy to even do the ritual."

So what's crazier: to deny the possibility, or accept it?

"What's crazy is I'm standing here arguing with myself."

He sighed, looked at the door, and decided maybe a little crazy was just what he needed.

※

Jonathan had returned to his office, thinking it would be the wiser course of action to call the group home, instead of just dropping by. However, as he waited to be connected to Althea, his gut told him he might have miscalculated.

"Mr. Alvey."

Althea's tone of voice wasn't much warmer than the air outside, but he continued with his hastily thought-up plan all the same.

"Hi, I was thinking it might be nice for Des—for Ina, if I took her out for some ice cream. Just, well, I guess sort of to apologize for saying I'd help her but then just dumping her back with you."

"We can't allow that."

There was a noticeable pause.

"There are certain rules, and as you are not her legal guardian, she can't leave the premises with you."

"Oh—I see." He cursed internally. "Well, I suppose that makes sense."

"Have a nice—"

"But I could see her *on* the premises," he interjected. "To explain."

Again, a chilly silence.

"I don't think that would be in the child's best interest."

Althea had changed her tune since last time they talked, and Jonathan wondered why.

"Please, I would just like a chance to—"

"No, I have to think of the child's welfare."

"Well, that's what I'm trying—"

"Mr. Alvey, under no circumstances can I allow you to see the child."

"If I could just have five minutes."

"No."

The dial tone sounded in his ear, and Jonathan slammed down the phone.

He had tried being nice. He'd even asked politely.

Perhaps the kid was right: perhaps it was time to use a little force.

He got up and, grabbing his doctor's bag of tricks, thought about strapping on his gun. He decided against it. He didn't want the cops to hear 'armed' in connection to this child abduction it seemed he planned on attempting.

Thinking of the cops made Jonathan realize Althea had probably spoken to them. If she had, being adamant that he stay away from Des made a whole lot more sense.

The cops didn't much like him, and his stint at St. Dym's wouldn't look good either.

"Oh, I'm going to get in so much shit for this."

Jonathan drew in a big breath, pushed his shoulders back, and marched up the walk to the front doors of the group home.

He made it only halfway before gigantic growls split the air from behind the place.

Cutting diagonally across the yard, he reached the side of the building and saw the source of the sound: three big motorcycles roared up the road toward the back play area.

They skidded to a stop on the other side of the fence and one of them popped a wheelie, unleashing black smoke.

All of the kids in the yard went running to the fence to watch. Jonathan turned and ran for the front door.

Barreling into the group home front lobby, he watched two workers push out the back door—they looked to be the last living souls in the place. He dashed into the playroom, but it was a graveyard, so he turned and headed down the first hall.

"Des?"

He tried to pitch his voice so it would only carry to a few rooms—not loud enough to attract any supervisors still inside.

All the rooms he passed were devoid of life. Halfway down the hall, he called out again, though he had started to believe she wasn't inside.

Why would she be? Everyone else is out in the yard.

"I'm here."

He turned and saw her step out of a room just ahead of him. A miniature suitcase was clutched in her small hand.

Jonathan bent down and took two small cow's horns from his bag. He had Des hold both of the horns, which, in her petite hands, looked immense.

Certain she held them securely, he took out mugwort, used for scrying, and nettle, which deflected energy, and dumped equal measures of each into both horns. He topped off the horns with dried heliotrope, which makes one's movements and actions undetected.

He noticed Des had a smug smile on her face. "I knew you were a Magos."

"Hold them steady."

He raised his right hand over the first horn and began to rub his ring and middle finger together. The fact that the spell he used to activate the properties of the herbs, and bend them to his needs, had Greek origins didn't escape him.

He felt the power rush through him and ignite his nerves. He almost shook with the relief of having the energy once again coursing through his atoms—the salvation and splendor of the magic coursing through his flesh.

It was referred to as Riding the White Dragon, but the withdrawal would come: the Dragon Black. He pushed aside that truth for the moment, snapped his teeth closed and squeezed his hand. He took a deep breath and tried to fight back the sensual demon inside him, clamoring for more.

The spell had worked. It wouldn't make them invisible—no spell could do that—but it would do the next best thing.

With each of them carrying a horn, the security cameras wouldn't be able to see them. Human perception would be warped, making anyone trying to look directly at them feel nauseous.

It might be the edge needed to keep the cops from being able to do more than breathe heavily on his neck for a day.

"Time to go." Jonathan grabbed his bag and then took one of the horns from her. "Okay, kid. Let's blow this Popsicle stand."

They walked out calmly, but quickly. Just before the front door shut behind them, Jonathan heard the voices of children filling the halls.

✦

The trio of bikers caught up to them a couple of blocks from the group home.

Jonathan pulled the Lincoln to the side of the road, but left it running. He turned to tell Des to stay put, but she'd already scampered out the door.

He didn't feel comfortable springing the kid just to hand her over to these three. He'd done this incredibly stupid thing on the crazy chance it was real—how would he explain that to them?

Maybe I don't.

"Thanks for the diversion," Jonathan said, going to stand by the bikers.

"Hey," said Berus. "We were coming by to see Des. Just coincidence."

"Coincidence," Jonathan said. "Right."

He watched Hound scoop up the kid in a big bear hug as his face bloomed with joy.

"So I guess you guys will take it from here then." Jonathan reached reluctantly for Des' suitcase.

"No can do," Cur told him.

"What?"

"Told you, we don't know where her folks are, man." He looked down the street. "And where do you think the cops are going to go looking for her, now?"

"You mean, after me?"

Cur shrugged.

"All right, fine," he said sharply to hide his relief. "But if that's the case, we better all get going—now."

Cur nodded and extended a hand. Jonathan looked at it for a moment before taking it in his own.

"The Acheron Pilots will know what you did, here; me and my boys will make sure of it. And we won't forget this—you understand?"

"Yeah."

Jonathan wasn't sure how having a biker gang owing him would work in his favor, but he wasn't going to spurn the idea either.

Cur nodded and let go of Jonathan's hand.

"Mount up, boys."

Hound set Des carefully back on the ground and swung one of his huge legs over his Hog.

Des gave Berus a squeeze around his waist and then, when the biker bent down, a quick kiss on the cheek. Jonathan wasn't sure, but he thought Berus might be crying.

Cur rubbed the top of Des' head, then jumped down on the kick start and his bike roared to life.

She watched them drive off for a minute before running back to the car.

"Do you know what we do now?" she asked, biting her bottom lip.

"We have faith, I guess."

Des smiled, and it was sunlight on gold.

※

Des had been silent as they drove through town, but he hadn't given her much to feed off. Jonathan had been keeping his eyes on the road, especially the one behind that might contain a cop or two.

She sat straight in the seat, her eyes wide and her bottom lip caught fast between her teeth. It made Jonathan terrified he'd stop suddenly, and she'd bite right through.

"You afraid?" he asked, partially just to remove the possibility.

"Uh-uh."

"It's okay to be afraid."

"I *was* afraid, but not now."

Jonathan let the conversation lie.

When he stopped in front of the burned-out building, Des looked at it with wonder. He got out, grabbed his doctor's bag of tricks, and circled the car. Des had already gotten out and was sliding her suitcase off the seat by the time he got there.

"Okay, we have to go in."

She nodded and reached for his hand to pull him toward the building. If she cared about the state of the building, she didn't show it, but walked quickly to match strides with him.

In the back room, Jonathan tried to catch the aroma of flowers again but, if it had been there, he couldn't detect it now. It didn't matter. He had come this far down the road, he might as well see where it led.

"Des, I think we have to get that door open."

"It leads down, doesn't it?"

"Yeah, I think it does."

"Can you get it open?"

"Maybe—with a little magic." He flashed her a smile.

She giggled and took a small step away.

Jonathan took his knife from his pocket and flicked it open, one-handed. He jammed the top of his finger on the tip. A drop of blood welled up.

Quickly, he drew the summoning symbol of Perses, the Titan god of destruction, beside both hinges on the door and, calling up energy from within, he cast a quick, dirty incantation, essentially cursing the door.

The spell sped up the rust, the corrosion, the aging, and weakened the whole structure. Alone, it wouldn't be enough, but Jonathan had another plan.

A cold part of him remained sure it was foolish to think the next spell he had planned would work. However, under the trust radiating from the young girl beside him, he found that part melting rapidly away.

He took white chalk from his bag and began to cover the door in inscriptions dedicated to Hecate, the goddess of crossroads, and death, and . . .

"Mommy's friend," Des piped up from beside him. "That's clever."

Jonathan was glad the kid thought so. Myth said Hecate helped find Persephone once; maybe she'd do so again.

Once he had completed covering the door with the appropriate words, he took out a bottle of mandrake and a brush made from dog hair. With these, he began to paint Hecate's symbol on the center of the door.

There remained only one thing left to do—an offering of blood.

He took out his knife once more, but didn't press hard enough to break the flesh. If this had any chance of working, if this was real, it wasn't his blood needed, as it wasn't his plea.

He turned to Des and her eyes grew wide as she took in the knife.

"I need you to be a brave girl, Des. But you are, aren't you?"

She gave one solemn nod of her chin. Then, biting her bottom lip, she turned her head away and stuck out her hand. Jonathan, never more relived he kept the knife razor sharp, slid the edge across the tip of her middle finger. Des hissed, but didn't pull away. He put the knife back in his pocket and guided her to the door.

"Okay, Des, make the offering."

She reached out and touched her bloody finger to the door.

LEGENDS AND LORE

It didn't just open or fall away—it blasted out of the frame. Smoke and embers shot out of the open portal. Jonathan wrapped his arm around the girl, spinning her into him, even as he turned his back to the flare.

He looked down to make sure she hadn't been hurt. Red flakes were plastered to his coat sleeve—rust flakes, not embers, and the smoke, nothing more than dust.

He turned his head and saw, through the floating debris, a woman standing at the bottom of a flight of concrete stairs. The door rested at her feet.

Even if he hadn't seen the pictures, he would know this to be Des' mother. She had the same smile, the same hair, and the same presence.

"Someone was looking for you." Jonathan turned the girl around.

"Des," sobbed the woman and clambered over the door.

Des pushed out of his arms and scampered down the stairs.

He watched as the two clung to each other. After a couple minutes, they ascended from the dark, hand in hand.

When they stood before him, Des said, "This is Mr. Alvey, Mom. He's the one who found you."

The tone of her voice made it hard for Jonathan to find his own.

"He's a Magos," she declared.

"He must be, darling." She looked down at her daughter and hugged her close. "And a fine one at that.

"I took the only passage open to me and it led here, but I couldn't get the way to open. I don't hold those keys."

Jonathan wasn't sure to whom the woman spoke, and so held his own tongue.

Then she looked directly at him with eyes the color of new leaves and said, "Thank you, Mr. Alvey. Thank you for bringing me my daughter."

Though her voice hitched with joy, Jonathan caught the way her eyes roamed outside. He saw the sorrow at finding that no one else waited there.

"I guess I'm not done yet." He looked at Des. "My client hired me to find *both* her parents."

Jonathan didn't like to do necromantic spells. He knew of no other way to call on those who ruled the underworlds, however. Kneeling on the ground among the dust, ash, and rust, he readied himself for the task at hand.

He took out a leather pouch of grave dirt and poured the entire contents onto the floor. Using his finger, he made four furrows in the center of the dirt and then drew a circle around those to represent the five rivers of Hades.

He slit his palm and allowed the blood to run into one of the furrows: Acheron, the river of pain. He poured bourbon into the next furrow: Lethe, the river of oblivion. Phlegethon he filled with sawdust and bourbon and lit it on fire. Cocytus he filled from a small vial containing the tears from a dying man. That left the outer ring: Styx, the river of hatred. Into that, Jonathan spat.

He heard Des' mother gasp, and knew she understood the truth behind the offering.

Jonathan held his right hand over the dirt. Rubbing his middle and ring finger against each other, he began the incantation. The energy flared in him greedily and ran through his nerves and muscles. He spoke the words of power and invocation. Beneath his hand, the 'rivers' began to flow.

Dark, ugly energy pulsed through him, pushing him to his limits. He focused and continued to chant the litany. With every cycle of the words, a new outer ring cut through the dirt and flowed around the one before.

Eight times he spoke the words. And eight times the outer river circled itself.

Holding fast to the power he'd summoned and now channeled, Jonathan spoke the incantation once more. The ring blew out of the dirt, and a putrescent wave of cold smacked him down.

Jonathan's guts clenched. He shook and trembled. His head throbbed. He felt half-dead, and it was no wonder. He had channeled the energy of death itself through his every cell.

He managed to get himself to sit up. Des came over and gave him a kiss on the cheek.

"Thank you, Mr. Alvey."

Jonathan didn't know what she thanked him for. Except for the state it had left him in, the spell didn't appear to have had any effect.

Then he saw the man standing at the exit. Tall, powerful, and dark, he filled the doorway. When he reached out a hand, Des' mother ran to him, with Des only a moment behind.

Jonathan got slowly to his feet and followed them outside.

A large black motorcycle with a black sidecar sat parked in front of his car. The trio headed to it. Jonathan went to stand by his own decrepit chariot.

Des' mother separated herself and walked back to him. She laid a warm hand on his arm.

"The river Styx is wide enough, Mr. Alvey. It does no good for you to feed it anymore." Having had her say, she turned away and climbed into the sidecar.

Then Des was suddenly there, wrapping her arms around his waist. She tilted her small head back and smiled up at him. Then, just as suddenly, she let go and scampered to join her mother.

Des' father nodded to him once. His eyes were hard, but the way he had held the other two spoke of a possessiveness rooted in love. He kicked down with one large black boot, and the motorcycle roared to life. Jonathan gave Des one last wave and opened his car door.

He still didn't know if he'd done the right thing. Had he helped a stripper and a gang member kidnap their own daughter from the system? Had it been something else? Did it matter which possible reality was true?

He heard them pull away, and the sound changed. Under the smooth growl of the engine, Jonathan heard a pounding. The new sound soon overwhelmed the engine noise, and Jonathan recognized it. Hooves.

He turned, already knowing there would be nothing to see.

The road stretched before him, empty. "I didn't even get paid."

A warm breeze came up from nowhere, and Jonathan shrugged his coat open. Then, he saw the color alongside the road.

He walked away from his car and bent down at the embankment. Before him, a riot of color bloomed—crocus, violet, iris, lily, and larkspur. Scattered amongst them, like mulch, were sheaves of wheat.

Jonathan stood up and, taking off his coat, walked back to his Lincoln. He didn't look back down the road.

※

When he got back to his office, Jonathan sank gratefully into his chair. He lit a fresh smoke off the end of the previous one, then took his bourbon bottle out of the desk drawer. He put it down on the desk and it tilted. From beneath it, he slid out one of the coins from the pile Des had dumped. With a smile, he held it up. It was weird—too flat and oddly irregular. He took a closer look and saw one side had been stamped with a face with curly hair and its tongue protruding.

Flipping it around, and seeing the anchor on the other side, he knew its purpose and origin.

He pawed through the rest of the silver and copper pieces, and though not identical, they were all similar. The coins on his desk had once been buried with the ancient Greeks for their passage to the underworld.

Jonathan remembered wanting to laugh when Des had dumped the coins on his desk as payment. He laughed suddenly, and felt a burden float from him.

He raised his mug and silently toasted the mysterious girl.

GRAIL DAYS

by A. F. Stewart

Some days, being an immortal witch by way of Camelot can be satisfying.

I sat in my favourite weathered chair, enjoying my garden. I had no clients staying at my bed and breakfast yet—it still being early in the season—so I decided to take the day and relax. I sipped from a glass of my homemade mead, and basked in the sunny spring morning. I gazed in satisfaction at the lovely sight of my blackthorn bush, and admired its delicate white blooms. Then I gave a nod to the tree, and laughed.

"Looking good, Merlin. You made a lousy wizard, but as a tree, you're delightful."

I wasn't spouting crazy talk, or drunk from the mead, because that particular bush used to be the famous wizard Merlin. The one and only selfish psycho of Camelot, the creator of glory and lies, and a realm of resentful immortals.

I thought I'd never see him again after we parted ways centuries ago—and he ended in a magical prison. Then, a few months ago, my old nemesis and lover whirled back into my life unexpectedly. Still the same narcissistic oaf, he haughtily demanded I return the sword Excalibur for some cockamamie scheme to resurrect Camelot. That being the worst idea since Jar Jar Binks, I refused, and dealt with the old windbag. He never saw the spell coming.

I smiled and stirred the memory like a dry martini, recalling the shocked look on Merlin's face after I slashed him with the spelled wand and the incredulity in his eyes as the transformation, well, took root. That night was the most satisfaction I ever had from that man.

Savouring my revenge, my poetic justice dished out for his web of lies and deception, I indulged my need to gloat. "How does it feel, Merlin, to be bested by me, your former pupil? I wager your massive, vainglorious ego is fairly bruised, you backstabbing trickster."

I tipped my glass to the erstwhile human practitioner of magic, and took another drink of mead. It looked to be the start of a wonderful day.

"Nimue?" A voice drifted out from inside my cottage.

Drat, that was Morgan's voice. Hopefully she didn't bring news of another Camelot catastrophe. Maybe I spoke too soon about a wonderful day.

With a sigh, I replied, "In the garden, Morgan."

I turned my head and watched the dark, lithe figure of Morgan le Fay as she emerged from the dim shadows into the sunshine. She looked immaculate as always, stylishly dressed in a black and white business suit. Sometimes I envied her beauty and grace. I'm no slouch when it comes to looks—the one perk of immortality is I still see a youthful, twentyish, brunette beauty in the mirror—but compared to her . . . well, it's no contest.

"Sorry to arrive unannounced, but we have trouble brewing—" She stopped talking, her attention caught by the blackthorn tree.

"Is that who I think? Merlin?"

"Yep, our one and only douche-bag wizard. In the bark, so to speak."

"I knew you succeeded, but wow. That's a heck of a spell, Nims. Remind me never to piss you off."

I smiled and changed the subject. "So, why are you here, Morgan? You said something about trouble?"

She nodded. "Big trouble. No easy way to say this, but it's the Grail. The thing's gone missing."

I nearly choked on my mead. "Again? I thought we finally had that detestable hunk of metal contained. Damn. Magic that powerful could wreak havoc."

I held my slightly ruffled demeanour, but internally, dread invaded my bones. The thought of the Grail up for grabs stirred an ominous panic in me. That thing possessed enough magic to level cities, countries even.

"There's worse news. Perceval escaped the mental hospital, and Galahad vanished, too."

"What? Tell me they didn't steal the Grail and go off on some harebrained crusade together. I swear I'll turn them both into toads if they did!"

The corner of Morgan's mouth quirked. "Toads?"

"Well, killing them won't do any good. They'd recover from that." I drained the last of my mead. "So, did those fools pilfer it?"

She shook her head. "They didn't steal the Grail. That cursed crock pot disappeared all on its own. But Perceval and Galahad may be off chasing it again."

I sighed. "Didn't those two idiots learn from the last time? Nothing good ever happens hunting that relic. Sit down and tell me the details."

I poured myself another glass of mead, and then one for Morgan, which she accepted. Then she settled in the chair opposite.

"Do you know when the dratted thing disappeared?"

"Not precisely. Lancelot discovered it was missing. He was on one of his revisiting kicks, indulging his maudlin nostalgia for the good old days. He swung by Glastonbury Tor, and no Grail."

"You sure he didn't just imagine the whole thing?" I grasped at a tiny straw of hope. "You know how he gets during one of his drunken binges."

She shook her head. "Not a chance. He swears it wasn't inside the Tor with Arthur, and you know Lance can sense when that wretched Grail is near him." She paused, looking pensive, and her voice lowered. "Something strange happened at the Tor. He won't talk about it, but the incident turned him sober, Nims. He hasn't touched a drop of alcohol since he arrived on my doorstep babbling that the Grail was gone."

That news made me choke on my mead. I sputtered, but managed to spit out, "Lance isn't drinking? That's serious. The world may be ending."

Morgan smiled, briefly. "I don't believe it's that bad, but something significant is happening."

I sighed. It never ends. Sometimes I wonder if I'll ever have any peace.

"You don't think the Fisher King is involved, do you?"

"No, he's still living in America, and I don't think it's the Grail playing its usual tricks." She gave me a look. "First Merlin is freed, and shows up on your doorstep after centuries, then the Grail vanishes. Do you think *he* might be behind the disappearance?"

Morgan nodded toward Merlin the tree, a slight tremor in her voice. "You don't think this is part of his plan, do you? Some sort of contingency, or maybe he had a partner?" She shivered. "I still can't believe he thought we'd go along with creating a new Camelot."

"I honestly don't know. The old bastard was capable of anything. I wouldn't put it past him to try and use the Grail again, despite his failure the first time. I don't think these two events are coincidental. I think someone is meddling with magic."

I quietly exhaled a breath and continued. "Maybe it's something Merlin did; maybe it's a new wizard, or a small-timer, thinking bigger. Could be someone messed with the confinement spell, and there were ripples. The Grail does tend to respond oddly to magic. Or it could be part of a power play."

"I hope it's another wizard. I don't want to deal with one of Merlin's schemes."

I nodded. "Amen to that." I took a long drink to settle my nerves. "Whatever's going on, though, we have to get to the bottom of it, quick. The Grail's too powerful to be let off the leash, and if some poor fool's pulling supernatural threads, there could be serious unintended consequences. I hope it's not the beginning of another Quest. In 1901, we chased it halfway across Europe, and it came damn close to destroying Berlin."

"I remember. Bedivere lost his left hand with that quest. Poor sap brooded for months until it grew back."

"Bedivere lost that hand in the Black Forest, wasn't it?" Morgan nodded, a touch of melancholy edging across her lovely face, and I let out a breath. "I never want to experience that again." My fingers tightened around my glass. "What a horrible and bloody time."

Morgan whispered, repeating, "I remember," and we both fell silent, lost in the consuming miasma of the past.

I shook off the melancholy first. "I'm just glad I won the blasted thing in the end. Hopefully all we have to deal with now is another foolhardy recruit to the live-forever club."

You see, that's the catch, the big consequence of living in a world full of magic: you absorb the energy as a sponge absorbs water, and you gain the unfortunate ability of not dying. And let me tell you, the glamour of that wears off rapidly.

"Those dumb idiots don't know what they're getting themselves into, do they? And messing with the Grail—not smart."

I shivered. The sudden thought of the Grail in the hands of an amateur wizard, well . . . it terrified me. Then, another thought hit me.

"It's strange though—if someone is casting spells, I haven't sensed a thing. They know how to hide."

A contemplative look crossed Morgan's face. "I haven't either. That means they're powerful enough, or clever enough, to stay off our radar."

"Hmmm. Off our radar maybe, but Vivienne might have sensed a disruption. You can't hide magic from her." I gave Morgan a wry smile. "Fancy a walk?"

"No, but I doubt you're offering me a choice." She wiggled her foot at me. "I'll need better shoes."

She was right, those pumps wouldn't do at all. "I think I have some sturdy boots that will fit you."

I put my glass down, and stood. So much for my day off, but at least it was a beautiful morning for a stroll in the Lake District.

※

I outfitted Morgan in a pair of hiking boots, donned my own Wellies, and the two of us set out down the trail to Vivienne's lake. Despite the circumstance, I enjoyed the fresh, bracing air as we walked through the woodland and across the hillside, even with my companion grumbling complaints under her breath.

We reached the end of the path, and our first sight of Vivienne's lake was stunning, as always. The cool, blue surface reflected the shore-side trees, the faint sound of the water broke over the sand and stones, and the majestic, emerald mountains framed the view, with the blue and white sky above it all. A breeze ruffled the reeds and grasses as we arrived, and I knew Vivienne sensed our presence.

"Time to rise, Viv. We need to talk."

In response, the surface of the water undulated and gurgled, and the liquid sprayed upward. A figure burst from underneath the lake, then floated effortlessly to shore. Vivienne, the Lady of the Lake, looked at me and smiled.

"Nimue! How wonderful. After our last meeting, I wasn't sure I'd see you again. I'm glad you survived. I take it Merlin's not a problem anymore?"

"Don't worry, he's history."

"I'm glad. Oh," her attention shifted as she noticed Morgan, "and you've brought a guest, how lovely. Who is . . . Morgan le Fay, is that you?" Vivienne clapped her hands in glee. "It *is* you! It's been ages. How are you?"

"It's delightful to see you as well, Vivienne. I'm fine enough, but we'll have to chat about the good old times some other day. There's trouble brewing."

"Oh, dear, I feared there was something else stirring. I'd hoped it was simply residue from Merlin's return."

I shook my head. "That might be part of it, and he could have shifted it into gear, but we have bigger issues. The Grail's gone missing, Viv. Morgan and I think there may be a new magician inciting mischief."

"Could be, could be. There's definitely a dreadful smell in the ether. Like rotted fish and pine."

"You think you can work your sorcery, and divine what's happening?"

"I can try, but no guarantees."

She waded back into the lake and slowly levitated above the surface until she hovered about three feet in the air. Above us, the sky darkened, the clouds turning the shade of soot, and the air thickened with the smell of ozone. Vivienne moaned, a hoarse, guttural sound, and began to spin violently. A whoosh of lake water ascended, sucked into a gyrating whirlwind, a waterspout funnel that surrounded her. Lightning flashed, the air temperature dropped, and the howling wind bent the trees. I could barely breathe, and I saw Morgan crouched nearly double.

Then the tempestuous weather ceased abruptly, and the sun warmed the cerulean sky again. Vivienne stopped whirling, and water plunged down in a cascading splash that sent a spray of mist over the shore. She faced us, her arms outstretched, and her eyes shone with an unnatural silver light. I knew she'd connected with . . . *something*. She laughed, a rather cold, haunting trill and spoke in a singsong voice.

"Behind all guises, the Black Knight rises. To chase the Grail, around the Vale. The games begin, who will win?"

With an ear-pounding shriek, Vivienne dropped from the air and into the water. She disappeared under the surface of the lake.

Morgan snorted. "Well, that was ever so helpful."

"I think it was very helpful. We know for certain someone's after the Grail, and it damn well sounded like we have a new

Quest on our hands. Also, we know the identity of one of our opponents."

"The Black Knight, you mean? And how do you propose we find said Knight? Do an Internet search? Or perhaps look 'Black Knight' up in a telephone directory?"

"Hardly." I threw her a dirty look. "You know as well as I do, the Black Knight isn't who we need to find—not yet, at any rate. We want the person trying to draw out the Knight, and spells to conjure a creature like that will leave a trail, even if you're shielding your magic. And the Grail, wherever it is, certainly leaves a trace you can follow. Figuring this out will take a bit of time, but it's feasible."

"I suppose." Morgan frowned. "I just hope we have that time. The last thing we need is that spectral monstrosity of a Knight roaming the country. It's bad enough some mad idiot is attempting to raise him from the netherworld. It'll be chaos if he succeeds."

Drat, she was right. I sighed.

"Let's head back to the cottage and see if we can craft a scrying spell to track down this wayward wizard."

Two hours later, with not much luck, we took a break from spell-casting and prepared some lunch. I reheated some leftover broccoli and chicken casserole in the microwave and dished out two plates. I also grabbed some sherry from the pantry, so we could drown our worries in a glass or two.

"Too bad one of the things we're searching for is the Grail. That pain of a scrying bowl could locate this annoyance of a wizard without the bother of a spell."

"There's some irony in there somewhere, I think. That we need to find the one thing that would help us find itself."

Morgan gave me a quizzical look.

"Yeah, that didn't sound right. Maybe I've had too much sherry. And the mead I had in lieu of breakfast probably didn't help."

"Oh, we're going to solve this problem, two half-drunk witches on the case."

Morgan raised her glass in salute and then downed the contents in one gulp. I smiled. One of the constants over the centuries has been Morgan and her love of wine.

"It's a shame we don't get together more often. When there isn't trouble, I mean." Morgan poured herself another glass of sherry and swallowed a large mouthful. "That's what I miss about past centuries: the camaraderie. It's all texting on your mobile these days. For all the nonsense, we had some good times back then."

"Yes, it wasn't all bad . . ." Something clicked in my brain, and the rest of my words trailed off into the land of the unsaid. "Wait a minute. I've got a stash of old spell books, tucked away in a trunk. Including some I acquired from Nostradamus."

"Acquired?" Morgan shot me a withering look.

"Okay, I stole them. But that hardly matters. The important fact is the books might help, especially one in particular. And

I think that trunk is in the cellar. Let's go take a look after we finish eating."

"Sounds good to me. As long as there aren't rats in your cellar."

"Oh, please. I've spelled this cottage against vermin. There isn't a rodent, reptile, or bug within a mile of my home."

She laughed, and we turned our attention back to enjoying our lunch.

After the meal and the washing up, we traipsed downstairs. I spotted the trunk in a corner, so Morgan and I dragged the thing into the centre of the room. I lifted the lid to reveal my secret hoard of books.

"Are these all spell books?"

"Most. Some are a few treatises on alchemy and medicine." I knelt down, inhaling the scent of aged paper and nostalgia, and started rummaging. "Keep an eye out for a book with Greek lettering; that's the one I'm most interested in."

Morgan joined in the hunt. "Why that one? What's so special?"

"The spells are old, powerful. Nostradamus claimed he found some ancient texts, and transcribed the spells into this book. Said the spells originally belonged to Circe, the mythological Greek witch."

Morgan stopped looking and stared at me. "What? You don't believe that, do you?"

I shrugged, stacking books as I searched. "Don't know. The fool may have been a bit cracked, but he did have a gift. All I know is the spells are old and formidable, and if anything can help, it's in that book."

I sorted through more books, and Morgan picked up a musty, leather-bound volume. I glanced at her. She was holding it with a reverence akin to how Lancelot would clutch a glass of thirty-year-old premium whiskey.

"Is this the Grimoire of Honorius?"

"Yes. And no, you can't play with it. You know how you get around necromancy spells. Put it down, Morgan."

She reluctantly set the book down, and I turned my attention back to the trunk. I lifted another book, and there it was, the Greek lettering on the cover staring me in the face. I picked it up and stood.

"I found it. Let's go back upstairs and take a look."

I pried Morgan's interest from the trunk and hauled her from the cellar and into my parlour. I plunked myself in a nice, comfy chair and flipped through pages, looking for the spell I remembered. Morgan paced while I thumbed through the yellowed parchment.

"Here it is. I knew I recalled this spell." I slapped the book in triumph.

"Here, let me see." Morgan peered over my shoulder and read aloud, translating the text into English., "The Seeking Whisper. A tracking spell. Be it hidden in realm far or near, this incantation will seek and find." She grunted. "A bit overdone on the language, but if it works—"

"Yes, Nostradamus was a tad pretentious. Just be glad it isn't cryptic, like some of his other work. And the spell performs, I've used it before. It should be able to track the magic."

"So, what do you need for the spell?'

"Hmmm, let's see." I scanned the list of ingredients. "Most of it is fairly basic, and I can raid my supplies, but the bloodstone and the juniper oil I'll have to get from a shop in town. Also, I'll have to go to the market for the pomegranate juice. I can probably have everything ready by tomorrow."

"Not today?"

I shook my head. "This will take some preparation, even after I gather the ingredients."

"Then, can you handle the spell from here on out? I have a board meeting day after tomorrow, and I should return to London."

"That's fine. This doesn't need the two of us. If I find anything, I'll give you a ring and fill you in on the details."

"Good." She checked her watch. "If I leave now, I can still make it back to London tonight." She scooped up her purse. "I'll keep in touch, Nims."

She strode out of the room, and the cottage. A few minutes later, I heard her car roar away. Typical Morgan: drop the problem in someone else's lap and then make herself scarce. I wondered if she realized how irritating that trait was at times like these.

No use fussing about her defection, though. Time to get to work and whip up a spell.

The next day, all ingredients and preparations ready, I waited for dusk to settle on the world so I could begin the spell. Contrary to popular belief, it's not midnight we witches work incantations, but twilight.

I decided to work the spell in the garden, as I do my best work when I can feel the earth. I inscribed a boundary circle with sea salt, then set my spell bowl in the centre. Some practitioners prefer to use stone or pottery bowls, but I've always found metal bowls to be best. I currently utilized a lovely decorative copper bowl, made in Victorian London by a weasel-faced merchant I used to know.

I stepped inside the circle, carrying both a wooden chest that contained the ingredients and a small glass pitcher of spring water. I reached into the box, pulled out the bloodstone, and placed it in the bottom of the bowl. I poured the water on top of the stone and filled the bowl, then mixed in the rest of the ingredients, stirring it well with a piece of dried cedar wood. As I mixed, I chanted the incantation of the spell in Greek, hoping my pronunciation wasn't that rusty. As the words faded, I stopped stirring and waited. Finally, the water turned black as obsidian, and with a sigh, I let out the breath I didn't know I'd been holding. It worked.

I reached into the chest once more and pulled out a twig of blackthorn, AKA Merlin. If errant magic had been responsible for his sudden appearance, the spell would find it. I dropped the twig in the inky-looking water and asked it what I needed to know.

"Who awoke Merlin?"

The surface of the liquid crackled and sparked, and bluish mist rose into the air. It coalesced into a shape, forming a face I didn't recognize—a pudgy face, with thinning brown hair.

I stared, incredulous, at the vision wavering in the air. "This is the wizard messing with the Black Knight and the Grail?"

At my words, the mist shifted and re-formed, this time fashioning into features I knew well.

"Bother and spit. Not her."

Elaine of Corbenic. Daughter of the Fisher King, mother of Galahad. It made sense that she'd be the one behind a move on the Grail. My mind buzzed with this information, thoughts tumbling out.

The pudgy wizard must be one of her pawns, like Lancelot was back in the day.

Poor Lancelot, he certainly won't be happy she's returned; nor will Morgan.

I wonder if Galahad's with his mother?

Why can't those medieval magic rejects stop causing mayhem?

I sighed and shoved aside my disarrayed notions, trying to concentrate on the task at hand. I whispered to the scrying bowl, "Show me where to find these two."

The mist shimmered, and then presented me with a map of London, and a very helpful address.

"Thank you."

The mist wavered and disappeared. The water in the bowl cleared. The spell was broken. I sighed again.

I bet it was the juniper oil. Good quality spell ingredients are so hard to find in this day and age.

I plucked the bloodstone from the water and picked up the bowl and the chest. Then I stood, broke the salt circle, and used the leftover liquid to water Merlin. After I was done, I went inside to pack for my trip to London.

※

I called ahead to Morgan and filled her in, so she was waiting at the train station when I arrived, looking none too happy.

"You really should own a car."

"I had one once. Didn't like it. Far too noisy."

"Cars have come a long way since the Model T, you know."

I stuck out my tongue. "For your information, it was one of those flashy American cars—a Mustang."

"Oh, fancy."

We stopped sparring long enough to retrieve my luggage, including one very special item, and loaded it into the boot of Morgan's Bentley. Then we drove through London traffic in the direction of the address I received, a place in Camden.

"Elaine. I can't believe that witch is back." Morgan thumped the steering wheel. "Stupid woman. I hope you have some spells up your sleeve, because the wench is no pushover."

"Don't worry." I patted my oversized handbag. "I tucked a few goodies in here that will help."

"What does she think she's playing at?" Morgan continued to rant, and I watched, amused. "You know, when I told him, Lancelot had the nerve to defend her? He said, 'It's not her fault,' and, 'She needs help.' That barmy man still has a soft spot for her."

I shot Morgan a worried look. "I'm not going to have another one of your love triangles to contend with, am I?"

"Not on your life. I set the fool straight, and he'll keep any sympathies to himself." She scowled. "If he wants to stay healthy and human."

I wasn't surprised Lance fell in line. The last fellow to cross Morgan ended as her lapdog—literally. But I didn't comment on her love life, simply replied, "Good. One problem at a time is all I can handle."

"Well, we have a humdinger of one in Elaine. Going after the Grail, I get. She's always been obsessed with the thing. I mean, she sired a son deliberately to groom him as a Grail champion. But what's with the Black Knight? Or Merlin? What's Elaine's game? What?"

"I don't know. The behaviour is odd, even for her. Maybe she finally snapped. It's not like that hasn't happened before with our Camelot gang. And her personality is as high-strung as you can get. But the bigger question is, how did she trigger a new Quest? She's never been powerful enough on her own before." All the unknowns in this mess worried me.

"You think that's why she wanted Merlin? That's the only reason I can think to want the old fart. Did she really think she could control him?"

I shrugged. "Maybe. She fancied him, you know. She probably thought Merlin would be grateful, and she'd be able to seduce him into her bed and her plans. She always did underestimate the crafty old wizard."

"And overestimate her own charms." Morgan smiled. "Served her right, getting rejected. I hope he laughed in her face." Morgan paused, then abruptly changed the subject. "So, what's her objective with the Black Knight, do you think?"

"My best guess, she's looking for a new Grail guardian to keep the thing safe once she has her greedy hands on it. And to run interference with people like us trying to stop her."

"And now it's starting all over again because of her. Perceval, Galahad, and some fool of a beginner wizard all chasing the dream of the Grail. I wonder how she convinced this new player to join in the madness?"

"Probably filled his head with the nonsense from the legends—the Cup of Christ, and those lies." I shook my head. "It still amazes me the stories they tell about a witch's scrying bowl."

"Well, it is more than just a scrying bowl, Nims; it's the source of all magic. The power in that simple bowl is astounding." She licked her lips. "The things a witch could do with that power . . ."

I snorted. "Oh, please. Don't *you* turn into a Grail zealot on me, Morgan. It's a battered old bowl with a mind of its own, and nothing but a right royal pain in the arse."

Morgan rolled her eyes at me, but she ended her speculating and her grumbling, and we drove the remainder of the way in comfortable silence. When we arrived, Morgan parked her car, and we walked through the clamouring throng of residents and shoppers, past the rows of brightly coloured buildings, hunting for the address. We spied it on the right-hand side of the street and entered.

We found ourselves in a smallish bookstore, crowded with shelves and stacks of new and used books. The place held a comfortable, wonderful aroma of stained wood and musty paper, with a hint of lavender and citrus from the candles on the sales counter. Behind that counter stood a gangly teenage girl, leaning on her elbows, feigning to look indifferent, but only appearing petulant and bored. Morgan snapped her fingers to get the girl's attention.

"You the only person who works here?"

"Nah. There's the manager."

Morgan tapped her foot impatiently. "Well, where is he?"

"In the back."

She pointed to a faded green curtain apparently concealing a back room. Morgan strode forward, and I scurried to keep up, the girl's languid voice following us.

"You're not allowed back there."

We stepped past the curtain, expecting a dingy back office, but emerged into a space as large as a car park, resembling an old castle set from a 1930's Hollywood movie. I gaped at the stonework, the dark mood lighting, and the flickering torches on the walls. I could smell the smoke, and a hint of damp mould mixed with peat moss. From somewhere, I heard a howling wind, and the faint roar of a dragon. Whoever worked the magic here liked the old-fashioned, melodramatic touch.

Morgan whistled. "Impressive. It's bigger on—"

"If you quote *Doctor Who*, Morgan, I'll smack you."

"Who dares trespass in my domain?"

A menacing, booming voice echoed from a dark corner. I tensed as a figure walked from the shadows, until I spied the balding, stout fellow, dressed in a tee shirt, denims, and sneakers—the fellow I saw in my spell. Over his street clothes, he wore a blue velvet robe, and he carried a homemade staff with a hunk of sapphire-coloured glass glued to the top.

Morgan giggled. "So, you're Elaine's pet wizard? She's definitely scraping the bottom of the barrel. I bet I could flick you down with one finger."

As she stepped forward, I saw it. I reached out and shouted, "Morgan, wait!"

Too late. She tread on the hex pattern scrawled on the floor and triggered the spell. Energy snapped around us with a piercing *crack*, forming an invisible barrier of magic, and binding us in a circle snare.

The stout man cackled. "You cannot harm me! I am Martin the Magnificent! I am all-powerful, and I have trapped you!"

He leered, his face fixed in what I surmised to be smug triumph. However, mixed with the pompous pronouncement, it only came across as asinine. Now *I* giggled; I couldn't help myself.

"You mock me? I, who have ensnared you, made you helpless? I, who anticipated your arrival? You truly didn't believe you could outsmart *me*, did you?"

I rolled my eyes at his continued grandiosity, and decided to end the charade.

I closed my eyes and whispered, "*Amddiffyn.*"

As I reopened my eyes, an amulet hanging around my neck activated, and, in an instant, the magic surrounding us ceased functioning. I grasped Morgan by the hand, and we both stepped out of the circle snare. Martin the Magnificent sputtered in disbelief. I smiled at the expression on his red, pudgy face.

"You truly didn't think it would be that easy to trap *us*, did you?"

I reached into my purse, pulled out a hex bag, and threw it at Martin. It smacked into his chest and exploded in a burst of magical energy that slammed the twit against the back wall. His magical illusion vanished, leaving us surrounded by the shabby reality of a cramped storeroom and office. I walked over to the moaning would-be wizard sprawled on the dusty floor and grabbed him by the shirtfront.

"Where is Elaine?"

Morgan leaned in, her face inches from my shoulder. "I'd tell her, if I were you. She can do some very nasty things to people who cross her."

He wiggled like a worm on a hook. "I don't care what you do. I won't tell! I won't ever tell!"

I slapped the snivelling little nutter across the mouth, and then gave him a quick jab to the belly. He folded like a paper fan.

"What did you do that for?" His whiny voice grated in my ears.

"Because you won't talk, you ninny." I turned to Morgan. "Did you bring your dagger?"

She smiled and drew out her blade, lovely and sharp. Martin blanched.

"What—what are you going to do with that?"

"Just a little torture. What do you think, Morgan? Start with cutting off the ears?"

"Sounds dandy to me."

"No, you can't!" Martin clamped his hands over his ears and started babbling. "Don't hurt me, don't hurt me. I didn't mean any harm, please don't hurt me."

"Then tell us where Elaine is hiding."

"It doesn't matter. You're too late. She left me here and went after it. She's taken her champions to chase the Grail."

"Champions?"

"Yes, Perceval and Galahad."

Wonderful. Those two yahoos were up to their ears in it with Elaine. This mess kept getting better. I glared at Martin, grabbed Morgan's dagger, and pressed it against his throat.

"Tell me everything."

Martin swallowed, and his bottom lip trembled. "She's been trying for months to find the Grail. She started by recruiting me to wake up Merlin, so he could break the spell concealing the Grail. He wouldn't help her, though—said he was only interested in finding Excalibur."

Morgan chortled. "Ridiculous. Why did she need *you*? Elaine's a powerful witch."

Martin's face turned red. "She needed my spell book, the one I inherited from my granny, and she couldn't use it without me. It needs a bloodline descendant to work the spells."

"Okay, that explains you. Now finish your story. What happened with the Grail?"

"After Merlin defected, she had me doing all these weird spells from my book, and most of it didn't work, but we lucked out a few weeks ago and located it in Glastonbury. Then, uh, something went wrong."

"Wrong?" I didn't like the sound of that.

"Well, the daft thing disappeared before she could steal it. Or, more precisely, the Black Knight took it. You see, we were trying to breach the barrier surrounding the Grail, and, well . . ."

"What did you do?"

"I-I don't know exactly. The idea was to channel as much energy as possible into the barrier and fracture it, but it didn't work. I mean, it did work, just not the way we thought."

I took a breath and then exhaled, to calm myself. "I repeat, what did you do?"

Martin's lips quaked, and his words came out in a rush. "We were channelling energy from the netherworld, and we didn't do it right, and we opened a portal, and the Black Knight came out, and he breached the barrier and stole the Grail. Then he disappeared, and we've been looking for him ever since. And we triggered a Grail Quest by accident."

"You triggered a Quest by accident?" I gritted my teeth. I wanted to stab the idiot. "Of all the moronic—"

"I'm confused," Morgan interrupted my would-be rant. "Why did the Black Knight take the Grail, if this dimwit summoned him?"

"Because this fool and his equally brainless cohorts didn't summon him. We had it wrong, Morgan. Elaine's not controlling the Knight. It sounds like the Grail itself invoked the Black Knight from the netherworld energy they used. As a protector, I'm guessing. By trying to steal it, they weakened the incarceration spell enough that the Grail escaped and defaulted to its primary purpose. Stupid, idiotic twits."

Martin nodded in agreement, vigorously.

I sighed. "Save me from fools and ignoramus wizards. What happened next?"

"Elaine was quite mad when the Black Knight and the Grail disappeared. She made the best of a bad situation, though, and recruited her Grail champions. We've been in full Quest mode ever since."

"Of course you have," I snarked. "She say why she wants the Grail?"

"No, she never told me."

"So, where did she go?"

He squirmed, but kept silent, and I pressed the blade tighter against his throat.

"Where did she go?"

"Oxford! She went to Oxford. But you'll never stop her; she probably has it by now."

I let Martin go, and stood, watching him as he scurried into a corner and cowered. I pulled a small silver box from my bag.

"Maybe we can't stop her, but we can try."

I opened the box and took a pinch of dust from inside, then closed the lid. I placed the box back into my purse.

"Nims, is that . . ."

I nodded, and dropped the dust onto the floor. I smiled as the portal opened.

"Show me Oxford, and Elaine."

⁂

"I'm going to kill that witch! Why did that stupid cow Elaine stir up trouble?"

Morgan was in a foul mood, and I didn't blame her. After we jumped through the portal, we landed underground, in a warren of caves. We now trudged through wet slime and moss, with water dripping down from the stalactites. Morgan's poor shoes would never recover.

"How did we get here? Caves, Nims, really? Where are the caves in Oxford? I was expecting hallowed halls and stuffy professors. Did your portal send us off track?"

"No, Morgan, this is where we're supposed to be, and Elaine is here somewhere. At least, technically. This place doesn't feel right. I think we're in a netherworld. We're in Oxford, just not the Oxford of our reality."

"What! You mean we've landed in some unnatural realm outside our world? I hate those places. They give me the shivers."

"I know, but what can you do? It's probably the Black Knight's influence."

"I hate him, too. Just so you know." She growled, "I'm going to fry them both."

I hid a smile and shifted the weight of the bundle slung over my shoulder. Before we departed London via portal express, I retrieved my very special item from Morgan's car. With all these champions and swordsmen around, I figured we needed to even the odds a bit.

"I just hope we don't get lost, and that you can get us home when this is finished. I don't want to be stuck here, and spend the rest of my eternity in this hole."

I had to agree. "Then shut the chatter, and pick up the pace. The sooner we find Elaine and her cohorts, the sooner we are out of this abyss."

Morgan stuck out her tongue at me, but she hastened her steps. We scoped several more feet of cavern before we heard voices coming out of a passageway to our left.

"Mum, this is nuts."

"Shut up! For once you'll listen to me, and keep moving."

I recognised the voices. We found Galahad and Elaine, at least. Hopefully, Perceval would be with them. I slung open my bundle and drew out my surprise.

"Excalibur." Morgan hissed at me. "Why didn't you tell me you brought that? That blade will make you near invincible."

I shrugged. "Didn't think to mention it, but it should come in handy. If I hold off our two champion buffoons, you think you can tackle that witch Elaine?"

"With pleasure. I'll scratch her cornflower-blue eyes out."

With mayhem in our hearts, and maybe a bit of exhilaration, we turned left and hurried along the passage to find our foes. We heard the shrill echoes of their argument as we moved forward, Perceval's voice now joining the fray, and we took them completely by surprise in a blitz ambush attack.

Morgan felled Elaine hard with a fireball, pitching her across the cavern in a rolling tumble, but she didn't stay down for long. She slammed a hex back at Morgan and the two witches went toe to toe, magic sparks flying, while I faced down a pair of would-be Grail Knights.

The grotto we burst into sprawled wide, with plenty of room to swing a sword, and I slashed at Perceval with all my momentum behind the swing. The blade caught his sword arm, slicing halfway through bone and sinew, all before he drew his own weapon. He screamed, the ear-splitting noise shaking the stalactites, and fell to his knees, his arm spewing blood. I moved to finish him, but then abruptly retreated as Galahad rushed to his friend's defence. Behind me, I heard the sizzle of magic and the grunts of the two women, but I had my own problems.

With one eye on Perceval—who now slumped forward, moaning—I circled, sword at the ready, with Elaine's son. We each sought an opening, but Galahad swung first, hacking at me from the right. I parried, and the ferocious clang of metal echoed off the rocks. He slashed again, and I dodged, pivoting Excalibur under his reach, to cut a nasty gash through his chainmail and flesh. He lurched, stumbling. I channelled my rage and smashed

Excalibur's hilt into his nose. His head jerked, and he staggered backward, dropping his sword.

A noise distracted my attention, and I instinctively swung my blade around; Excalibur cut through Perceval's throat with little effort. He fell like a sack of potatoes from a lorry, with his wound spurting blood. Staring at his lifeless body, I felt ill, the pointless crap of this Quest rushing in at me. My only consolation was he wouldn't stay dead. Shaken, I wiped his sticky blood from my face with the back of my hand.

I looked up from Perceval and saw Morgan and Elaine doing some weird witchy hand-to-hand combat, but didn't have more than a minute to take it in before I faced a screaming, enraged Galahad.

"You killed my friend!"

Shrieking like a drunken banshee, he charged. Too bad he forgot his terrain. I did a quick step aside and let him ram into the cave wall to knock himself senseless. Then I helped matters along by bashing the back of his head with a large rock. He crumpled to the ground, unconscious.

I looked around and spotted Morgan sitting on the damp earth, groaning, and Elaine missing. So much for scratching her eyes out. I rushed to Morgan's side.

"Are you all right?"

"No. The blasted witch sucker-punched me. Get after the hellion, I'll stay with these fools."

I left Morgan with the no-brain twins and hastened after Elaine. I could hear her running ahead of me, the sound of her

LEGENDS AND LORE

feet splashing through puddles and scraping over rock. I chased pell-mell to catch her, brandishing Excalibur, until I skidded to a halt to avoid careening into her back. She stood still, seemingly not bothering to notice me. Then I saw why.

We were in a cave, a dead-end, completely enclosed but for the passage entrance I'd just used. The Grail floated in mid-air a few feet away, haloed by a golden, ethereal light. Behind this display, the Black Knight maintained a vigil. Elaine stood as if mesmerised, and I carefully slid past to stand by her side. The Knight's gaze followed me.

I sucked in my breath. I'd forgotten how menacing he appeared, with his black chain mail and helm, his spiked gauntlets, and his emaciated face, both pale and shadowed, with crimson, soulless eyes. The resurrected dead do tend to unnerve a person.

Instinctively, I thrust forward Excalibur. A big mistake. The Knight stepped back and drew his sword.

"Lower the sword, you ninny," Elaine hissed at me. "Stop causing trouble."

"Look who's talking," I shot back, but lowered the blade. The Black Knight sheathed his weapon. Neither Elaine nor I moved.

"So, what's the plan, Elaine? You going to out-stare him to death?"

"No. Before you arrived, I was planning to do this." She stepped forward. "I come to challenge for the Grail."

The second the words left her mouth, the cavern exploded in light and magic, and I knew I was in trouble. The air felt charged with the power of a thousand storms, reeking of sour and bitter blood. I tasted metal on my tongue, and wheezed for every breath. When the glare and energy cleared, the cave had sealed itself, and the three of us stood enclosed in a room of stone.

"What have you done?" I could have kicked myself for not anticipating her move.

She laughed. "What I had to do to win the Grail."

"Then you'll have some competition." I turned to the Black Knight. "I, too, come to challenge for the Grail."

"You just can't let me win, can you? I guess it's on, then. Now one of us takes the Grail, or we spend eternity here, with him."

"Just tell me one thing before we begin. Why did you start this again? Why now, after all these years?"

She laughed again, only this time it exploded with frenzy and fury as an unruly screech that made my skin crawl.

"Why? Why not? Aren't you *so* sick of this existence, sick of the pretence, sick of the everyday routine? I miss the old days, the fun. I just decided I'm going to take what I want, show the whole world what I can do, and finally enjoy myself."

Listening to her shallow, self-centred whining, I lost it. "You stirred up this mess because you're bored? Of all the selfish, childish, moronic reasons to cause trouble! I'd expect such stupidity from Lance or Perceval, but I thought you would have a better reason. For pity's sake, Elaine, you awakened Merlin! Of all people, how could you bring that narcissistic ass back into this world? Do you know he wanted to start Camelot again?"

She spit, the glob of phlegm flying off into a dark niche of the cave. "Oh, I know. He droned on and on about it. I tried to make him see going after the Grail was a better option, but he's a stubborn bastard. And he responds to flirting as well as a tree stump. He must have been a real treat as a lover, Nimue."

I glared, her petty needling raising my temper. "So, that's truly it? No grand scheme? Rather pathetic. In the old days, you were at least creative in your plans. You're slipping, Elaine, getting lazy. What happened? You just woke up one morning and said, 'I'll screw the world'?"

"What's so damn good about the world?" Elaine stamped her foot, and her face turned a pale shade of crimson. "You wouldn't understand, because everybody loves Nimue. When anybody from Camelot has a damn problem, it's 'let's ask Nimue what to do,' or 'Nimue will fix it.' Hell, even my own son defers to you. It's not like you're better or stronger than me, or even that skanky Morgan, but you still get the adoration. Even that damn Merlin went to you in the end."

I rolled my eyes. "Same old story, isn't it? Whining like a little baby about not getting attention? Well, tough. Life isn't roses and sunshine on my end, either. You think dealing with you nutters is my idea of fun? Grow up, Elaine."

"That's your answer for everything. Be responsible. Be practical. Behave yourself. Nimue is the nice one. Elaine's so horrible. Be more like Nimue." She scowled. "You're nothing but a sham."

Elaine tilted her head and put her hand on a jutted hip. "Your hands are as dirty as mine, so why am I the bitch? Because I know what I want, and go after it? Because I don't play by those damn Camelot rules? Even in the legends, I'm reviled. Your story's just as bad, but you ended barely a footnote in Arthurian lore."

She took a breath, her chest heaving from her fury. "And for your information, I *do* have a grand scheme. Why the hell do you think I awakened Merlin? We were supposed to recreate Camelot together, rule together, except he couldn't be bothered with me. No, it was you he wanted. Well, to hell with him, he got what he deserved, and to hell with you! It's my time! I'll show everybody!

"When I bring back magic, raise Camelot to its glory again, I'll be the one people come to, listen to; I'll be the one in charge! I want the damn world you think is so wonderful to stand up and see me! To bow to my rule, or die! And if I have to embrace what they made me, to embrace my inner bitch, then I'll do it!"

My fingers itched to slap her haughty, self-righteous, power-mad face. Or grind it into the rock wall. I clenched my jaw instead, and tightened my grip on Excalibur. "You embraced your inner bitch a while back, Elaine. Now you're simply crazy."

She shrugged her shoulders and sneered. "Maybe, but crazy is more fun than being sane. You should try it sometime, Nimue. I bet you'd like it."

"*Are you ready?*"

The sonorous, disturbing, slightly cantankerous voice of the Black Knight interrupted our discussion, and our full attention snapped to him.

He repeated his question, "*Are you ready?*"

We nodded, our animosity temporarily silenced.

"*Only the worthy can claim the Grail. Only those quick of mind can answer my riddle. The first to speak, the first to veracity, will claim the prize. Tell me true, the answer rare: What is it that all women desire most?*"

My voice and Elaine's chimed simultaneously, "Free will."

For a moment, stillness reigned, and then he spoke, "*You have both answered correctly. The Grail is not won.*"

Beset by a sudden wave of irritation, frustrated with a thousand lifetimes of shenanigans, I snapped at him. "Of course the Grail *is not won*, and we both answered correctly, you moron. What did you think would happen with you rolling out that old chestnut of a riddle? Everybody from Camelot knows the answer. Try for something a little different, a little fresh this time."

The Black Knight turned to me and stared. His look seemed to freeze the breath in my throat and slow my heartbeat. For a moment, I perched on the edge of that deathly abyss, lost in a petrified millennium of one unmoving second. Then the spell shattered, but my bravado dropped a few notches, and I wanted to faint.

"*As you wish,*" he growled. Then he smiled a chilling grin that looked more like a celebration of death than humour. "*Answer this riddle true and rare, with wisdom deep, if you dare: I will disappear every time you say my name. What am I?*"

Elaine stomped her foot. "What? We're supposed to know what that gibberish means? What kind of Grail riddle is that? Stick to tradition."

It was my turn to smile. "I'm not surprised you don't know, Elaine. You don't avail yourself of it much."

I addressed the Black Knight., "The answer is silence."

"You are correct. The Grail is yours." He bowed his head. *"As am I, milady."*

The cavern shook and erupted with the ear-splitting noise of breaking rock. I looked behind me to see the entrance restored, and the way out.

"No!" Elaine's shriek rattled the walls, and she stormed toward me, her hands curled, her fingernails ready to claw. I gave her a thump of a right cross to the jaw, knocking her onto her plump backside.

"Knight! Restrain her."

He obeyed my command, hauling Elaine to her feet and pinning her arms behind her. She struggled, but he held her fast. I reached into my bag of tricks and withdrew a potion I'd prepared especially for her. I opened the stopper and grinned. I would enjoy this.

"Yank her head back."

The Knight grabbed a handful of her hair and forced her head backward. I pried open her mouth and shoved the potion down her throat, holding her mouth and nose shut so she'd swallow. Then I stepped back and watched her scream as the magic coursed through her system, as the transformation spell morphed her human form.

Her bones and flesh shifted and warped, cracking, tearing, breaking, muscle and tissue altering and disappearing. Her blond hair shed itself as her new flesh grew mottled fur. The long minutes ticked away, filling the cavern with gruesome echoes, until the Black Knight held not Elaine, but a rat.

I was of half a mind to leave her in the netherworld caves, but I decided against it. I wrapped her in some sacking from my purse and stuffed her into my bag. She made a squeaky fuss, but I stowed her in safely.

I walked over to the Grail, the Knight at my heels. I ran my finger over the chipped rim of gold. It would be so easy to take it, and make myself the strongest witch this world would ever know. I could re-make the world to my own satisfaction, silence all the bothersome fools forever and have my peace. Maybe fashion a quiet paradise of my own, with magic and tranquillity. All I had to do was pick it up, and leave this place.

I sighed and pulled my hand away from temptation. Trouble always followed this thing. "It's not worth the aggravation."

But still, something must be done about the Grail. I turned around.

"Black Knight. I hereby charge you with guarding the Grail for all time. You are its protector, its defender. None may challenge to claim it; you may let none touch the Grail save me. Is that understood?"

"Understood, milady."

I didn't know if this tactic would actually work where the unpredictable Grail was concerned, but it would slow down any future fools who might take a notion to come looking for that accursed bowl. Besides, I had one last trick up my sleeve.

"Take your post, Knight."

I watched the dark spectre take his station behind the Grail as I slung Excalibur over my shoulder. I almost felt sorry for him. I pulled out one last thing from my purse amid angry squeaks. I opened my hand and showed him.

"Do you know what this is?"

"The Grail Stone, created by Merlin. The talisman used to hide the Grail from the world and suppress its power."

"Yes. I used this before, to secure the thing inside Glastonbury Tor before you retrieved it. I'm going to seal it away again, here. With you."

His eyes flickered, but he exhibited no other reaction.

"As you wish, milady."

I gave him a smile, a last goodbye. I walked out of the cavern and placed the stone against the outside rock of the entryway.

"Cau'r drws."

The earth rumbled, and the magic poured from the stone into the caves. It ripped through me like a million sharp needles piercing my skin, and I screamed, but I persevered—until the entrance sealed itself away, and all trace of the cavern room, the Grail, and the Black Knight disappeared.

Exhausted, in pain, and spent of magic, I managed to trudge back to Morgan and the boys. I found her waiting, Perceval alive again, and both he and Galahad looking bad-tempered and morose.

Galahad scrambled to his feet at my appearance. "Where's Mother? What happened?"

"Did you kill her? Or maim her a little?" Morgan sounded too gleeful about the possible harm to Elaine.

I reached into my bag, pulled out my prisoner, and unwrapped the sacking, amid angry squeaks and attempted bites to my fingers. I handed Elaine-the-rat to her son.

"There's your mother." I heard Morgan's hysterical laughter behind me, but ignored it. "That's what happens to people who try to steal the Grail." I gave him and Perceval my best glare. "Do you both understand? No more Grail hunts!"

They hung their heads. "Yes, ma'am."

Galahad cradled his rat of a mother in his arm, and I dug out my silver box, withdrawing another pinch of dust.

"Let's go home."

~☙❧~

A fortnight later, and things have gone back to normal—well, as normal as they ever get for me and mine. Morgan went back to her business, Lancelot went back to boozing, and for some odd reason, Galahad and Perceval decided to open an animal shelter. Elaine's even helping them, as some sort of mascot, or something, for their adverts.

Now I'm back in my garden, enjoying the sunset.

"Here's the tea." My new employee set down the tray and settled into a nearby chair.

"Thanks, Martin."

Well, I couldn't leave old Martin the Magnificent on his own to wreak more magical havoc, so I, uh, persuaded him to come

North and work for me. Which turned out for the best, for it seems Martin's "Granny" was one of us—my old acquaintance, Iseult. That's probably how Elaine located Martin in the first place. It seems Iseult settled down for a bit, then disappeared in 1951; my guess is Tristan or Mark started stalking her again. Whatever the reason, she left behind her very interesting spell book, forgotten until Martin found it.

So, all in all, it's a good thing for Martin to live here. There were a few adjustments, especially with my housekeeper Millie—who threw a fit—but it turns out he's a whiz with the accounts. My books haven't been this organized in years.

"Sorry about screwing up the spell, earlier. I didn't mean to set Merlin on fire."

I sighed and poured some milk in my tea. Maybe there are a few glitches still to be worked out in this new arrangement. I picked up my cup and glanced at the well-singed blackthorn bush. Still, it could have been worse. I'll give the idiot a break.

I sipped my tea, and then smiled. "Don't fret over it, Martin. The old fool wizard deserves to be scorched a little."

NATURAL ORDER

by Lance Schonberg

Carlos woke in darkness, the taste of dryer sheets coating his mouth.

And not just the taste. His cheeks bulged and he couldn't move his tongue much. Something pressed into the corners of his lips, adding to the pressure and forcing him to breathe through his nose. That meant the darkness had to be a blindfold and a little twisting and pulling led him to conclude duct tape surrounded his wrists and ankles.

He remembered the Laundromat, dumping clothes from the washer into the dryer and reaching into his pocket for quarters. A loud crash. A scream. Then . . . then waking up blindfolded, bound, and gagged with a mouth full of paper fabric softener.

Trying to suck in enough oxygen to jumpstart his brain, Carlos shook his head to get the sound of waves out of his ears. They wouldn't go away, and he eventually had to decide they might be real and not far from his resting spot.

Wind. He could definitely feel wind on the right side of his face, and the surface under the back of his head had some grit and give to it, so unless someone had gone to a lot of trouble to fake it, he was lying outside on the ground somewhere near the ocean.

Which didn't make any sense. He lived two hours from the coast.

He'd been kidnapped. Why should anything make sense?

With his wrists crossed and far too much duct tape involved to turn one of them around—but at least they were in front of his body—he had a hard time hooking a thumb under the gag beside his ear. He had an even harder time sliding that thumb over far enough to make even a tiny gap he could start to press his bottom lip up and past. Sawing up and down, he worked the digit closer to the centre, feeling like he was using his thumb to rearrange his face instead of freeing the gag. He winced the first time a canine tooth bit into the inside of his lip. The third time, he tasted blood but didn't stop.

A little pain, his step-father used to say, was a good thing. It let you know you were alive. A lot of pain might make you wish you weren't, but the alternative was worse. Carlos had never found much use in the statement when he'd just smacked his thumb with a hammer, but it made a lot more sense now.

Most of his raw upper lip eventually fit underneath the gag. One after another, he freed the dryer sheets, counting a dozen before he'd emptied his mouth.

Then he started on the blindfold. Forcing it up over his eyebrows proved, if not easy, at least easier then moving the gag had been. Tiny shafts of sunlight squeezed through clusters of shadow to hammer into his left eye, the brief flash of pain forcing his eyes to squeeze shut, even as he slipped the blindfold over his right eyebrow and off his head.

Two major accomplishments down, he let himself relax, his body not quite conforming to the ground under it. Slowly, he began to let a little light past his eyelids. Details took sporadic shape, not that there were many of them. Green and brown, needles and cedar leaves—some waving gently in the wind, some weaving a thick net above him, some strange scraggly fingers clawing at the air. A small break in the foliage to his left let the sun warm that side of his face a little, but the cool spring wind still forced a shiver through him as shadows rippled across the ground.

Trying to steer his mind to something positive in the situation, Carlos exhaled hard through almost closed lips, enjoying the feel of the air puffing them away from his teeth. Until now, he'd never realized just how much he took breathing freely for granted. It was nice, even if he could still taste the dryer sheets.

Someone moaned to his right, and Carlos tried to roll away from the sound even as he turned to look. A dark-haired woman lay with her back to him, a yard or so away. With both arms in front of her, he couldn't see her wrists, but her ankles were crossed and coated with enough duct tape to choke an elephant, and she lay in a tangle of scraggly grass and weeds. Thinking about the itching and scratching in her future, Carlos didn't feel so bad about his dirt mattress.

Flopping around a little, he tried to crane his neck to see more of his surroundings, but the effort didn't reveal anyone else, and he couldn't decide if that made him feel better or worse. After a moment's reflection, he decided on worse, but couldn't quite figure out why.

It took Carlos five tries to lurch into a seated position, due to some combination of his ankles being crossed and the squishiness of his middle area, but he didn't think about it too closely. Breathing heavily, he held out his arms to keep balance and dug in with his heels, pushing himself backward a few inches at a time until he managed to lean against a thick cedar. The support was so welcome that he let himself slump against the yielding trunk, closing his eyes and revelling in the softness of the bark. Questions rolled through his head, but with a little effort, he pushed them all aside. They could wait. They could all wait. The only two important things were getting himself free and then getting out of here, wherever here was.

He opened his eyes to a man's face, eyes and grin wider than anyone's should be, just close enough to his own to make focusing hard. "Good afternoon, brother. I see you're awake and ready to participate in the celebration. A little early, but that's okay. It'll give us time to catch up, or it would, if I had the time to spare, but I have to get things ready for our company."

Carlos opened his mouth, shut it again, and changed his mind. "Um . . . what?"

The man straightened, his grin not shrinking at all, and glanced toward the woman. "Don't worry too much about it. Not yet. It's been so long, forever really, and we really should catch up a little, but maybe you're not ready. She definitely isn't." He turned around and started to walk back into the forest.

"Wait! What do you want? Why are we even here?"

Without looking back, the pale man waved over his shoulder. "Nothing to worry about yet. Just relax. The bait should always be fresh and well rested." Branches seemed to reach out for the man as he spoke over his shoulder. "Happy birthday, by the way. Make sure you tell her that if I'm not back."

Carlos gaped as the forest swallowed the man, his brain still trying to unpack everything from those few short statements. Far too much of it depended on information Carlos just didn't have, so he latched onto the one thing that made any sense at all: it was his birthday. And more, it was the woman's birthday, too. That was too much of a creepy coincidence, made worse by their captor—whoever he was—knowing it.

Happy birthday. So, he'd been out for most of a day. Trying to dig back through his memory, he remembered doing laundry, needing clean clothes to go out for his birthday dinner and to go drinking after. Crap. He probably had dozens of texts and messages waiting. Everyone would be freaking out.

With the realization that he hadn't eaten in more than twenty-four hours, his stomach began a low growl, but he lost his new-found hunger when the woman moaned again, suddenly rolling over in the dirt. Frowning, he tried to figure something out about her based on how she was dressed, mentally subtracting the few stains and smudges on her face and clothes. It didn't help much. Jeans and a fake leather jacket, jewellery he couldn't focus on, and too much makeup spread across her pale face. Too much, but still not enough to make her look older than fifteen or sixteen.

She was just a kid.

A kid who shared his birthday. Carlos wondered if that was why they were both here, but what did birthdays matter for anything? Except they did, or the nut job wouldn't have pointed it out. It didn't make any sense, either way.

The girl's eyes flew open, locking on Carlos' face, and she screamed. He just waited. It wouldn't do any good and wouldn't make her feel better if he told her to relax or that everything would be fine. Platitudes wouldn't help either of them, so he just let her scream. Three times. Considering the duct tape and whatever clogged her mouth, he was impressed by the volume.

At the end of the third, she was working hard to get enough air through her nose to stop panting, and she'd stopped trying to scrunch back into the harsh scrub. He wondered if she'd pass out if she screamed again. Her wide eyes didn't leave him the whole time, as if her being there could somehow be his fault. He held up his hands to show off the duct tape around his wrists and one little stringy spot caught his own gaze. He lifted his hands, bringing them almost up to his mouth before the nut job who'd kidnapped them suddenly popped back into the little bare space, the same idiotic grin on his face.

Big eyes flicked to the girl, then back to Carlos. "Did you wish her happy birthday?"

She made a little sound, but Carlos managed to keep his eyes on their captor. "No. I didn't want to scare her any more than she already is."

The man made that half huff, half sigh Carlos used to give his parents as a teenager. Did he do the eye roll, too?

Before she could flinch, the nut job reached down and grabbed the corner of the duct tape. A quick twist of the wrist pulled it off her face, and Carlos had to wince. Leaning in, not quite sticking his face in hers, the smile got wider. "Happy birthday, Megan. Fifteen already. Wow." With two fingers, he pulled what looked like a tube sock out of her mouth and she sucked in a deep breath. "Since Carlos got rid of his own gag, there's no reason you shouldn't be able to express yourself, too."

Words hissed out at the end of a puff of breath. "I'll express myself. Come a little closer, you giant piece of—"

Tossing the sock over his shoulder, he used the same hand to pat her cheek. "Now, now. There's no need to be unpleasant. Can I get you anything?" It almost seemed like an honest question to Carlos, and he half expected the man to pull a can of soda or a candy bar out of his jacket pocket.

She tried to bite the hand as he pulled it back. "You can untie me so I can kick your ass."

He laughed. "Well, I was going to offer you the chance to pee behind a bush, but I suppose it doesn't really matter if you're comfortable or not. You're only here to help me catch Dad, after all." Standing up, he turned to walk away again, and Carlos wondered where he kept going. Probably just far enough into the woods that they couldn't see him.

Then the words sank in, and Carlos churned them through his brain. "What can we possibly have to do with your father?"

Turning just far enough back to see Carlos with one eye, the man winked. "Now, that would be telling. But it doesn't hurt for you to know that I'm going to kill him and take his place. It is the natural order of things, after all. Time for me to inherit." He chuckled as shadows reached out from under the trees, and then disappeared without taking a step.

Megan began to thrash around as soon as he was out of sight, not feeling or not noticing the sticks and twigs that had to be jabbing into her from almost every direction.

Not knowing what else to do, Carlos brought his hands back to his mouth and started trying to chew through the duct tape. One strand at a time, it began to give, just enough to give him hope, just enough to make him impatient. How long before their captor came back? He tried not to think about it too much, tried to focus on his wrists. After a few minutes, he realized the girl was staring at him, had been staring at him the whole time.

He read fear in her eyes, but a lot more than that. Her face creased and her teeth ground back and forth. She'd long since stopped flopping around, but he could see her pulling at the tape, twisting her wrists back and forth in what was probably a completely misguided attempt to loosen the bonds. If he listened closely enough, and he tried not to, Carlos was pretty sure every muttered, not-quite-under-her-breath word would be an obscenity. As he chewed at the tape, he watched her while trying to look like he wasn't. She seemed a lot more intense now that the screaming was over, and the gaze, blinking out of the long, sharp grass, made him too aware of himself and the task he'd set.

He spit out a small hunk of tape and stopped for a breath or two.

Megan chose that moment to be a teenager. "How's that working for you?"

Ignoring the sarcasm, he shrugged. "Slower than I'd like, but any progress is good. You?"

She snorted. "Stupid duct tape. I hate the stuff." With a sudden twist, she pulled hard against the bonds. He had to admire her determination; one wrist got almost halfway to vertical before she relaxed. "Stupid."

Not correcting her took a lot more effort than it should have. She was just angry and not at him. He should have been, too—angry, frightened, and ready to climb a tree to get away from the situation. In a flash of honesty, he could admit to all of those things, but since none of them would help him at the moment, he focused and tried to tell himself it was like any other project deadline. Feel the pressure when you're done. Until then, buckle down and focus on the work.

He spat another chunk of tape from the end of his tongue, trying to decide if it tasted better or worse than dryer sheets, or just different. With a sigh, Carlos gave an experimental tug, pulling hard to see if the thick strands of tape might start to give. The outermost layer—of at least ten, a helpful voice in his head reminded him—frayed just a little bit more where he'd last been working his teeth. Wrenching his wrists apart as hard as he could, a tiny tear rewarded his efforts. Maybe, if he had enough time, it would work.

And maybe he didn't need as much time as he thought. A long strip of tape came away in his teeth. The noise surprised him, and Megan's head jerked up. "Did you get it?"

Afraid to let the strip go, he shook his head gently and spoke around it. "No, but I'm a lot closer than I thought. Give me a minute." Carlos tried to twist his hands around to make the strip longer and longer until he ran up against the next loop. More strips followed quickly and his heart started to beat faster. After every strip, he twisted and pulled his wrists apart as hard as he could, until finally a loud tear freed one hand. He heaved a huge breath and reached for his ankles.

"Hey, smart guy."

He looked over at Megan.

She wiggled both sets of fingers at him. "If you get my hands free, we can both work on our own ankles and get out of this shithole. Unless you were planning to leave me?"

The feigned innocence in the statement made him laugh, but she had a good point. "Sorry. Hadn't thought that far ahead yet." Rolling away from the tree, he seal-walked over to her, dragging his feet through the dirt. By the time he put his fingers on her wrist tape, the blood had started flowing in them again.

Her skin felt hot to the touch as he tried to pick at the edge of the tape, and he wondered briefly if she might be sick, but decided it was probably him. "Give me a second, here. I'm still trying to feel my fingers."

"Oh, take your time. I'm in no rush."

He almost laughed, but couldn't quite make the sound out loud, as he finally got enough of a grip to start peeling. Her tape was much easier than his, in spite of how she'd warped it with her struggles, and it took less than a minute to unwind. She flashed him a smile before almost diving for the tape around her ankles, attacking it with a ferocity that didn't surprise him at all.

"Yeah, I'm sorry guys, but you being free isn't convenient quite yet. I still need you to bring them to me."

A dark line whipped in from each side, cedar tendrils locking around Carlos' wrists, holding them in place a few inches apart, and at least a foot from his ankles. Megan snarled at the same moment, but Carlos' eyes followed one branch up and over his shoulder, into the thin tree behind him—the same one he'd found so comfortable a couple of minutes before. Traitor.

"Let me go!" Megan strained against the thin limbs holding her, and Carlos felt his jaw drop as he watched more branches stretch out toward Megan, even as the first two started to drag her back. Pressure on his own wrists just preceded the ground moving beneath him until his back rested against the tree again. It seemed a little straighter now, but didn't manage to dig into his back.

"I don't think so."

More branches wrapped around Carlos—shoulders, ribs, and waist—fitting him snugly to the trunk. Two thin roots reared up out of the soil to slip over his ankles and knees, locking him in place. In a few seconds, he couldn't move anything but his head.

Carlos looked at the man, the cocked smile, and tried to make sense out of the world. A tree had reached out and grabbed him, a tree somehow directed by the grinning man standing on the edge of shadow. A shake of his head brought one cheek into the light, and Carlos swore the skin showed a tinge of green. The thought made him cold without knowing why, and scared him more than being on the receiving end of the tree hug. "What are you?"

The man tilted his head, ear almost touching his shoulder. "Hmm. That's a good question." He patted his side, something bulging under his coat. "I should be able to answer that just a little after sunset. Which"—he looked up at the sky, already growing darker—"is about half an hour from now." He smiled. "Hang out for a couple of minutes. I'm just about ready." This time, without turning, or walking, or moving at all, he receded into the forest, swallowed by the green.

"Hang out?" Megan pulled against the branches holding her tight and practically growled. "What is this crap, a fairy tale? Trees that tie people up? And where did the jerk even go?"

Not exactly polite, but the words summed up Carlos' thoughts pretty well, at least once he got past the haze of confusion. He didn't see how it was possible, didn't understand what had happened to him. He felt like he'd stepped off the edge of the world into some strange, lucid dream he had no control over. Fairy tale wasn't a bad analogy. Trees that held onto you. A man who almost literally became part of the forest. "This doesn't make any sense."

Megan spat and turned her gaze on him, her brilliant green eyes so intense he wanted to shrink away. And she was fifteen? He didn't want to be around her, angry, at twenty-five. "You're just figuring that out now?" She shook her head. "Why do you think things have to make friggin' sense? Take it for what it is and fight against it. Me, I just want out of here and back to the world."

He rolled his eyes. "You're the one who asked the question, but I'll spell it out, since you don't have enough patience to complete a thought. If you can figure out the logic something follows, you can solve whatever problem it represents."

She grimaced, shaking her head and just barely missing the jagged, broken branch beside her left cheek. "Sure. That sounds like something a teacher would say."

"Educational software developer, but whatever makes you happy."

"Ooh, a teacher's geek."

Carlos tried to shrug. He didn't see any reason to fight with her, but wasn't interested in letting her get away with what she thought was an insult either. "And the geek shall inherit the Earth."

"Yeah, whatever."

He shook his head, almost the only motion he could manage. "I just wish these weren't so tight. A deep breath or two would be nice to help me think." Almost as soon as he said the words, he felt the pressure against his chest ease a little so he could take those deep breaths.

The fading scowl on Megan's face told him she'd noticed it, too, and it caught her enough by surprise that she forgot to be angry for a moment. "My branches just got looser. Did you do that?"

"I don't see how."

"Do whatever you did again."

"Nice and specific. All I did was wish the branches weren't so tight. It was just timing. Or imagination." Except Megan had felt it at the same time, and they had loosened. He couldn't possibly wriggle free, especially with his ankles strapped down, but maybe he hadn't imagined it. Maybe. "I think I'd like the trees to let us go."

They loosened a little more, giving him space to actually shift his weight around, but stopped well short of actually releasing them. Megan had enough encouragement to start trying to climb out, but the branches started to tighten around her again until she stopped. She growled. "Give me space!"

While Carlos watched, the branches holding her stretched and warped to form a loose cage, confining her, but leaving plenty of room to breathe or stretch or scratch or whatever else she might want to do. "Interesting." He frowned a little, wondering if he imagined the thick, rough bark and jagged points of shadow.

She glared at him. "That's all you've got to say? What's friggin' wrong with you? You should be angry enough to tear those branches apart."

"Well, I can see how much good it's doing you, so I thought I'd save the energy." Sarcasm: first and best refuge from having to actually deal with feelings, but it was still a good point. "Maybe if—"

"Oh, you're starting to figure things out. That's wonderful, but we don't have time for it right now." Their captor seemed to glide into the space between them, and the branches constricted again, if not quite so much as before. "Maybe later, after Father's dead. But for now," —he bowed—"the forest and I have everything ready for our little walk to the beach."

"Frig off. What makes you think we're going to cooperate?" Megan's voice bit into the wind, and Carlos could almost feel thorns take shape against his back. There had to be something more going on here. He just needed more time to figure it out. And probably more information.

The man shrugged. "Because when I'm done, you go home." Turning around, he began to hum a random, jerky tune, and the trees in front of him seemed to lean apart, stretching branches out toward each other to form a long fence on either side. The space stretched out for at least a hundred yards, ending in a view of rolling waves. "Come along. It's almost time. Our guests are nearly here."

Roots slipped back into the soil, leaving only frozen ripples on the surface, and the branches around Carlos pulled back, one of them taking a moment to somehow slip between the layers of tape binding his ankles and part the sticky mesh.

Caught by surprise, Carlos didn't react for a moment, reaching to get rid of the scraps of tape only when he saw Megan tear at hers. She was on her feet before he could blink, turning to run in the opposite direction, but brought up short after only two steps. He followed her gaze even as he pulled the tape free from his pants.

The forest behind them somehow made a solid wall, trunks and branches overlapping so tightly that he couldn't see more than a few inches into the gloom. He stood up as Megan turned back with an expression he couldn't read. Every moment since she'd woken up, there had been some strong emotion etched across her face, anger or hatred or fear, but for this one instant, she seemed completely blank.

And then her lips twisted, and she ran after their captor.

Not knowing what else to do, Carlos followed, but at a slower pace.

The man hopped down onto the thin strip of rocky beach just before she caught up, and the last trees leaned in, flinging branches out to bar Megan's way. Unable to stop quickly enough, she crashed into them. Thin and brittle with the last vestiges of winter, she should have smashed through the flimsy barrier, but instead, the branches bowed and stretched for a moment before flinging her back to sit in the dirt.

Carlos stopped beside her before taking a single step forward to offer her a hand up. To his surprise, she took it, pulling hard to get to her feet even as she inhaled to yell at the man, but she never got the words out.

The trees wrapped around them both, jerking them from their feet and stretching out so that half of Carlos' body stuck out over the stones. Megan moved out a little farther as the trees arranged them according to some master plan.

A thin branch curled around Carlos' left arm, jerking it straight out so his palm hovered four or five feet above the wet sand. Was the tide coming in or going out? He'd never spent enough time on the coast to recognize the difference.

His left palm twisted down and locked into place. After a second or two, Megan's right hand appeared beside it, forced into the same position. Heat built through the line of contact on the knife edges of their hands, and he thought he might feel her trembling. Probably not scared.

The man walked into view almost underneath them, still smiling. "Not too uncomfortable, I hope; not that it matters." He grinned again, wider than ever. "Don't worry. This will be over soon."

Before Carlos could ask what he meant, or do more than think the question, a knife appeared in the man's hand. He had just enough time to wonder about its colour, warm and brown, before their captor flicked it across his palm and then Megan's.

Carlos hissed as the wound burned for a moment before a roar washed over his ears, a thousand years of wind rustling through the trees drowning a stream of curses from Megan. His vision narrowed to the string of blood extending from the wound, bulging at the bottom as it stretched, reaching for the stony beach below them. The second drop came faster, racing to catch the first. As the third slipped free, one joined it from Megan's hand, the two drops striking rock together just before the leading edge of a wave licked high enough to catch them. The wave pulled back, tiny swirls of blood leaving with it.

"Answer me, jerk wad!"

Carlos tried to focus beyond his exaggerated heartbeat. Megan was yelling at their captor, swearing at him, threatening him, trying to make him say something, maybe say anything, but he just stood there smiling up at them as the waves curled around his feet.

Opening his mouth, Carlos took a deep breath, tried to form some words in his mind, but nothing would coalesce. Nothing, except . . . something. He felt something. Something he couldn't put a name to, something all around him.

The man turned away to look out at the ocean as Megan sucked in a deep breath to scream at him again, but Carlos almost didn't notice. His eyes stayed glued to the branch wrapped around his wrist and forearm. The supple wood seemed to glow. He exhaled deeply and kept staring, suddenly not wanting it to let him go, but instead to turn over his hand so he could see the wound making a line of fire across his palm.

The branch rotated slowly, bringing the line of blood into view. It stretched across his entire palm, running below the inside of his knuckles, skipping across all of the thick lines. From somewhere above and behind him, another branch stretched down, placing a small bundle of buds across his palm, dragging them back and forth through the blood. It stung for a moment and then started to burn, not unpleasant exactly, but something like a concentrated fever. As he watched, the skin pulled itself together and the blood stopped flowing. In a dozen thrumming heartbeats, the wound was gone, a small smear of red remaining to mark it.

"How did you do that?" Megan's soft words surprised him, and he wondered idly if that might be her natural voice when she forgot to be angry. Grinning, he looked up, forgetting any words he might have been about to attempt when he saw the mermaids.

No more than a dozen yards away, twin fairy tales stretched out on the rocky strand as waves washed around them, everything and nothing like he'd pictured as a child. If he looked past the scales covering them, he could see either adorning the cover of any men's magazine. Above the waist, at least.

One looked straight into his eyes, and Carlos found nothing he recognized in the giant pupils. When she opened a too-wide mouth to suck at the air, the teeth inside belonged to a predator, but that didn't matter. The dark gaze reached into him, stirring the ancient and primeval heart inside him, instincts far more primitive than any rational thought or impulse, and he tried to shift his weight, leaning forward in the branches to drink in those eyes.

"Oh, well done, Carlos. The blood drew Father's Spring Brides here, and now he'll have to follow. A nice change—him coming to them. Yours and Megan's blood instead of Father's—male and female, the taste familiar and new at the same time—a far more potent mix than mine alone. But now you're learning, and that's got them confused. Can you feel them wondering where Father is?"

Could he feel it? A cool breath started to build behind his eyes, but a tickle in the back of his head pulled him away from the sensation. Growing stronger with every breath, it swallowed the sound of the tide kissing the edge of the forest. He felt a burning beside him—Megan's raw emotions a flame to kindle the forest's rage—and something else in front of him, a hole in his thoughts where their captor stood, where there should be more.

The man didn't look back, but stood a little straighter. "Oh. Yes, it's perfect. Our father approaches." A giggle escaped him. "And when it's done, *I'll* share blood with them, share the surf with them, share the world with them, and the seasons will turn to my will, not his."

Something stirred among the trees far off to his right. Carlos felt it through the branches wrapping him, as if the trees somehow knew something approached. Maybe the forest amplified the feeling, but he suddenly wondered how he could have gone through almost three decades without really noticing the life all around him, the throbbing, flowing veins of pure, living energy.

There couldn't be a coincidence to his new awareness. Whatever approached was not merely alive, it radiated that life in every direction, so much that every bit of vegetation nearby thrummed with each step it took. Carlos half expected the trees to start purring. He couldn't visualize what it could possibly be, couldn't think why he should be able to. Nothing lay in his past experience to bridge the gap to where he currently stood. Hung.

He took a deep breath, now seeing the world around him with more than just his eyes, and let his senses stretch out along the branches touching him to feel the beat of the forest, the steps of the approaching stranger, the purpose driving it to the shore. He could almost grasp the forest creature, but when he reached out over the waves to the ocean legends, they seemed completely alien—two cold presences in the surf. Whatever they felt, however they felt it, remained hidden from Carlos, even down to their expressions. He wondered what strange bond connected them to the forest, to the approaching being.

Their strange captor, human, but not—and what did that say about Carlos?—now ankle-deep in the slowly approaching waves, turned to Carlos' right, toward that green presence, a frown creasing the side of his face as he tucked the strange knife back inside his jacket. When his hand came out again, it held a gun.

Before Carlos could do more than recognize the weapon, the man raised it, smiling as he pointed it straight ahead into the forest, and squeezed off three quick shots. Harsh above the waves, those hollow snaps startled the mermaids into motion, and in less than an eye blink, Carlos saw only retreating ripples.

The growing awareness of the creature in the forest disappeared under a spasm that racked Carlos' body. In the same moment, Megan screamed, and the vegetation around them reacted with a quivering, shaking violence so intense he lost one shock under the other. Two branches stabbed out of the trees, leaves sprouting and filling out with an entire summer's growth. They sliced through air, serrated tips almost gleaming in the twilight, to spear flesh.

One went through the back of the grinning man's hand, knocking the gun into the water and the joy from his lips. The living, wooden tip curled up and around his fingers, while the second branch lanced through the meat of his thigh on the same side. Their captor screamed, and Carlos felt echoes of the pain even as he felt Megan's rage spread through the forest around and behind him. More branches seemed to rear up, spreading apart to get a dozen different angles, ready to finish turning the man into a grotesque pincushion.

Carlos turned his head to look at her, saw the pain and rage etched across her face. "Megan. No." He forced the words out on a shallow breath and willed her to look at him.

When she met his gaze, tears leaked from her eyes, drawing some cheap mascara with them to create dark cracks in her face. "Don't you get it? He's trying to kill our father."

"I know." Maybe he'd known for a while. Maybe some instinct had wormed its way into his consciousness the moment he heard the phrase 'happy birthday' applied to both of them. Our father. "Does that mean you have to kill *him*? He's our father's child, too. Our brother. Think about that."

Carlos might not understand everything, might not ever, but he began to make sense of the world in a new way. Our father. My sister. My brother. Warmth and peace flooded Carlos' body. He cleared his throat and spoke to the trees. "Set us down, please."

The branches loosened, twisted, turned, cradling their fragile bodies to place their feet on the ground rather than in the water. And if the trees understood his intent, they wouldn't let Carlos counter what Megan had demanded. Their former captor, their brother, stood with his feet submersed in the surf, face twisted, two branches growing through his body. Blood dripped from the fist clenched around one branch, each droplet of life pulled into a retreating wave, and a dark spot slowly spread across the denim covering his thigh.

He turned toward them, teeth grinding loud enough to hear. "You won't take this from me. I have the right."

"No, you don't." Carlos shook his head. "The only life you get to decide on is yours."

"But it's natural. This is the way things work."

"You're wrong." A few pieces fell together in Carlos' mind, bits of feelings and half-remembered legends. "We're not here to pick winners or losers, individuals or species. We're here to make things possible."

"No! It's my right!"

Smiling, Carlos shook his head. "No, it isn't."

The trees around them trembled, but almost instantly smoothed themselves out again. The almost forgotten feeling exploded in the back of Carlos' head, and a figure appeared beside him.

He had always wondered about his father. His boyhood fantasies all seemed so normal now, never coming close to the not-quite-human thing in front of him. Accepting the truth of the stranger as his father—their father—asked far more questions than it answered. What new truths would he have to embrace about who and what he was—what they all were?

Dressed in shabby clothes, almost rags, it looked like a man—old without being ancient, thin without being weak, tall without being imposing. Carlos stared into eyes that were a thousand shades of green all at once, glowing in a bland, expressionless face. A thick, bushy beard and tangled hair created a single snarled mass around his head, complete with twigs and leaves. The three wet spots spreading at an angle across the man's chest didn't seem to bother him in the slightest, and Carlos wondered if he'd even noticed the bullets.

Trees spread, leaning away from the old man as he took the last few steps to stand in front of them, green moss and grass spreading from each spot where his bare feet touched the dirt. Without warning, he reached out and put one hand on Carlos' forehead and the other on Megan's. Warmth and joy spread from the touch, and Carlos felt more awake and alive than he could ever remember. The touch lasted only a few seconds, but it changed Carlos' world more than the rest of the day already had. He resisted the urge to reach out and hug the man, and from the corner of his eye, saw Megan trembling.

Their father turned away from them then, opening his mouth. "Ahhhhhh." Not a word or a sigh, but a long, deep musical note.

The trees around them responded, reaching out to pull their brother from the water and place him gently before them, restrained but intact. The pair of branches that had pierced his flesh retreated, and he pressed forward against his bonds.

"It isn't fair. I would have let you go, and what has he ever done for any of us?"

Megan's hands balled into fists as she leaned forward, but the old man shifted, the ground pushing him into the middle of the little group, turning him to face the other man. He put both hands on him, one on either side of his face, took a deep breath, and let out another long '*Ahhhhhh.*'

The man didn't struggle, didn't try to fight, didn't do anything other than stare into their father's eyes. "I hate you. I've always hated you. I'll die hating you. It should be mine. I have the power, too."

The note went on longer than Carlos would have thought possible, and just when he thought the old man should be gasping for air, the change started. The tree branches blossomed and sprouted, covering his brother's body with leaves a hundred shades of green and dozens of too-early spring blossoms. Twigs and branch tips fractured and spread until, in a few seconds, they completely concealed him.

And still the note went on without pause. The forest vibrated and the note swallowed the waves, stealing the sounds of Carlos' breath and heartbeat. He stood transfixed, not having the faintest idea what might be happening, but completely unprepared for the note to just stop and all of the branches to whip away, revealing a naked infant on the cold grass.

Megan reacted first, whipping her pleather coat off and scooping the child up with it, a smile softening her face even before she straightened. In the same moment, their father turned his back, took three steps into the forest, and disappeared.

The trees around them settled quickly back into a more natural state, growing and standing as trees should. The foot-sized green places on the ground remained, as did the fresh leaves and scattered flowers. Never mind an early spring, parts of the space around them looked a little like summer.

Normal, natural. But Carlos could still feel the life all around him. The world might not have changed, but his perception of it certainly had. He looked down at the baby Megan held. One tiny fist wrapped around her index finger and bright green eyes blinked up at her sleepily. "Cute kid."

"Mmm." She didn't look up.

"You don't hate him?"

She did look up then, one side of her mouth lifted in a smile. "That wouldn't be fair, would it? This baby hasn't done anything to me, and neither will the person he grows up to be."

He had a surprisingly easy time agreeing with that statement. Even if the baby was just the same person, regressed to a natural infancy, he'd have a completely different childhood. And there was a lot of future between now and whatever time Megan had in her head. He wouldn't be the same person. "I suppose."

"Don't suppose. Believe. He's one of us. We'll be a good influence."

There were a lot of assumptions in that statement, but Carlos let them go. First step was to figure out where they were. Anything else was just asking for trouble. "He never told me his name."

Megan shook her head. "Me neither. I guess we'll have to pick one."

Carlos looked out over the ocean. The tide had begun receding again, and the sun had half its head hidden under the waves.

Not the birthday he'd expected, but when you were born on the first day of spring, a little bit of growth and change seemed right. He had a lot of questions and knew he'd have to figure out most of the answers on his own, although maybe Megan would help a little. "I guess we will."

PERADVENTURE

by Sarah E. Seeley

Delilah stood rooted to the gritty mud floor of her hut with a mixture of awe and terror as a goliath of a creature with pointed, bat-like ears and glowing yellow orbs for eyes reached for her with a massive hand through the night's darkness. That hand could have easily crushed her throat or broken her neck before she could think to scream. But she didn't scream. And the giant, claw-like fingers merely stroked back the hair that had fallen into her face.

The creature's skin was surprisingly silky, dark blue like the night's sky just after sunset. A glowing blue vapor curled off his skin in pale wisps and illuminated his features. A single lock of black hair, tied in place at the top of his head, fell snarled and loose over his shoulder. He was bare-chested, wearing a pair of loose muslin trousers that gathered at his ankles. The jawbone of some large animal was pinned to his left side by a striped sash at his waist. He smelled like scorched sand, like fire and brimstone.

He smiled at Delilah. Though menacing to behold, the creature's methods were beguiling. A part of Delilah still wanted to flee for her life, but she was inexplicably transfixed.

"Do I frighten you?" the creature asked. His voice was deep and unearthly. It seemed he could have churned the underworld with a single rumbling breath. Yet it was as gentle and silky to her ear as his touch was to her cheek.

Delilah knew that voice. She couldn't deny it belonged to the mysterious man from the south who had been pursuing her the past three days. The man she'd been avoiding, yet unable to chase from her thoughts and dreams for the same three nights. In daylight, he had been a mere man. Just as massive. Just as ominous. But a man. Only a man.

"What are you?" she whispered, her voice trembling.

He took a step closer. "I am jinn," he said. "By daylight, I take whatever form pleases me, be it a man or any other creature. By night, I take my demon form."

"And your name?" She dreaded the answer he would give, her heart pounding in her chest.

"Among my kin, I am known as Afzal. Among men, I am called Samson."

"Samson!" His words confirmed her fear, and she stumbled back into the water pots against the wall. She kicked over one of the vessels by mistake, and it shattered on the floor.

"It seems my reputation precedes me." He flicked his wrist, and the base of the broken water pot righted itself. The clay shards flew back into place, leaving no seams or cracks. Water slurped back inside over the lip of the vessel.

Delilah clutched her chest and shuffled away a little farther from the pot in astonishment. "Have you come to curse me?"

"Nonsense."

"Why have you come, then?"

"For the same reason any other man comes to you from time to time. Though, I could not have come into your humble abode of my own want if you hadn't invited me. The laws of magic forbid it."

"What do you want with me, Samson the Jinni?" Delilah surprised herself with her sternness. She was doing everything in her power to avoid his fiery gaze. Afraid he might seduce her to her doom if she let him stare into her soul too long.

The jinni paused. His bare feet were even more massive than his hands, yet they had a graceful toning instead of the flat, lumbering stock she might have expected for someone his size. Strong tendons stretched across his knuckles. His toenails were long, black, and pointed, like his fingernails. His callouses even seemed aesthetic in a way: not too thick or thin somehow, for a creature that clearly enjoyed journeying everywhere he went without shoes. "Delilah, isn't it?"

"Who told you my real name?"

"There was no need."

Delilah's face grew hot with shame.

"I mean that I can look upon your heart and see for myself who you are and what your intentions are. I saw your true name there."

Delilah said nothing, continuing to stare at his feet, or the ground, when she could manage to look away.

"Tell me what you've heard about me?"

Delilah lifted her eyes ever so slightly. "I know that you revel in luring men to their ruin. You claim you will grant riches to any who should solve your riddles or win gambling bets with you. And whenever one or two are clever enough to outsmart you, you slaughter and plunder whole villages out of spite because you are bound by your magic to honor your pacts."

The jinni plucked a few figs from a basket on Delilah's table and popped them into his mouth. He gave a masticating smack of his jaw. "This is true enough," he said. "I do take pleasure in causing humans mischief, watching them crumble beneath their own vices. You humans have such base and petty appetites. Avarice. Malice. A sense of entitlement. You're so easily corruptible, it's hard to resist toying with the minds and hearts of your race."

"For a creature who has no material needs, I find it ironic that a base and worthless creature like myself has so much power over your emotions as to make you lose your temper."

"Among other things," he added. The jinni's figure shifted before her eyes, morphing into the form of a man with ebony skin. He had the body of a god. At last, Delilah looked up into the dark human eyes that had first captivated her before she knew they were merely a demon's facade. The glowing vapors didn't dissipate, pouring off him like sweat in the night's heat. In the absence of daylight, that seemed to be the only thing Samson couldn't mask about his true form. He crept closer, lingering over her as she pressed her back against the angular brick wall of the hut. He slipped one last fig into his mouth, chewing it slowly. "Do you like mischief, Delilah?"

Something bubbled up inside Delilah that made her want to giggle. She remained silent, but couldn't stifle the smile curling her lips. How did he know just what to say to entice her? She wouldn't dare lie to a jinni, knowing he could read her intentions so keenly. A creature that could shift forms at will and fix water pots with a mere wave of his hand was not one to be trifled with. And she couldn't deny that she did delight in the thought of mischief and malice and other things the jinni had mentioned, from time to time. At the moment, she knew she was indulging a little too much in his figure and his closeness. It was, indeed, human nature.

"If you want me to leave, I'll leave," he said. "I never force myself or my . . . mischief on anyone." He stroked her cheek with a human hand this time. His skin was a little rougher, but the touch just as gentle and inviting. It sent a shiver through her spine.

Still smiling, she replied, "I don't do business with jinn."

"Why not?"

"I've also heard that you've seduced many women, some to their shame and ruin."

Samson laughed and dropped his hand from her cheek. "You are right, Delilah. I have indeed broken the hearts of many human women. But I have shamed none of them, unless for some reason they think they should be ashamed of themselves."

"How can you be so cruel? There are other jinn who choose to help us overcome our weaknesses. Why do you choose instead to vex and destroy as many of us as you can?"

"I don't wish to destroy *you*," said the jinni. "Any other human fool enough to make a bet with me doesn't deserve to win my little games. They deserve to fall. My torment is reserved only for humans who are too weak and desperate and stupid to make the right decisions for themselves."

"Clearly you must think I'm one of them."

"Not so. You're different."

"How?"

"I'm in love with you."

Delilah put a hand protectively to her throat to stop herself from laughing at him. "Love is a strong word," she said. "We've only spoken a few times in passing since you approached me three days ago. I doubt you're in love with me. Maybe you're smitten. Maybe you've got an itch in your trousers. Or, most likely of all, you're simply the snake you've already confessed to being."

"Tell me you're not intrigued, that you don't desire me as well."

Delilah held her breath a moment. She couldn't deny those things either. "What is your game?"

"My game?"

"The deal you want me to make."

"I'll grant you whatever your heart desires."

"Marry me, then. If you truly love me, you can wait one night and commit yourself to me alone. Come back in the daylight tomorrow in your man form and declare your love for me in front of the priest. Take vows with me in the temple of Dagon, lest you ruin me tonight and break my heart."

"It's strange that you would ask so much of me when you require so little of human men."

"Not so strange if you knew, as you claim to know, what it is my heart truly desires. Unlike human men, you are bound by magic to keep the vows you swear."

Samson simply smiled and pressed in a little closer. Not touching her, but almost. "Shall I vow to you tonight to come back on the morrow?"

"No. That will be your choice."

"You are wise indeed." He lingered there, close, his lips an inch from hers. His breath was warm and pleasant on her face. Tempting her to kiss him. She bit her lip and diverted her gaze from his eyes to what she could make out of his perfectly clean-shaven chin.

At last, he retreated, kissing her hand instead. "Goodnight, Delilah," he said. Then he turned and disappeared once more out her doorway into the night. Delilah wondered what mischief this jinni truly had in store for her. Whatever it was, she wasn't staying in Sorek long enough to find out.

Delilah shut the door and rushed to the wall behind her table. She removed two loose bricks. From a shallow crevice, she retrieved a dusty woolen blanket that protected the few valuables she owned: a clay lamp her mother had given her as a child; a silver dagger that had belonged to her father; a beaded necklace with an abalone shell that came from a seaside village many miles away; and a purse containing what few silver and copper pieces she had saved from day to day.

Delilah wrapped the bundle in the few extra articles of clothing she owned and stuffed all into the bottom of an old camel-hide sack. Next, she gathered up the figs and pomegranate on the table. She was reaching for a pot to fill her water bag when the door crashed open behind her. Delilah gasped and spun to face the intruders, clutching her sack to her bosom as she shrank against the wall.

Torchlight flickered over the walls and modest accouterments Delilah planned to leave behind as five soldiers barged into her hut with scimitars drawn. The last to enter was a slender young man dressed in dark silk robes. He wore a feather turban, with many rings on his fingers and fine gold chains about his neck. A metal scabbard encrusted with jewels was tied to his waist by his sash. His beard was ornately braided, strung with beads and ribbon that clearly set him apart as nobility.

"Are you Delilah of the valley's north end?" the young nobleman demanded. His tone was strangely elegant, like his appearance.

Delilah's heart leapt to her throat, and she simply nodded. How did *this* man know her true name? What was happening?

"I am Prince Husam, son of Basim."

"Your Highness." Delilah quickly fell to her knees and bowed low to the figure, touching her brow to the floor.

"Are you the same woman who stole precious wares from her husband's guests to feed her expensive tastes for fine apparel?"

"I was thus accused and punished by my former husband."

"Do you still deny you stole those things?"

"I do, my lord, though I know none believe me. I can't betray my own heart in this thing." Had someone brought new accusations against her? The thought churned Delilah's stomach.

The prince approached, standing just a pace from where she bowed. "We are in pursuit of Samson the Menace and lay in wait outside your hut for him to emerge. We heard you speaking with someone, and I thought I recognized your name. Did he not see you tonight?"

Relief washed through Delilah. She focused on the prince's dusty boots so as not to disrespectfully meet his gaze. "Yes, my lord. He spoke with me here but a moment ago, and then vanished into the night. If I knew where he went, I would straightway confess it to you."

The prince tapped the sack in her arms with his foot. "Where are you going in such a hurry?"

"I wish to escape before Samson returns for me on the morrow. He says he is in love with me, and I fear he will curse me."

The prince laughed and slid his scimitar into the scabbard at his side. He paced back and forth across Delilah's hut, shifting objects with a dull *clink* like he was examining them out of curiosity or amusement. "Do you really think you can escape from a jinni?"

Delilah shook her head. "I don't know what else to do, my lord."

The prince crouched before her on one knee. "Look up," he said.

Delilah met the prince's eyes, hoping her own expression didn't reveal too much of the shame and apprehension she felt in his presence.

He smiled at her with a wide set of clean teeth. "Fear not. My brothers and I have set a bounty of eleven hundred pieces of silver for anyone who can find a way to bind Samson's power and deliver him to us."

Delilah swallowed. "Eleven *hundred* pieces of silver?"

"Each. With this bounty, you would no longer have to survive as a harlot."

Delilah felt her face grow hot once more. She looked away.

"Marry the jinni. Get him to confess to you how a human might rob him of his powers."

"It is a dangerous thing you request of me, Your Eminence. I fear greatly for my life should Samson return. I fear his wrath even more should I cross him. There is little I can hide of my heart's true intentions from a jinni."

"Do you harbor any malice in your heart for Sorek?"

"None, my lord."

"Do you value the lives of our people?"

Delilah met the prince's gaze earnestly. "Yes, my lord."

"Do you care if Samson corrupts the souls of the people and wreaks havoc here?"

"I wish he would not have come back to this city. He will bring great evil upon us."

The prince chuckled as though genuinely pleased. "You seem to me a humbled woman who has borne her suffering well. If your heart's true intention is to deal with Samson for the good of the people, he will not be able to perceive more than this."

Of that I am not so certain, Delilah thought.

"Help us stop this demon from destroying Sorek the way he destroyed Gaza. Swear it, and I will swear to you before my men that all this bounty will be yours. You will not know poverty or shame the rest of your days."

Delilah frowned. Astounded as she was by the prince's kindness toward her, she feared granting his request. "What if he will not confess his weakness to me?"

"He will. He is a jinni, bound by magic, and must choose his words carefully. If he says he is in love with you, he will have no choice but to confess his heart to you."

Delilah swallowed again, steeling herself to accept the prince's offer. "Very well. For the sake of the people and for this bounty you have offered, if Samson returns on the morrow, I will marry him. I will test his claim of love for me to see what he will confess. When he tells me his weakness, I will reveal it to you."

"It is agreed." Prince Husam extended his hand. Delilah shook it. Her grip was weak and clammy in the man's palm. He tightened his grasp when she tried to pull away, and gazed firmly into her eyes. "Do not flee until this task is done. Otherwise, you will be guilty of breaking this pact and forsaking your duty to your people. Understood?"

"Yes, my lord." When the prince let go, Delilah bowed her head to touch the ground at his feet once more.

The prince rose and waved his men toward the door. "Rest well tonight, Delilah of Sorek." He disappeared after his soldiers and their torchlight.

Left in darkness once more, Delilah returned her things to their places. She tried to calm her nerves by fashioning twine bracelets to sell at market before curling on her side on her straw mat. "This is madness," she muttered to herself, closing her eyes to welcome the escape of sleep. "Fate has dealt me a most cruel hand this night."

꧁꧂

The amethyst blue waters of the Mediterranean Sea heaved against the sandy shores of Ashdod like a living, breathing entity. Delilah had never seen anything so beautiful in all her humble existence back in the Valley of Sorek. She was awed by the power of the sea, by its seemingly endless expanse against the beaming afternoon sky. Every breath she drew was pleasantly humid and peppered with salt.

The water, rhythmically combing the sand at her feet as it rushed around her ankles then pitched back out with a roaring *swoosh,* was clear as crystal and pure as the daylight that kissed it. Warm. Enticing. Teeming with life mysterious. Despite the wonder of it all, Delilah dreaded the unseen perils lurking, deep and patient, beyond the marvelous, sparkling shoal.

Samson's hands lighted on her shoulders like great birds. Even in human form, he smelled like sand and fire. "What do you think?" he murmured in her ear with his deep, rumbling voice.

Delilah frowned at her feet with uncertainty as water and shifting sand continued to tug at her toes and ankles. "It's breathtaking," she said.

Samson's fingers traced the red beaded sash draped over her shoulder. "This dress is most becoming on you."

"Thank you. It feels good to wear something respectable for a change."

"There was no need to spend your money for it. I could have easily conjured a duplicate."

"I didn't want a duplicate. And I'd been saving my pennies for it a long time."

"Why didn't you get it before?"

"I never knew if I would need the money for something else. And I didn't have the right occasion to wear it, until now."

Samson chuckled. "Shall we go for a swim?"

Delilah lifted her eyes to take in the endless expanse of sea and sky once more before turning to meet Samson's gaze. She forced a coy smile and shook her head.

"Tell me why not?"

"You will laugh at me," she said. "The waters are so great and powerful, and I am so small. I'm afraid the sea will swallow me up should I dare to venture any further."

Samson grinned with a devious gleam in his eye and took her hands. "Peradventure they do?"

"Then peradventure I should drown." Delilah tried to hide how uncomfortable she really was at the thought of disappearing into that great expanse, hoping to find a way to convince Samson to take her back to Sorek instead.

"Is love the same with you?" asked Samson.

"Oh." Delilah looked down at her feet once more. "Life is the same with me, I suppose. Fate has not been kind to me."

"Your former husband was not kind to you?"

"Would I be what I am now if he was?"

Samson pulled her close and wrapped his great arms around her. His chest was smooth and hard, like a polished river stone. "You're a harlot no more. You belong to me now, and I to you."

Delilah shivered at the loveliness of those words. She had to remind herself that this man was really not a man at all, but a monster she'd agreed to bait for silver and for the good of her people.

"Do you think that I, the great and powerful jinni that I am, would let you drown?"

Delilah's smile wilted, and she said nothing.

"You still don't believe that I love you?"

"It's not that simple, Samson."

"It is for me. I swore my vows to you before the priest this very morning, didn't I?"

Delilah squinted into Samson's deep brown eyes, searching them carefully. "You told all gathered there and round about that you were the great and dreadful Samson."

"And why not? None will dare harass you now, fearing my wrath should come upon them."

"Except you also told them *my* real name."

"It's a lovely name."

"It's a tainted name I left behind. And for good reason."

"No one on this end of the valley has heard of you."

"None except. . ." Delilah bit her lip to stop herself from mentioning Prince Husam. "Can't you understand? By revealing to others who we really are, you have put me in greater danger, not less."

"If you weren't up for a lifetime of danger, why did you marry me?"

Delilah gasped and turned out of Samson's embrace. What kind of fool had she been to think she could hide her heart's true motives from a jinni? Surely he would curse her now, or drown her in the very place she had so often yearned to see. A part of her wanted to flee, but another part of her knew there was no escape. Running from a jinni would be pointless. This had been a most cruel trick of fate.

"Have you not always longed to behold the sea?"

"Yes," said Delilah, her voice trembling. "And it's even more stunning than I could have imagined."

"But you never imagined it would frighten you so much?"

Delilah said nothing.

"What a shame. The wound you carry must be deeper than you thought, too." Samson approached her and lifted her chin so her eyes would meet his gaze. He frowned this time. Delilah feared she couldn't hide her dread anymore. "Tell me what happened with Faraj?"

She was not expecting that request. Realization sank deep into her heart that she had never met someone who could discern her name and perhaps her innocence also. Someone who might actually believe the truth of what she said for once. But Samson liked mischief and cruelty. Opening up her past would make her vulnerable to his vices. Her mind stumbled to find words, wanting to escape the question but unsure of what to say. So she gave in. "I . . . I was not . . ."

"You were barren," said Samson. "Faraj said you weren't good enough for him. When he got his mistress pregnant, he set you up and publically decried you as a thief and usurper of his household. He turned you out and took his new wife before anyone could notice his infidelity. Then your father said he was so ashamed of you for the things Faraj had accused you of that he didn't want to see your face again. The old man passed away a few months later without reconciling."

Delilah's eyes grew hot with tears. She fought to keep them from spilling over as she glared at Samson. "It hardly seems fair. You can discern everything about me, but I can't know anything about you unless you tell me."

"I can't read your mind. Only your heart . . . Are you going to weep?"

Delilah clenched her jaw. "No."

"Why not?"

"Because I think you want me to."

"You really do think I'm cruel, don't you?" Samson took her face in both of his massive hands. Delilah shrank a little, clutching his wrists. "What do you wish me to tell you?"

"What do you mean?"

"You wish me to tell you something about myself. What is it?"

Delilah swallowed. She gazed firmly into his eyes. "If you love me, tell me how a human may take your powers away and render you mortal."

Samson laughed. He kissed her lips sweetly. "Very well," he said, to her astonishment. He took a step back and held his hand out to her. "You accused me of reveling in destruction while others of my kind seek to help humans. Come for a swim with me. Let me help you conquer your fear so that you may enjoy the beauty of these waters without being overwhelmed by the thought of their dangers. Take this chance with me. Let me earn your trust, and I'll trust you with my greatest secret. I'll tell you how a human may render me powerless."

He is going to drown me, Delilah thought. *He knows my heart. . . . He must know my intentions.* An idea came to her then, one she knew in her heart she would be willing to die for. "Grant me one more request, and I will go with you into the sea."

"Name your wish."

"Promise me you won't destroy my people in the Valley of Sorek with your powers."

Samson hummed and paced in a circle, stroking his chin like he was thinking. "The lure of my greatest secret is not enough to entice you?"

"Perhaps you only say it is your greatest secret because it is the one I desire most to know. I desire this more."

"Any other requests?"

"None."

Samson picked up a stone and skipped it across the waves. "You are a tough bargainer, my love."

Delilah folded her arms. "Is it so hard for you to shed your cruelty and spare the souls of one city for me?"

"It would be of no use if those souls were already lost."

"Perhaps we should go back, then, and forget that I ever mentioned the sea." It felt like an oddly selfish thing to say.

Samson sighed and shook his head. "I will do it," he said. He extended his hand once more. "I will grant both of your requests. Soon we will make love, and you will forget the sea was ever at odds with you."

Delilah took a deep breath, then took Samson's hand. They left their clothes in the branches of an old tree, and he led her away into the surf.

※

"You treacherous worm," spat Husam. He kicked rubble with his boots as he paced a dark alleyway outside a tavern in the southern hub.

Delilah squirmed in the grip of two soldiers who pinned her wrists behind her back. "It is what he told me," she pleaded. "He said a measure of lemon juice mixed with a measure of vinegar and a bulb of ground garlic thrown upon his head would weaken his magic. He said he would lose his ability to shift forms and be powerless, like any human. I swear it."

"All while uttering the 'magic words' *ufoolio ufoolio*." The prince threw a stein of the lemon-vinegar cocktail in Delilah's face and smashed the vessel at her feet. She shrieked at the white-hot burn of the liquid and squeezed her eyes shut. Tears of pain flowed down her cheeks. She would have shrunk to her knees if the soldiers hadn't kept her upright with a sharp tug.

A hand squeezed her jaw, sending a stab of pain to her ears. "Do you think this is some sort of game?"

"No, your eminence," Delilah managed.

"Because of your folly, fifty of my finest assassins have been turned into dung beetles and squashed beneath the heel of that cursed jinni!"

"He must have lied to me somehow. Please, my lord. Have mercy. I wouldn't betray your men to Samson if I knew."

"Oh, I don't know about that." He gripped her beaded shoulder sash. "You clearly seem to be enjoying his *gifts*. Perhaps I should withdraw my ransom."

"I bought this dress myself, with my own money. Samson didn't give it to me."

"And where did you get the money?"

"I came by it honestly. In the market, I make and sell bracelets made of twine with clay beads."

"And on the side you slake men's passions." Prince Husam thrust her back against the grip of his guards. Delilah's head spun with nausea. "Perhaps he doesn't love you," he said. "Perhaps you are merely another harlot to him, one more passing conquest to drown his cares for a few nights."

"Perhaps," Delilah agreed.

There was silence. Nothing but the roar of torches carried by Prince Husam's remaining men, and the echoes of other people traversing distant streets. The soldiers released Delilah. She fell to her hands and knees on the gravel with a huff. Immediately, she began wiping the lemon juice from her eyes and the snot dribbling from her nose. She desperately craved water to wash out the sting.

"Go back and press him for the true answer of his undoing," said the prince.

Delilah was stunned. "*Go back?* I can't go back to Samson. He will murder me."

"Pray that his means are quick and painless, then. If you fail me again, or try to flee, the wrath of my brother Elazar in Hanna's burning will seem to you like a great mercy compared to how severely I will deal with you."

"Hanna?" Delilah asked, confused.

"Has Samson not told you of Hanna?"

"No."

"She was the first human woman to capture his heart, and the last one to break it." The prince gave a final shout to his men to clear out, and Delilah was left alone.

She stumbled blindly along the street until she found the back alley well. There, she drew a bucket of water and rinsed the smart from her eyes. Her new dress was a bit sooty, but otherwise no worse for wear. The lemon juice hadn't left as much of a stain on the white fabric as she'd expected.

"Samson had another wife?" she whispered in disbelief. "If Samson loved her, is it possible he could . . . ?" Delilah shook the idea from her head. She couldn't allow herself to believe that Samson loved her. It was far too dangerous. The jinni was up to no good, and the prince was eager to stop him. Delilah only wished she wasn't caught up in this mess as the expendable, thieving harlot who'd married him.

"Maybe he will spare me," she whispered. She was only half convinced. Half was enough to send her back to her hut. With any luck, Samson wouldn't be there. Maybe he'd go into hiding for a few days. If she was really lucky, she might be able to catch a few hours of sleep before things got horrible. That's what she told herself.

❧

"Faraj?" Delilah croaked. She reeled in shock at the sight of her former husband, the woman he had shamed her for, and the couple's son, all bound and gagged on the dirt floor in the middle of her hut. The child sobbed. The woman squawked hysterically. Faraj glared at Delilah over his shoulder with a dark, brooding hatred she had never forgotten. His expression inspired her own hatred, like an itch in her spine that wouldn't leave. As if seeing them all like this wasn't upsetting enough, the other woman, Ihab, was wearing a blue dress that had once belonged to *her*.

"Hello, Delilah."

The hairs on the back of her neck prickled.

LEGENDS AND LORE

Samson rose from her table in the shadows behind the abductees. Pale blue wisps of light flickered about him. His jinn eyes glowed, golden and menacing, in the darkness.

Delilah's eyes darted from Faraj and his family to her jinn husband. "Samson... what's going on?"

"Faraj would not confess the evil he has done to you, so I burned his house and all his fine possessions. I brought him here, captive, to prove my love for you."

"What do you mean to do with these people?"

"Whatever you and I shall please." He gripped Faraj by the shirt and hoisted the man to his feet. "Let's start with this one." Samson waved his hand. A puff of black smoke enveloped Faraj. His clothes fell to the floor in a pile. A shiny black scarab scuttled out across the floor, and Samson lifted his massive foot as though to crush it.

"Don't!" Delilah dove to catch the beetle. It escaped and scurried toward the doorway. She shut her door and blocked the space beneath it with her body. "Got you," she said, scooping up the beetle as it came straight into her hands. But the beetle pinched her, and she tossed it away again.

After chasing Faraj around her hut, Delilah pulled the loose bricks from her wall and retrieved the one blanket she owned, spilling its precious bundle on the floor. Her mother's clay lamp shattered. Delilah threw the blanket to catch the beetle, but it fluttered out the window.

"Faraj!" Delilah bolted out after him into the street. The beetle was halfway to the edge of the slope when a blackbird swooped down and plucked him out of the air. The bird tossed Faraj down its throat and disappeared over the sandy cliff. Delilah clutched her stomach in revulsion.

"It's a shame he didn't heed your warnings," Samson called. "Do you think these two will be wiser?"

"Samson! No!" Delilah hurried back inside.

Samson already had Ihab pinned against a wall by her throat. He gripped the front of that blasted blue dress. "This isn't yours," he said. With three dreadful strokes, Samson ripped the dress from Ihab, along with all her undergarments. The garments smoked in Samson's fist. He tossed them on the floor, where they curled and blackened as though on fire.

"STOP!" Delilah snatched her father's dagger from the floor and plunged the curved blade into Samson's back. Samson chuckled, extracting the knife without leaking so much as a drop of blood. Jinn didn't bleed, she realized. Mortal weapons were useless against them.

Samson tossed the dagger aside. "This would be the second time you've stabbed me in the back tonight. Didn't I tell you that I never force myself on anyone?"

"Yes."

"Am I not bound by the things I say, according to the laws of magic?"

Delilah hesitated, still unsure what to make of Samson's lie about the lemon-vinegar concoction. "Don't curse them. Please. You're angry with me for betraying you. Curse me instead and let them go."

"She has wronged you."

"There are laws to deal with wrongs of this nature."

"Clearly your people's laws have utterly failed you."

"Please, Samson. Just let them go."

Samson waved his hand, and the cords fell from Ihab's wrists. He released her throat. The young woman pulled the gag from her mouth and hurried back to her son. She untied the boy, clutching him protectively to her naked bosom as they sobbed together.

"Go," Samson growled at the woman. "Get out."

"Wait, you can't send her out like that," said Delilah.

"Why not? She and Faraj did the same to you. She even wore the apparel she stole from you that day."

Delilah shook with shame and anger. The memory was still as fresh as a cut. She hid her face in her hand.

Samson returned to Delilah's table and took a seat. He perched his head comfortably in his palm, curling his fingers about his lips as if intrigued. "If you can forgive this cruel wretch for her hand in destroying your reputation, I will let you do with her as you please."

Delilah turned back to Ihab, clenching her fist. How oft she had wanted to give this woman a good beating.

"I'm sorry," Ihab blubbered, her eyes wide with terror. "I'm sorry. I'm sorry."

No, you're not sorry at all, thought Delilah. *And you never will be. You'd do the same thing to me again and again if you had the opportunity.* Angry tears filled Delilah's eyes. "Why do you hate me?" she asked.

"I . . . I don't hate you," said Ihab.

"Why did you do it, then? Why did you take Faraj's heart from me?"

"Faraj had no heart. I only thought he loved me more than you, until I married him."

"What do you mean?"

"I caught him twice with other women. He threatened to divorce me and leave me penniless like he'd done to you if I told anyone."

Delilah huffed. She wanted to laugh. She shook her head. "You planted those goblets in my chamber, didn't you?"

Lip quivering, Ihab nodded.

"Why did you help him shame me?"

"Because I was weak. Because I wanted . . ." Ihab curled in on herself and squeezed her scalp with one hand, sobbing even harder.

"You have wronged me most grievously, Ihab. For my man, his house, and all my fine clothes and jewelry, you helped him destroy my good name. You have condemned me to a life full of suffering and humiliation beyond what I even *want* to describe to you. My heart withers some days to the point that I think I could not defeat my own shadow if it were to take aught with me. I'd done nothing to you, nothing to deserve this fate. And I have hated you and Faraj both with all the bitterness of my soul these three years."

"S-sorry," Ihab stuttered. "I'm so . . . I'm so sorry . . ."

Delilah noticed for the first time that Ihab had three large bruises on her back, and many scars that resembled lashings.

LEGENDS AND LORE

She touched one of the bruises, and Ihab flinched. "What are these?"

"Faraj was not a p-patient man," Ihab gasped. "When he d-didn't get his way or th-things weren't just right in the house, he would g-get angry with me and beat me."

Delilah sighed. The anger fizzled out of her. She could never trust this woman. That wouldn't be right, and it wouldn't be smart. But she felt reassured about her desire to show mercy. Perhaps Ihab had seen enough natural consequences for her actions to think twice about taking advantage of others again. "Maybe I am the lucky one after all," said Delilah. At last she held out her hand to Ihab. "Come on."

Hesitating at first, Ihab took her hand and got to her feet. The young woman took her son's hand, and Delilah led them over to a new cedar chest in the corner. Samson had conjured it for her, along with all the clothes it held from their three days at Ashdod. When Delilah opened the chest, however, it was empty except for her old street urchin clothes. "Samson?"

"Those dresses aren't yours to give away," he said.

Delilah pulled out a tattered black robe she'd made herself from discarded sackcloth. Someone had been kind enough to offer the material to her to hide her nakedness all those years ago. "I'm sorry, Ihab. All I have is . . ."

Delilah caught a glimpse of her own sash and gown. Immediately, she was furious. She was repulsed by the idea of giving up this one small luxury she had worked so hard for to the woman who had taken away everything in the world she had ever owned. But she didn't want to be merciless, and she feared Samson would send the woman into the night without a stitch of clothing if her forgiveness was not sincere.

"Curse you, Samson," Delilah whispered. Fighting every ounce of spite and anger in her body, Delilah unwrapped her dress. Naked, she offered it to Ihab. "Here. It's the best thing I own. No one will think to take advantage of you in this."

Ihab stared at the dress, still clutching her young son protectively at her side.

"It is a gift this time," said Delilah. "Take it."

"Why are you being so kind to me?"

"Because I know you can't handle the hordes of pitiless vipers that are going to come pouring out of the alley crevices, whistling and groping at you if you go out with anything less. These streets can be a dangerous place for a woman. The child is innocent and doesn't deserve to see his mother treated that way."

Ihab took the dress and put it on. Delilah donned the old black robe instead. The other woman touched her shoulder. "Here." She offered the red sash with both hands. "It is beautiful, but it is more than I need."

"Thank you." Delilah took the sash and wrapped it around her hand. "I guess you can't go back to Faraj's house now. Do you have a place to go?"

Ihab nodded. "I can go to my mother's house. She lives in Hiblion."

"Do you know how to get there from here?"

"Yes. It will be a few days' journey."

"Here." Delilah retrieved the bejeweled dagger and sheathed it. She offered it to Ihab. "This was part of my dowry when I married Faraj. It's the only thing I truly stole from him. There is an exchanger down the street named Fatsam who will give you three hundred pieces of silver for it. That should be enough to cover your journey to your mother's house. Enough, if spent modestly, for you to live on for two years."

Ihab bowed on her knees as she accepted the dagger. She offered one more "thank you," then left with her son. Delilah sagged against her crooked doorway, feeling haggard as she watched the sunrise. Missing sleep at night made her anxious. Samson likely wasn't finished with whatever retribution he had in store for her.

"Tell me why," said Samson.

"Why what?"

"Why you granted them mercy. Why you gave Ihab your new dress and your father's silver dagger."

"You did burn the dress she was wearing."

"True." His hands gripped Delilah's shoulders more gently than she expected. She flinched all the same. "You betrayed me to Prince Husam's men."

"Yes."

"Why?"

"Because you're a monster. Because there is a bounty on your head and . . . because I'm afraid."

"You're still afraid of me?"

"Yes. You. Prince Husam. Everyone."

"Why don't you run away if you're afraid?"

Delilah shook her head, almost laughing. "I want to. But I can't." They were both silent for a while. "Were you married once before, Samson? To a human woman?"

"Yes."

"Did you love her?"

"I did."

"Did she love you?"

Samson pulled away. Delilah turned and watched him pace across the floor of her hut. "Almost," he said.

"What happened to her?"

"Like you, she was afraid. I was causing mischief in Sorek many years ago. Prince Elazar came to her because he had entered into a bet with me. If he could solve a riddle I posed to him by the time the sun set on a certain day, I would take all the gold he coveted that had belonged to a certain man in the town and give it to him. If he could not, I would turn him into a monkey."

"A monkey?" Delilah tried very hard not to sound amused.

"He said he would burn Hanna if she didn't learn the answer to the riddle. She was very upset, so I told her the answer, and she told Elazar. I had no choice but to grant his wish, but I also burned his father's grain fields in my anger."

"Then what?"

"I abandoned Hanna. Because I burned the fields, Basim's son burned her and her father to avenge his honor."

Delilah frowned, tracing the beads on the sash in her hand with her thumb.

"You don't believe me, do you?"

"I've heard Prince Elazar can act a bit . . . spoiled sometimes," said Delilah. "I didn't know he'd made such cruel threats to anyone. Were you really so angry with Hanna when Elazar threatened to burn her if she did not press you for the answer?"

"No. There is another reason I abandoned Hanna. Someday I will tell you why I did it."

"Was it a noble reason?"

Samson put his claw-like hands on his hips and shook his head. "I thought it was a *good* reason at the time. But there is something humans have which I lack."

"What's that?"

"I think you humans call it *empathy*."

Delilah raised her eyebrow and turned once more to look out at the city below the hill. She just wanted to sleep. Nightfall seemed so far away. "If you love me as you have said, do the right thing for once. Stop causing mischief. Stop cursing people. Answer to the law for the wrongs you've done."

Samson said nothing.

"Or if you will not, get on with cursing me and . . . if you have any room for mercy in your heart, make your vengeance quick."

"Surely I will curse you to keep my promise, but only for the day."

"Only for the day? Why so generous?"

A dark cloud swirled around her head. The sunlight and city below quickly faded to blackness. Delilah stumbled backward, gasping and rubbing her eyes. She would have tripped over herself if Samson hadn't caught her.

"Steady," he said. "I have made you blind. Sleep, then go straightway at dusk when your eyesight has returned. Tell Prince Husam that my power may be taken from me by throwing a net over my head made of green reeds and gold thread."

Delilah was so confused by what was happening, at what Samson's motives could possibly be. "Green reeds and gold thread? Is it the truth this time?"

"What do you think?"

"I thought you couldn't lie, but obviously you can."

"I can lie. But if I ever break a promise, or a vow, or a bet, my magic will obliterate me."

"You promised you would tell me your weakness."

"And so I must."

"Husam has vowed to torture me, perhaps to death, if my information proves false again."

"Your life is in fate's hands, then. Sleep well, Delilah."

Wind whipped about her. There was a loud *crack*. The smell of hot glass—sand and fire—filled Delilah's nostrils, and the wind died away.

Delilah groped about the darkness. "Samson?" The jinni was gone. Delilah found her mat on the floor with her feet and curled up there on her side. Though she led an isolated existence, interrupted by brief interludes with strange men to satisfy their passions, she felt surprisingly empty sleeping by herself, without Samson. To her thankfulness, sleep came to her much more quickly than she thought it would.

※

The setting sun reamed the desert sky in a reddish-golden hue as Delilah made her way through the bustling market streets near the main trade road. It was hot, and the stale air stank of human sweat and animal manure. Most of the sellers, rich and poor, were packing up their wares and heading home.

Some stared as Delilah passed them. Thanks to Samson, everyone on the southern end of the valley now knew her name. How many of them would not let her sit in the shade beside their stands to sell her bracelets? How many who had been kind enough to share food or water with her from time to time would now refuse? The thought of having to fight harder for daily meals made her empty stomach growl unpleasantly. Many took pity on poor beggars, but few took pity on thieves.

Delilah sighed. Could Samson not have sent her back in three days' time, or three weeks'? Surely Prince Husam would not believe she had reconciled with Samson and learned his secret so quickly. The thought of betraying Samson made Delilah feel guilty this time. Was it possible the jinni did love her? He took her into the sea at Ashdod to make love and help her conquer her fear of drowning. When she betrayed him to his enemies, he sought justice for her wrongful shaming instead of cursing her. He filled her eyes with blackness so that she could sleep out the day and be refreshed. A small part of her hoped a gold-threaded net wasn't his true weakness either.

She approached a white building with a shallow flight of steps leading up to the entrance. It wasn't the prince's main house by any means, but a much smaller city outpost used by nobility as they passed through. She was surprised to see none of the prince's entourage outside. Even when he was away, there was usually someone present to keep watch and relay messages.

Smoke billowed up over the courtyard walls. It smelled like spoiled meat. Delilah wrung her hands, pacing back and forth at the foot of the steps. Something wasn't right. No guards? No horses? But a servant was burning a dead animal in the refuse pit behind the house?

What would Samson do if she turned back? It seemed absurd that he would curse her. But forgive her? Praise her? No. Samson knew her heart. He would know her fear. He sent her here tonight so that when she turned back, he could shove her weakness in her face. She hated Samson for persuading her to think, just for a moment, that he loved her.

As the daylight faded further, Delilah noticed torchlight flickering beneath the double doors. She climbed the steps. "Hello? I seek Prince Husam on an urgent matter." She felt extremely foolish to think she could be admitted this way.

No one, not even a steward, came to the door or answered back.

Delilah knocked. The door gave a little at her touch. It wasn't bolted. Cautiously, and feeling ever more intrusive, she pushed the door open. There were two torches burning, one on either side of the room.

"Hello?" Delilah called again. Again, there was silence. Heavy curtains were drawn over all the windows. Three massive cedar chests stood side by side in the center of the room.

Delilah was itching to leave. Perhaps there were real thieves here, trying to steal the prince's treasure. It would be difficult to carry away everything with chests that size. But why would the prince be so unwise as to leave his treasure unguarded in the middle of an outpost room?

As Delilah studied the beautifully carved chests longer, she noticed that they bore the insignia of a wealthy merchant named Asra. The man was last seen caravanning on the way to Sorek about a week ago, but had mysteriously vanished, along with all his cargo.

Casting a quick glance back and forth, Delilah crept inside to take a closer look. As she snuck toward the chests, she stumbled over something bundled on the floor in black cloth. There were three or four of them, side by side. Delilah unwrapped the bundle at her feet. The bloated face of a boy stared up with wilted eyes. She shrieked. *Husam slaughtered Asra's caravan!*

The front doors swung open before Delilah could reach them. She stopped just short of colliding with Prince Husam and another man who resembled him in too many ways to be anything less than a brother. The sleeves of their robes were rolled up to their elbows. Between them, they carried another body bundled in black cloth.

Husam dropped his burden and caught Delilah by the wrist. *"Delilah,"* he snarled. He pushed her back into the room while his brother bolted the door.

"Wait!" Delilah cried.

Husam thrust her on the floor and pinned her arm behind her back. He put a knife to her throat.

"The jinni has told me his secret!"

"So soon?"

"I would not have come otherwise."

"Tell me his weakness, then."

"Swear you will let me live and I will tell you."

The prince laughed. "You really must think me a great fool."

"I won't tell anyone. I saw nothing. I know nothing."

"Of course you won't tell anyone." He took the knife from her throat and pressed his lips against her ear. His breath was sharp. "I'm going to make sure of it." He slid her robe down her back.

The walls shuddered and a fiery blue pillar swirled up in the center of the room. When the tongues of flame receded, they coalesced to form a figure. A demon.

"Samson!" Husam hissed. With a sickening *crack*, the prince twisted off Delilah and thudded to the floor. Blood oozed beneath his head. His eyes lay open, lifeless. Delilah stared at the dead prince in shock.

"Elazar," Samson growled.

Delilah snapped her head around. The other prince unlatched the door and ran screaming out into the street. "Guards!

Guards! Samson is upon us! He has killed Husam and the company of Asra!"

"Delilah." Samson secured his jawbone club and extended his hand. "Come, quickly."

Delilah grasped his arm, and he pulled her upright against him. He fixed her robe and wrapped his big arms around her. She was shivering.

"Hold on tight."

Delilah squeezed her eyes shut and clung to Samson's waist sash. The ground fell away. Her stomach lurched like she was falling.

When her feet touched solid ground again, the surface was hard, and the air was cold. Delilah opened her eyes. It was dark, except for a single beam of moonlight that trickled down from an opening in the rock above them. Her eyes adjusted quickly, and she realized they were standing in the heart of a small cave.

Delilah laughed, releasing all the terror that had gripped her since Samson threw her life into chaos. She glanced around in wonder at the rocky walls of their underground oasis. "Where are we?"

"About a mile west, outside Sorek. Not as far away from the city as I'd hoped to get."

"What do you mean?"

Samson shook his head. "Nothing." He shifted to his human form, gazing at her with eyes instead of light-filled sockets. There were no wisps of light streaming off him this time. He was getting better at concealing his true form. "Are you all right?"

Delilah nodded. "Can you forgive me for not believing you?"

"About what?"

"That you love me? That you . . . ? You were trying to stop those men from getting away with murder, weren't you?"

Samson smiled that lovely, succulent, ghoulish smile that was his in any form. "Do you believe me now?"

"Yes. With all my heart."

Samson kissed her. Sweetly. Then hard. Full of passion. "Shall I tell you my secret now?" he whispered. Sweat trickled down his face. She had never noticed him sweat before.

Delilah shook her head. She stroked Samson's cheek. "I don't want to know your secret any more. I wish never to betray you again. And . . ."

"Yes?"

The words fluttered in her chest. "I love you."

Samson laughed. It was soft and breathy. His eyes drooped and he began to buckle. Delilah gripped his shoulder to steady him. He looked at her hand as though surprised.

"Are you all right, Samson?"

"Yes, my love. I'm just weary." He was still smiling.

"I didn't know jinn grew weary."

Samson nodded vaguely. He took her hand from his shoulder and held it in both of his without speaking for a long time. "Do you mind if we rest for the night?"

"Of course. We can do whatever you please."

Samson led her around the cave until he found a place to stretch out. Delilah curled up beside him, resting her head on his shoulder. He put his arm around her. Stroked her fingers at his chest. He closed his eyes, still smiling like he was in a daze. "Good night, Delilah."

"Good night, Samson. Sleep well . . . my love."

⁂

Delilah awoke to Samson's laughter. He stared at his hands, trembling as he clenched and opened his fists. His cheeks were damp with tears.

"Are you weeping, Samson?"

"Yes . . . Delilah, I am mortal."

She sat up, searching his eyes earnestly. "What?"

Samson stretched and sat up beside her. He stared at his human hands once more, front and back, laughing and laughing. "The moment I gained your full trust last night, my powers began to slip away. That is why I grew weary after I brought you here. I had to make a choice last night at the outpost—to leave you in Elazar's hands and betray your trust once more, or to take you away from that place and lose my power."

"Samson, how will we escape Prince Husam's brothers without your powers?"

"We can't."

"We *can't?*" Delilah got to her feet, pacing back and forth in the muted light of the cave. "Could you not have taken us away to some very distant land that's never even heard of Sorek before you went to sleep and lost your powers?"

"Alas, I could not. I tried, but I had not the strength to take us both any farther away than this cave."

Delilah went to the wall of the cave and squinted up at the crevice, where daylight beamed in a narrow, blinding pillar. "We are outside the city. Perhaps we can make a run for it."

"The time for escaping on foot has passed. By now, the princes have sent their men out this far and farther to search for us while we slept. I'm . . . I'm truly sorry for bringing this mischief upon you, Delilah."

Delilah curled her fingers in the sleeves of her robes and continued to pace. "We perish, then? Is there truly no means for us to escape?"

Samson rose and took her hands. His answer was calm. "The princes are still bound by their oaths to the people, and by Prince Husam's personal oath to you, to pay their ransom for my head."

Her anxiety withered. She felt hollow inside. All she had cared about until now was her own survival. All Samson cared about was her. "No. I won't deliver you into their hands, Samson. I can't."

"I have a plan."

She gazed at him, skeptical.

"Take the bounty they give you and flee Sorek. I will find you again."

"Peradventure they kill you before you can escape?"

"I will find a means to escape before the princes of the city can kill me."

"Peradventure they will not spare me, either, and we are both killed?"

"Then the princes and their city will indeed be ripe for destruction. I am not afraid to die, Delilah. Not for you. You are the most worthy thing that could undo me."

She shook her head. "Why are you doing all this for *me?* I am no one."

"The first time I fell in love, I withheld the secrets of my errands to keep my wife's trust at bay. In the end, I found I could not love Hanna and keep my powers both. I abandoned her to a fate most cruel. Never before had I known grief or regret, nor any pain at all. I realized my powers were no substitute for what my heart had lost. I vowed that if I ever fell in love again, I would make a different choice."

"Why did you choose me?"

"You were fair and caught my eye. When I looked upon you, I saw your heart also, and I knew you didn't belong here in this evil place I had come to destroy. That thing mortals call love swelled inside me then, and I knew I had to find a way to spare you."

"But I . . ."

"You were innocent. You knew I could see it. You also knew I could be cruel. It was hard work, earning your trust. I wouldn't sell it for all of Dagon's omnipotence."

Delilah shook her head in disbelief. "What will I do without my Samson?"

He took her face in both his hands. "Fear not. Let us spend one more day together in peace. Tomorrow, we go to meet whatever fate awaits us."

Delilah led Samson toward the city. His hands were bound behind his back as he'd instructed. He was going to pretend that, because Delilah had taken his powers, he had to do whatever she commanded. It was a hopeless plan in Delilah's eyes. But Samson refused to go into Sorek hand-in-hand with her. He said that if she did not appear to be at odds with him, Husam's brothers would not spare her.

Before they could reach the entrance to the city, a legion of soldiers swarmed them. Delilah folded her arms to hide the tremor in her body. As Samson predicted, the circle of men would not come closer than about thirty paces because they feared Samson would curse them.

"Kneel," she told Samson, and he obeyed.

"Hear me, good soldiers, and fetch the princes of Sorek! Yesterday, I took away Samson's power. He is bound to obey every command I give him."

The sea of soldiers parted. Delilah's knees went weak as the young prince she recognized as Elazar came to the fore. What were she and Samson thinking? Elazar would not spare them. She took a deep breath.

Elazar pointed at Delilah and snarled, *"You."*

"Your highness." Delilah bowed, but not to the ground. "I bring you Samson the Menace. I come to collect my bounty and wish nothing more than to be on my way."

"Ha! How do we know this is not a trick?"

"Cut me," Samson whispered. It was quiet enough that the circle of men would not have heard it.

"If one of your men will bring me a sword, I will show you he is mortal."

The prince waved his hand. One soldier came forward, cautious, and held out the hilt of his scimitar. Delilah took the weapon. A few laughed as she stumbled to balance its weight.

"On my shoulder," Samson whispered when she returned.

She pressed the curved tip of the blade into his skin until blood oozed out. "Behold, he bleeds," she said. An astonished murmur rippled through the assemblage as she showed the bloodied tip around the circle before returning the blade to its owner.

Elazar clapped his hands, bringing silence. He paced in front of Delilah. She avoided his gaze as though to show respect.

"What is your name?"

"I . . ." she licked her lips. "Delilah is my name."

"Tell me, Delilah, how it is that you rendered the jinni powerless?"

She glanced at Samson, then back at her feet. "It was what I would have told your brother, had Samson not killed him. I wrapped him in a net made of green twine and gold thread for the night."

"Where did you find such a net?"

"Would you believe the fool conjured it for me when I told him he must do it or I would not believe that he loved me?"

"Where is this net now?"

"It . . . melted into him," she fumbled. "It has become a part of him somehow to make him mortal."

"You say he is bound to obey your every command?"

"Yes, my lord."

"Order him to obey *me* now."

Delilah glanced at Samson. He gave the slightest nod.

"Samson. You have a new master now. You are to obey Elazar, son of the king of Sorek."

"As you wish," said Samson.

Delilah turned back to Elazar, bowing once more. "He is yours now. If you and your brothers will give to me the bounty I was promised, I will be on my way."

"Not just yet," said Elazar.

Delilah swallowed.

"Samson, stand up and do a jig for us."

Samson rose to his feet and leapt about in the most awkward sort of dancing Delilah had ever seen. The prince and his soldiers laughed. Surely Samson meant to make himself look graceless, but she didn't like seeing others make a mockery of him.

Elazar waved his hand. "Come here, Samson."

Samson stopped dancing and came forward.

"Take off these cords." Two soldiers cut the ropes from Samson's wrists. The prince drew a bone needle from his robes and held it out to Samson. "Take this pin and gouge out your eyes."

Delilah pressed the back of her hand to her mouth. It took everything in her power not to shout or shake her head.

Samson took the pin. He clutched it with both hands, pointing it at his face.

"Samson, don't!" Delilah cried.

He shoved the pin into his right eye, then into his left. He howled in agony as blood ran down his face.

Delilah turned away, screaming into her hands.

Elazar chuckled. "Delilah . . . Are you not the thief who robbed her husband's guests?"

"I am not a thief. Faraj was a fraud!"

"You *are* a thief. And thieves shall have none of our bounty." The prince snapped his fingers. "Samson, break this woman's neck and dispose of her in my fire pit."

Delilah stared at Samson, heartsick. Why had she let him do this? Why had she agreed to escape without him? She knew the answer, and it stung her heart: she was afraid to die in disgrace, branded as a thief and a harlot, without anyone knowing the truth about who she really was or what had happened to her.

A perplexing smile spread across Samson's blood-slicked lips.

Elazar's smug grin vanished, and a glimmer of fear returned to his eyes. "Why do you not obey me, Samson?"

"You and your brothers promised anyone who could render me powerless a ransom. Breaking that oath would be a grave mistake."

"Seize them!"

Two soldiers pinned Delilah's arms behind her back and forced her to kneel before Elazar. The prince stood over Delilah with his scimitar drawn. "Your time is not yet come, Samson. I have much torment reserved for *you*. But as for your Delilah, she is a thorn in my side that must be removed."

Elazar raised his weapon. Delilah squeezed her eyes shut and braced herself for the fatal blow. The ground shook. Elazar screamed. The soldiers' grip fell away. She looked up.

Samson's skin had returned to its natural jinn blue. He was covered in brighter blue seams that resembled cracks in a clay pot. A dark flame billowed out from him in all directions. It burned everything in its path, except Delilah.

Elazar clawed at the demon hand clamped around his throat. His flesh shriveled in the flames. At last, his body crumbled into dust and scattered about with the furnace-driven wind.

"Delilah," Samson called.

"But you lost your powers!" she cried over the roar of his fire.

"When Elazar broke his vow to deliver the ransom, he broke your trust and freed my powers."

Delilah watched in dismay as the bright blue seams continued to spread across Samson's flesh. "What's happening?"

"I had to use magic to kill Elazar and his men in order to save you. Thus, I have broken my promise not to harm the people of Sorek with my curses. My powers are conflicted, and they're tearing me apart."

"Samson, no!" Delilah rushed to him. "I don't care about that promise anymore. You have my permission to break it!"

He took her in his arms. "Delilah, Delilah." He kissed her. It was a beautiful kiss. Sweet, yet filled with his sand and fire. "I love you," he whispered. "Goodbye."

He waved his hand. Delilah was enveloped in the dark, swirling flames. Her body left the ground and she seemed to be hovering, weightless, like the other times Samson had whisked her away. She settled facedown on a hilltop to the west of the city. The wind roared, whipping violently at her robes as she pushed herself up on her hands and knees.

"Samson!" she called to the wind. There was no reply. She ran to the crest of the hill and looked down. Smoke and fire poured into the air. The burning cloud was so thick she couldn't see the buildings of the city or its people.

Delilah sat on her knees and buried her face in her hands, weeping bitterly for the loss of her lover. Her Samson was no more. When she looked up again, she spied an old camel-hide sack slumped against a rock behind her—the same one she had left behind in her hut.

When she opened the sack, she found a bundle of fine new clothes Samson had given her on their honeymoon. Beneath the bundle were seven bulging purses. She opened one and discovered it was full of silver coins. The purses contained the ransom Prince Husam had promised her. And everything managed to fit into that old sack.

Nestled between the purses, bundled inside her dusty little blanket, were her treasures. Her mother's lamp was whole once more, without seams or cracks. The seashell necklace and the red beaded sash Ihab had returned to her were wrapped together with a lock of Samson's black hair.

She took off her tatty beggar's robe and left it on the rock, donning a new dress. She hoisted the sack onto her shoulders. It should have been unbearably heavy, but with Samson's unknown enchantments, it seemed light as any other load she had carried in that sack. Delilah gave one last longing glance at the burning city. "I love you, Samson. I wish I'd been yours forever."

Turning her back on the valley and all its vices forevermore, she took courage and made her journey toward the sea and a new life. For the first time in a long, long time, fate had been kinder than cruel. Her name was no longer tainted, and her destiny was in her own hands. Most wonderfully of all, she had grown to love herself again because the jinni loved her.

DOWNWARD MOBILITY

by M. K. Wiseman

Amelia listened to the man at her desk blather on about "unexpected career changes" for about a minute, amused by the turn in conversation. *You don't know the half of it* . . .

The law firm was quite a switch from the hospital. For one thing, people here seemed much more contented with standing around making chitchat, even with a lowly legal assistant such as herself. The office seemed friendly, clean, businesslike—not at all the gruesome battlefield she'd come to expect from a high-end litigation firm. The Valkyrie wondered if perhaps she'd been mistaken in jumping ship, *again*. These bland, business-suited people didn't look like they could get blood on their hands.

Law: field of modern warfare—bah! The only thing akin to battle she'd experienced in this, her first day, was the lingering scent of anger, the senior partners having argued in the conference room down the hall but an hour before.

She kept the smirk off her face and cocked her head attentively. Best to get on with the new staff—easier access that way. At the thought, Amelia wondered if her "other sight," her Valkyrie powers, were yet practicable in the new office. Even though her transfer had not gone through celestial channels, the powers up in Valhalla surely had figured out her next move by now.

After all, her restless moving about had become common knowledge amongst the few remaining Valkyrie. The last time Amelia had abruptly moved, the lag in getting her set up with new souls to escort had been less than a day. Curious as to who would have been assigned those she'd left in limbo when she left the hospital, she tried to remember which other Valkyries did work in the metro New York area.

Called back to the present as her colleague cleared his throat, Amelia struggled to pay polite attention to the fellow chatting her up in her cubicle. He was now comparing Amelia's recent move from a hospital setting to the legal field to his own from a big firm to a massive one. Same tired jokes, same tired overtures of friendship. But Amelia laughed and smiled along, eventually offering, "Nursing in the trauma unit was a total hell. My move here was a bit of a godsend."

Obligatory "Ha ha ha" from the other party. He moved on, concluding, "Nice meeting you, Amelia. See you around."

"Yeah, later!" she waved to the receding backside. *Bit of a godsend, Amelia?* She could not believe her cheek. Speaking of Odin—*phooey! I forgot to check this Peter, Dan, Tony, what-ever-his-name-is!*

Cursing her oversight, Amelia rose and followed in the direction she'd seen the man leave, hoping her interaction with him had been long enough for her to access his spiritual state. Not that she wanted the man dead—he seemed rather nice. Rather beige, of course, but altogether an okay guy.

She didn't find him. Fine by her, since he was likely not her . . . *jurisdiction?* anyway. Amelia blushed with pride. *See? I already know the lingo here.* She turned to find her cubicle, instead coming up short against a red silk tie, crisp white collar, and jet-black suit.

"Beg pardon." Both apologized at once. Amelia wasn't sure which astounded her more: the collision itself, or the fact that the gentleman she'd just bumped into glowed blindingly bright in her Other sight. She quickly turned off the observation, trying to assess the situation.

Partner. No, an associate, judging from his I'm-trying-too-hard power suit combination. *That, and he's now stopped to talk with me, a lowly secreta—legal assistant.*

He was rather good-looking—well, he was in Amelia's opinion. While she had a thousand years of experience under her belt, her taste was anything but conventional. Amelia always told herself this was because fashion changed with the ages; however, her friend, Val, always maintained that Amelia was the unfashionable one.

Yes, like her, he was definitely a lower-rung "nice guy." Amelia forced herself to look away from the handsome face, instead seeing again how bright the man shone in her Other sight. *If I were you, I'd get going on whatever I still had to get done instead of chatting up the new girl . . .* Amelia couldn't help it. Charming as the man seemed, she couldn't get past the glaring knowledge that he was marked for death. Real death, too, not just the career suicides with which she'd lately been assisting.

Shame. He seemed very nice. Amelia caught a name. Michael. *Pleased to meet you, Michael. You're going to die soon.*

Scolding herself—she never lost control like this—Amelia smiled and made her escape. Only once she was safely at her desk did she notice the absolutely mortifying spread of coffee staining her shoulder and sleeve.

How embarrassing. Not the stain—though that was a problem she'd have to live with for the rest of the day. No, it just pointed Michael's attentions in a less complimentary direction. *Yeah, Amelia, be upset that the dead guy wasn't flirting with you.*

༺༻

A tentative knock at the doorway to her cubicle roused Amelia's attention. Never the best typist, she had been making good headway on that morning's work and was momentarily irked at the interruption. Amelia looked up to find a somewhat severe woman frowning down at her. She held out a package, her dour face turning pleasant as she eyed Amelia., "Michael said he'd loused it up with the new girl. Now that I see your coffee stain, this makes a whole lot more sense."

Puzzled, Amelia accepted the soft wrap of brown paper and sliced through the tape with a fingernail. A sweater. Light enough for the weather, not too big, not too small—it was perfect for covering up the stubborn stain that had set into her blouse.

It came with a note:

Again, my apologies for inadvertently sharing my morning coffee with your shirt. I did not want to seem presumptuous with this gift, but thought I owed you. I know what it's like to be new—so if you're ever needing a lunch companion, let me know.

—Michael

Amelia looked up to thank the messenger, but she was already gone, leaving Amelia to enjoy her sweater with a side of guilt.

※

The cat greeted Amelia at her door. "Hi there, Wolf the 142nd." The feline companion yowled in answer—demanding nothing more of Amelia than food and a quick cuddle. Not for the first time, Amelia wished that animals were sent to Valhalla at life's end.

Settling down on the couch with a bag of chips and the TV remote, Amelia reflected on the day with a clinical detachment, trying not to feel depressed. Maybe the hospital was easier on her. After all, people died all the time in hospitals. Amelia paused in her channel flipping, eyeing the scene with amusement. It was one of those action flicks from a couple summers back—full of battles and impassioned speeches by actors she didn't know or care anything about. CGI effects: nothing like the real thing.

You've come a long way from the real thing, Amelia. First, an antiseptic-laden hospital, now a law firm? How far from your duties will you try to stray? She turned off the TV, preferring the silence.

That was what was getting to her. The noise. The constant noise and laughter, traffic and chatter.

It was like Valhalla, in a way—but also deliciously mortal and maddeningly out of reach for one such as her.

Mortal. Amelia gave Wolf's head an affectionate rub. Already he was telling his age. In a few years, she'd have to get another one. Wolf the 143rd. In looking at the cat pawing its way across her lap, trimmed claws gently pulling at her new sweater, Amelia allowed what was bothering her to really creep in.

Abject familiarity with death. That's what my life is. Only I keep looking at it from the wrong side. I have to keep coming back over and over and over . . . I can't just be one in a long line of house cats. Oh, no, I must cull the warriors and soldiers of this world, offering life or death, always promising reward or damnation at the end of the latter.

Amelia strode to the window, fingers absently exploring the hem of her new sweater as she looked out on a world positively humming with the excitement of being alive. Somewhere between the dull and constant lights of the skyscrapers and the moan of the occasional siren, Amelia threw caution to the wind—she'd have lunch with Michael tomorrow.

She told herself it was so that she could keep an eye on him.

LEGENDS AND LORE

Lunch became drinks, became dinner-and-a-movie, became so much more. It had been ages since Amelia had taken a lover—*had America even been a country yet?*—and even so, Michael felt special. It hadn't taken the work of a genius to realize why he glowed so brightly in Amelia's Valkyrie sight, despite their never having met. Their souls simply knew one another.

A thousand years of life and I finally find an answer to why it is worth it, Amelia sighed happily, her lover gently kissing the underside of her wrist in the dark privacy of her bed. While the death of a good man is never a thing to rejoice—a stance she'd long held against that of her numerous sisters—the idea of spending eternity in Michael's company, enjoying the loud pomp that was Valhalla . . . for this man, Amelia could do it.

⸙

"Amelia?" Michael's voice sounded from the depths of his pillow.

"Mmmm?" her answer came with a kiss. "Yes, dear?"

Propping himself up on an elbow, Michael furrowed his brow, a gesture Amelia had come to adore over the past several months. Michael's "work face", she called it. Intense, thoughtful, and always boding ill for the party on the other side of the courtroom; to have such scrutiny turn toward her now was unusual and put her on guard for his next words.

"Amelia, I need you to tell me the truth on this, okay? Do you remember last week on the Anderson case, when I mentioned Rutgers?"

Oh, Odin, here it is! Amelia felt herself pale. Rutgers was her most recent alma mater, one she'd adopted for the last half-century. She'd often wondered what she'd do when that lie grew stale. In the digital age, it was becoming harder to fabricate an identity, especially if you did it on your own, without divine intervention.

It was now that Amelia wished to Odin that she'd at least *visited* her purported alma mater at some point. She tried to laugh it off, hoping he'd let it drop, and praying that his sharp litigator mind would just let it go., "It was a slip of the brain, Michael. You can't tell me you remember every little detail about every single building or professor."

Michael backed away, hands hunting around for shirt and pants., "Three months together—"

"It is the *truth*!" Amelia groveled. "It *is* the truth, and I love you—"

Whirling around, half-dressed, Michael stopped her short. "No. Don't you dare say that you love me with the same conviction you put into that pack of lies you've told the world.

"I looked into it, Amelia. I called the school. You never went there. And from there, it only got worse. Where do you think I work? What do you think we do at the firm? Once I knew about Rutgers, I had to know the rest. Your driver's license, birth records, your very age is a mystery.

"That aside, it's dating in the twenty-first century. Didn't you think someday this would come to light? If you're in witness protection, or some sort of weird situation like that, fine. I'm willing to hear you out if you'll just, *please*, trust me with the truth. Trust me."

It was Amelia's turn to move further off. *What do I do? What can I say? That I'm a thousand-year-old Norse messenger of the dead?* She thought fast . . . but not fast enough.

"Okay, then," Michael interpreted her silence in the worst way possible. Amelia could tell she was losing him, and she could feel her heart die with his next words. "Please understand this makes us a thing of the past. And as for work . . . Damn it, Amelia, I tried to give you the benefit of the doubt, give you a chance to explain, but you know I have to say something now. We've confidentialities to protect. Think of me, think of my clients. You're a liability."

His eyes pleaded with her for an answer. She offered none, instead wishing to Odin—or any god—that this conversation had waited three more days. Three more days and she could give Michael his answers, along with an eternity to explore them.

⁂

They canned her. Of course the firm had to. Michael had done what he'd promised—what he'd had to—and Amelia couldn't blame him. This wasn't the first time the World Wide Web had ratted Amelia out as a ghost, a woman without a past. On the flip side, not existing certainly made it easy to set up a new identity for the next job, for the next role she had to play.

But her caseload—no, not the office caseload, of course— her *real* work would have to be reassigned. Mostly a painless process. After all, when you worked in the employ of a divinity, these things generally took care of themselves. She briefly wondered if the Valkyrie who'd inherited her hospital cases would now also acquire her souls at the firm to escort.

This last thought made her feel slightly guilty. She really ought to go through the proper channels this time. Through Asgard, she could again secure proper credentials, a better backstory, perhaps even a more permanent position ushering souls.

But she just couldn't handle the scrutiny again: "Why are you switching, Amelia? Maybe it's time to take a break and return to Valhalla for a century or two . . ."

Ugh. Valhalla—where the stink and sound of countless valiant men enjoying eternity eventually grew more oppressive to Amelia than what one found on the fields of battle. Yes. All she had to do was find a new job, a new life, make new acquaintances, check her Other sight and pick things up from there . . . something she'd done countless times within the past century.

And forget all about what happens to Michael tomorrow night. While she'd never had the option of ducking out of her duties towards his fate, she'd taken comfort in the idea that she would be there in the end. She'd harbored a faint hope that perhaps she might finish him off in a car wreck—with her by his side, cradling his head and talking sweet hopes in his ear to ease him from his mortal coil.

In her despair, she nearly reached out with her Other sight. With his brilliance, she could likely see him from just about anywhere. But no, that was cowardly. What she needed to do was confront him, tell him some version of the truth that his human brain might process—he was a smart guy, after all. And hadn't she always been taught that when you led a soul to its fate, you were to encourage the finishing of business, give them a safe and secure route to the grave so that their soul might truly enjoy its reward?

The phone rang.

"Soooo glad you could meet me for lunch, dear Amelia!" The speaker practically gushed the words, embracing Amelia like an old friend. And old friend she was, Amelia supposed.

"Goodness, Val. It's been—what? Ten, maybe fifteen years?" Amelia took a seat opposite her lunch date, glad to be dining al fresco. Val was known to be pretty loud, and, right now, fresh air seemed the only thing that would diffuse the growing pit of unease in Amelia's stomach.

Flipping back her bottle-blonde hair and giving the waiter a wave and a "Yoo-hoo!" Val certainly did not look the role of a Valkyrie. Trim, well-dressed in tiny suit and sky-high heels, Val was everything her friend was not. Which was likely how they had managed to stay friends these past several hundred years.

There was something so opposite about each that they refreshed the other, something that made their ancient work somehow bearable in the modern day. Neither quite enjoyed their jobs any more—and who would, after a thousand-odd years? Although, Amelia often suspected that Val got a kick out of the secrecy of it all.

"Never talk years with me, dear," Val sighed indolently. "You know I'm the timeless one." She leaned forward, toying with the stem of her wine glass—most likely to highlight the freshness of her ruby-red manicure. "You, on the other hand, change like the wind. How many jobs have you hit and run in the past few years now?"

"Six." Amelia wasn't in the mood for a full-on catching up. She knew that her numbers were far below that of the other few remaining Valkyrie, and that her constant moving about was partially to blame. But, unlike Val, she didn't like sticking out, much preferring to blend into the hubbub and anonymity of the modern world.

Amelia tested her pet idea on her friend. "Ever wonder if we mightn't see what it's like . . . to get a little older this time? Just for a while, you know."

Val was nonplussed. "You know we—or at least I—don't look like this on accident, dear. Who doesn't want to spend immortality looking like this?"

"Like a co-ed?" Amelia teased, sensing she'd hit a nerve and trying to make amends. She couldn't help at least one more dig, however., "And if it's all by your grand design, why don't you just make yourself a natural blonde?"

"Darling Amelia, I do this for the *fun* of it. Being dissatisfied with one's own image is part of their game. It amuses me to play along." Val's eyes turned a gooey sort of sympathetic. "If you're bored with all this, you could always return to Valhalla. Party is still going, you know." She paused, dramatic as always., "Buuuuut, then you'd have to go without him."

"Him." Amelia narrowed her eyes. There it was. The *real* reason for Val's call. Not some 'you're short on souls again, Amelia. It's time for a real bender. Let's show them what a true harpy looks like' social visit.

"I knew it. I knew I should have just appealed his case from the start."

"You wouldn't have, darling. And anyway, you know what they say. That only the good . . ."

"Shut it, Val," Amelia snapped, rolling her eyes. Val claimed years ago to have had a one-night stand with the great Billy Joel. Said the bastard had used the night to steal one of Val's better lines. Amelia didn't believe a word of it. But she appreciated her friend trying to cheer her up.

Val leaned forward again, her low-cut sundress not doing her any favors as she practically pressed herself into the table., "Hsst. Raise your glass, Amelia. Like me." Val hadn't stopped her toying with the wine glass and it seemed she'd good reason for it. "There's another one here. Michael's new case manager," she spoke low, through lips that barely moved.

"Where?" she spoke the monosyllable through the straw of her water glass.

"Your ten. I'll tell you when she looks away." Val flipped her hair again, leaning back. "Now."

Amelia risked a quick glance. She didn't recognize the woman, but it seemed Val certainly did.

"Yes. Her." Val glanced about as if in search of their waiter. "And you know as well as I that her souls go to Folkfangr for Freya's use."

"But why?"

"Because you got involved with him, and your numbers this past century have been deplorable, my dear. We all know that you'd likely never leave Asgard again. It's nothing against Michael. And Folkfangr is a lovely place in and of itself."

"No..."

"I'm so sorry, hon. I... I wanted you to know before—before you lost the chance to see him again. My recommendation would be to catch him tomorrow evening. 8:45. As he's leaving the office." Val took out her compact, touching up lipstick that matched her wicked-looking nails. "I'm only telling you this on the guarantee that you won't interfere, Amelia. We all know you want out of this gig, but even you don't want it *that* badly."

∽⋄∾

Checking her watch for the tenth time in three minutes, Amelia couldn't help but smile at the little bit of plastic and metal wrapped around her wrist. She hated progress, and the constant changing of technology upset her job more than most, but she found wristwatches amazing.

Michael wore a wristwatch—a habit he found funny and old-fashioned due to the relatively recent encroachment of mobile phones. But he liked that Amelia liked it. Recalling such details made her heart skip a beat as she waited in the dark of the alley.

A familiar form stepped from the glittering office building upon which Amelia kept her vigil. She waited until Michael had crossed the street, knowing him to be intent on the substation down the street. Suddenly unsure of herself, Amelia froze—the man had told her off three days prior, gotten her fired. What if approaching him in a darkening street was seen as, well, stalker-ish?

Val would be amused.

At that thought, determined not to feel the fool and realizing that this was really it, truly her last chance to say goodbye to the man she'd come to love . . .

Amelia stepped out of the shadows. "Michael—"

His shoulders hunched in alarm and, for a moment, Amelia was certain that her intrusion into his walk home had been unwelcome. But Michael turned then, and she quickly recognized the brief tension as merely the reaction of a startled man on a dark street. Her ex's heart was in his eyes and he took a breath, letting it out slowly, waiting. Clearly, he still wanted an explanation. And it appeared he was going to allow her to give it.

"I'm sorry." If a thousand years of watching humanity had taught her anything, it was lead with the apology. "Michael, I'm so, *so* sorry. And I . . . I would like to tell you the truth, if I may."

She couldn't tell if he was receptive to the idea or not. Most likely, Michael himself did not know. But after a moment's pause, the love that he'd had for her still shone in the corners of his smile, and he nodded gently., "I'd like that."

They'd taken all of three steps when the thug approached—his threat of a gun a demonstration rather than mere words. Wallet. Phone. Briefcase. The demands were simple. Michael acquiesced, promising that they didn't want any trouble.

"You, too, lady." The gun's barrel trained itself on Amelia . . . Amelia who rarely carried much of anything in the way of a wallet or phone. This was apparently less satisfactory to the mugger, and he cocked the gun as a warning.

"Don't you dare, you son-of-a—"

Michael leapt, the man panicked, and Amelia simply stood watching as if removed from the scene. The gun going off. The love of her life taking the bullet meant for her. The mugger swearing and running off with naught but the briefcase that Michael would shortly no longer need.

Amelia would have liked to claim that it all happened too fast. Michael's act of bravery really *had* caught her by surprise. But she knew she could have done something. 8:45. Val had given her the place and the time.

Amelia knelt, cradling Michael's head in her lap, knowing the wound to be fatal and telling him lies. He'd be okay. The ambulance was on its way. She did tell him one truth, however: she loved him with all her heart.

~ · ~

"Oh, my gods. Oh, my *gods*," Amelia swore under her breath. "I cannot believe I just did that." She checked that he was still beside her, hand clasped firmly in her own. And, yes, he was. Bloodstained shirt and dazed expression, but still fleet of foot, Michael ran alongside her as they made their escape from the scene. Already sirens could be heard—of the emergency sort, not the Valkyrie—flying along the street.

It was a good thing he was in shock.

"Amelia—" Michael wasn't going to be held off for long. Already he was glancing behind him anxiously. "We have to talk to the police about this, we have to—"

Amelia shushed Michael, gripping his hand all the tighter and feeling bad about the unbreakable hold she'd had to put on his soul., "Almost there, 'kay?" Slowing, they ducked into an alley, Amelia relying on her Other sight to ensure their safety. She debated throwing some Valkyrie fire further down the street—insurance against any of her kind pursuing them in their wild flight—but thought better of it. After all, Michael didn't need to see a demonstration of that type of power just now.

"Amelia. *Amelia.*" Michael's words cut through with an urgency of their own. "We need to go back. We can't flee a crime scene." Even in the midst of her own anxiety, Amelia noted the mastery with which Michael assessed the situation, became the lawyer, comforted her. She let him continue, still expecting a wild-eyed Valkyrie to come swooping in at any moment. "Maybe you've got a past that you may not want to expose to certain authorities. I don't know. But, babe, I will help you, okay? I promise that. We've just got to go back and talk to the cops."

Amelia refocused on her companion. "Michael, dear. I-I've done a terrible thing." She covered her mouth with hands that shook.

"No, no, sweet." Michael reached out, held her close. "You're in shock. Do you remember? There was a man with a gun. A man with a gun and he—" Michael paused, shook his head as if clearing a strange thought. Passing a hand absently over his chest, Michael noted the hole in his shirt and the large dark stain that surrounded it. It didn't hurt. Also of note, his heart didn't beat.

Amelia saw the look of alarm on her lover's face and nodded. "You were shot."

"I remember that,"—Michael breathed the words—"but . . . but I also remember dying. That's not possible. I . . . It's like I remember you pulling me out of me. Like I was still lying there when you grabbed my hand and told me to run." He sank to his knees and started to shake.

"Michael." Amelia crouched to meet his eyes., "Michael, listen to me. Remember when I told you I couldn't tell you the truth about myself?"

◈

"So, you're a Valkyrie . . ." This part Michael was having trouble wrapping his head around. Odd, as he seemed to take being dead calmly enough.

"Yes. And now we need to go see Odin. He can get you reassigned, at least." Amelia handed him a clean shirt—one of his that she'd still had in her apartment. Going back to Michael's . . . out of the question.

"If he can just reassign me, what's the problem? Why are we hiding?"

"Because. I did a stupid thing, stealing you—your soul—like this. If the Valkyrie to whom you've been reassigned gets to you first—then, boom, it's a permanent one-way ticket to Folkfangr. I need to find a way to reason with him."

"If Odin is all god-like, can't he just undo that when you eventually see him?"

"No."

"Well, that's stupid. If he's all-powerful—"

"Never said he was 'all-powerful.' And he's a god, not 'god-like.' There are rules. Unbreakable ones."

"Why?"

"All right. I know you don't have children. But think on it—if your children knew that, technically, any rule could be broken, what would that do for their faith and trust in you? In your steadfastness?"

"But we're talking a little rule . . ."

"For Odin's sake! You're a lawyer—think of the slippery slope argument, or something."

Michael sulked. "Fine. How do we go see this Odin?"

Amelia thought for a long moment. "I don't know."

"You don't *know*?"

"How do you go see your God, Michael?"

"I'm an atheist."

"Well, probably not anymore . . ." Amelia allowed herself a small smile.

"Yeah," Michael agreed, a tone of misery coloring his attempt to appreciate the weak joke. "Amelia, are you in trouble? For what you did for me?"

She didn't answer.

"So, where are we going?" Michael eyed Amelia's hasty packing of a duffle bag.

"North."

"To Az—"

"Asgard," Amelia corrected, "No."

Tears again threatened to blur her attempts to pack for their ill-planned escape. *Or is it even an escape? Are we just buying time? Have I damned the man I love?* Not once did thoughts of herself cross her mind, even after Michael's pointed question.

Strong arms folded around her then, gently pulling Amelia from her frantic task. She almost shrugged away, but gave in to her anguish. His silent embrace spoke to the most pressing of her fears, soothing her own soul as she was supposed to have done his. And though Michael was a man known for his compassion, she couldn't help but hope that this tender act meant that she was forgiven, that she was still loved.

She fell freely and gratefully into his embrace, and wondered at it. He should, by rights, be in absolute turmoil, and here he was comforting her, instead.

It was a lot to take in, even for a brilliant man like Michael. Alone, the truth of who and what she was, it was more than she could ask him to understand. But she'd also played a role in his death and *then* denied him his rightful afterlife . . .

Perhaps she shouldn't have interfered.

It wasn't that she regretted saving Michael—if stealing a soul could be called that. Faced with never seeing Michael again, and an immortality to ponder it, she'd have done it all again.

Amelia just didn't know what to do with him now. How do you hide from your god? From his servants?

Her only hope now was that nobody up top had bothered enough about her life to note the private retreat she had long kept for herself in upstate New York.

❧

Amelia had taken precautions. Though nothing was ever certain, unleashing a good deal of her Valkyrie fire in several spots throughout her neighborhood might well be enough to hold off any immediate pursuit. Closing her eyes, she could still see the fear in Michael's eyes when the white-hot soul fire had left her fingers, leaving to dance upon cars, coffee shop tables, her bed . . . *And you wondered why I didn't tell you.*

Now, safely away on the train—and three cab rides later— Amelia and Michael shared an uncomfortable vinyl seat. This precaution had amused Michael.

"We're taking a cab? We're running from a god and his host and we're taking a New York City cab?"

If Michael had met Val, he'd understand. Most other Valkyrie— besides not being well-acquainted with New York—would never stoop to such pedestrian modes of travel. Michael and Amelia were, essentially, hiding in plain sight. Well, plain enough. Amelia couldn't help but be amused by the sight of Michael in a ball cap.

But, incognito as they were, Amelia did not dare a sigh of relief until the skyscrapers grew to matchsticks and the trees multiplied, then became the predominant scenery.

Michael eyed the cabin with a bemused eye. The look on his face made Amelia wonder if he was surprised or disappointed at her keeping a wooded retreat. She'd certainly never spoken of such a place. But his hesitation had another purpose. "Before we go in, I need . . . I need to apologize. And thank you." He glanced down at his hands. He really did look normal, save for the occasional strange glint that his skin reflected in the early morning sunlight. "I was going to say for my life but . . . I'd say that 'for your love' is more appropriate in this case."

"Michael." Amelia's face threatened to cloud over with tears once again.

"No, really. Odd as all of this is, it's really sweet. And I'll admit that, unbelievability aside, you really did have a good reason for not telling me about . . . about you. And if it weren't for . . . all of this . . . I would still—" He pursed his lips, clearly regretting where that sentence led.

Together, they entered the safe haven of Amelia's cabin.

It was a well-appointed little place. Old—but then, she'd had it for nearly a century. It was Amelia's personal Valhalla. One without the noise and stink of countless warriors carousing and drinking mead. Had Michael not been, well, a ghost, and Amelia not been an ancient battlefield harpy, it would have been an idyllic scene. Despite those differences, they quickly set about making it livable, while Amelia thought through their next move.

"I can honestly say, Amelia, this side of you does not surprise me one bit." Michael looked around, admiring the cozy getaway.

"How so?"

"Don't take this the wrong way, but . . . I think what initially attracted me to you was your detachment from the rat race. You played along well enough, were diligent in your commitments to work, life in general, but something seemed to be missing. This. This place fills that hole. Even the rest of you—the part I only know about as of last night, the unworldly stuff—that, too, doesn't quite fit."

"Thanks." Amelia looked down at her hands, unsure how much she wanted to give this man.

They sat in silence.

Amelia was the first to reach out. "You know that I didn't start things with you because of my—"

"I didn't think that, no."

"Okay, good," Amelia breathed a sigh of relief. "I do love you. And if I wasn't me . . ."

"If you weren't you, I wouldn't have loved you one whit, Amelia. I just don't know what we do now. You've got to give me some credit—what I've learned in the past half-day would drive most people to the funny farm. I'm gonna need time."

Amelia felt the hair on the back of her neck prickle to attention as a voice sounded from the doorway. "Unfortunately, time is what you won't have."

Val certainly knew how to make an entrance.

Amelia jumped to her feet, a mix of surprise, fear, and hope on her face. "Thank the gods. We needed a friend." She felt Michael's hand on her arm, gently pulling her back.

"I thought this was a place nobody knew about." He eyed the leggy blonde who still stood in the doorway, highlighted dramatically by the morning sun behind her.

"The name's Val." She entered at last, shutting the door behind her. "And Amelia seems to have forgotten that I have a most excellent memory for detail." She turned to Amelia. "I'm more than just a pretty face, dear." Her words carried a touch of sadness.

"Michael was reassigned to you."

"Yes. And my hope was to give you at least a chance to explain things to him, like you had wanted to. I never expected that you'd do something like"—she gestured at their surroundings—"all of this. Did you actually believe you could run? With an undelivered soul?"

Amelia hung her head, "No. I just . . . I'm tired. I'm tired, I'm in love, and I reacted. We'd hoped to speak with Odin, plead our case for Valhalla over Folkfangr." She raised her eyes to Val, pleading.

Val sighed. "You know that Michael cannot see Odin. And you know that I am to do my job. We've already one Valkyrie in the room who's betrayed the order of her god; I'm not keen on making it two. You see, I still like what I do."

She raised her hands. White hot, Val's soul fire exploded outward, toward Michael. It lasted only an instant, blinding all.

LEGENDS AND LORE

It captured the first soul it hit, binding it to Val for the journey into the afterlife.

❦

"You git! You absolute idiot!" Val screeched at her companion.

Amelia set her jaw and glared back at her friend with as steely of an eye as she could muster. Inside, she was trembling.

And she had every right to tremble. Just as Michael had stepped into a bullet for her the evening before, Amelia had now done much the same thing. Striking back with soul fire of her own, she'd drawn Val's power to her.

Admittedly, her only thought had been to, once more, save Michael from an unfair, undeserved end. But it seemed that Amelia had accomplished yet another surprising feat. For she and Val stood in the home of their god, within the hallowed halls of Asgard.

"I command a revered silence in my home, Valerie." At the booming voice, both Valkyrie lowered their eyes, falling on bended knee. "That's better. Now, it would seem we have a problem here."

"Yes, Lord Odin." Amelia acknowledged the quiet rebuke, quaking at her god's displeasure. To use soul fire on another Valkyrie. Unthinkable. Damnable. And with her years of avoiding divine guidance, striking out on her own when the fancy took her . . . she knew that mercy was too much to ask.

Tears sprang into Amelia's eyes as she knelt in the achingly beautiful hall in which her god resided. In spite of her inner condemnation, she felt her heart swell. She knew full well that her path had strayed far from its original course. But Amelia ardently believed in her wayward passage through the changing world. She *had* done good; she *had* managed to make being a modern Valkyrie worthwhile. It made no difference upon which battlefield they were found, every soul she had escorted to Valhalla had known peace and contentment in its final moments.

In her journey, searching for meaning in a world gone cold, Amelia had found her own spirit. There was so much she wanted to tell Odin—to explain the anguish that her life had become. She wanted to tell him of Michael, and how his humanity touched her so, had made her happy for the first time in her long memory.

But Odin, being a god, knew all of this. And so he turned to Val. "Amelia's fate has already been decided. Yours, however . . . Valerie, what explanation will you give for your behavior?"

Had Amelia been anywhere other than kneeling at the foot of Odin's throne, she might have found delight in Val's lack of speech. It was the first time she could remember the woman being caught without anything to say.

Satisfied, Odin supplied his own explanation. "Your humility and lack of desire to justify yourself do you credit, Val. And your love for your friend does you even more." He paused, giving weight to the judgment that was to follow. "Valerie. You've long been straying from your true calling. You flit about using your powers, reveling in the opportunities your station provides, while forgetting that your purpose is to escort souls.

"Being a Valkyrie is to soothe aching spirits and provide a kind arm to lean upon, a familiar face to guide them into the bliss of eternity. Valhalla is not some 'never-ending cocktail party,' but a heavenly reward for a life well lived. You've forgotten that, relying upon Amelia's love of humanity to fill what you lack in yourself.

"And so, Valerie, you are hereby forbidden from Valhalla and Folkfangr for the duration of Amelia's life. You are not yet stripped of your powers, but are only to escort souls to the afterlife, not stay."

"Amelia's life?"

"Yes. Amelia. As I said, her fate has already been decided by her actions." Odin now turned to the still penitent Amelia. Feeling his hallowed eyes upon her, she trembled again—this time not from fear, but from the ecstasy of a heart filled with the joy of being fully understood.

"Rise, dear child, and find your burden lifted. You are Valkyrie no more. The punishment I give you, I am sure you will find more of a reward. I thank you for your service and dearly hope that Val finds new love for humanity through yours."

※

The scream of ambulance sirens bled into Amelia's senses even as the transcendent beauty of Asgard faded from sight. Stopping mid-stride, she tried to grasp where she now was and how she'd come to be here.

The white-coated gentleman behind her nearly bowled Amelia over, clumsily side-stepping her while trying to keep a steady hand along the gurney.

The gurney...

Absently, Amelia looked down at the cart as it rolled to a stop. The three-person team shouted incomprehensible syllables at her. It was the first time in Amelia's long memory that she could recall having completely lost her grip on the English language.

It was like drowning. No, it was rather like dying. She, of all people, would know.

"She's in shock."

"Watch her, she might drop."

Blinking, Amelia felt the roar in her ears subside and coalesce into the sterile rush and whirr of a hospital ER. She worked to find the words, "I'm okay. Just..."

Michael.

Michael was on the gurney.

And she was in a hospital.

Memories came flooding back—sharp, galvanizing.

She spotted a familiar face. "Maude! We need a room! Victim is a white male in his thirties, single GSW to the chest. And he's my boyfriend, so step on it."

"I told you I used to be a nurse, right, babe? This is where I used to work." Amelia bent and huskily whispered the words to the white-faced occupant of the ambulance gurney. Warm and affectionate, Michael's hand squeezed acknowledgment.

Life, vivid and palpable, coursed through Amelia as she trailed the gurney down the long, white hallway. The nurse in her recognized it as mere adrenaline, but inside her ears, the words rang out: *Rise, dear child, and find your burden lifted. You are Valkyrie no more.* Even her fast-fading memories of Asgard's celestial beauty seemed to pale in comparison to the vibrancy of a life being lived, trauma and all.

"Thank you, God. Thank you, Odin."

Her prayer was interrupted by a beckoning gesture from the gurney.

With a start, Amelia found she could not read the state of Michael's soul, but his eyes sparkled bright and clear. "Where's Val?"

SKYFALL
by Emma Michaels

"It's nearly time," I whispered in the Hall of the Gods, the ornate central dome in our community, and swam in tune with my people. We softly rotated together, like a school of fish, around the tower in the center of the room. I was glad I wasn't the only one having a hard time staying still as we awaited the choosing ceremony, even if I was one of the only sirens who feared it.

"I know." Marek, my mate, looked confident, though our hands were clasped so tightly I could feel bruises forming. We both knew this tradition could tear us apart. I stared at anything but the crystalline tower above the gathering. I didn't want to remember the great honor once bestowed upon us, nor did I want to be the first to repeat our vain efforts of instigation.

Atlantis sirens were known for being curious, but we'd taken things too far and now delved deeply into the lives of humans, researching them constantly in the hopes that one day we might be able to reveal our existence to them. We couldn't settle for the peace we'd found beneath the waves.

We felt a need to address the problems of other species because we had already solved our own. No sickness, no secrets to unveil, no mysteries to discover, no wars to fight occupied us. So we did as we have always done: ferried souls with our songs and gathered information until the day we would be able to truly help those above us.

We were running out of new selections. No matter who was chosen, this would be their second trip, because, although we numbered in the hundreds, our slow aging meant multiple trips were bound to happen. With our extended lifespan, whoever visited would be greeted by a completely different world than the one they had faced before.

No true child could be sent out. Comparatively speaking, Marek and I were actually close in development to humans in their twenties. It had simply taken a few hundred years for us to get there.

One couple would be selected to play the traditional roles of our ancestors: to keep an eye on the human world above and the Underworld below. One to leave the water and return to earth as a human, while the other would ferry their souls to their proper destination in the Underworld. A set of relay stones would connect the minds during their assignment, helping the couple to cope with the journey and stay vigilant. Every year we made the same mistakes; always repeating a vicious cycle in our efforts. However, to refuse meant punishment, or worse, banishment.

"Do you hope you'll be chosen again?" the siren next to me asked, and I smiled without answering. If I said no, I disgraced the family I'd found in Marek. My neighbor didn't know what had happened the last time we were chosen, didn't realize what a mess we made of things. Only the elders knew the lives we'd destroyed in the process; those leaders whose songs were so powerful that their questioning spilled the information from those who returned during the gleaning.

We remembered more when we listened to their song and gave clearer information as it was dictated for the archives. My shame was written there, and I hoped it would never be found.

Marek was the first to choose to travel upland as a teenage human and ended up living a year as a high school student. He collected so much information, we ended up leaps and bounds ahead of where we had been in tracking their progress. After our first assignment, we'd brought back more information than many generations of sirens, and that was all that mattered.

It had always been difficult monitoring how far behind us the humans lagged on the evolutionary scale, and how their customs had changed from our own. When we turned from violence, they turned toward it, when we stopped having our wars, they started theirs, and somewhere along the way, we realized that it meant their knowledge of us would only lead to another war and bring violence back to my people. Even the legends sprung from their memories of us scared humans: legends of sirens' songs leading sailors to their deaths, and the ferrymen who carried damned souls to Hades. They turned us into attackers of seafaring men, and greed-driven debt collectors hounding the dead.

I resented humans for it, and for what I'd learned from my own experiences. I'd been the ferryman and seen the horrors they committed from beyond the veil of their dead. Meanwhile, on the land above, Marek had grown to love their kind and found them admirable. It evened out to most of us who were sent, but I could never look past the innocents I saw suffering. I couldn't stop caring and lead the souls while ignoring the lives they had lived. They had such short life spans, and yet, it was spent in struggle and, at times, humiliation.

The ceremony started. We heard the song begin at the front of the gathering, and soon enough it spread throughout the crowd. I couldn't help but sing. No matter how much I feared returning to the Underworld, I would always love singing the 'promise to protect.' I had sung it for millions of souls to melt their pains away and allow them to pass, but now, it was easing my own fearful heart.

I slowly let my grip on Marek's hand loosen until our hands were clasped as they normally would be, reminding me that I had all I need standing with me.

The song rose until we hit the crescendo and the name was pulled, still unannounced in the eldest's hand as he slowly walked up the tower's stairs to the pedestal. I let my emotions swell in my voice, and release. If it was our fate to be the ferryman and the wanderer again, then so be it. It hadn't torn us from each other the first time, and we wouldn't let it now.

"Thank you. We call upon our ancestors for guidance. May the ferryman bring peace to those who wander, and the wanderer find their place on land. May these two stones bind and hold them. We ask your guidance for . . . Estra and Marek Ari. Please return them to us in one year from now, by skyfall."

"By skyfall," the crowd chorused, but my response wouldn't leave my lips.

My body went cold. I wanted to scream, to cry out and wail, but my body knew better than my heart and plastered a smile on my face. My people needed this. Even if it killed me, they needed this. This ceremony helped us keep peace; knowing that we were helping others who were less fortunate gave sirens purpose. A reason to exist. We'd moved too far beyond the rest of the world and were left with nothing else to solve, no questions left unanswered other than the few scientific mysteries deemed better left alone.

Marek's grasp was firm, but I knew mine had to be painful. I couldn't help it. It was my only way to keep myself moving forward. The only way I let my body glide to the beat of the song from the sirens below and take my place in the second half of the ceremony.

I didn't let go of Marek's hand when the summoning began, and this time the elders didn't try to make me. They let us stay together, almost as though they knew what they were doing to me.

I cried silently as I felt my beautiful scales turn to flesh and bone. My fin separated painfully, splitting into two legs that couldn't keep me moving the way my body normally would. I repeated in my mind: *You can once again help them. You can bring them the peace they were denied.* But then the small truths crept in between: *this could destroy me, you aren't strong enough not to feel*, and, the thought I had to fight hardest to ignore, *flee!*

LEGENDS AND LORE

The ceremony ended, and neither of us moved. Marek and I stared at each other, knowing what this meant. His face wasn't a mask this time. He knew this honor was no honor to us. He mouthed words to me as everyone left, words of love and strength, and I let myself focus on them. I fixated on them, and it kept me calm enough to stay still until only the elders were left. Even then, I may have stood a chance until I heard Elder Cassius softly say, "We are so very sorry."

⁂

It was time to choose our roles. One of us would be the ferryman and the other the wanderer. I thought I knew what role I had to play in all of this until I heard Marek plead with me.

"See their world the way I saw it. Choose to be a child again. I know you feel this is wrong, but maybe this can help. You already saw the bad; why not give the good a chance?"

"I am not sure I am strong enough to look past what I have already witnessed."

"Violence doesn't fill your everyday life. Sometimes it happens. Sometimes. And, you don't see them all. Uplanders rarely see death. You only live in one area, and you are lucky if you get to travel beyond it. Please, won't you try, for me?"

I didn't have the nerve to tell him that I was more worried about his own opinion of them being shattered if he were the ferryman; that it would haunt him as horribly as it did me—especially now that he had come to know them. He might even end up singing to someone he had known the last time, now that they would be the elderly generation.

"Wouldn't you rather return there?" I was honestly curious.

"Perhaps, but not if it means sending you back to the Underworld." I'd seen this side of him once before, during the gleaning when the elders questioned us and I first realized how much my pain had tormented him, knowing that every happy moment he was having was counterbalanced by a moment of my emotional turmoil. The first time around, I had been too weak, and we both knew I was unable to go back. I couldn't handle it, not really, not the way others always had.

". . . Thank you." I said it softly. I knew I should fight him, tell him he deserved the happiness the first time and I wouldn't stand in his way now but . . . I would. The dreams never left, and maybe this way I could find something to help ease them, some sense of—whatever they are other than death. There were wars, murders, and much worse. It was terrifying, the lengths they would go to destroy each other. The worst had been the serial killer in the very town Marek had been assigned.

"Have you decided?" Cassius asked, and we turned toward him. He gave me the same smile he'd always saved just for me, but it didn't give me the same pleasure it once had. I'd always been in his favor, and though it still meant a great deal to me, it didn't make up for the situation. Nothing could.

"I am the ferryman," Marek said, emanating strength. Cassius' face brightened, surprised by the choice. He turned to me, and the warmth of his smile gave me the strength to say the words aloud.

"... and I the wanderer." I made my voice deceptively strong. I needed Marek to know his choice to let me be the wanderer this time held meaning, that it might save me. We were the first couple to be selected together twice who decided to switch places. We would be the first with the chance for each to experience both sides.

When the proceedings ended, I fell into his embrace.

"Upon our return, from the moment I first saw you, I knew I would accept the ferryman, were we to ever go again." He ran his fingers through the streaks of white in my deep black hair. "You were a fantastic ferryman. Loving them wasn't a weakness. It was a strength. I only hope I can live up to your example."

I froze. What? What did he mean? But then the elders were guiding us away from each other, separating us for our journeys, and thrusting a small relay stone into each of our palms. As our minds connected, I just kept repeating, '*I love you*,' as Cassius led me to a side room.

"Cassius, why?" I asked it softly, giving him an opportunity to ignore me. I had always been gentle for a siren, possibly too gentle.

"Your kindness kept the Underworld in order. You ferried more souls to the light than any other siren. Marek gained more data on the humans than anyone had before. We need that now. There is change above."

"It resulted in my carrying a soul he had caused to fall," I said. My anger got the better of me, even though the events had always had a stronger effect on me, more than they had on my mate.

"Your empathy can work in our favor again. We all care about them, but you have a special connection. Don't fight it. We need you both to exceed expectations again. We need this more than you know." He was pleading. It was much more effective if an elder pled. Their charisma bled from them because of the age of their powers. "I am sorry it hurt you, but this time will be different. Now, time to choose your features."

"Dark hair and water-colored eyes—to remember myself and Atlantis."

"Age?"

"Seventeen." It was the age Marek had chosen before.

"You've chosen well," he said, watching as I backed into the chamber and started the song of change. Ferrymen do not require it, so I had never felt this before—the sense of purpose the song gave as your body morphed into a new shape. Marek's voice entered my mind through the stones' connection, softly singing along in my honor, although he was already in the Underworld. I could feel his joy at my own strange exhilaration in this new feeling. This new . . . hope.

※

I woke on the shore the moment the sun hit my skin as the water receded. We weren't used to sun, for obvious reasons, and the warmth was unusual. I'd bathed in the open air before, but human skin felt different, more compounded. The way ours moved against water felt almost like thicker water, but this new skin was so solid and warm. Everything felt heavy. I couldn't lift myself at first—my arms tried to support me and failed.

'*Ari,*' I heard Marek's nickname for me, and remembered the relay stone still in my hands. '*Remember you are strong; you were underwater, and you are here, the movement just feels different. Try moving faster.*' I did as he asked, and it worked. More effort was needed even for the slightest of movements, whereas underwater, once you had found your motion, you were a force of your own. Less thought was needed when swimming than the strange way I had to think each time I wanted to take a single step forward. I managed to get my bearings, and as I looked up, I saw what I had seen the dead wearing before.

'*When I was upland, my caretaker was a man. A family line passed down the tradition. There is a beach shower. Use it before putting on the clothes.*'

"Shower?"

'*Yes, it pours water on you.*'

"Why? I just came out of the water."

'*Salt water dries out their skin. You need to get the salt off, especially being this new. I don't know why your contact isn't there to help you yet.*'

He walked me through my actions and explained temperatures to me. Even once in this form, we still didn't need to worry as much as normal humans, but enough warmth or cold could still make us uncomfortable or blister this skin.

He tried his best to talk me through putting on the clothes, but I skipped a few steps, namely the things he was calling boots.

Once I was ready, I started walking, his voice singing in my mind as he ferried souls and kept count for each one as though it were a game.

'How many did you ferry?'

"I didn't keep track. I should have. It would have made passing the time easier."

'See, I am already doing better, for all we know.' he joked, and I laughed aloud. Then, I saw my first Uplander standing there, staring at me as I laughed by myself. *'Remember, they can't hear me. Humans who speak to themselves are thought to be unhinged.'*

"But you did." I said it aloud again.

'I didn't much mind being thought to be crazy, but then again, I had a contact by my side, so I was never alone.'

"Should I try to find him?" I asked softly.

'Yes. You'll need his help to get acclimated.'

The human was walking toward me. He was wearing blue and had some large box behind him with blue and red lights on top of it. "You aren't due for another two hours," he said, stomping toward me. "You disorderly lot have no sense of time."

"I'm sorry. Who are you?"

"Felix, your 'contact,' 'caregiver' . . . whatever the others have called it."

"You don't seem happy about it."

"Should I be?" His eyebrow rose, but the expression wasn't one sirens used, so I simply watched him, confused. "You're younger than the others. I wouldn't have realized what you are if you hadn't been wandering around talking to yourself like a nut job." He grumbled and grabbed my arm, pulling me toward his box.

"My name is . . . Ari." I chose the nickname Marek had given me so that I'd have the reminder of him, but regretted it as soon as the man spat the name back at me.

"Ari? Nice. Like Aria. Not obvious at all or anything." He shook his head.

"I shouldn't have come," I whispered, already ready to give up on humans if this was supposed to be a nice one. Screw them. Let me be the ferryman—at least there humans had shown me kindness in return for my own.

'*Oh, come on. Give it time. It will be an adjustment, but just like we all have different personalities, they do, too. He is just surly.*'

"Marek, this was a mistake. I should have been the ferryman." I said the words to the relay stone, but the man froze and stared me down.

"Marek?"

"I am not talking to you."

"I realize that. Is Marek your husband?"

"Yes."

"Oh." He went silent and opened part of his box. There were seats inside, so I guessed and sat. He sat in another part of the box, and when it started to move, I nearly jumped out of the hole next to me—until I realized it was sealed with glass. He was silent for a while, and I felt like I was wasting time, but looking out the opening, it was strangely beautiful and filled with so much color. The plants were vibrant and green, or even orange, like the fish that would swim through our city.

"Tell Marek that Ralph is still kicking."

"Ralph is kicking things still," I said to the stone, and heard roaring laughter in return.

'You just mean 'kicking.' It means the man who helped me is still alive. What is the name of the man you are with?'

"Felix." I waited for Marek to respond. He was silent for a long time, long enough for me to worry. In the silence, a memory surfaced: Ralph had been his sponsor. *'I'm happy to hear that Ralph is doing well. Tell Felix that I hope he kept his promise.'*

I felt sweet relief hearing his reply, but my concern hadn't faded. After I passed on the message, I only had one response to give from Felix to Marek: "I'm a cop now, aren't I?"

It was difficult to remember the details of Marek's visit here, but those words helped the pieces fall into place and made me look on Felix with more respect. He'd been a friend to Marek; I was lucky to have him as my sponsor.

※

"Now, to start with, you are going to learn how to use a computer. The public school around here doesn't make it easy for an outsider to fit in, but education is available online now, and it means you can cover more searching in less time. I know you only have a year. I've been mapping out what everyone else has covered, but you're the first to come through at a school age since Marek, so I guess school is your focus.

"My daughter can help you when you need it. She may only be twelve, but she understands computers better than I do, at this point. I've signed you up already for an 'at your own pace' learning experience, and the rest of the information is in your e-mail."

I looked at him like he was the crazy one this time, but his daughter walked into the room and something about my resolve to dislike him, despite my respect for him, lessened. I couldn't dislike someone if they had any part in creating the beautiful little human walking toward me. I had saved many like her, and while the memory stung, seeing one that I was certain would grow made my heart swell with love.

"Okay," I said simply and turned toward the device, still utterly confused.

The child pressed a circle, and the square screen lit up.

"I have a murder case. I'll be out for a few hours, but I have siren-safe food in the fridge, and Iggy can help you. Ralph is around here somewhere, too."

"I'm Iggy," the girl said. "I know. Weird. But I'm named after my great-grandmother."

"Ralph's wife?"

"Yes, she was beautiful, like you."

She explained the device to me, and my fascination grew. It was a knowledgeable machine that could search for nearly anything, but risked giving you lies just as easily as facts, because other humans were providing the answers. She walked me through my classes after finding a shortcut to the link on the 'desktop,' and before I knew it, I was able to handle some of it on my own.

We both stumbled our way through the technology together until I got a better grip on it. It was similar enough to Atlantis' old archives that, after a while, I got it. I still asked the occasional question, and in return, she asked about Atlantis. She would be in Felix's place one day, helping someone like me, just like she was now. The more she knew, the better.

"Ari, why do you call yourself Ari instead of Estra?"

"How do you know my name?" I felt cold shock run down my new form; I hadn't even told Felix. But, then again, Ralph had known Marek. I tried to remember his story from the gleaning, what had happened to him up here other than 'the incident' and the things he told me directly during our time back home.

His human contact had been kind to him, like he was his second child. Of course, second son would account for the first being Felix, even though Ralph was Felix's grandfather. If Felix and Marek were that close, then of course he would have spoken of me. I just hadn't thought about it. Then again, with the age gap between Ralph and Felix . . .

The person he had killed. Oh. Of course.

If Ralph was Iggy's great-grandfather, and Felix her father, then that left only one missing member of the family. One that Marek had been forced to kill for his crimes—the crimes I had paid witness to on the other side.

LEGENDS AND LORE

Eli. Felix's father.

I steadily worked away at my classes. I had studied past human knowledge and, when he was the wanderer, made Marek tell me about his studies as he did them, because I was bored in the Underworld as the ferryman. These modern classes were more organized and shorter. I made steady progress, and before I knew it, I looked up, and Felix was back.

"Good progress," he commented, as he looked over my shoulder. "Actually, that is pretty darn impressive. Did Marek help you?"

"No, but he'd talk to me during his homework when he was here, and I studied the materials we have in Atlantis. Listen, I want to thank you for your hospitality. I'll understand if you would prefer I stay elsewhere." As I finished the sentence, I felt his eyes on me, but I didn't meet them for a moment. I wasn't ashamed, but I wasn't about to put him on the spot either. His silence didn't let up, and my curiosity got the better of me. When I looked up, he stared into my eyes.

"Now, you listen. Marek did the right thing. Even as a kid, I knew that. Without the two of you, who knows what would have happened." He paused then, and looked up at the ceiling for a moment. "I do have a question, though. Had you returned before it was time to ferry him?"

"He chose the light. He nearly didn't, but my song called to him before he went too far. I knew what Marek had done and made a point of paying extra attention. The ferryman always takes longer to return."

"Thank you." His voice was filled with an outpouring of unexpected gratitude, and before he said anything else, he walked away. Not knowing what to do, I continued to study. It was what I was here for, after all, wasn't it?

※

'The math is the same; if they let you take the tests out of order you can get through those quickly. We are so far beyond them that even their highest math levels are still incomparable. English is close enough to ours, as is customary. You will want to focus on history, social sciences, and reading their modern literature. Some of the classics have already been covered, but not all; not everyone likes to read out of water, which is the biggest reason they choose to return as adults. If these classes are really going as fast as you say, then you may be able to start on some college courses and gain even more knowledge about their education system than I did.'

"Marek..."

He went silent. He'd been rambling as a distraction to both of us because he knew the tone in my voice. Even the lengths of my hesitancies gave away my emotions.

"He says you did the right thing. I remember what you said at the gleaning, but he says you did the right thing, and he is grateful his father went into the light."

His silence was overwhelming. Had I underestimated how much it had hurt him?

LEGENDS AND LORE

"Marek?"

'Yes?'

"I love you."

◈

It had been two months, and studies were unusually quick, mostly because the information in the first two years was mainly things I already knew. It was silly that they wouldn't let me skip ahead, but when Felix explained the education system to me, it made sense.

I knew I shouldn't stick my nose where it didn't belong, but as I passed Felix's desk one night, I saw a photograph.

I didn't mean to.

I shouldn't have.

It changed everything.

Life had been simple while landlocked, until I looked at that photo. I knew the girl. The one with the cuts and blood pooled around her; I had ferried her the first time Marek and I'd been chosen. She was one of Eli's victims.

Just as I started to recover from the shock, Felix walked in and watched me for a moment, the way my eyes studied the picture. I remembered her reversion from that beaten girl to the girl she became when walking into the light. It had been a truly beautiful transformation.

It hurt at the time, knowing she had been stolen from this world, but now, somehow, I saw it differently. I guess because Felix had been so grateful his father had gone into the light, it helped me realize that it counted for something.

"They're happening again." He broke the silence, and my heart. Humans were still human. They still murdered.

"You know it isn't him."

"No, it is a copycat. That's why I found your timing so peculiar. Now, I am wondering if it isn't fate."

"What do you mean?"

"I mean, there is a copycat killer, and you have a direct line to the other side, just like Marek did the first time. I mean, you can help. I know you came here with the intention of helping your people, not mine, but Marek told me how much it hurt you, and this time you can do something about it. You can help make it stop."

"I'm not strong like him."

"You're wrong. He told me all about you. About what your love was like. You're stronger than you know. Everyone is, if they just give their self the chance to prove it." He walked away, leaving me alone with the file and my thoughts.

After a while, I got up the nerve to speak. "Marek, keep an eye out for girls between fifteen and twenty-five."

'What? I just had one not two minutes ago. Very young, she reminded me of . . .' I could feel the moment he realized she was a victim of the copycat. I ran out to Felix.

"He's killed again. Just now." I was out of breath; this world still made everything feel so heavy to me, and the breathing was too easy, too quick.

"I need details. Ask him what he once asked you."

"Marek, we need to know—"

'About sixteen, but could have been older or younger; I haven't adjusted to the differences yet. Black hair, blue eyes, birthmark on her neck, but a nondescript shape in a darker color than her skin. She was fair, but still had obviously spent time on the beach. She smelled like seaweed, and when she first arrived, she was scared, but had no memories of her death. If this is another killer targeting the same kind of girls, he isn't killing them the same way. He keeps them unconscious and makes sure they feel no pain.'

I repeated the information, and Felix took it down. He started moving as soon as I said birthmark, so I followed him into his car, and we sped off, leaving Ralph, who was old enough now that he tended to sit and read by the window, with Iggy, who was enjoying the television set and tablet game.

"I know who she is. Her mother was in my father's files as a prospective victim when we found them. Same description, only she has a birthmark her mother jokes is shaped like Texas. They're local."

So this was how it started. How Marek started to feel like he was really making a difference, and I got to know the stories of the dead before they passed. How we had broken all the unspoken rules when we shared their messages to their families from my world to his before skyfall, only to find out they weren't rules at all. Now here we were, only this was my world this time, and he was far from me.

'I don't want to say this, but we both know . . .'

"I know . . . It's happening again."

'I will question the next one for details. I'm sorry. I didn't know.'

"It's not your fault. It never has been."

'We know what to do this time,' he assured me. We wouldn't waste precious months without it occurring to us to question the girls. We had barely managed to catch the man the first time, and even then, Marek had only one choice. He couldn't tell anyone in time, and skyfall was approaching. So he did the one thing he could do to stop it.

Then I did the only thing I could think of to make the entire situation any better. Yes, I had been tempted to throw the man into the fires and let him burn, but I knew Marek wouldn't want it, so I sang my sweetest song for the man who had killed the girls who somehow managed to become my only friends and company that year.

It is strange the way fate turns on you.

This time, Marek was the untouchable one.

And my life was the one at risk.

Why had I chosen dark hair and light eyes?

What was I thinking?

⁂

"Ella was first, then Angie, Crystal, Cynthia, and Devyne. All within three months, before the murders stopped, until the next cycle. I've been here for two months already. How much time do we have?"

LEGENDS AND LORE

I remembered the last three girls whose deaths still haunted me. The way they had spoken to me over the course of their time on the other side before crossing. They had so much to sort through before they were able to be at peace that the songs hadn't been enough. Then, once they were, they wanted to see justice done before moving on, so they stayed with me, watching me ferry others.

"Two weeks. He has already taken three, so if the pattern holds, then there will be two more. I feel so... How is this happening again? I should have been able to stop this!" Felix was getting angry, the kind of angry I knew, the kind I had felt as each girl joined me in the Underworld. I stepped away softly and let him cool off, walking to the office to go through his files. So far, the girl with the birthmark was still considered a missing person. We couldn't very well tell them why we assumed she was dead, but without a body, we couldn't prove it either.

I sorted through his files like I had sorted through my schoolwork, systematically arranging everything into its proper place. Even in Atlantis, everyone had a job. I sorted things, mostly information, but almost always mathematical or scientific. I tried to look at the files like an equation, and since Iggy was already fast asleep, I laid them out on the table. Five girls over the course of three months, twice a year. If I didn't stop it this time, there might only be the two deaths, or there might be the second cycle. I couldn't let that happen.

'*Ari?*'

"Yes, my love?"

'What are you thinking?'

"I'm wondering why he did it. Why five girls, and why twice a year? His method is so specific, but his motive isn't in his files. We know who his next cycle would have been, but we still don't understand how he chose them, other than dark hair and light eyes."

'I have wondered for years. Every night when you would dream and I would awaken, I would ask myself the same thing.'

"I made a foolish decision."

'What? Are you okay?'

"Yes, but Marek . . . I chose dark hair and light eyes."

'. . . Why?'

"Because I wanted them to remember Atlantis by." I turned and realized Felix had heard me. He'd been standing by the door, watching the pattern I had laid the images out in.

"Interesting," he mused. "Two of these are the daughters of the women whom he had selected to be victims. The others on his list have sons. I'd just thought of it; what made you?" He pointed to the table, and I realized that I had set out both the police files I likely wasn't supposed to have available to me, and Eli's files.

"I compile information about mathematics at home, keeping track of schematics and the latest in technology, and entering it into our database for comparison of our timeline to yours. I'm just not the one who enters the other half of the information."

"You said you chose dark hair and light eyes because of Atlantis. You aren't the only one. I always wondered if he did it because of sirens. They're the features nearly all of you choose."

I was struck. I hadn't thought we would all choose similar features. Would the elders even allow it? How would it not become obvious after a time?

Or was that the issue? That it had become too obvious, and now someone knew. Now someone was targeting humans who looked like us.

"Marek, we have a theory up here. Felix noticed that almost all sirens choose dark hair and light eyes."

'Like the victims.'

"It would make sense."

'Yes, I am not quite sure how, but at least with Eli . . . it would with him. But what about this new killer? He wouldn't know about us. I mean, it isn't Felix. He's a cop, and if he wanted to hurt a siren, he would know who to hurt.'

"Wait . . ." Felix said, then looked up sharply and ran from the room. I was too startled to follow him, too absorbed in our conversation that seemed to be coming to a point neither of us could quite make out yet.

"But so would Eli."

'We only have a few days until the next one.'

"If this were an equation, I would wonder who of the other victims shared the same features or were even a part of the same family line, before you ever came here." I still couldn't break the habit of speaking aloud to the relay stone. When Felix returned, he had Ralph in tow.

"Tell her."

"No," Ralph responded and tried to leave, but Felix blocked the doorway.

"Please, it is happening again. *Tell her.*"

"Again?" Ralph's face fell, and he sat back into the nearest chair. Apparently, he hadn't known. Everyone knew two girls had died, but he didn't see the pattern yet, or had happened to miss the newspapers one day, not being prone to leaving the house for anything but apple pie on Tuesdays. He hung his head and clenched his fists in his lap. He looked close to tears for a moment before he found his composure.

"Did Marek ever tell you that I wouldn't say anything about my boy's mother or how she died?"

"No, not that I remember," I answered honestly. Knowing Marek, he probably just thought it was a matter of privacy and didn't want to reopen old wounds.

"She didn't die. She left, and I knew she wouldn't be coming back . . . not in my lifetime anyway."

"She was . . ."

"She was only here for a year. It only takes nine months for a human body to have a baby, and she knew only the elders would know what she had done—what we had done. She even suspected others had done the same, though more likely men than females. She said some sirens below were weaker, and she wondered if women sometimes came back secretly pregnant—that some were part human."

His words sounded like justification as much for his benefit as mine. I didn't know how to take in the information.

'You're using the stone silently now. I told you you'd get the hang of it, Ari. Not everyone is like us. Some of them view it as a vacation. As a chance to be someone they aren't when in Atlantis. Or perhaps they fall in love. It's not that outlandish. You and I met and knew quickly. Would you say it was about a human span of, what—a few months before we knew it would always be us? I can't blame him, if he really loved her, for wanting some part of her to stay behind.'

"I understand," I said softly, coming up to Ralph and laying a hand on his shoulder. "Marek does, too. You wanted some piece of her to stay with you. And when . . . what happened . . . happened." I held him as he cried in earnest.

"She's gone . . . She's gone . . . I will always love her . . . Always."

"What was her name?"

"Anara."

"I'll make sure she knows. I promise."

⚜

"He seems to be all right now," Felix said, coming back into the room. I was devouring my second jar of pickles that day while organizing photos and using the computer to research family histories. We were creating our own maps of the families these tragedies were affecting, and trying to find the first incident.

"Felix, these seem to date back from before your family was even living in this town."

"We only started being the contact for sirens when we moved here. My fourth great-grandfather met one on the shore one day and gave her his jacket. He took her home and helped her, and we've been doing it since." He looked at my work appreciatively. I'd made good headway once I realized that it really was a math equation. There were causes and effects to everything. I just had to discover the cause, and we would be able to trace the effects.

"Could someone have fallen in love before? Like Ralph? I know the location of where we emerge changes every few years, but it's here most often. Here and an island in Greece we have particular interest in." My comments seemed to perplex him. He stayed silent, his mouth a thin line.

"You don't start hunting and killing women because you loved one. Do you?"

"Unless . . . Do the victims have a special sort of charisma? Almost like they hold more push when they ask someone to do something? No matter what they are asking?" I stared at my human hands, so like my siren ones, and remembered what it was like to change from child siren to adult—the pain and confusion. I could only imagine how difficult it would be if everyone around you was susceptible to your abilities and catered to your whims instead of knowing to teach you to control them.

"What are you thinking?"

"When we mature, something happens to our gift. Siren children have abilities, but they are very light, things that no one would notice even here. It would be unusual, but not enough to attract too much attention.

"That being said, teens—specifically when they come into their abilities—they have a hard time controlling their charisma. They ask you to do something and one day, you just start listening and do it, even if it isn't a good idea. It wouldn't work very well on others at their level. Someone like me wouldn't even feel it. But normal humans without any siren blood—if hybridization theory holds true—would be susceptible."

"Are you saying these families could have siren blood?"

"That's exactly what I am saying. In this small a town, it wouldn't have to be a lot of sirens who fell in love, just one or two somewhere down the line long ago, so that the blood lines split and split and . . . This is all speculation, of course."

"More than we had before."

"Eli was able to lead them because of his charisma, but that makes me wonder why this killer is putting them to sleep first. How is this happening? What is the sequence of events? The bodies are all found on the beach, in the caves, like the last case, right?"

"Yes, though they're more obvious. Less hidden and just more protected from the elements."

We stayed there in silence, going through the rest of the files and expanding the family lines. The more we expanded on the family histories, the more they converged. It was hard to see—we couldn't see the full picture—but the more we worked, the clearer it became. Something was going on here, something old but new.

The only thing was, Ralph knew who his love was. Had this person even known the person they had a child with was a siren?

If so, what siren, and how far did this go back? How was any of the bloodline even so powerful? I had more questions than answers when I fell asleep upright in my chair, a pen still in my hand, and a half-eaten cupcake on the counter.

※

'Ari, are you awake?' I awoke to Marek's tentative voice.

"Yes . . ." I knew my voice would still be scratchy, but it was true, I was awake . . . now. Soon, I recognized my surroundings and remembered the desperate mystery we faced that laid out before me on all the flat surfaces around me.

'I was thinking about what you told me last night. Everything we've learned. Have you ever heard of a siren not coming back?'

"Once. Just Halcyon. When I was younger, but that was thousands of years ago."

'Why did the elders choose us? Why was Cassius so sure it needed to be you and me?'

"I'm not sure."

'Ari . . . I don't know who my mother is.'

"I know, neither do I. Many of us don't, with the way our society works."

'What if . . . ?'

"What if Halcyon is your mother and still here? Seems a bit farfetched, doesn't it?"

'I suppose.'

"But Marek?"

LEGENDS AND LORE

'Yeah?'

"If you are worried, I will keep it in mind. I do trust you and respect your opinions, no matter how farfetched they might seem to me."

I heard his soft response, but got distracted when Iggy came down the stairs, and I rushed over to steer her clear of the room. Felix walked through the front door just in time.

"Let's go out for breakfast!" I said, nodding toward the table.

"Sure. Why not? You haven't seen much of the town yet." He smiled at Iggy, who squealed and asked if she could get waffles with sprinkles. "Yes, sprinkles and milk shakes and even..."

"Curly fries!" she shrieked, and it occurred to me that she had siren blood in her as well. Sugar and salt were her favorites, just like mine. She was so young. Felix would have siren blood, too, but he was putting it to good use as a cop. I wouldn't want to be the one questioned by him.

We ventured out to the car after locking up and deciding we would bring Ralph back a whole apple pie. He always slept a bit later than the rest of us, and there were still a few hours until Iggy would be expected at school. I'd never been so thankful as I was on that car drive, knowing that Iggy was far too young to be a target if the pattern held true.

'Ari?'

"Yes?" I said; by now Iggy was used to my ramblings and was too distracted by entering the diner to care about anything I might be telling Marek.

'What if Eli was influenced by her? What if he was told by someone to do the killings?'

I froze mid-step. He had a point. These had been happening before him, and now were happening after him. The person doing the killing was a manipulator, but the way they disposed of the bodies, protected them, suggested they were being manipulated. "I think you're right," was all I said. I didn't want Iggy to catch on, and I knew she would be off to school after this.

I could tell Felix soon enough. He was too distracted by Iggy's jubilant reading of the menu as she spun on the red and silver bar stool at the counter. A jukebox in the corner completed the ultimate diner stereotype. I'd been watching movies lately with Ralph, and it looked like this place could have come right off a set, whole pie in a glass case on the counter and all.

The moments passed slowly as we sat together, and for the first time, I truly understood what Marek had felt during his time. This sense of . . . family—something our people didn't quite have, not the way humans always have. We had mates, but children were raised by those who chose to raise them, and often birthed by a completely different couple who just happened to be at that point in their life cycle.

We all knew and cared about each other in a way, but not like this, not in a way where even though you know everything will come crashing down and the people you are learning to love will die before you, you can't help but want to spend forever with them. You want to live forever, but only in that moment, living forever in their loving gaze with their laughter and their joy.

I'd only ever felt that with Marek before that moment, but watching Felix and Iggy, I realized just what I would do to protect them and just how much they had come to mean to me, even in so short a span of time.

We enjoyed our unusual meal. Each of us had a waffle with ice cream and sprinkles, dripping in raspberry syrup, with a side of fries with extra salt. The waitress ended up bringing us a small salt dispenser, and we laughed as Iggy added some to her ice cream. Yup, definitely part siren. She reached her hand out toward me expectantly, and I barely paused before taking it. She just held it, the same comfortable way Marek always had, as a simple sign and silent whisper: "I am here. You are here. We are together."

As we got the check, I felt something else, something confusing that made me think of Atlantis. *'Marek.'* I thought silently, almost second nature, needing to know he was all right.

'Yes?' He answered automatically and let me hear he was still singing beautifully, ferrying souls with more joy than I had ever managed. *'I can see why you didn't like it, but . . . I've never felt so much purpose,'* he said as soon as the song for that soul was over. I smiled and simply sent the feeling of my happiness, ignoring the looming feeling creeping through me for the moment. I could tell it seeped through the communication when he commented, *'What is that?'*

"I don't know," I answered, aloud again because I realized all of my emotions bled through when I tried to communicate the other way. I didn't want him to feel my fear and the unfamiliar feeling.

'Someone is watching you,' he said, the feeling more familiar to him than me. *'A predator. I've felt that before. You're in danger.'*

"Directly at me?" I asked, hoping it meant I was the target and not Iggy. I couldn't stand it if Iggy was the target. I didn't want anything to ever steal her smile.

"What is going on?" Felix asked, and I gave him a look that said enough; I didn't have to speak aloud.

'Yes. It only happens when you suddenly become a target. It could be a human thing, but I think it could also be heightened for us. I felt it once, before I was attacked. Wherever you are, get out of there.'

If I was the target, then Iggy was in danger. I needed her to be safely away before I could escape. I wouldn't be the reason she needed a siren's song in the underworld. Not after all the souls I had sung for.

"Look at the time! Iggy, you're going to be late! Felix, you'd better go ahead and take her. I still have a bit to eat. Mind coming back for me on the way home?" I was overly cheerful, and Iggy looked disappointed, but content with her belly full of sweets. Felix, on the other hand, instantly knew something was up. I didn't say anything, I just stared into his eyes and flicked my eyes to Iggy and back. I would wait until they were gone to look around. I knew the feeling now and could tell the eyes were still on me.

'What is happening? Are you safe?'

'Can't talk,' I thought back, trying not to lose my focus on the feeling.

'Then let me feel.'

I did.

'Tell Felix that he forgot to turn off the radio. I hope he understands. I know you have every good intention, but don't you dare let yourself get hurt. Even for that precious child. I need you.'

"Felix, I think you left the radio on." As soon as I said the words, his resolve melted. I looked at Iggy and back again, and he nodded, his eyes full of emotions I understood. He didn't want to leave, but felt like me: she was more important.

"I'll be right back," he said, sounding confident, even though his eyes told a different story. He put on a smile to walk out, and I realized he must have known what I meant—that whoever it was, was here. Whether the killer or the puppet master.

'You're fine in public. Stay there until he is back. The killer has never attacked when there was more than one victim.'

'This is someone from Atlantis,' I thought, and realized that I was right as soon as he received the thought, and I felt his mix of shock and confirmation. I wanted to look around, but I couldn't deny I was frightened, even to myself. The feeling was getting harder to ignore, stronger, as though moving toward me. I dared a glance and saw the diner was still full of the breakfast crowd, then I felt the person directly to the side of me before I saw her. She slid into the booth, and I tried to act normal, like I wasn't what I was, even though it was likely just as obvious to her as it was to me that she was a siren like me.

"You have the most beautiful eyes. They remind me of a place I once visited." Her voice was full of her luring call, so potent and powerful that it gave away her age. I wanted to play dumb, and was about to, when she grabbed my chin suddenly, her expression changing as she raised my face and looked into my eyes directly. "Finally. It's you."

I wanted to respond, but something held me still, waiting for an explanation. She stayed silent, and I looked away. She was so beautiful. Still so much a siren, though her age did show more than it might have underwater. How long had she been in human form?

"Do you know how long I have waited?" She continued to stare, though I was watching my food now. She was a predator, and I was not. I couldn't be. It wasn't a part of me like it was supposed to be. Like it was in both humans and sirens. It was what was missing from me all this time. I knew I'd have to respond soon or we would attract attention, and while I didn't want to be in danger, I also didn't want to put anyone else in danger by attracting attention she might not want.

"No," I said simply, only a single word, but it seemed to give her a great deal of pleasure.

"I wanted them to be you."

"So you want to kill me?" I whispered softly enough that no one but her might hear.

"No, of course not. They weren't you, but I'd said too much. I needed to know. I thought I would know for sure when I saw you, but until now, I hadn't known I was right." She seemed earnest in her demented eagerness, her voice quaking like something extraordinary was happening—something other than me being cornered by someone I knew was an attacker, a killer, and a threat.

"I don't understand." I said it softly, losing my nerve under her stare.

"You're kind. I didn't think about it, but that is how I knew. How I knew who you were . . ." She said the word 'kind' almost desperately, so much emotion in her voice that I didn't know what to do. My own emotions were too much for me, and I could feel Marek there with me as I grasped the stone tightly. I remembered what he had said, that maybe she was his mother. He had been attracted to me for my kindness; it was a stretch, but . . .

"I am Marek's wife."

"What would I care whose wife you are?" she said, confused. Leaning forward, she lay her hand against mine. I yanked mine away too quickly, and it spurned her. "You're my child. I would never harm you."

"What?" The word left my mouth slowly, like I was back underwater, only unable to breathe . . . like I was drowning for the first time in my life.

"They took you from me. They said I wasn't fit to raise you. You were kind and I . . . I know I am not the best mother, but I'm yours, and you're all I ever wanted."

"Then why kill those girls?" I asked, my voice raising a fraction too high. I needed to calm down or we'd attract attention.

"Because they weren't you," she said as though it were obvious, as though her actions followed some form of logic I simply didn't understand. "I wanted them to be you. I needed to find you. I needed you, but they weren't. They weren't even close."

My anger was starting to push its way around in my heart like a wave rolling through me. I'd never been this angry. She was the reason they were gone? She had killed them? For me? She was going to blame all of this on me?

I stood and started to walk outside. It was too late for a public place, there was no way to hold my temper as my powers radiated from me. One wrong word and those innocents wouldn't be in nearly as much risk from her as they would from me. I had to get away from them. I had to get to the sea.

'*Ari, don't!*' I heard Marek screaming inside of me, but without meaning to, his understanding bled in, his love and desperation for me to be okay. We both knew that if I died as a human, I died as a siren.

"Where are you going?" she asked, following me.

"I need to see the sea."

She wanted to blame me for this? She wanted me? If she wanted me, she never should have done any of this. She had destroyed so much. I had blamed myself for her actions even without her instigation. Now, in my mind, it was both undeniable and impossible.

I didn't do this. I would never do this. I'd do anything to help and had never done a single thing in my life with the intention of hurting another being, whatever race. When we got to the sea, the waves both soothed and roiled my emotions, pushing and pulling until I felt something I hadn't felt before, something I craved and hated at once. Power.

"I love you," she said softly, and when I turned toward her, I realized she was just beginning to realize her mistake.

"Why? Why do this if you loved me? I could have loved you. I am foolish: I love everyone without meaning to. Why would you destroy your chances? You knew I was kind? Then why act out in destruction? Would someone kind truly appreciate that kind of action?"

"Estra . . . please . . ." she pled, and my name left her lips for the first time. That was when I remembered the briefest glimpse of her, smiling and warm. What had she become? How?

"Tell me. Now," I said. I needed to know. I needed to understand, and the woman in my memory didn't make sense compared to the one standing in front of me.

"They tricked me. They sent me here as a human and never took me back. They wouldn't have me back, and you were there. I realized it was Cassius' plan all along. He knew. I knew he knew the other side of me, that I wasn't like you. He said I would corrupt you, but I didn't believe him. You were my salvation, and he took you from me. You may have been half his, but you were half mine, too. The half of me that was good and pure went into you. You could have made me everything I no longer am . . . You still could."

"I blamed myself for their deaths. They were my friends on the other side. I loved them, and you . . . You . . . You really think I could redeem you?"

'Ari, don't be a fool. I beg you.'

"I don't know what to do."

'I wish I did. I've done all I can.'

"What do you mean?"

'Stall, I'm coming.'

"No, don't you dare desert those souls."

"I . . . I'm sorry." She knelt, her hands in fists, her tears a crystalline blue. She wasn't lying, they weren't the false clear tears—they were the ocean inside of her, flowing over.

"Sorry isn't enough," I said softly.

"What is?" Anger was returning to her voice, and for a moment, I wondered if she might go against what she had said in the diner and hurt me. If she couldn't have my forgiveness, she might decide I was like the other humans she had destroyed. But then, she hadn't done them herself. Why?

"Why didn't you kill them yourself?"

"They looked like you. Once I knew they weren't, I never wanted to see them again. If I was going to stay here, I had no choice. I couldn't live like that, looking at you, but never being near you. It was torture I endured for a thousand years before I first took anyone from here. I made a man do it for me; I couldn't see you die. I still . . ." Everything she said made a morbid kind of sense, but it only angered me more, breaking my heart further and further with each word.

A storm was rolling in, one so vicious, its wind was whipping at us like leather. It took me a moment to realize it was me—I was doing this. I didn't want to, but it was pouring out of me after years of being that person who constantly took the higher path, who bottled the anger or fear down into a jar that had finally cracked and ruptured.

"Stop this, Undine." A voice rippled through the thunder, and a form started to emerge from the water . . . Cassius.

"No. Stop! Go back. She blames you," I screamed as she launched herself toward him.

"I am your father. It is about time I learned one lesson from the humans and act like one." He stood strong. He had legs as his individual morph, but his differences from my form were obvious. It was strange to know that even then my appearance was so my own that my mother had recognized me.

"I have done this to you, and there is no one to blame but me," he said, though even I knew his words were faulty. There *was* someone to blame. The woman behind the killings that, even now, I hated myself for forgiving. Because somehow, hating myself was easier than hating her . . . than hating anyone else.

She launched at him, and he held her firm. Her humanized form wasn't as powerful as his, fresh from the water. "WAIT!" he yelled. "Before you kill me, listen."

"No! YOU did this to me. You made me this. I wasn't before. You're wrong. YOU did this."

"No. I didn't," he said, and I felt fear ripple through me; it was true, but true didn't make it smart. "Before you kill me, you should know . . . you can come home." She had her hands around his neck as he said it. She nearly didn't loosen them, until he croaked out, "I confessed to . . . the others."

Her grip loosened, and he was able to speak clearly., "I've explained what you did and why. I explained about Estra, the murders, everything. I told them I was the reason."

"You were."

"I know. I realize that now, Undine. I was wrong to let you go."

"You knew what was happening?" I asked, now furious with him as the realization dawned.

"Yes. I'll pay the price. I've been a fool and let others sway my beliefs. Not like you, Estra. Undine, you'll pay a price, too, but they blame me; they'll have you back. You and Estra can be together again, like you always wanted."

His words read false, but she only needed the slightest bit of hope to hold her heart at bay. She collapsed at his feet, and, as I ran toward them, he held out his hand to stop me. "Forgive her or don't, but this is mine to fix. I am sorry . . . I am sorrier than you will ever know." He took her into his arms and walked back into the water just as Marek started to come out of it. He looked at Marek and nodded.

"I'll be the ferryman this round. Alone. I can't undo what has been done, but I can give you both a few months together here. I can take her back and pay the price for her actions. I know what I did was wrong. I've done . . . more than you know. I don't mean to justify my actions, and I'm not asking for your forgiveness. I don't deserve it. I just want you to understand. I thought I was doing what was best for everyone. But then I saw how much Marek cared for the humans and realized why being the ferryman had hurt you so much. You cared for them, too. I couldn't let her continue, no matter the cost to Undine—to me."

"I . . . don't want to hear anymore." My voice was broken. I was already overwhelmed and needed time more than anything.

"I understand, just . . . take these months and use them. Not for us sirens, but for you both. Please . . . have the happiness we robbed you of the last time." He made sure it was loud enough for me to hear before he disappeared, and I was left with more emotions than I could bear, or understand. The storm was still raging as they left, still unstoppable, until Marek drew me into his arms and it lightened just the tiniest bit.

"Was he lying to her? Are they going to kill her?" I sobbed, knowing he was the one person I could truly be fragile around, but also the person who made me brave.

"I don't know. I don't know what the future holds, but Ari, I am here. I'm not going anywhere." He held me so tight that I leaned into him, and the storm slowed, step by step, until my emotions were on track enough for me to move. It felt like the entire day had been a physical blow, but I needed to know that this had stopped the murders. I needed to know Iggy was safe, and somehow, that was the one emotion I was grasping fully with everything I had.

As we approached the diner, I realized that the storm made me look like I had been through a hurricane, and all Marek was wearing were pants left on the beach that had flown from the line. Felix spotted us before we even made it close to the window, Marek's arms still wrapped around me. He was shocked at

Marek's presence, but his inner cop overcame anything else as he came directly to me to make sure I was okay.

"It's over."

It was all I could manage, but it was enough.

※

Iggy was adding more sprinkles and frosting to a three layer cake than there was cake itself. It was her birthday, and the last three months had proven to be peaceful. The cycle ended, and the murders along with it. It was a small comfort, but a rewarding one. We'd found the last body and given her a proper burial. The time had been difficult, but oddly beautiful. With Marek there, we made quite the family: Felix constantly helping the community, Ralph joking at every turn, Iggy always a bundle of sunshine, and Marek being just as human as anyone else in the room.

I guess when it came down to it, there weren't as many differences between humans and sirens as we thought. Only the ones we created. We weren't sure what the future would hold, but we knew we had a few months left to be a family, and, for that moment, that was all we needed. The rest would come, but we'd stay strong. We got stronger every day we were together, each of us.

A true family.

How beautifully... human.

FAELAD

by Sarah Hunter Hyatt

I didn't see it coming. I was so captivated with the atmosphere in Galway, the quaint little shops that lined Quay Street, that I didn't notice the men that had followed me from the pub. After turning down a side road, headed back to the bed and breakfast, the attack came from behind.

Snatched around the waist and a hand clamped over my mouth, I was unable to scream out for help. They yanked me into a dim alleyway and farther from any chance of rescue.

A man with a swollen red nose threw me up against a stone wall. My head made contact with such force that I heard a crack on impact. I nearly blacked out but forced myself to stay awake and fight. I kicked at the air, hoping to make contact with either one of them.

The stench of stale whiskey reeked from their clothing. And Red Nose was close enough that I felt his breath on my cheek. I tried once more to scream, but a sudden punch to the gut left me breathless and choking for air.

"Shut yer mouth, ya blasted American." A husky Irish accent filled my ears.

"Doesn't she smell good? Not like the bogtrotters we're used to," the other voice said, just as Irish as the first.

Images filled my head of the kind of horror that could take place. I tried to squash the thoughts from my mind and began thinking of ways to get away. My head throbbed, and something wet trickled down the side of my face.

I kicked out one last time and made contact. Unsure of where I hit him, my shin exploded in pain with the thrust. Red Nose yelped and hollered at the other guy as he lost the grip on my arm. I stumbled away and began to run as fast as I could. My head ached and my vision was blurred, but I had to keep going.

My freedom was short-lived.

"Where ya think yer goin', lass?" The younger man was right behind me.

With tremendous force, I was knocked down to the ground. I looked up and saw the man clearer now.

"If ya don't stop fightin', I'll have to silence ya fer good. Understand?" Cold metal slid across my neck. I froze, looking my attacker right in the eye. He appeared younger than Red Nose, but just as dirty, stench and all. His dark hair shot out at every angle around his baseball cap that read "Guinness" across the front. He had a crooked smile perched at the corner of his face, his cold, black eyes fixed on mine.

He sank down, clenching his hands around my throat, and I struggled to breathe. I thrashed against the weight, but he only tightened his grip. A black haze swirled around my vision. I felt on the brink of unconsciousness. Death wasn't as scary as I'd imagined, more like slipping into a dream.

LEGENDS AND LORE

The blackness had nearly consumed me, when a flash of . . . something . . . jumped over me, followed by a horrible scream, not my own. It filled the air. Then all went black.

※

I first saw her walking down the cobbled street of the historic district. Her ebony hair caught my attention. I hadn't seen hair that thick and black for about 150 years. Her beauty stopped me in my tracks, and I felt compelled to watch her. She walked slowly but with grace, gliding along, her eyes full of wonder.

Her blue jeans were faded, and her white sweatshirt with "Ireland" written across the front in green, branded her as a tourist. Her bright blue coat hung loosely on her shoulders with a matching blue– and white-striped scarf wrapped in a droopy knot at her neck. No one in Galway dressed in such bright colors.

Even the way she strolled gave her away as a traveler. Her head darted from side to side, lifting her phone to take pictures of the stores and people. It was like watching a child experience grass for the first time—that smile that forms and never seems to end.

I followed her the rest of the afternoon, careful to keep her from discovering me. As the sun began to set, she stepped into The Quays, one of the most popular pubs for tourists. I came in behind and studied her as she sat across the room. I was at the bar. She was a few steps away in the restaurant area. It took her well over ten minutes to place her order. I nearly laughed out loud at the frustration written on the waiter's face.

It wasn't until near the end of her meal when I realized that I wasn't the only one watching her. Two foul-smelling men were whispering in the corner, clear enough for my fine-tuned ears to hear them.

"Look at 'er lily-white skin," he spattered with a mouth full of beer. "We could dirty 'er up, ya know, give 'er a proper Irish welcome."

The younger man laughed and nodded his head.

My anger boiled over as they followed her outside. I knew what was in store and I couldn't allow it to happen. I snuck out quietly behind, careful that no one saw me leave, but I was too late, the yelp of pain came from the shadows and was quickly silenced.

In an instant I was on them, the animal taking control, stopping them forever from hurting another soul. I don't like to harm others. I don't want to kill, but the beast inside is hard to direct, and when my anger takes over, I have no control.

I took her in my arms and her eyes flickered. "Yer all right, lass," I whispered into her ear, "no one will hurt ya again."

∞⟨⟩∞

A sound brought me from the darkness swimming through my mind. My head pounded like drums beating away inside. It took several minutes to realize what I was hearing. My eyes fluttered open and I could see a gaping window above me. Swaying evergreens lined the open view, but the birds caught my attention. Crows filled the branches, all squawking and calling out.

The trees looked black with the swelling crows. The cries of the birds resonated in my head like chanting.

Still dazed, I looked around. I was lying on an old couch, a faded flower design woven into the frayed cushions. How did I get here? Panic sunk in as I realized I had no idea where I was. The slightest movement caused an explosion of pain, so I sat up slowly. It wasn't until I was almost sitting straight up that I saw him.

Sitting in the corner of the room, half shadowed, was a man. He watched me but didn't say a word. My first instinct was to scream, but my severe headache made my response time sluggish. Our eyes met and I froze. Piercing emeralds stared back at me, accompanied by a boyish grin. It wasn't either of the men from last night.

He stood up and stepped into the light from the window. His jeans were worn and hung loosely from his waist, secured by a black belt. His grey, V-neck sweater hugged tightly to the muscles underneath. My cheeks flushed and I felt awkward staring at him.

"How're ya feeling?" His voice was smooth and calm.

"I'm . . . I'm fine." My words came out like stale broccoli. I tried to stand, but the room swirled and I was forced to sit back down. "Who are you?"

"I'm Collin O'Shea. I brought ya back here two days ago. Do ya remember what happened?"

I would have certainly remembered a man like that saving me from those drunks, but I didn't. I shook my head. "It's been two days?"

"I'm just glad I got to ya in time. Who knows what those men could've done?"

"Thank you for helping me, but I really need to go home now." I tried to remain calm, but the alarm building inside made my voice shake.

Collin shifted his weight and looked uncomfortable, although he still smiled, and when he spoke, his words were slow and decisive.

"I know who ya are, Morrigan. I've watched ya since ya arrived in Ireland. I've waited for yer return fer over a hundred years."

I'm sure the look on my face gave away my confusion. Nothing he said made sense except for the fact that, apparently, he'd been stalking me. My nerves kicked in.

"First of all, my name isn't Morrigan. I'm only here for a few more days and then I'm heading back to America." I forced myself to stand. "Thank you for saving me, but I think I need to leave now." Wobbly legs didn't stop me from heading for the door. He didn't move to stop me, but his grin faded.

"I know that yer name is Claire, but there's much more that ya don't remember."

My hands felt clammy and I was sure all color had left my face. This guy was crazy. How did I always attract psychopaths? Even as gorgeous as he was, he was downright nuts.

"Collin, I really think I need to leave now." I put all my energy into each word to make my point.

"Claire, ya have no reason to trust me, 'tis true, but I promise I won't hurt ya." That time his voice cracked. First sign of desperation.

"Do ya know this woman?" He reached out, holding a picture in his hands.

I took the portrait and realized the woman looked just like me, her eyes the same cloudy grey. We could've been twins. The painting was very old, set in an antique gold frame. There were brush strokes visible through her raven hair. She held a pink flower that matched her ruffled dress. I looked up. "Who was she?"

Collin's face relaxed. His lips parted and I could see a sliver of white underneath. "T'at's Mary Elizabeth Henry. She lived at Kylemore Castle an' gave me this portrait before her death in 1872."

Collin had to be around my age, maybe twenty-one or twenty-two? This wasn't helping his case for sanity. He continued before I responded.

"This woman is you. T'was the last time ya lived here in Ireland. But now yer back and ye can be restored to what ya once were."

"Well, that does make sense. I think I better get back to my room so I can pack up some clothes, and I'll meet you back here later, okay?" I grabbed the doorknob. I wasn't going to stay here another minute.

As I was about to open the door, Collin's hand touched mine. I stopped, my body rigid with something I didn't understand.

There was a spark of memory trying to break through. His face, clouded in a fragmented memory, came into view. I knew I'd seen his green eyes before, but how was that possible?

"Claire," his breath next to my ear, "please, try to trust me. Can ya give me a chance?" The warmth between our touching hands grew and his voice lingered in my ear. Why did he seem so familiar to me? I nodded but couldn't turn to meet his gaze.

"Ya need to meet the Faelad Clan. They'll not believe yer here."

"Faelad? I don't understand what you mean."

"The Faelad are . . . Well, ye'll just have to meet 'em to understand." Collin opened the door and the sunshine burst into the room. It was then that I saw the books. One wall was filled with bookcases, one after another, each bulging with books of every size and color. Hardbound, softcover, new and old, unlike anything I'd ever seen.

Collin wrapped his fingers around my hand and gently pulled. "Ade will want to meet ya."

We stepped outside into a clearing, the forest a few feet away filled with dense, dark trees. I looked up at the blue, clear sky, the sun only penetrating the clearing where the cabin sat.

I followed behind Collin, his hand still guiding mine. I wished I had packed the mace that Dad encouraged me to take. Even though a part of me—a part I didn't understand—trusted him, I was nervous about where he was leading me.

The path was barely visible in the green moss and dirt. We walked for a while in silence. I didn't know what to say, still trying to process this nonsense. I kept my eyes on the ground to avoid staring at Collin's muscular arm and to avoid tripping over anything.

"We're almost there, Claire. Just a few more steps and ye'll see why I brought ya here. These are the sacred grounds of the Faelad Clan of Ossory. These people are me family." There was reverence in the way he spoke.

I heard voices ahead and looked up to see a large cave that sat at the foot of the mountainside. Inside the opening were shadowed figures in the muted light.

I looked down to see if there was a rock or stick to grab for protection. I feared I had made a huge mistake and took a deep breath.

We stepped inside the great opening, and everyone gathered there froze. They looked like mannequins set in a store window display as they stared back. A man stepped away from the crowd and walked over, arm extended. Collin let go of me to meet up with him. They shook hands and embraced. The other man was brawny like Collin, tall and broad. His dark red hair hung to his shoulders with the hint of a crimson beard on his face. He, too, was stunning to look at.

The man looked past Collin towards me and stiffened his body, making him appear more massive. "Who've ya brought to us, Cúchulainn?"

Collin turned around and both men stared at me. My cheeks burned with embarrassment.

"Ya don't know her, Ade? This is The Morrigan, returned at last."

Ade looked me up and down, eyebrows furrowed. "Are ya sure, lad? Could it possibly be her?"

"I'm sure, me' brother, look at 'er eyes." They leaned in, staring me down. Uncomfortable wouldn't even begin to describe how I felt, and I was ready to turn and run.

"Stop it! No one wants to be gaped at like that. If you have something to ask, then do it." I was surprised at the force behind my words, but I was at my limit for lunacy.

"Yep, that's Morrigan all right. How'd ya find 'er?" Ade chuckled.

I didn't get the joke.

⁂

I knew that Claire didn't trust me. The world she'd known was about to change in a way that even I couldn't comprehend. It was hard to believe she was here. Since the curse she put on herself to separate us, I'd only seen her one other time. Nearly 150 years ago, at Mitchell Henry's castle. I knew right away who she was, her flowing black hair, those beautiful grey eyes. I had no idea that she herself wouldn't remember who she truly was.

My greatest sorrow was that I couldn't convince Mary Elizabeth that she was The Morrigan before she died of a mysterious illness. She was gone, just as quickly as she had come into my life. But here stood my second chance, and most likely my last. Waiting 150 years to see her again was torture, the time before that, unbearable. I had to restore the woman I loved, but more importantly, I had to break the curse that kept us apart.

"I'm sorry, Claire. It wasn't nice to gawk at ya like that." I sat down on a blanket lying on the floor of the cave. "Ya must have questions; let me clear things up."

Surprisingly, Claire sat down, but on the edge of the blanket, away from everyone. Clearly she didn't trust me or anyone else.

"This must be confusing. What can I tell ya to ease yer nerves?"

Claire didn't say anything, but her eyes darted around the faces in the cavern. I wished I knew what was going through her head.

"Claire, don't ya have questions?"

She looked at me, those silver clouded eyes locked on mine. All of my memories, good and bad, came flooding back. She was real, sitting here, and I would do anything to keep it that way.

"I'm sorry." Her chin quivered. "I just don't believe anything you're saying to me." She looked away, and lowered her head.

"I know ya don't, Morrigan, but shortly, ye'll know we're tellin' the truth."

"Please don't call me Morrigan. I don't know how to convince you that I'm not this long-lost woman that you think I am."

On instinct, I reached out to touch her hand, but she pulled away. It was too much for her human brain to grasp. The shell of mortality kept her subdued and fragile; The Morrigan was anything but. I had to delve deeper, to reach The Morrigan and there was only one way.

The sun was slipping behind the mountain and night was closing in. I only had to keep her here a little longer so she could see the truth.

I stopped pressing and focused on her needs. Claire must be hungry and cold. The temperature dropped quickly as the sun disappeared. I offered her a blanket from Tressa, Ade's sister. Eadan, who was an amazing cook, had a stew simmering, filling the cave with smells of turnips and caraway seeds. I offered a bowl to Claire and she took it.

※

The soup was delicious; the warm liquid trickled down my throat. It was a new flood of spices I'd never experienced, and yet it felt like something I'd eaten before. It was wonderful. I slurped down every drop. The soup kept me warm and filled the emptiness inside.

It was a relief to eat in silence. I didn't know what to say. It was true that I was full of questions, but where would I start? These strangers were all convinced that I was the reincarnation of a woman from the 1870s. The only reason I stayed here was to figure out the fleeting connection I felt towards Collin.

The darkness was closing in and I was hopeful it meant I could go home and forget this day. Returning to Portland became my primary focus. Not even staying for the Winter Solstice meant much anymore. I wanted to be back in my apartment, all 500 square feet, and cuddle up to Perkins, my calico.

Once the light from outside completely vanished, the mood changed. Energy around me emerged strong enough to fill the air. The cavern became alive with movement. Three women crowded towards the back were smiling and seemed eager. The other men, Collin, Ade and five more I didn't know, also stood up. Collin held his hand out; I took it and he pulled me up.

"Stand back, Claire, and try not ta panic. I promise it'll be deadly."

"Deadly?" I shrunk back. That wasn't the word I was expecting.

He laughed. "In Ireland, it means fantastic."

Our eyes connected and all uneasiness left. Once again, a feeling of familiarity filled my mind. I did what he said and took two steps back, keeping my eyes on him.

Shrieks, like tearing fabric, muffled with howls and snorts filled the air. The people standing in front of me transformed, taking on beastly features over their human frame. They were unlike anything I'd ever seen. Covered in coarse hair, each had pointed ears and large eyes, but none looked exactly the same. A scream slipped from my mouth, and I was running before the thought crossed my mind. My "fight or flight" instinct kicked in and I was out of there. I couldn't stop my feet, nor did I want to.

"Claire, please stop."

Collin's voice broke through my fear and I stopped. I'd witnessed him change before my eyes, but his voice was the same. I was too terrified to spin around and face what stood behind me, and yet, deep down in my memory bank, I knew his voice. I turned slowly on my heels.

Within the bright rays of moonlight, I could make out a figure. The beast before me had to be seven feet tall. It was covered in fur and both pointed ears stood straight up. The jaw was extended, white canine teeth protruded from its mouth. Its emerald eyes, glinting in the beams of light, looked back at me. It was Collin.

Seeing Collin as a werewolf was scarier than anything I'd ever experienced in my life. But within this creature was a voice so familiar that the fear slowly dissipated. Deep inside my brain I knew more about this clan and the life they lived; and it was all centered around The Morrigan. But these new thoughts brought more confusion as I battled the unlikelihood of it all out in my mind.

"Bet ya didn't expect this." Ade emerged through the trees behind Collin. His fur appeared bright red, as if on fire. "Well, Cúchulainn, looks like ya succeeded. The great warrior triumphs again."

"Cúchulainn?" I wasn't sure why they called him that.

"Aye, this is the legendary Cúchulainn, fer whom the poets write sonnets and all the floozies swoon." There was hardness in his voice. "And now he's brought home his greatest conquest, the long-lost daughter of Ireland, The Morrigan." Ade mockingly bowed towards me, his hand extended to take my own.

Collin stepped between us. "What is it, brother? Why're ya acting like an eejit?"

Ade snapped up, burning fury in his eyes. "Because she can change everything; she has the power ta make things right, but ye'll not do it."

Tension built quickly and I didn't understand what was happening. Collin jumped in front of me, yanking me behind him with his massive arm. His grip, firm and quick, moved me like a rag doll.

"She hasn't returned ta wreak havoc on the humans. The Morrigan is here to break her own curse, to be free of the bonds of mortality." His voice grew louder. "Would ya have her take the lives of those we're sworn to protect?"

"Aye. I would have 'er release us from our servitude, no matter the cost." Ade's voice rose to match Collin's.

The rest of the clan came running to where we stood. In the darkness, the shadows divided into two distinct groups. Most of the clan stood behind Ade, while the remaining took the space behind Collin and me.

※

How could he betray his clan, his family? My mind raced, but I remained firm. Whatever Ade's plan was with The Morrigan, it didn't sound like the covenant we'd made centuries before. Our blood oath was still binding and only she could break it.

I'd taken the oath as a young boy, after killing the wolf hound of Culann. The hound had bitten me, and I was thereafter cursed as a wolf to protect the Culann family forever. I joined other wolves, already under oath, and formed a clan. These men and women were my family and I, their brother. But here we stood, divided, our brotherhood hanging by a thread.

"Ade, what 'as changed in ya? We've roamed these hills of Ossory for hundreds of years. We've drunk ourselves gammy, and battled side by side. Why would ya part with our clan now?"

Ade, still fixed on Claire, answered heavily. "This goes beyond our clan; don't ya see the world has changed? We need not be slaves to the weak and useless humans; we need to rule them, be who we truly are—gods over the mortals."

It was strange hearing my friend speak like a tyrant, ready to rule the world with power and fear. And it was how he'd break the oath that worried me most. That was why he focused on Claire; her direct line as The Morrigan was Culann. Her father, Lord Ernma Culann, had power beyond mortality. He created the wolf hounds and bred them for war. Having The Morrigan to tip the balance on the war against the humans would release the bond and set us free.

"Without order, the clans will fight fer power and supremacy. Human casualties will be the price of yer pride. Do ya want that blood on yer hands?"

"We've that blood on our hands already. You've killed without warrant and so have I. That's the beast we subdue. Why not let it out and stop hidin'? Humans don't need protection any longer." His words spat from his mouth, dripping with arrogance.

Anger coursed through my veins and the Faelad beast raged. "Why, Ade? Why are ya doing this?"

"Ya know she's the only one who can set us free. Her power will release the curse. Don't ya want to be free—free from this hellish life as a guard dog?" He took a step forward, his chest heaving up and down.

I steadied my stance. I didn't want to fight my brother or my clan, but what he wanted was more than I could give him. The

Morrigan deserved to be set free, not used as a pawn for our release. I promised Claire she'd be safe, and now that promise was broken. I'd already failed her.

"Olcán." I motioned to the wolf on my right. "Take her back to me' cabin. I'll join ya shortly." I heard Claire behind me, each heartbeat matched her quick breaths in and out.

Ade took another step closer and leaned in as if to strike. I barred my teeth, growling deep from my throat and he froze.

"Ade, ya know what'll happen if ya try to take her, even worse if ya try to hurt her. She's human and a threat; the oath is clear. The pain of boiling blood is excruciating."

Ade looked up at me, teeth barred to match mine. "Pain is worth the price."

"Olcán, take her and leave now!"

⚜

The beast grabbed my arm, and before I knew it, I was being dragged through the thick ferns and bushes. Collin remained behind, leaving me with this animal. I began screaming, shouting to Collin and thrashing around, hopeful to get loose.

"Morrigan, I'll not hurt ya. I'm taking ya back where it's safe."

His voice was young, and filled with fear. This creature of thick black fur and dark brown eyes was just as scared as I was. I stopped thrashing and let him lead me. As we stepped further away from Collin and Ade, I couldn't help but look back over and over again, not wanting to lose sight of the only person I trusted.

Once inside the cabin, I sat down on the musty couch. Olcán remained outside, as a guard, I assumed.

A large fire raged in the hearth, which kept me warm and also lit the room. I studied the log beams that ran across each wall, a mud mixture crammed in between the gaps to cover holes. The beams were weathered, faded to a light gray, with dusty cobwebs in the corners where the roof met. This cabin was ancient.

I didn't know what time it was, but with the darkness outside, I knew it had to be late into the night. There wasn't a chance I could sleep knowing werewolves were outside, and some—if not all—were willing to kill me. I shuddered and stood, headed for the bookcases. Maybe there was a way I could push one in front of the door.

I tugged and pushed, but the bookcase barely budged. I gave up, sinking to the floor. In frustration, I slammed my head back, striking the wooden shelf. I rubbed the back of my head, sure I'd see blood, when a book toppled into my lap.

The brown leather binding was frayed and torn. I carefully picked it up and brought it to the fireplace for better light. The cover was made of green linen with a band of brown, cracked leather down the binding. In the center was a circular leather piece with a symbol burned into it. A Celtic pattern wound around the inside shape of a bird.

I opened up the book to see yellowed pages, inked with elaborate lettering. It was the most beautiful book I'd ever seen.

Slowly turning the pages, I studied the artwork. The top of each page began with an ornate letter, hand-painted with intricate

LEGENDS AND LORE

weaving in green, red, and blue. On the sixth page, I stopped. The first words written were "The Morrigan." The M was painted with Celtic knots at each point. Halfway down the page I saw "Cúchulainn," the name by which Ade referred to Collin.

It was the tale of the great warrior Cúchulainn, who had defeated the wolf hound of Culann. He was strong, powerful, and a great leader. He had won many battles and seemed undefeatable. And then he met The Morrigan. She was the goddess of battle, sent to oversee each war and to help the right army prevail. She had fallen in love with him and tried to stop Cúchulainn from going to the battle at Cooley. The warrior in him wouldn't stop, bound by the wolf-curse to protect. He fought, and she witnessed his death.

"Death?" I whispered, looking at the depiction painted on the opposite page. The caption read "Battlefield of Cooley," and there was Cúchulainn, lying against a rock, bloodied and dying. "But how could he be dead?"

I read on, anxious to learn how Cúchulainn survived. When The Morrigan saw the death of her love, she set a curse upon herself—a curse of mortality so that she could never remember the lost love that had broken her heart.

I stopped reading, my mind whirling from the dark tale. There was so much of it that matched what I'd already heard, but this was folklore: words made up centuries ago to scare the locals.

Outside there were low, muffled voices, too muffled to understand. I slammed the book closed and held it tight against my body, like a shield.

The clan was divided. It was hard to believe that it'd happened this way, and by my own brother. Ade had been my companion, was with me from the beginning, the first Faelad I had taught after my own oath. He was strong, smart, and fierce, like me. He had always been eager to please and serve. What had changed? The beast I saw tonight was not my kin; he was a stranger to me. What was worse was that he knew how much The Morrigan meant to me. How could he threaten her?

"Do ya not remember what happens in two days' time?" I had warned him. "The Solstice arrives and then we can settle this."

The only thing I could do to stop Ade and his fellow traitors was to remind him of the solstice. Winter Solstice was the most important day for the Faelad. It was a time of renewal, a time of rejuvenation. In two days, the solstice meant that we were at our most powerful.

Ade had relinquished his position, for now, and retreated back to the cave with his followers. As he disappeared into the forest, he let out a long, snarled howl which echoed through the silent forest.

I turned to assess who had stayed with me and was shocked to see Tressa standing with the small group. Carrek, Eadan, Kasey, and Tressa. Adding Olcán still didn't make for a strong clan. Three men, three women.

"Tressa, ya stayed. Ya risk the wrath of yer brother now."

"I don't share the feelings of me' brother." The pain was present in her eyes and her ears, once pointed, now drooped.

We only had a few hours left of night. I knew the clan was tired and hungry. I sent them out to find food, and I walked back to the cabin to release Olcán for the night, as well. Ade wouldn't return this night; wanting to prepare, he needed time to do so.

Claire sat on the couch, shivering. She looked small and scared as I entered. I had to remind myself that she wasn't used to seeing a monstrous form, so I remained in the doorway.

"I'm sorry, Claire, sorry that this is happenin'. But ya must know now that I only want to protect ya."

She eased slightly, bringing the book to her lap. "Can't I just go back to my old life? I want to see my dad, be back on campus, and hang with my friends. I don't want any of this."

The pain in her voice hurt me as well. I knew nothing of her old life but only wanted to see her happy. However, I knew that she was destined for more than the confines of a mortal life.

I changed the subject. "Ya found me book, I see."

"It fell from the shelf. I'll put it back." She moved to stand, but I held out my hand to stop her.

"No, read it. In truth, it's yer book." I reached over to a basket on the floor and took a folded quilt from it. I held it out to her. "Read as much as ya'd like." She took the blanket from me and nodded.

Turning to head back outside, to guard her until morning, I paused. "Try to get some sleep, lass. There's much to do in the morning."

I dozed off after reading a few more pages. I was able to learn that The Morrigan was a shape-shifter, most often taking the form of a crow. The tale told of a beautiful goddess who was fierce but merciful. She alone could decide the fate of those who went into battle. She was fearless and strong; The Morrigan was nothing like me. How could this clan think I was that woman?

The painting on the inside cover showed a woman wielding a sword, black hair flowing in the wind and a crow perched on her shoulder. I wasn't her, and I never would be, no matter how much our faces resembled one another. I was the English major who lived in a loft apartment four blocks from my father. I came home every night to cuddle with a cat. My friends consisted of a group that met at the gaming shop to play D&D for hours. I was nothing special.

The morning was gloomy as I awoke. The clouds formed a wall against the sky, blocking out any hope of light. The gray outside matched the wooden beams of the shack, and the lack of light cast shadows throughout.

The wooden door creaked as it was opened, giving away any chance of a surprise entrance. It was Collin, back to his human self, wearing casual jeans and a brown button-up shirt, sleeves rolled up to his elbows.

"I thought I heard ya getting up. Do ya want some breakfast?"

I shook my head; it was far too early for me to eat. I needed to ease into the day and collect my thoughts.

Collin sat on the couch next to me, picking up the book from the floor where it had fallen the night before.

"How much did ya read?" Holding the book, his fingers rubbed across the bird image on the cover.

"I read some." I couldn't look into his face, knowing the moment I did, my cheeks would flush a nice shade of raspberry.

"This is the closest account to what happened between us. It will tell ya how we were separated."

Questions swirled in my head and I hoped Collin could clear a few things up.

"If The Morrigan is the daughter of Culann, how is she immortal?" The book didn't clarify.

"She's the mortal daughter of Culann but the immortal daughter of Badb, the Queen of the Banshees. The Morrigan was born, like a mortal, but she will never die."

"Okay, but if you're Cúchulainn, like Ade said, why does the book say that you died?"

Collin inhaled deeply, then let out his breath in a slow puff of air.

"The Morrigan saw me get wounded—mortally wounded, if I hadn't been Faelad. She didn't know that I was part of her father's oath, didn't even know it existed." He bowed his head, his hands beginning to shake.

"She found me as I lay there in the sand. I remember her crying out and holding me in her arms, but I was too weak to speak." Collin's voice quivered. Clearly holding back emotions, the memory must have been unbearable for him to recount.

I reached my hand out and touched his arm. Like a flicker of light, an image popped into my mind of Cúchulainn lying in my arms. My chest filled with a combination of agonizing sadness and overwhelming love for him. The emotions were jarring and I let go of Collin's arm, feeling dizzy.

"May I have some water?" Coughing through my words, I leaned forward.

"Of course." He reached out his hand, but pulled away. "I'll be right back."

As soon as he walked from the room, I stood up. Needing fresh air, I opened the door and stepped into the crisp Irish morning. I filled my lungs with the cool breeze, closed my eyes, and leaned my head back to feel the wind on my cheeks.

December in Ireland felt a lot like Portland. Cool temperatures, rarely cold enough for snow, left the land green year-round, with rolling hills and evergreens. Shades of red, orange, and brown were sparsely scattered across the landscape. The overcast sky and thick fog were also familiar sights for this time of year, and if it had been raining, I would've sworn I was back home.

I opened my eyes to see the tree line, tall evergreens reaching up like soldiers guarding the forest within. A flutter in the branches caught my attention and I saw the silhouette of a murder of crows.

I scanned the perimeter of the cabin to see that all the trees were filled with black birds, swaying with the branches in the wind. Strangely, they didn't make a sound, not one caw escaped a beak. A scene from the movie *The Birds* came to mind and my nerves kicked in. Being out in the open with hundreds of birds might not be the best idea.

I turned around and knocked right into Collin. He wrapped his arms around me and chuckled. "Where're ya off to?"

"It's the birds, they're freaking me out." I buried my face into his chest, even though my cheeks burned.

"The crows? They're the least of yer worries. They've been waiting for ya."

Pulling away from Collin, I lifted my head. "What do they want with me?" The silence of the fowl-covered trees was unnerving.

Collin stood behind me and lifted my arms with his. "Call to 'em, they'll come."

I felt ridiculous standing there, arms raised, like some kind of circus performer. And for my next trick, I'll summon the birds. The thoughts in my head were as absurd as I felt! I dropped my hands, quickly folding my arms. "I'm cold, can we go inside now?" Without waiting for an answer, I retreated indoors.

※

The Morrigan was present, if only a flicker in Claire's eyes. Maybe if she'd tried to call the crows, she would've freed the power that was inside her. It was hard not to press her, though. I had to remind myself that she didn't remember anything from her past—had no idea the force she could display. And sadly, she didn't know the love we once shared. The touch of her cool lips to mine, her delicate porcelain skin, her stormy eyes of gray, all burned in my memory for centuries. Those memories were what kept me from trying to find love again.

Claire sat at the table in the corner of the miniscule kitchen. The chipped paint on the chairs left flecks of green on the floor like glitter. She looked defeated, slouched with her elbows resting on the edge of the mahogany.

"What can I say to help ya feel better?"

Claire looked up from the table and shrugged.

"The power of The Morrigan is in ya, ye'll just have to release it."

"Like I did with calling the crows?" She scoffed at her own words.

"Are ya starting to accept yer destiny then?" There was the glimmer of hope I was looking for.

"There's a slight—and when I say slight, I mean less than 10% chance that I'm this Morrigan you're talking about. Honestly, it all seems crazy to me; however, there's something familiar that's keeping me from leaving . . . for now."

I wanted to grab and kiss her with the passion I'd only felt for her. She was sitting right there, my lost love, and yet she didn't know me. It was difficult, but not as much as her being lost to me. I pondered on all the lives she must've lived. Once her body died, she moved to a new one, reincarnated over and over by her own fateful curse.

"Claire, come outside with me. You can try again." It was a light push, one I hoped she'd accept.

Claire stood and followed me back outside. The sun peaked through some cracks in the clouds, sending rays down on us. She was stunning in the sunlight. Her hair shone as it blew to the side of her face in the breeze. I was drawn to her, like the moment I first saw her in Galway. The fates had aligned that day and I'd be forever grateful.

Placing my hands under her elbows, I raised her arms to shoulder level. This is how I'd seen The Morrigan do it many times. I hoped it would spark Claire's memory. I leaned in close, whispering, "Now, call to them."

Claire's head shook. "What am I supposed to say, 'Come here, little birds'? I feel stupid standing here."

"Don't move yet." I moved my arms to around her waist to steady her. "Close yer eyes and listen to the sounds 'round ya. Breathe in the smells, taste the air, let the forest invite ya in."

I stepped back, giving her over to the Earth Mother, to fill her senses with all that was beautiful in nature. I watched Claire's body relax with each breath, her countenance changing before my eyes.

Claire's arm reached higher into the air; the breeze picked up with her movement, swirling around us both. The trees swayed left to right, but the crows' feet were stayed. Not one fluttered.

"Chairde dilse mo, preachan, teacht anseo!"

Clear and strong, The Morrigan's voice called out.

The birds came alive, flowing from the trees in a beautiful parade of black feathers towards her. They swirled in a pattern, following the rush of air, gaining speed as they descended.

Headed right for Claire, the birds blurred together as they forced themselves closer and closer into the path ahead.

I held my breath as they came at her.

When the birds reached Claire, the beautiful spectacle shattered into hundreds of lone birds in a mad dash for escape. Many cawed in protest as they soared by, finding comfort in the branches once again.

With my attention on the trees above, I failed to notice Claire. When I finally looked back, she sat in the dirt, sobbing.

※

It was hard to describe what'd just happened. I wasn't sure myself. One moment I stood in the open air, breathing in the forest and the next moment, a black cloud was rushing towards me. I panicked and collapsed into the dirt. Pain coursed through every limb; my lungs felt empty as I gasped for air. I hadn't realized I was crying until the tears dripped from my cheeks onto the soil below.

Too weak to stand, my head throbbed, making me nauseated. Whatever had happened was a huge jolt to my system.

"Claire, are ya all right? Please answer me . . ." Collin's voice slowly made it past the ringing in my ears and I looked in his direction. His face ashen, his clammy hands held my own.

"What—what did I just say?" My last memory before the birds was yelling out unfamiliar words.

"Ya called 'em, Claire. You said, 'My friends, the crows, come to me,' in our native tongue, and they obeyed ya."

I didn't know Gaelic, and I certainly didn't know how to speak to birds, and yet, something had happened. Collin seemed sure that I'd called some ancient power from deep within me to get the crows to come. Having them fly, at ramming speed, didn't seem the right way to go about it, however.

Collin asked if I was okay over and over. I reassured him each time that I was fine. I needed rest, to let my body recover, before I could stand up.

"Can I have a few minutes alone? I just need to pull myself together; I promise I'm okay."

Collin's right eyebrow cocked up in disapproval, but he smiled. "I'll be right inside if ya need me. And ya only git a few minutes before I come take ya inside to rest."

Collin's hovering was worse than my father's. Living close to Dad meant that I'd often come home after classes to find him in my kitchen making dinner. He always had an excuse for being there, but I knew he was worried about me living alone. He had to be lonely himself, now that Mom was gone, so the visits were nice for us both.

It was strange to think that Collin had only saved me four days ago, two of which were spent unconscious. But he was kind and observant, making sure my needs were met. No one, besides Dad, had ever treated me like that. Not one of my old boyfriends had pampered me the way Collin did. I felt safe with him and wished I could return the favor, but my feelings for him were confusing.

I tried out my legs, making slow movements to stand. Once on my feet, the guilt of not reciprocating Collin's feelings made me feel worse. I had fleeting memories that stirred up a connection, but nothing more. I decided to slink into the cover of the woods so I wouldn't have to look Collin in the eyes yet.

"I didn't think Collin would let ya outta his sight." A voice broke my concentration and I turned to face Ade, who was grinning at me.

"Collin will be here any minute. You'd better leave, Ade."

Ade's arms were loosely folded, his ankles crossed as he leaned against a tree. "That's why I'm here; I want to tell ya me plan, without Cúchulainn whispering in yer ear."

"Why would I care what you have to say?" Still weak, I hoped Ade couldn't see how much my legs shook.

"He's not telling you everything. He's only focused on his feelings for The Morrigan and not the reality of the situation. Can ya give me a chance to explain?"

"What's this really about, Ade? Why are you here?" I scanned the foliage for any sign of Collin. It was obvious that if Ade attacked, I was in no shape to fight back.

"Morrigan, you have a valiant destiny. You alone can bring about a great change for us. With you as our leader, the balance of power will sway and the Faelad will be released. We don't deserve to be slaves any longer."

Ade stepped away from the tree and I tensed. His stance remained casual, however, as he placed a thumb into the corner of each pocket. He didn't resemble any part of the wolf that snarled the night before.

"Why should I believe anything you say?"

"Why shouldn't ya? I only want what's best for me brothers. Cúchulainn has been blinded by his quest to find ya. He fails to see the agony of our oath. I only want to be released from it."

My thoughts turned to his words from last night. "Aren't you the one who said, 'pain is worth the price?' You were talking about killing me, weren't you?"

Ade's smile diminished. "That's what I call 'Plan B.' If ya don't want to accept yer fate, I'll make yer fate. You have Culann blood in ya, and yer blood spilt on the *Brú na Bóinne* will break the curse."

His words made little sense. My head swirled and my legs gave out from under me. I stumbled, grabbing a branch, to keep from hitting the ground.

"Look at yer weak human body, ya can't even stand properly. Break free, Morrigan; join us and never return to this wretched existence." He pointed at me, as I struggled to remain standing. "The authority is there; just let it out in all its fury. Yer Faelad army is ready; accept us as yer destiny."

"What exactly do you want with me?"

"It's simple, Claire. You become our leader. You're the goddess who decides fate in battle. Choose us to break the oath over the humans and set us free." His left eyebrow cocked in a high angle. "Or I'll be forced go with Plan B."

I stood up slowly, balancing my weight between my wavering legs to appear steady. I didn't want to look frail in front of Ade, so I mustered up every bit of strength to let go of the branch and stand on my own.

"Your proposal sounds honorable on the surface, but other than speaking of the power within me that you wish to control, all you've done is insult me."

Ade's eyebrows furrowed; I'd touched a nerve.

"Yer going to help me, Morrigan, that's all there is to it. Help me or die."

If Ade knew the power inside me was worth killing for, could I use it on him now? Trying to recreate the control I felt earlier, I closed my eyes and slowed my breathing. I raised my arms, willing The Morrigan to take hold.

The words came from me, but I didn't know their meaning. *"Mo preachan teaghlach, troid!"* I opened my eyes ready for the birds to appear. But nothing happened.

Ade chuckled. "Trying to call yer birds to what, peck me' eyes out? Truly, Morrigan, ya can do better."

I fell to the ground, this time unable to grab anything to stop the impact. Crumpled in a pile of exhaustion, I couldn't move. Above me, a canopy of branches swayed back and forth in a rhythmic dance to inaudible music. Lying in the dirt and leaves, I heard Collin's voice.

"Ade, what have ya done?"

※

I rushed to her, desperate for signs of life. Why had I left her alone so long? I knew she needed space, to catch her breath and gather her strength, but I'd left her vulnerable. If Ade had hurt her, nothing could stop me from ripping him apart.

Claire wasn't unconscious but made no attempt to move. I didn't see obvious signs of trauma, so I picked her up. She fit perfectly up against my chest, and I hoped I could get her back to the cabin without Ade trying to interfere.

Ade had fled deep into the woods as I came upon Claire. He was a coward, unwilling to face me and the consequences of his actions. But Ade would have to wait; Claire's safety took priority.

I headed back towards the cabin, Claire cradled in my arms. My chest felt tight, regret filling up every space left inside me. I'd almost lost her again. How could I face her when she recovered? Her vacation to Ireland had turned into one nightmare after another; first, the filthy low-life drunks, and now at the hands of the wolf sworn to protect her.

"Cúchulainn!" Tressa's voice pierced the forest.

I broke into a sprint, headed in the direction of her screaming. It was hard to move as fast as I needed with Claire. After what just happened with Ade, I couldn't let her out of my sight.

I emerged from the forest and stopped at the edge of the clearing. There, standing in a line, blocking me from the cabin were Ade's men. There were seven and I knew them all by name. Days ago, we'd been one clan, our Faelad brotherhood stronger than if we were blood kin.

"How can ye come here and try to take away all that I have?" I looked them each in the eye as I spoke.

Gaeth stepped forward. "Cúchulainn, what Ade wishes is fer freedom. Is that not a valiant desire? We protect undeserving souls. I don't want t'at anymore."

He didn't have the same anger that Ade displayed earlier, and I wondered why Gaeth would follow him.

I was the strongest in the group in both forms but didn't use that power to control. I used it to protect the people I love. And now these men I'd give my life for were standing against me.

"Gaeth, this woman needs to be released from her mortal captivity and return as The Morrigan. Once she's restored, let her decide what our fate will be."

Filib spoke up from the end. "We know what she'll do. Yer her mate, and she'll do whatever ya want."

"What about Eaden and Brady?" I nodded towards Brady, whose face hardened. "Did Eadan choose out of love?"

Eaden and Brady were betrothed but now stood on opposite sides. I could see Eadan, to my right, shaking as she sobbed. Kasey and Tressa stood on either side, arms wrapped around her. Carrek and Olcán were missing.

Ade was also absent and that worried me. He wasn't the type to skip out on a fight, always eager to hunt at night after we transformed. For years, our biggest opponent was the brown bear. But they'd all been killed off by the tenth century, leaving us with deer, wolves, foxes, and boars. Not much of a hunt.

"Where do we go from here? Ya know I won't just hand Claire over to ya, and I know yer desire for liberty is fierce." We were at a stalemate.

Before anyone could answer, Ade broke through the woods near the cabin. His head was bleeding and he toppled to the ground. In heavy breaths, he yelled out to his men, " 'Tis an ambush! Carrek and Olcán attacked me as I approached."

In an instant, all the men charged. I had seconds to decide what to do with Claire. I knelt down, resting her next to a grand fir, its trunk reaching well above my head before green boughs formed.

I called out to Eadan and she rushed over. I trusted her to protect Claire at all costs.

Filib came at me first. In human form we were still stronger than the average man, but I didn't want to fight him. Filib was the comedian of our clan, the one that kept the atmosphere light. The rage in his eyes was a new side to him.

"Filib, stop!" The words had barely left my lips when I was hit at the waist with Filib's entire body. I was almost knocked to the ground but kept my footing. His arms were around my waist, trying to knock me off balance. I pushed down on his arms, trying to break his hold.

My anger quickly erupted and I pushed back with more force. I had to get him off me and keep a barrier between Claire and them. Focused on Filib, I didn't see who'd come up behind me.

Claire screamed out as everything around me faded.

◈

The haze within my mind was clearing, and I sat up. The yelling brought my mind into focus, as well as the realization of my circumstance. A battle raged in front of me. I saw Kasey and Tressa first, holding back a dark-haired man with a beard. Both of them hung on to his arms while tears streamed down their faces. Then I heard Collin. He yelled at a man named Filib who had him around the waist. They fought only five feet in front of me.

I saw Ade slinking in from the side, Collin unaware of the threat. Ade held a large club, raised high into the air. In one swift movement, the club came down. I only had time to scream. Collin went down hard, the impact to his head was solid, and I heard a crack as the wood met with his skull. Was Collin dead?

Eadan grabbed my arms, holding me back as I tried to stand. I struggled against her hold, but was too weak to fight back.

Filib and Ade had Collin by each arm and dragged him away. Filib gave a quick whistle and the rest of their men stopped fighting and joined them. Tressa pursued them, yelling something in Gaelic. I didn't know what she'd said, but it didn't sound good.

Kasey joined us, followed by Tressa. We sat under the tree in silence. Carrek and Olcán were still missing, and now Collin was taken. They all stared at me and I could see the pain in their eyes but didn't know what to say. Eadan's tears flowed in a stream down her cheeks, although she, too, remained quiet.

"Do you think Collin is dead?" I had to know the truth of the situation.

"No, he's alive, but he must be badly hurt." Kasey kept her head down, playing with a frayed edge of her sweater. "What're we going to do now?"

Getting Collin back was my first impulse, but the two missing men took priority. We had to find them. I stood up with the help of Eadan and staggered to the cabin.

LEGENDS AND LORE

The warmth of the fire felt good against my cold skin. I sat close to the hearth and far enough away from the questioning eyes of the broken clan awaiting direction from me. I wasn't a leader, I wasn't Faelad, and I wasn't The Morrigan. Everything they believed in me was a mistake.

I felt defeated, broken, and alone. Collin protected me, believed in me, and had faith that The Morrigan's love could be restored. Now, he was gone, along with all of my confidence, and I was losing the conviction of my purpose here.

I pictured the book of their love story, the warrior and goddess, who fought to the end to be together. What a disappointment I'd turned out to be. By now Collin had to be second guessing his decision to bring me into his world.

His world: the Faelad Clan of Ossory, and The Morrigan, Goddess of Battle; the myths were real. A few days ago I was happy to sit in a pub and drink a Guinness. Now, the balance of humankind teetered on my decision.

The front door swung open with a bang, and I spun around, expecting another assault. Instead, in staggered Carrek, arm around Olcán, supporting him. They stumbled a few steps and Olcán collapsed onto the couch. Carrek's gaze found me in the room and he walked straight towards me.

"It was Ade, m'lady. He attacked us in the forest." He was out of breath and a large gash above his eyebrow dripped blood down the side of his face. It was clear that he'd tried to fight back. I stood to face him.

"I'm sorry, Carrek, so sorry."

"No, Morrigan, I'm sorry we failed ya." He raised a bloodied hand to the gash on his head.

"You are not shamed; you're a brave warrior—all of you are." My eyes filled with tears as I looked at the clan. They were willing to stand by me, with or without Collin. They weren't following because he told them to; they followed because they believed in me. I couldn't let them down; no matter what, I'd find a way to get Collin back.

"Whatever his plan," Olcán spoke up from the couch, "it will most likely have to do with the Winter Solstice at Newgrange." The rest of the clan nodded in agreement.

I'd been to Newgrange on the first day I'd arrived in Ireland. It was a fascinating structure, dating back five thousand years—older than the pyramids of Egypt. Built by the Neolithic people before the invention of the wheel, the workmanship was astonishing. The building consisted of three chambers and was believed to have been used for religious purposes.

I didn't understand how Newgrange applied to me, but knowing that was the place Collin would be, nothing would stop me from going there.

In less than twenty-four hours, I'd face Ade for what I hoped would be the last time. Trying to exude confidence, I was terrified inside. How could I save Collin's life without destroying humankind by releasing werewolves on them?

I woke up as the sun peeked above the horizon. This was the beginning of the solstice. A small group of people from around the world, lucky enough to win the Newgrange lottery, were standing in the passage tomb, watching the light fill every crevice. The light only remained for a few minutes until the sun moved past the opening and the tomb was plunged back into darkness.

I would've given anything to be there, to see the beauty of the event captured in the structure made so long ago. The sun meant life to the humans then, so much so that they built an enormous structure to catch its purity one day a year.

I'd be back tonight, far after the tourists had left and the reporters had broadcast their last story on the event. I'd come at the pinnacle of night.

I spent hours isolated in the cabin, reading from the book. I had to learn all I could about The Morrigan: who she was, her life before Cúchulainn, and how she'd fallen in love with the warrior. I hoped to reach down to the goddess inside of me, my soul with eternal amnesia.

The clan left me alone, giving me space. I didn't know what they were doing in preparation, but it didn't matter. They would escort me to Newgrange, standing by my side the entire time.

As the afternoon sun burned bright in the sky, I decided to test my power one more time. Letting out The Morrigan was the only way I could think of to save Collin. I'd only just recovered from the frail state the last attempt left me in, so it was safe to say I was nervous.

In the solitude of the trees, I steadied my footing and slowed my breathing. I pictured the air filling my lungs and then pushing it all out. The rhythmic drumming of each heartbeat echoed in my ears.

Once my breathing balanced out, I turned my attention to the surrounding noises: the rustle of branches swaying in the breeze, the tiny flying insects buzzing near my head. In the distance, faint chirps of woodland birds fluttered throughout the trees.

What I didn't hear were the crows. Were they close, watching me like before? I gazed into the leafy canopy above. The dense trees made it impossible to see the sky. No crows perched in wait, no black feathers to come at my command. Where did they go? I wondered if they were with Collin, watching over him, waiting for his command, not mine.

I closed my eyes and raised my arms despite the birds' absence. If the crows were near, they'd hear me.

Once again, beautiful Gaelic words flowed from my mouth, but this time with a glimmer of understanding to their meaning; I was calling for my bird family to fight alongside me.

My body tingled and the sensation grew stronger with each passing second. Heat filled my chest and spread up into my throat and down my arms. The buildup was overwhelming. I knew something was inside, pushing to break free.

Then, I heard my crows—their melodious calls from the sky. I could feel their presence as they pressed closer, soaring towards the ground. They needed to be reunited with me as much as I needed them.

A raging force was consuming my body and I wanted to let it out.

Would I be able to accept the change that my soul was craving? The deepest senses called to accept the power of The

Morrigan. As if each cell within me cried out for release, I wanted this power, this release, this change that I was on the precipice of.

But in one fragment of doubt, it all ended. I gasped for air, coughing and choking. The connection to the birds was gone, the buildup and power dissipated. I was back to just being Claire in the blink of an eye. I fell to the ground, catching myself with my outstretched arms. I continue to gag, bile burned up my throat and I felt the nausea roll around in the pit of my stomach. My legs were heavy and felt brittle, as if my bones would shatter if I tried to stand.

❧❦☙

Blackness surrounded me as I awoke. Startled awake, I tried to stand, but the bands around my wrists kept me from much movement. I had to break free and find Claire, to protect her from Ade.

The darkness kept me from my most important sense and I couldn't tell where I was. I knew it wasn't dark yet because I was in human form. But it was close to dusk, the energy in the air was building. Once I was a wolf, I could break free of the straps and get to Claire, hopefully before Ade got to her first.

The thought of what Ade might have in mind for Claire made my body shudder. My anger grew as time slipped away.

"Hello? Who's there?" I called out, trying to control the edge to my echoing voice. No one answered, so I began pulling on my bands, which were connected to a thick metal chain. I followed the links that led to a post against a cold stone wall. It felt like I was in a cave, the rocky cavern made by nature.

I yanked at the metal, which clanked loudly at my pulling. I was making a lot of noise, but didn't care. If Ade or his men heard me, what could they do? I continued to tug at the post, which was firmly secured in the ground. If it took me the rest of the day, I was going to set myself free.

"It's no use, Cúchulainn." Ade's deep tone echoed off the walls, making it hard to determine where he was.

"Don't keep yerself in the shadows, brother. Step out where I can see ya." I wanted nothing more than to find Ade's smug face in the darkness; the beast inside was emerging.

"In a few hours, it'll be over. Be patient, brother; soon you will see the truth of my plan." Ade's voice was relaxed, lacking the anger I'd expected.

I jerked on the chains as hard as I could, trying to get the pole to loosen or the thick metal rings to weaken. But after several attempts to budge it, I stopped and listened for any sign of Ade. The cave was silent; my breathing the only muffled sound.

I didn't want to be left alone to face my thoughts, filled with scenarios involving Claire being killed, or becoming a dark angel bound to a new Faelad leader who would usher in the age of human servitude.

I knew now that it would've been better for me to have left Claire alone that day in Galway. I should have rescued her from the drunken lowlifes, and then walked away. Claire was better off to move on, find love, and live another normal human life than to be controlled by a tyrant seeking world domination. She could get married, travel the world, and forget the things she saw here. Her eternity was about to be decided and I feared that my life was the ransom.

A light lit up the space I was chained to. Brady approached with a torch in his hand. That's when I realized that I was inside Newgrange. I looked up at the corbelled ceiling, each stone slab precisely layered to keep out the elements. It hadn't changed since it was constructed.

I stood in the main chamber and could see the three additional recesses. What I had felt earlier as I explored was the slabs lining the long passage into the chamber. It was eighty feet to the opening and my freedom.

The chain didn't stretch long enough to step into the cruciform chambers. But I could see each carved alter with the tri-spiral markings throughout.

The *Brú na Bóinne*, as called by the locals, was lush and green, built along a bend of the River Boyne. This was a place of reverence. It had been a place to remember those who had died, and celebrate the gods for their rich blessings upon the land. This was also the place where I was born.

And now it would be the place that I would die.

"What happens now, *mo charaid*?" Maybe reminding him that we were friends would soften his anger towards me.

"Claire will be here soon, and then we'll begin. There's no turning back, Collin, and ya know it." Brady spoke matter-of-factly about the situation.

"I know her better than anyone, Brady. I know what she'll do, and Ade will be proven wrong." Deep down, I prayed my words were true.

※

The clan gave me clothing to wear to Newgrange. The skimpy fabric was hardly what I'd call clothing. I discovered it didn't cover much, as I slipped on the green plaid skirt with slits up both thighs. A brass buckle tied with a leather strap kept the cloth from falling off.

The leather breastplate was curved in an elegant swirling pattern that formed neatly against my chest, as if tailored just for me. This was the most I had ever exposed, adding to my apprehension.

Carrek took the red cloak off his shoulders and draped it around mine. The white streaks within his red hair reminded me of my dad. I wondered how old he was, as he seemed like the father figure of the clan.

"Don't ya worry, lass, it'll be fine. Yer The Morrigan, remember? Only ya can decide the fate of this day." He stroked my cheek with his finger, then turned and walked out of the cabin.

It was time to go.

Only a few steps behind Carrek, I crossed the threshold of the door and was greeted by the rest of our bloc. They had each painted their bodies with Celtic symbols of swirls and knots.

Tressa smiled and bowed as I walked passed her. I could see an eel, painted in black, wrapped around her leg from her thigh to just below the knee—another beautiful display of Irish artwork. She wore the same plaid fabric, but her skirt was short and tight against her legs. She had braided leather straps that crisscrossed over her chest and a sword sheathed at her side.

All of them had the same three bands painted around their arms. Carrek, paintbrush in hand, was working on his arm bands. I couldn't help but stare at the art they created on themselves. They looked like true warriors.

Although our numbers were small, the power within each of them was far greater than their stature. My spirits rose; maybe there was a chance to save Collin without anyone having to sacrifice their own life.

"It's yer turn, Morrigan." Eadan, a green sash draped across her body, held a small paintbrush in her hand.

They all nodded and stepped forward. I closed my eyes and let them work their artistic magic. Once the last brush stroke lifted from my skin, I opened my eyes.

A delicate swirling pattern started from my shoulders and ran down both arms. At my hands, a tri-circle pattern intertwined. The swirling continued down my legs, but at my feet I saw what appeared to be bird talons on the top of each foot. Kasey held up a mirror.

"Look at The Morrigan, transformin' before us."

Taking the mirror, I held my breath in anticipation. A large crow, painted in black, was across my chest, the wings extended to each shoulder and the head rested just under my neck. On the left side of my face, in beautiful Celtic lines, was the image of a wolf.

Tears filled my eyes and I gently wiped them away before they destroyed the art on my cheek. I wasn't Claire anymore. The woman staring back at me looked like them—a warrior, too.

"There's one more thing." Carrek held out a small leather pouch. "You need this." He dropped the leather bag in the palm of my hand and I pulled at the twine to open it. I turned the pouch over and a ring plopped out, falling to the ground.

Embarrassed, I quickly scooped it up. The bright blue stone in the center gleamed as if lit from within. Four prongs held it in place on the thick band. On each side was a delicate carving of an animal in white gold. One side was a crow, wings spread in flight, and on the other side, a wolf, like the figure painted on my cheek. Within the band, I could see writing. It read, Chéile Deo.

"Cha-lay Dee-oh." I knew I'd butchered the pronunciation.

"It means 'Together Forever.' Cúchulainn had that ring made for ya." Carrek took the pouch from me and motioned at the ring. I tried it on and it fit perfectly on my middle finger.

"Now, she's ready." Olcán's smile washed all tension from his face.

We arrived outside of Newgrange just before sunset. The surrounding gates were secured with large locks, all evidence of tourists long gone after the hype from the morning. I could see some of Ade's men standing around the perimeter of the mound; two stood in front of the entryway, but no sign of Ade as we approached.

My body trembled with anxiety, and beads of sweat formed on my forehead, even though the temperature dropped as the sun sank below the horizon. There was no turning back, and I had no idea what was about to happen.

The darkness closing in meant transformations shortly. The men would soon be wolves and I would be surrounded, unable to defend myself.

Dermot, Hagan, and Gaeth met us halfway, each man with broad shoulders and bulging muscles. It was intimidating to be near them.

"Ade wanted ya to come alone."

"Ya know we couldn't allow that, Gaeth." Carrek stood at my left flank.

Piercing eyes stared down at me. Dermot stepped forward, holding out his hand. "Come with me, Claire, don't make this difficult."

As I took Dermot's hand, I couldn't look at Carrek or Olcán; the disappointment in their faces as I willingly turned myself over was more than I could take.

I heard a scuffle behind me, heated words I couldn't make out. But I had to find Collin and trade places; Carrek and Olcán would eventually understand.

I thought we were headed to the passage tomb, but instead, we walked around to the back. Along the perimeter of the mound, I noticed large stones resting at the base with delicate carvings. I counted four as we walked along. What struck me was the pattern carved into them, the same tri-circular pattern painted on my hands. I wondered what the significance was.

At the back of the mound, a pathway led to the top. Dermot stopped, dropping my hand; he nodded towards the hill for me to continue alone.

Once I made it to the crown of the grassy hilltop, I saw Ade.

"I knew ya'd come willingly, not wanting any bloodshed." He held something in his hand, and it wasn't until the last rays of light hit the metal that I knew what it was; Ade grasped a dagger.

"Looks like I'm the only one unwilling to spill blood tonight." I stood still, my voice steady, but inside I started to crumble.

"Come closer, Claire. We're about to begin." In one movement, Ade reached out, grabbed my arm, and yanked me next to him. The knife was at my throat, the cold metal rested against my neck.

I let out one long breath. This was how I would die.

※

The last bit of light sank behind the hills of Ossory. I hadn't wanted to release the beast more in my entire life. As the wolf took control, I howled out Ade's name, loud and deep so it would echo throughout all three chambers and through the passageway. The time had come to take my vengeance.

I broke the chains easily and made my descent through the tunnel. Near the opening, the passage was tight, even for an average human; I had to push and stretch to fit, my frustration building in my chest with each passing second. Once freed of my prison, I was met by my Faelad clan. They rushed to me, yelling in my face. But I heard nothing; I scanned the grounds for Claire—my Claire.

"She's up there!" Tressa's words finally broke through the fog in my head. I turned to where she pointed. "She's there."

In one jump, I found myself on top of the grassy knoll, and in the center stood Ade, one arm wrapped tightly around Claire's waist and a knife to her neck with the other. Claire stood stiffly in his massive arms but didn't scream or cry out. She simply looked at me, eye to eye.

"There's nothing you can do now, Cúchulainn. She came to me of her own free will." His guttural voice pierced my ears.

"She doesn't choose to die of her own free will." I kept my eyes on Claire as I spoke. "This is yer plan? Kill her because she came to ya without a fight?" My hands curled into fists as my human soul wrestled within the beast.

"Killing 'er will release us. I wanted to be free from the curse the moment I became a werewolf. Serving humans? Hah! Nothing but wasted pieces of flesh; I'd rather exterminate 'em than protect 'em. I won't fail again."

I hadn't known Ade's true feelings until now. He'd never talked that way around me. How could I have missed something so extreme? But then his last words resonated in my ears: Ade had said, "again."

"What do ya mean, again?" I scanned through my memories of a time where he tried to kill a human, but nothing surfaced.

"Mary Elizabeth."

As soon as the words slipped from his tongue, I knew what he'd done. Mary Elizabeth Henry had died quickly of a sudden illness. I thought back to her portrait, the flower I'd given her held tightly in her hand.

"Ya poisoned 'er." The memory of my last moment with Mary Elizabeth, at her bedside, as she thrashed around in pain. Her death, pure agony.

"But it didn't work, ya see; all that fer nothing." Ade filled in the missing pieces. "The Morrigan was simply reborn into another life. So, I failed." The knife he held pushed into Claire's skin and I saw her flinch at the blade.

"How do ya know this will work now, Ade? What if it doesn't and ya have her innocent blood on yer hands?"

"Innocent? There's nothing innocent about 'er. She's the daughter of Culann, the very man who cursed us right here on this spot. Spilling 'er willing blood is the only way to free us." Ade's grip tightened on her waist and I knew he was preparing to end it all.

My clan appeared behind me, their presence strong to my senses. All were willing to fight with me to save Claire. But as my clan came to my defense, so did Ade's men. All standing at opposite sides; massive beasts, ready to battle. I turned my attention to Claire, her eyes still locked on mine.

"Ya know what I must do." The words came out and my decision was made. I'd die for her to set her free.

I squeezed my fists tight, and jumped.

Collin's words resonated in my ears., "Ya know what I must do . . ." I did know. He was going to attack Ade to keep him away from me. The only way to save Collin from death was to call the birds and free The Morrigan. I'd felt her force before and knew she could save us now. There wasn't time for debate. I reached deep down to let her out.

Even with Ade's tight grip and knife at my throat, I steadied my breathing. I saw Collin disappear in a flash of movement as he jumped into the air. Suddenly, everything slowed down. The air around me stopped; the sounds, smells, and energy all halted. I closed my eyes and focused on the crows. I called to them inside my head, reaching out, begging for the help of my feathered friends.

A voice bellowed from behind me, "Mo preachan teaghlach, troid! My crows, attack!" But the words didn't come from behind me, the voice came from within me—a melodic, powerful voice I'd never heard before.

The birds obeyed. I felt them as they filled the sky and then descended towards me. They were like my children; deep love burned in my heart as they neared.

I saw them from the sky, like a fog bank, rolling in my direction. The power from within me reached and pulled at the crows, aching for their return. I closed my eyes, took a deep breath, and let go of my soul.

A rush of feathers and beaks hit me with a brutal force. Ade and I were knocked to the ground. I rose quickly as the murder swarmed me. Like the funnel of a cyclone, they circled round and round. I could feel my body contort, changing into something free and beautiful.

Consumed in the moment with my birds, I didn't feel the knife plunged into my chest. I only saw the hilt of the knife right between my breasts, piercing the leather breast plate.

The world around me spun like a violent storm, thrashing me to the ground. I heard the shrieks of my crows, screaming in agony as I fell.

※

I was too late. The knife came down before I could reach her. I cried out as my heart tore in two. This was the third and final time I'd lost my love.

Letting the beast take control, I willed it to do whatever was needed to remove the threat. Killing Ade couldn't mend my shattered heart, but it would prevent him from living one moment of freedom.

With outstretched arms, I clawed at Ade's shoulders and took hold of skin and fur as we toppled to the ground. With all my might, I pinned him down as he scratched back. With teeth bared and growling, I looked him in the eye.

"How could ya do it? Yer me brother, me family."

"It had to be done and ya were too weak to do it." His breath was labored, but he gave no sign of backing down.

The fight erupted on top of the mound; hell broke loose with the rage of the beasts. Our clan had turned against one another and now fought on holy ground; everyone but Eadan. She and

Brady stood a few feet apart, staring at one another, neither one willing to take action.

Claire lay still in the grass. The night sky made the blood pooled around her head look black. She didn't move and I feared the worst. Images of her first death on the beach filled my head.

Her pleading for a mortal death was something I'd never be able to forget. "*Mé pléadáil le haghaidh bás marfach.*" To those words, she fell to the earth, her body in mortal form. The sky filled with terrible shrieks as the banshees spread news of The Morrigan's death.

I glared at Ade as I held him down, the pain of his deception sunk deep. I bit down on his neck, tearing into his flesh. My mouth filled with his blood. I wanted his death—an eye for an eye. He took my Claire and I would take his life. Ade struggled under me, but as the blood poured from his wound, he stopped resisting. As he lay dying, I looked at my friend, my brother, and anger turned to anguish. I'd lost everything.

"Cúchulainn." Her voice broke through the noise. An immediate hush fell among the clan as they froze where they stood.

Standing before me with a halo of crows hovering around her was my beautiful Morrigan. Her ebony hair flowed to the side, a feathered dress extended around her body down to a long train at the back. She raised her arms, high in the air.

"Síocháin ar ais chuig an talamh; let peace be restored to the land." She lowered her hands and her crows descended. The crows swarmed Ade's body and I moved out of the way. Each Faelad wolf changed back into human form.

"Morrigan." Her name left my lips as a whisper.

The birds burst away from Ade's body; the wound on his neck was gone. His chest moved as he breathed. He was alive, thanks to The Morrigan.

"How?" The only word I could bring myself to form.

"It was Claire. She released me before she died." Morrigan smiled, eyes filled with tears.

"Is she gone?" A part of me had fallen in love with the brave little mortal, and I wondered how much of her remained.

◆◆◆

Claire was very much alive inside of me. I felt every moment of her human existence; the love for her parents, the fear of losing Cúchulainn to Ade—everything was locked inside my memories. I could recall every life I'd ever lived; every name, every person that I had met along the way, too. It was an eternity of memories. Although it started with a curse, I was grateful for the experiences I had as a mortal. Lives full of love, laughter, and pain. I would never have understood the humans the way I did now, having lived so many of their lifetimes.

"Claire is within me; she'll always be." Tears of gratitude streamed down my face.

Cúchulainn looked over at Ade., "What will happen to him?" The pain of loss was evident in his eyes.

"Peace has been placed in his heart. The Faelad Clan of Ossory has been restored to its original grandeur—the servitude to humans for the benefit of peace amongst the land." I stepped towards Cúchulainn, wanting nothing more than to touch him.

He stood up and walked to me. His arms wrapped around me, and warmth radiated between us. I never wanted to leave him again.

Cúchulainn touched the ring on my finger. "*Chéile Deo.*" And he pressed his lips to mine.

TWO SPOONS

by Danielle E. Shipley

This once happened to a friend of mine.

That's how these urban legends always start, right? You never say *you*, you say *a friend*, or a friend of a friend, and you either mean yourself or no one who ever lived outside of a cheesy campfire story. And if you say it happened *once*, you either mean upon some never-mind-exactly-when time or just plain never.

So, you know if I say *a friend* and *once*, I mean something else. I mean us. And twenty years later, it's still too soon to forget.

It started out perfectly real, stupidly normal. Two kids in high school who felt grown-up enough to do grown-up things, until they recognized the just-beginning-to-grow-inside-of-her thing they'd created between them, and it struck them a little too late just how young and far from ready they were.

She didn't have much of a family to turn to. He had two or three times a normal family to help make up the difference. When his parents and grandparents, aunts, uncles, and cousins heard there was another one of them on the way, they absorbed the budding mother into their number, and the baby along with her.

LEGENDS AND LORE

That's what the family always did: feed and grow, feed and grow. They grew a restaurant and fed their community—straight from their hearts to the mouths of their neighbors. Their niche was soul food, and food was the family's soul.

The new little one, to whom the family gave a proper name only to generally ignore it in favor of calling her Tidbit, practically lived in the restaurant. She sat in a highchair or was passed from arms to arms, lap to lap, while her father scrubbed dishes and her mother scrubbed countertops. With all the kitchen noises around her—banging pots and pans, clattering plates and cutlery, sizzling, whipping, blending, splashing, and orders shouted back and forth—she grew to find less and less reason to add to the chaos.

Past her first birthday, she never screamed or cried. By her second, the family was still unsure whether she'd learned how to talk. By her third, they knew she could, though she didn't do it often; didn't open her mouth much at all, except to take in food or drink or her thumb. Having watched the disorganized dance of the kitchen her whole life, she'd figured out walking and staying out from underfoot at about the same time. With her general lack of sound, size, and nuisance, Tidbit was forgotten about as often as she was remembered.

The late spring evening the Black Man came, the girl was four years old and out of the kitchen, watching the less chaotic show of the diners on the floor.

He wasn't black in the way Tidbit's family was black. His narrow eyes were black, the sleek hair swept back from his forehead was black, his shoes, pants, and jacket over his black shirt were black, but black wasn't what he wore, and it wasn't what he was. It was *who*.

If anyone were to say I should have no way of knowing what happened next, they'd be right. I shouldn't know. None of us should—or *would*, if this wasn't the story it is. This story is made up of shouldn'ts that were.

Escorted to his table—a halved circle in a small semicircle of a booth upholstered with crimson vinyl—the Black Man's gaze pierced the menu, slashing left to right as he read all the things a determined team of chefs could do with meat, beans, potatoes, and buttermilk. His eyes were knifing the list of beverages when he took notice of the fact that he was being watched. The gaze cut to the side, and there was the girl, standing by the hosts' and hostesses' station. Feet spread a bit apart. Thumb in mouth. Eyes on him.

Each stared at the other staring back. He did not smile to appear safe, as adults often will, for small children. She did not duck her head, scurry away, laugh, or treat this like a game. He was not a game to her.

When minutes passed and nothing changed, the Black Man returned his attention to the more obviously important matter of his dinner. Only after sending his server away with an order of an appetizer and wine did he think to look up again. He startled back upon realizing that, by then, the staring child stood at his table.

Again, the Black Man did not smile. Nor did he frown. His thin mouth was straight, his slender brows at rest, his eyes resetting to narrow after their flare of surprise. Measured and silky, he asked, "Where are your people?"

Eyes and thumb still fixed in place, Tidbit half-turned her body toward the swinging double door to the kitchen at the dining room's far end.

"I see," he said, flicking a glance where she'd directed, then back down to her. "And do they allow you out here to creep upon their clientele's tables, or are you an escaped convict?"

This elicited a smile from the girl, a quiet giggle slipping out around her thumb and between her rows of tiny white teeth. The word *clientele* was beyond her current lexicon, but cartoons had painted an entertaining picture of escaped convicts—dark and dangerous circus clowns in zebra-striped prison shirts, slithering through shadows to avoid The Law's searchlights. Striped shirt though she wore, unnoticed though she'd been when she'd disappeared from the kitchen jail right under the noses of the cooking, cleaning, serving guards, she did not see herself as an escaped convict, though she found it gratifying that the Black Man seemed to see otherwise.

Tidbit hoped the Black Man would speak again. She liked his voice, so far removed from those of her family's variations of loud, louder, and loudest. Where theirs were sloppy, and comfortable as a warm casserole, his words were ice cubes clinking in smooth, dark tea. She waited, but he remained as silent as she did, his eyes once more on the oversized menu pages covered in plastic and the persistent memory of syrup drips and soda spills.

As before, when his eyes moved, so did the girl. Since he sat near the booth's left edge, she climbed up onto the right. When his gaze rose again, she sat across from him, her curly head peeking above the tabletop. The flat line of his eyebrow bowed upward. Her eyes at the table's horizon stared.

Scoot. She moved one inch further into the booth. Scoot. Another inch. Scoot, scoot, scoot. He watched without commentary as the girl curved around in half an orbit, until he had to turn his head to see her just beyond his elbow. Around her thumb, she smiled. Around the straight line of his mouth, he smiled, too.

He angled the menu. "What do you recommend?"

It sometimes happened this way, Tidbit was aware. The people who came in for lunch and dinner weren't always sure what to ask for, so they asked their servers to help them choose. Tidbit wasn't employed at the restaurant, but she knew its food. She pushed herself up to her feet on the seat's hard cushion and studied the menu held open before her. After some consideration, she pointed with the fingers of her free hand to one of the lines of letters. Though she didn't yet know how to match all of them to the sounds they made, she recognized the *n* nestled between tiny symbols like six and nine. Six-n-nine meant mac 'n' cheese, or franks 'n' beans, or chicken 'n' dumplings, all of which she liked.

The Black Man nodded. "Chicken 'n' dumplings it is."

When she spotted the Black Man's server—one of her first cousins—making her way across from the kitchen, Tidbit slipped down from the seat and underneath the table, where she crouched with an arm hugged around a long, lean, black-covered leg. Above her, the Black Man said nothing about the girl to his server, only ordered the recommended chicken 'n' dumplings.

Tidbit waited until the serving first cousin moved out of sight before climbing back to her place beside the Black Man, who'd been brought his glass of dark wine and a basket of mini corn muffins. He sipped from the glass, plucked a muffin from the basket, and held it out for the girl to take, which she did. They chewed together until the serving first cousin's return sent Tidbit back under the table, then resumed, he with his entrée, she with another muffin baked smaller than her fist.

Eating with her family meant talking. *Everything* with her family meant talking. They talked over her, around her, at her, about her. The Black Man talked little. "Good choice," he said of the food, then was silent. "Server," he said when someone approached from an angle the girl couldn't see, then was silent. "All clear," he said when it was, then was silent. "Goodbye," he said when he'd paid his check, then was gone from the table.

Tidbit scooted to the booth's edge, descended to the floor, and followed the Black Man with all the escaped convict-like stealth she possessed. She made it out the door and several squares down the sidewalk before the Black Man turned with a grim little smile. "No you don't," he said. "Back inside with you."

It didn't occur to Tidbit for one second to protest, let alone to disobey. The Black Man had given her a direct order. If the order had been to place her hand on a burning stovetop, she would have found a way to reach the height and do it, defying every lesson about fire she'd ever vicariously learned through the pain of careless others. She couldn't have told you why. The best reason she had to give was, "He's the Black Man." For her, that was enough.

Lips turned down in disappointment, Tidbit retraced her steps to the restaurant door, which the Black Man returned to pull open for her. With the girl where he wished her, the Black Man departed again. Tidbit stared at his back through the glass of the door until he'd crossed at the corner—the farthest she could see from where she stood with one hand pressed to the glass, the thumb of the other held at the listless level of her chin. And she waited for him.

❧

I couldn't tell you how this would have ended if he'd never come back. Another kid Tidbit's age would have forgotten the encounter—maybe not that first night; maybe not the next day. Maybe not for weeks, or even months, if the kid in question had settled on it as their temporary childish mania.

The Black Man might have featured in dreams, for a while, before fading into the back of the mind where memories gather dust until some arbitrary thing uncovers them some twenty years later. Maybe today would have been the day the small girl, all grown up, would have glanced at that booth from a certain vantage point, or ducked under its table to retrieve a drinking straw dropped from her server's apron, and laughed at the unexpected remembrance of that man in black she'd once thought was so fascinating for some four-year-old reason.

It might have happened that way for Tidbit, but I suspect now that it wouldn't.

There's little point in speculation, though, since he *did* come back.

'Til then, as I said, Tidbit waited for him. Not standing at the door, of course. Not the whole time. She soon left the high-traffic area of the restaurant for less troublesome spots. A few hours before closing, she allowed her parents to shuttle her to the house they shared with her grandparents. She picked at a late dinner she wasn't hungry for, took the weekly bubble bath (less pleasurable than usual), and crawled into her bed with its cloud-patterned sheets, all while waiting for the Black Man's return.

It would be tomorrow, she told herself.

Tomorrow came and went.

The next day, then; she was certain.

The next day passed without him.

Every day, she watched and waited. Two weeks of slipping out of the kitchen, scanning the dining room from one side to the other, hopes rising as she turned toward the opening door, hopes falling when it wasn't him, and returning to the kitchen for the ten, fifteen minutes she could stand before slipping right back out to look around again.

Nothing changed, until it did. And then, there he sat. The same small booth as before. Still head-to-toe, inside-and-out black.

Unlike the girl, the Black Man hadn't been waiting. To him, their first meeting had been unexpected, unusual, a little amusing. If he'd had any friends or went to parties, it would have made for a cute anecdote. A quirky supplement to a delicious meal, that was all. He'd returned for the chow, not the child.

But he knew the moment her searching gaze found him.

He waited until she'd crossed the floor to stand at his table before he turned from his menu to her. His mouth smiled a little, his eyes blackly bright. "Hello again."

"Hi." The first word she'd given him, soft as a private sigh.

As before, she climbed onto the far side of the semicircular seat and scoot, scoot, scooted around until she sat beside him.

"I've already ordered dinner," he said. "What should I do for dessert?"

Tidbit stood to scrutinize the menu's dessert page. Recognizing the word *banana* from its pattern of *a*s and *n*s, she pointed to the banana pudding, a house specialty. The Black Man nodded, and after the meal, when his server—one of Tidbit's second cousins—came to take away the dinner dishes, oblivious to the child huddled beneath the table, "Banana pudding, please," he said.

"Cup or bowl?" the serving second cousin asked.

"A bowl," he said, adding, as if in afterthought, "with two spoons."

The server regarded him oddly, but even a customer asking for extra silverware is always right.

Banana pudding served, the coast as clear as it would ever be in the dining room, and two gleaming spoons dancing in and out of the cream-and-yellow dessert, the girl and the Black Man consumed in silence.

Then, again, he left. Again, she followed. Again, he turned before the corner and ordered her back inside. Again, she obeyed. And again, she waited.

But this time, the wait was shorter. The very next evening, the Black Man came back.

❦

He didn't come every day. Four days a week, sometimes five. Never more than one day missed between visits. The hosts and hostesses began recognizing him on sight and leading him, out of habit, to his usual table in the same little booth. The servers laughed and shook their heads together over his dessert orders—sometimes the banana pudding, sometimes the peach or apple cobbler, sometimes the double-fudge brownie with fresh-churned vanilla ice cream on top, but always with the same eccentric request which, by the third time, had earned him a nickname in the kitchen.

"Table nine," they'd assign one another, jerking their thumbs in the general direction of the dining room. "Two Spoons is back."

Most lunchers and diners who frequented the restaurant often enough to be known by face and name became less like customers and more like an extension of the family, which seized at every chance to grow. It was different with Two Spoons—though, early on, no one could put their finger on any real reason for it. He was not impolite, didn't generate unnecessary hassle for his servers, and left consistently generous tips. Maybe his voice was a little unsettling. Maybe something in his smile was a little bit off. Maybe meeting his eyes felt a little too much like staring into the face of your death.

Of course, the explanation was obvious, once the man himself gave it. Until then, to the family that couldn't quite bring itself to think of him as in any way one of them, he was just Two Spoons, their irregular regular.

It was the hottest part of summer when they learned why he always asked for two spoons. One of Tidbit's third cousins chanced to glance toward table nine on her way back from refilling drinks for a family of three, and there, more than half-hidden by the table's height and her companion's body, was the girl, with her cheerful curls and soulful eyes, scarfing strawberry pie in Two Spoons' black shadow.

The restaurant had no official policy against children of the staff sitting with customers at their tables and sharing their desserts. It was just one of those unspoken rules. The serving third cousin rushed to table nine, full of apologies for Two Spoons and restrained reprimands for Tidbit, until an unsettling voice, a smile that was a little bit off, and eyes like the face of death's cut her short.

"It's perfectly fine. She's welcome to join me. It's our little arrangement, isn't that right?" he said, directing the question to the girl at his side.

LEGENDS AND LORE

Her mouth pulled into a strawberry-sweet smile. "Yes."

While there *was* an official policy suggesting customers who chose to dine with the staff's children were as right as customers always were, this specific situation made the serving third cousin uneasy nonetheless. Upon her return to the kitchen, she aired her concerns to everyone who wasn't too busy to listen—plus those who *were* a little too busy, but couldn't help listening anyway, once they got the gist of the subject at hand. All agreed that, official and unofficial policies aside, it wasn't a good idea to let the arrangement of the pair at table nine continue. When Two Spoons' server—a second third cousin—went back to the booth, he picked up both the check and the girl, who took the second third cousin's hand with great reluctance and a pronounced furrow between her brows.

❦

Most people don't believe in love at first sight. Tidbit hadn't even been introduced to the concept yet, her picture books focusing more on problem-solving puppies, socially savvy snails, and other colorful critters whose adventures and misadventures contributed to her knowledge base of how to get by in life. She'd been told few fairy tales, and fewer horror stories. Logically, there was no reason for her four-year-old heart to fall so deeply in love with the Black Man on sight.

I'm inclined to believe there isn't much that's logical about the Black Man.

Following the evening her secret trysts were found out, being an escaped convict was no longer feasible. The eyes of the kitchen were everywhere, no fewer than a pair trained on Tidbit at any given time. When she crept too close to the door, voices and hands shooed her away, steering her back to the corner's tiny table of sturdy plastic with its matching chair, coloring books and crayons, even a small serving of banana pudding, if she wanted a bite of dessert so badly.

The dessert, of course, had nothing to do with it. She'd have sat beside the Black Man if it meant starvation.

"Please?" she said, edging toward the door yet again. The word *please* was magic in the world of picture-book snails. But in the story she lived, the word held less power.

Denied again and again, Tidbit stood with her small hands tugging uselessly at the ribbon on her shirt, her head and heart pounding out the same tortured rhythm. *The Black Man. The Black Man.* The Black Man was out there, or he would be soon, and she was locked up where she couldn't even see him. Her wide eyes would not cry, her mouth would not whimper, but her insides wailed louder with every passing minute.

Out in the dining room, the Black Man raised his head. Taking this as a sign that he might be ready to order, his server—Tidbit's young father—made a beeline for table nine.

"What can I get you?" he asked.

The Black Man answered, "The girl."

The pen over the notepad in Tidbit's father's hand paused in the air. "I don't believe we have any girl on the menu."

"Not to eat," said the Black Man, with exaggerated patience. "Bring her to me."

LEGENDS AND LORE

Tidbit's father kept his face clear of the frown he felt. "No."

"No?" The Black Man's voice was the sort of polite that felt more dangerous than a verbal threat.

"Look," said the father, "I'm sure you don't mean any harm—"

"As I'm sure of the same of you," said the Black Man, "which is why you would do best to bring me the girl."

"She's not here."

"Liar." He said the word with disdain and relish. "I hear her in the kitchen. Her mind cries for me."

The father looked at the Black Man with understandable skepticism. "You hear her mind? What are you, psychic?"

The Black Man said, "Yes."

"Really." The father folded his arms over his chest. "All right, mind-hearer, what am I thinking?"

It was actually kind of a trick question; the father couldn't decide which of a half-dozen unlikely things to think about, and so jumped back and forth between them. Hooded eyes appraising the father with a malevolent gleam, the Black Man listed the six thoughts one by one. With every word, the father's cynical expression slackened. For anyone to guess even one of the competing thoughts would have been tricky to dismiss out of hand. Naming all six defied all reasonable coincidence. And the Black Man wasn't done.

"That," he said, "is what you're trying to think about. What you're *not* trying to think about, yet what you're *always* thinking about, is how much you regret having a child before you were ready; how the child came too soon, or your readiness too late, for you're reaching the point, now, where you feel you'd like to be a parent, but the girl you've got is not your own, belonging more to the family as a whole than to you."

Two gazes, dark and darker, held each other as well as the father's repetitive blinking allowed, the viscous silence between them nothing like the one the girl and the Black Man shared. Pain long suppressed oozed up in the father's mind, drawn like blood by eyes glinting sharp and cruel as a knife. For one hazy moment like a hellish eternity, he would have sworn those eyes had cut their way inside of him just to revel in the sight of his psyche's seeping wound.

The voice of the Black Man sliced through the haze. "The girl?"

Another blink. ". . . One moment, please."

Had the father shoved through the kitchen door two seconds earlier, he would have knocked his daughter to the ground. His cousin—Tidbit's first cousin, once removed—had herded her back toward the kiddie table none too soon. The father barked his cousin's name; demanded, "Have you been talking to him?"

"Who?" his cousin asked.

"Two Spoons!" he exploded, as if it were obvious. As if everyone's mind was fixed on the Black Man, not just his and his daughter's.

"No," said his cousin, his expression as puzzled as that of everyone within earshot, save for Tidbit, whose expression was all rapt attention. While Two Spoons was not what she called the Black Man, she knew who the name meant. "I don't think I've said one word to him yet. Why? What's the issue?"

The father dragged a hand down his apron, since running his fingers through his hair was a no-no while on the clock at a job that required handling people's food. "The issue," he said, "is that he told me things. Things I've never told anyone, except, that one time, *you*. So I'll ask you again: did you say anything to him?"

His cousin raised his hands, palms out. "Not a thing, I swear. You think maybe, I don't know, he's just psychic?"

The young man blew an agitated breath. "Sure, that's what he said, but . . ."

Tidbit's small voice moved into the space her father's hesitation left open. "What's psychic?"

"Y'know," said her father's cousin. "Like, occult stuff."

"What's a'cult?"

"Dark arts stuff. In league with the devil and tarot cards and whatnot."

Tidbit blinked at this equally unhelpful explanation.

"Like she knows what tarot cards are," the father snapped at his cousin. To Tidbit, he said, "You know how you play cards with Gramma, sometimes? Go Fish and Old Maid?"

She nodded. Her grandmother always tried to let her win, so Tidbit switched objectives, playing to lose. The games were far more interesting that way.

"Well," her father continued, "some people use cards sort of like that to tell the future."

Tidbit's eyes went round. "Can he do that?"

"I don't know." The father grimaced. "He can sure seem to tell the past and the present."

"You should ask him," his cousin advised. He tipped his head toward Tidbit. "And you should take her with. She's been trying to break out all afternoon. Maybe she'll cool down if she gets to see him for a minute. It'll be fine if you're there with her, right?"

Dubious, but too shaken to protest, the father crouched down to scoop his daughter up into his arms, and carried her out to table nine. The Black Man watched them approach, his eyes in a smile of partial satisfaction. When they reached him, he said, "No."

"No, what?" the father asked.

"No, I'm afraid I can't read the future." He folded his long hands over his napkin, smile moving toward a smirk. "Unless the future is in your mind."

Tidbit asked solemnly, "Are you a'league with the devil?"

The smile tightened around his eyes, vanishing from around his bared teeth almost altogether. "In league? No. I'm only his son."

"Seriously?" asked the father.

Every degree of warmth hissed from the Black Man's voice. "All too."

The father shifted the girl in his arms. " 'Kay. What's that like?"

"*That* or *he*?" said the Black Man. "I don't talk about the experience, so you'll get none of *that*. But as for the *he*, I've got a picture."

The Black Man reached into his wallet and extracted a thin, wrinkled rectangle of paper. He held it out by the very tips of his fingers; snatched it back when the father reached for it; offered it again, his gaze on the girl. She took the paper—using just her fingertips, as the Black Man did—and studied the face it wore, sketched out in angry slashes of ink, smudged either in the act of drawing or over time.

The Black Man's father, she noted, didn't look much at all like the depictions of the devil her cartoons had shown her. Whether or not this devil's skin was red was more than the black and white rendering could tell her, and since the portrait didn't continue below the level of his shoulders, there was no knowing whether he had hooves or a tail. But there weren't any horns sprouting up from his head, or a pointed beard stabbing down from his chin. No pitchfork or dancing flames to set him apart from any regular person. More than anything, Tidbit thought, the devil looked like the Black Man.

While Tidbit was held transfixed by the picture in her fingers, her father regarded the Black Man with a faint frown, less fully frightened than quietly disturbed. Maybe the man was the devil's son, as he claimed. Probably he could read minds, as he'd demonstrated. Those weren't the important points. What mattered to Tidbit's father—the question he asked and could only hope the answer he'd get, *if* he got one, would be honest—was, "Are you evil?"

The Black Man's lashes hid his eyes' knife glint as he lowered his gaze to somewhere just above the table. "I don't have to be."

Not quite an answer.

Unsure what to do with what he'd been given, the father tried again, probing from a different angle. "Are you dangerous?"

One side of the Black Man's mouth tweaked upward. "I won't harm her."

The air leaked from the father's lungs in a long, long sigh. "She likes you."

"A little," the Black Man agreed.

"It's probably just a phase."

The Black Man sipped from his glass of water. "Probably."

"We'll be watching," the father said. "All of us."

"Naturally." The Black Man's eyes swiveled to cut from their corners. "She belongs to the family."

His face wiped carefully blank, the father lowered Tidbit to the seat in the table nine booth. If her radiant smile broke his heart—and it did, a little—he allowed none but the one with a view of his mind to see. His hands no longer occupied with the girl already scooting her way toward the Black Man, he drew the notepad and pen from his apron pocket. "Ready to order?"

While the Black Man's mouth named the dish he desired, his mind murmured to the girl at his side. *Don't try to follow me out today, little convict. You're only on parole.*

Mouth to ear or mind to mind, it made no difference to Tidbit. If the Black Man commanded it, she would listen. She would not try to follow him.

That day.

∽⁂∾

She thought about following him the next day.

"No," the Black Man told her.

She thought about following him the day after that.

"No," he said.

Again, on the third day, she thought of following him.

The Black Man thought at her, *No*.

That was when the realization of her mistake sank in.

She'd learned early in life that no one around her could know what she was thinking or wanting or feeling unless she told them. Her mind was a private place, full of secrets that *stayed* secret unless she put in an effort to make them understood. That was how it worked with people.

But that wasn't how it worked with the Black Man, the psychic son of the devil. He could hear inside of her. Instead of hidden away where he couldn't go, her mind was an open room, her thoughts laid out all over the floor like books and toys she'd neglected to put away as she was supposed to. If Tidbit wanted to follow the Black Man, she couldn't leave the thought out where he could see it. The thought had to be tucked safely out of sight, or he would tell her *no*.

Tidbit wasn't sure why he didn't want her to follow him. It couldn't be that he didn't want her. He'd let her into his booth, hadn't he, and become Two Spoons so they could share his desserts? He had to know as well as she did that they were supposed to be together. That she needed them to be. And if he *didn't* know, she unconsciously reasoned, he *would*, if only she could find a way to make it home with him. If only she were always there, he would have to love her.

It was the sort of logic that could only make sense to a four-year-old or a stalker. And Tidbit was both.

Training herself to put her thoughts away didn't happen overnight. Summer was one chilly night away from conceding to fall before the evening came when she sat through dinner and dessert with the Black Man and he never once told her *no*. It pleased her so much, she forgot to keep the thought hidden.

"No," he said.

She hung her head.

The next time, she was better prepared. Her thought stayed locked in a drawer from the meal's start to its end, and she was out of the booth before it could burst free and betray her.

"What's your hurry?" the Black Man asked, since she'd never left the table in advance of him paying his check before.

"Potty," she said. It didn't seem wrong to lie to the Black Man. With the devil himself called the father of lies, who knew? Maybe the Black Man himself was a lie.

Tidbit had learned a few things in her many attempts to follow the Black Man. One, it was easier to leave the restaurant unnoticed if she waited to slip through the door during a customer's entry or exit. Two, the Black Man always parked his car, black as the rest of him, along the curb just past the corner she'd never been able to cross before he turned around and told her to go back. Three, on those occasions when the Black Man made it across the street before forbidding her to do the same, he would pull a key ring from his pocket and point it at his car. Since a number of Tidbit's relatives did the same thing with their key rings and cars, she understood what the action meant. And since she was, in many ways, an extraordinarily smart child, she knew how she could use this habit of the Black Man's to her advantage.

Ahead of the game, for once, Tidbit hurried down the sidewalk, looked twice both ways before crossing the street, then crouched between the rear of the Black Man's car and the vehicle parked behind it. She hadn't been in position long when she heard the sharp click of the car's doors unlocking.

Without hesitation, she crept out to the street side of the car and pulled open the door behind the driver's just far enough for her to crawl through. Once inside, she closed the door behind her—quick and firm and hoping the sounds of the neighborhood would cover up what little noise she'd had to make—and lay down flat on the floor, as far under the backseat as she could wriggle.

Keeping her mind tidied up of all giveaway thoughts, as the car rumbled beneath her and carried her toward the Black Man's home, was the hardest thing she'd ever had to do.

When the car came to a full stop, when the engine cut out, when the front door opened and closed as the driver made his way to wherever he lived, only then did Tidbit squirm out from her hiding place. A short walk paved in bricks away, just a step and a twist of the key from the far side of his red-painted door's threshold, the Black Man froze at the sound of his car door's opening.

He turned, slowly, back toward his driveway. Thumb in her mouth, eyes crinkled in a smile of self-satisfaction, the girl stared back.

"What—" he began. Stopped. "How—" Stopped. Drawing her proper name out into twice its rightful number of syllables, he pointed to the car. "*Back.*"

His mouth on the return drive had little to say, but his mind was angry. At the restaurant, he bodily handed her over to the surprised hostess at the station. "Terribly sorry," he said, his smooth voice hissing toward a snarl at the edges. "I seem to have accidentally absconded with the little one. It won't happen again."

Tidbit knew it for a command. Knew that smuggling herself into the Black Man's car was no longer an option.

She now also knew his home address.

⁂

The Black Man had said he didn't have to be evil, and it was true. He didn't. Though he often chose to be.

There were few things in the world that gave him pleasure. Causing fear and distress was one. A good glass of wine, dark as bloodshed, was another. The color black was a third, anything that could be tastefully covered in ice cream was a fourth, and a recent fifth was little Tidbit's company. Children in general—*people* in general—did not interest him as anything more than his cruel mind's playthings, but she . . .

More than interested in him, she was obsessed. And at first, after more years than he cared to count of going entirely unappreciated, that, too, had pleased him. But after her stunt with the car, he was annoyed.

He didn't need her family's trust. He didn't *deserve* her family's trust. However, it would be awfully difficult to get any service in his new favorite restaurant without it, and he was skating on thin ice there as it was. If the girl kept making it look like he was trying to kidnap her . . .

The Black Man will come.

His foot, already hovering over the brake pedal as he eased his car into the driveway, slammed down.

The Black Man will come.

He heard the girl's inner voice, soft and steady as a weary heartbeat. She was near. She was suffering. The Black Man's teeth clenched with fury and dread.

Surging from the car, he rounded the house to the rear, where Tidbit drooped over the back doorstep. She looked up when she heard him speak her name, and her face broke into a smile.

"How in the world . . ." he breathed hoarsely, but didn't bother to complete the question. He could see the answer in her mind as clearly as if he'd been there with her every step of the way.

Remembering the brass-colored numbers against the red of his front door had been easy. Keeping all the letters on the street sign straight took more concentration. But with a little trial and error—poking at the letters on her parents' computer keyboard one by one, sucking intently at her thumb as she compared what she saw on the screen with what she'd seen displayed near the Black Man's house, backspacing and retyping until it was a perfect match—Tidbit plugged the information into the online mapmaker.

By the computer screen's glow, the dominant source of light in the room at that predawn hour, she painstakingly drew a copy of the directions in colored marker; simpler and quieter than trying to unlock the secrets of the printer. Then, map in hand, the girl left the house and set out for the home of the Black Man.

From a driver's perspective, he didn't live far. Just a handful of miles from the family's restaurant, which was only a handful of blocks from Tidbit's starting point. With a car, or even a full-sized bicycle, the trip could be made in a fraction of an hour. On foot—on small feet at the end of four-year-old legs—the travel time was the entirety of the morning.

The Black Man's palms stung as his tightening fists drove his fingernails' edges in deep enough to cut. His hands trembled with the need to do violence, and as the two nearest potential victims were himself and the child, it was he who bore the pain.

He'd said he wouldn't harm her. That was true, too.

Tidbit's sunshine smile clouded over as she watched the thin trickles of red form. "Black Man. You're bleeding."

"And you're hungry," he said. Moving past her, he unlocked the door and stepped through. "Follow me."

He growled aloud at the elation he heard his words cause. *Follow me.* The opposite of *no*. It was working.

What? he thought, his mind turning to look square into hers. *What does she think is working? What is she trying to achieve?*

LEGENDS AND LORE

An exhaustive search, performed while he fed and watered the girl, showed that her thoughts had nothing to tell him. None of what she'd done could be attributed to reason. It wasn't a matter of the mind; the roots went far deeper, into the well of her spirit. So it was there he looked, and what he found astonished him, for the aching hole in her center was a mirror image of his own.

"How strange," he murmured.

"What?" she asked around her apple slices dipped in yogurt.

"Normally," he said, "with people like me, the people like you are older. Women, or men. Not little ones. Your soul is ahead of your age." He glanced again at her precocious mind. "So much of you is.

"Nature abhors a vacuum, you see. As son of the soulless devil, I am half-soulless." He pressed a still-stinging palm to his chest. "Half-empty. Half-alive, waiting for a receptive soul to be drawn in by the void and fill it." He contemplated the girl, so little like her family, yet little like him either. That would be his black pleasure to change. "It seems it will be you."

As the concepts he spoke of were strange to Tidbit, the Black Man opened his mind to her, sharing the words' intent. Her eyes upon him shone with hope. "So, I can stay with you?"

"Not yet," he said, reaching for his phone. "First, I perform a courtesy."

He didn't have to be evil. He would wait to see whether he was driven to it.

Tidbit's father snatched at the phone at the first ring. The hopeful part of him—the part that gave speed to the hand yanking the restaurant's kitchen phone from its base—believed it was the police or one of the numerous family members out combing the neighborhood for their little girl. The pessimistic part of him—the part that held his voice steady when he spoke into the mouthpiece—warned it was probably just another customer wanting to place a seating reservation or catering order. Even if any part of him had expected the chilling voice that entered his ear, it did nothing to stop the shiver that racked his spine.

"Two Spoons. Where is she?"

"In my kitchen," the devil's son answered. "Receiving a much-needed refueling after she walked from your house to mine. Her determination knows no bounds."

The father sagged in relief against the wall. "It's okay," he called out to the rest of the kitchen, and summarized where Tidbit was and why. Returning to his phone conversation, he said, "You'll bring her back at dinner, then?"

"Actually, no," said Two Spoons, "that wasn't the plan. I was thinking you'd let me keep her."

The father frowned. "What, like for a sleepover? I don't think—"

"Permanently."

"Permanently?" the father repeated, began to ask why, realized he didn't care why, and said, "Absolutely not!"

"Let me be clear," said Two Spoons, coolly precise. "I will be keeping the child, with or without your permission. I just assumed you'd prefer to feel like you had a say." His voice turned taunting. "You've had so little say, when it comes to your family's daughter."

The phone squeaked in the father's tightening grasp. "What do you want with her?"

"What I want," the devil's son said, "is to feed her. Open your eyes, pitiful boy. Your family's life is soul food, yet her soul goes hungry. And you can never fill it—none of you can—for the hole you've left inside her spirit has reshaped itself into a counterpart for mine. So I will save her from starvation, and you will not stop me."

It took the grip of one hand over the other to keep the phone from shaking. "We'll give your name to the police. Your actual name. We do know it, you know; it's on the credit card you pay with every night!"

A shade of scorn swirling amid the black, the voice said, "One would think a father in title only would know how little power there is in a name."

On the phone call's other end, the Black Man rang off, turning an arched eyebrow on the girl. "They're choosing to be uncooperative."

Tidbit blinked back at him. "Are we going to a'scond?"

A wicked smile crept across the Black Man's face. "Like an escaped convict."

❧

We never found them.

Oh, we looked. Everyone looked—friends and neighbors, police and other officials, strangers who'd seen the flyers and reports all over the news. People with badges and guns and enormous dogs with well-trained noses stormed the Black Man's house, tearing it and the car he'd left sitting in the driveway apart for clues to his whereabouts. They dug into his accounts, his correspondences, any record he'd left of connections to any person, place, or thing. They had eyes at every border on vigilant watch for the face that so closely resembled the devil's.

Nothing. Not a trace. The last piece of proof that the Black Man existed had been that phone call. After that, he was nothing more than a myth.

Tidbit had been told few fairy tales, and fewer horror stories. I've been raised on a legend that was both.

By the time I was born into the picture, she'd been missing for two years. Her absence rocked her family's life like an earthquake, but didn't stop it altogether. In the cracks and crevices around the calamity, there was still room to feed and grow. Her parents had another child—one they held close as truly their own. Not as a replacement for my sister. Just what they wished she could have been.

I don't belong to the family, but I'm still a part of them. Still have my place at the restaurant, just like all of us do. My sixteenth birthday present was a serving apron, and I've been waiting on tables ever since. I don't think it will ever feel anything other than weird, waiting on table nine.

A young black lady sat there this evening. Not just black in the way my family is black. Her glossy curls were black, her buckled boots were black, her skirt and the matching jacket over her black shirt were black, the glittering jewel in the ring on her marriage finger was black, but black wasn't what she wore, and it wasn't all that she was. It was a part of *who*.

When I asked if she'd like to start out with a drink, maybe some appetizers: "No, thank you," she said, and went straight to dessert. "A bowl of banana pudding, please." I'd retracted my pen with a click, when she added, "With two spoons."

I stared at her. She stared right back with unblinking, solemn eyes, her gaze only breaking away when another body slid into the booth beside her. "Just for tonight," he said smoothly, his black eyes piercing past my own, "why don't we make it three."

His mind's voice murmured into mine, *You've starved for answers long enough.*

I brought them their order. Joined them in the booth. And, three gleaming spoons dancing in and out of the cream-and-yellow dessert, my sister, the Black Man, and I consumed in silence.

About the Authors

Alyson Grauer

Alyson Grauer is a storyteller in multiple mediums, her two primary canvases being the stage and the page. On stage, she is often seen in the Chicago area, primarily at Piccolo Theatre, Plan 9 Burlesque, and the Bristol Renaissance Faire. Her non-fiction work has been published in the "Journal for Perinatal Education" for Lamaze International. Her short fiction can be found in *Tales from the Archives (Volume 2)* for the Ministry of Peculiar Occurrences and in one other anthology from Xchyler Publishing, *Mechanized Masterpieces: A Steampunk Anthology*. Alyson is a proud graduate of Loyola University of Chicago and hails originally from Milwaukee, WI. Her debut novel, *On the Isle of Sound and Wonder*, will be released in November 2014 from Xchyler Publishing.

Sarah Hunter Hyatt

Sarah Hunter Hyatt grew up outside of Salt Lake City, Utah. As a child, she kept notebooks of stories that she would share with her little sisters at bedtime. Now, an adult, her stories have matured but still occupy her thoughts (and notebooks). "Faelad" is Sarah's second short story for Xchyler Publishing, her first being "Stunner" which appeared in *A Dash of Madness: A Thriller Anthology*. Along with writing, being a mom to three wonderful kids, and a wife to a patient husband, she also dabbles in graphic design.

Emma Michaels
Emma Michaels is a cover artist, blogger, and author of the *Society of Feathers* series. Her love of blogging started when she created a book blog in 2009 which gave her the courage to finally submit her own novels to publishers. Emma Michaels' publications now include *Owlet* and *Eyrie* (Tribute Books), *Holiday Magick Anthology* (Spencer Hill Press), and *Cirque d'Obscure Anthology* and *Cogs in Time Anthology* (Crushing Hearts Black Butterfly). To find out more, stop by www.EmmaMichaels.com

R.M. Ridley
R.M. Ridley lives in rural Ontario on a small homestead, raising a menagerie of animals, including a flock of sheep and a swarm of fowl. He has been writing stories, both long and short, for three decades, the themes of which range from the gruesome to the fantastical. As an individual who suffers from severe bipolar disorder, R.M. Ridley is a strong believer in being open about mental health issues because myths should be kept to stories.

Lance Schonberg

In the middle of lecturing one of his children on the importance of following dreams, Lance began to wonder why and when he'd stopped following his. Gathering up a few salvageable shreds of unfinished stories, he began his first novel. He's written several novels and many shorter works in the years since, and has had twenty or so stories see publication. At any given moment Lance is working on a novel and at least one short story—probably more—most of which fall into the broad buckets of Science Fiction or Fantasy.

Lance can be found lurking on his blog at www.lanceschoberg.com, on Twitter as @WritingDad, and sometimes even on his Facebook author page.

Sarah Seeley

Through two wonderful mentored research experiences, Sarah E. Seeley had the opportunity to work with dead sauropods and ancient odonates while acquiring her undergraduate degree in geology from Brigham Young University. She hopes to study more dead things in the future and contribute to scientific discussions about what makes life on Earth so amazing. In the meantime, she explores the bright side of being human by writing dark fiction. Sarah's independently published works include *Maladaptive Bind* and *Blood Oath: An Orc Love Story*. Another short story, "Driveless", appears in "Leading Edge Magazine" Issue #66. You can learn more about Sarah on her writing blog at www.SlithersOfThought.com.

Danielle E. Shipley

Danielle E. Shipley's first novelettes told the everyday misadventures of wacky kids like herself.... Or so she thought. Unbeknownst to them all, half of her characters were actually closeted elves, dwarves, fairies, or some combination thereof. When it all came to light, Danielle did the sensible thing: packed up and moved to Fantasy Land, where daily rent is the low, low price of her heart, soul, blood, sweat, tears, firstborn child, sanity, and words; lots of them. She's also been known to spend short bursts of time in the real-life Chicago area with the parents who home-schooled her and the two little sisters who keep her humble.

You can find her blogging at EverOnWord.wordpress.com.

A.F. Stewart

A steadfast and proud sci-fi and fantasy geek, A.F. Stewart was born and raised in Nova Scotia, Canada and still calls it home. The youngest in a family of seven children, she always had an overly creative mind and an active imagination. She favours the dark and deadly when writing—her genres of choice being dark fantasy and horror—but she has been known to venture into the light on occasion. As an indie author she's published novellas and story collections, with a few side trips into poetry and nonfiction.

She is fond of good books, action movies, sword collecting, geeky things, comic books, and oil painting as a hobby. She has a great interest in history and mythology, often working those themes into her books and stories.

M. K. Wiseman

M. K. Wiseman is a librarian who recently decided that it would be fun to try her hand at the creation of books instead of mere curation. A 'method' writer, she likes to first try out the worlds that she builds. This has, admittedly, led to some strange results. (For example, she once elicited funny looks at her daily coffee shop by adopting a British accent for one day. We're all in trouble once she decides to write a space novel.) In addition to the dozens of stories currently marinating on her hard drive, she maintains two blogs, "Flying the Blue Pigeon" and "Millicent and Rue."

ABOUT XCHYLER PUBLISHING

At The X, we pride ourselves in discovery and promotion of talented authors. Our anthology project produces three books a year in our specific areas of focus: fantasy, Steampunk, and paranormal fiction. Held winter, spring/summer, and autumn, our short-story competitions result in published anthologies from which the authors receive royalties.

Additional themes include: *The Strange Island of . . .* (Steampunk, winter 2015), *Losers Weepers* (paranormal, spring/summer 2015), and *Worldwide Folklore & the Postmodern Man* (fantasy, autumn 2015).

Visit www.xchylerpublishing.com/AnthologySubmissions for more information.

Look for these releases from Xchyler Publishing in 2014 and 2015:

Accidental Apprentice, a young adult fantasy by Anika Arrington, October 2014

On the Isle of Sound and Wonder, a Shakespearean Steampunk retelling by Alyson Grauer, November 2014

Fantasy anthology, January 2015

Mechanized Masterpieces 2: An American Anthology, February 2015

To learn more, visit www.xchylerpublishing.com.

Need more things that go bump in the night? *Try Shades and Shadows: A Paranormal Anthology.* Here's a free sample.

SHADES AND SHADOWS

A PARANORMAL ANTHOLOGY

FOREWORD
Ben Hansen

Why has mankind always been so sated with the here and now? By here and now, I mean our world: our problems, our living flesh and blood, our present time, our tangible experience. Why are we so fascinated with what lies beyond this existence or the rumors of life on other worlds?

I don't mean to suggest that these age-old questions are not some of the most intriguing ever to plague mankind. This is not the matter that puzzles me. However, it seems that religions, faith, and even science have provided enough answers to quench the thirst of our exploration into these subjects.

Yes, the details of life after death may be fuzzy. We don't all agree on what *that* world or worlds may look like, what *we* may look like or consist of once we reach that place. Yet, why is the interjection of legend and folklore into the arena so prevalent? Why do we entertain ourselves so frequently with ghosts, spirits, and other versions of the undead?

Television shows and movies, fictional books and stories, ghost tours and paranormal investigators—fascination for the "supernatural" and death appears consistent, if not ever increasing. Even the most religious of people join ghost hunting groups, and some are found among the most ardent fans of vampire and zombie literature.

Are we trying to confirm our beliefs or just speculating on the details in an entertaining fashion? On one hand, it makes sense. Maybe it's an escape, a distraction from the mundane, an alternative to the unbearable circumstance that life can become.

One the other hand, could such intense curiosity originate from a mystical force which frequently demands our attention, regardless of what we think we may already know? As the host of a television show that investigates paranormal events and evidence, I find myself living this dichotomy nearly every day.

My own interest in the paranormal started really by accident. Like many children, I was taught that ghosts didn't exist. I believed in spirits, yes. But, those were departed relatives who might return in a dream or vision to impart an important message of comfort or warning. Ghosts who haunted a location by appearing at random or who inspired fear with their trickery and antics were simply nonsense in my reality.

It wasn't until I was in college and took a group of friends to a war memorial park for some fun around Halloween that my reality was challenged. We brought a tape recorder. A voice was captured on the tape that wasn't ours.

Fast forward a decade, and I can tell you that during investigations I've seen several instances of objects moving by themselves or flying across the room, audible voices responding to my questions, spheres of bluish light zipping through walls, shadows marching past doorways, and the occasional light touch of fingers on my back and top of my head.

If you would have told me when I was younger that I would have more belief in the supernatural as an adult than as a child, I never would have believed it.

May you enjoy the following collection of ghostly stories which will inspire your imagination. Maybe you will regard them as entertainment, a diversion from the world as you know it. Or maybe one day you will have your own experience that too closely resembles what you once considered fiction. Whichever the case, if you always stay curious, you'll never be bored.

—Ben Hansen
Lead Investigator and host of SyFy's *Fact or Faked: Paranormal Files*

MUSIC MAN
Eric White

I should have died that night, not Michael. For the last twenty years, I have thought of nothing else. This undercurrent drifts below every waking moment, followed by a simple question: why? Such a small word to consume a life.

In the end, it doesn't matter anyway. I must shut my eyes tight and resist the urge to turn towards the tinkling music box song coming from outside the bedroom window.

Most people call midnight the witching hour. My night terrors steal my dreams away at 3:30 in the morning. I learned the reality of nightmares at that hour. Darkness filled my dreams when I glimpsed his shadow through a sliver-crack in covers curled around my head.

It happened at my cousin's house. I was nine. I still see the red digital alarm clock from the nightstand flashing that dreadful hour over and over, like the silent lights of an emergency vehicle washing their dead glow over some fatal accident. 3:30 a.m. marks the last moment I saw my cousin Michael alive.

We always had sleepovers at Michael's house. Just a few years separated a half a dozen boy cousins in our family. Jeff and I came first. Greg, Ross, and my brother, Terry, made stair-steps behind us. A handful of years later, the youngest joined the family—Michael.

He was only five. Five. The years of his life splayed out on one gentle hand. What did evil want with someone so young? Why did our Uncle Jim tell us such a horrible tale? Did he know it was true? Why didn't he warn us, instead of treating it like a ghost story to scare us into going to sleep? And, why didn't the Music Man take me? Questions I'll ask God—if there is one—someday.

All of these memories flood my mind like the overflow at the spillway where we had spent most of the day before that horrible night. The contrast between that glorious sunlight and the wretched hours of darkness to follow slice my mind like a razor on soft skin.

༺༻

Terry and I woke up with the sun that Saturday morning. We wolfed down our Captain Crunch in front of the TV. Terry snorted sugar-soaked milk through his nose as Wile E. Coyote first went kersplat off the cliff and then got squished by a boulder. The big goof was never going to catch the Road Runner.

After breakfast, we hollered hasty goodbyes to our sleeping mother through her open bedroom door and jumped on our bikes to head off to our cousins' house. I can still hear my little brother's cry as I followed him out of the house: "Step on it, Petey!" And with that, we took off.

Dad bought us both Huffys, but getting the hang of riding mine eluded me for some reason. Then, one night he brought home a silver bike with Harley bars and a banana seat, and I shot off on it like a rocket. I flew like the wind. The nickname "White Lightning" stuck with me through high school. I made that silver bike scream.

※

Three light taps on the window behind me break my thoughts apart like shattered glass. "Tap . . . tap . . . tap . . ." The raps of long, bony fingers on the windowpane come soft and slow.

My mind brings up the image of the Billy Goats Gruff and their "trip-trapping" across the bridge to eat the sweet, green grass of the field on the other side. A troll lurked under that bridge. And I know a spectral figure leers in at me through the fogged-up window over my shoulder now.

Just knowing his shadow drapes over my body as I sit with my back to the window makes my blood stop and my stomach curl. I fight back the bile creeping up my throat. And still the tinkling song chimes on, a slow lullaby that leads not to sleep but death.

I shut my eyes tighter and try to remember that wonderful day again. The importance of remembering weighs heavy on my heart. Somehow, I know it is necessary, just as I know the necessity of returning here to this place and hour, on the anniversary of it all. I don't know how I know this, but I do.

The maddening truth lies behind my eyes like a bloody weight. It hangs on a thin, fraying cord, waiting for the certainty of gravity to make its full measure known. That measure will find me tonight. But first, I must remember the sunlight.

❧

We sped off, racing up Locust Street towards Main. A few blocks later, we curled past the Sunoco Station, jumped the curb at the Sesser Post Office, and veered left at the public library. From there, we raced past the park, only planning to stop if we saw Roy or Ryan in the ball field shagging flies. That day they played elsewhere.

We rode on. The green leaves of the huge oak trees cast flickering shadows over the street. We crossed over the culvert we sometimes played in at the base of the hill where our great-grandma once lived. Once we crested the rise, we slalomed down the slope on the other side. The wind whipped around us.

Only the sight of our Grandma Hutson tending the roses in her garden slowed our course on the way to our cousins'. She waved and we stopped, dumping our bikes in the yard. She made us come in and take a break. She filled our bellies with buttered raisin bread and ice-cold Coke, and our hearts with love. She smiled and laughed at all the adventures we shared with her. I can still hear the "Wheee!" she let out when something we said tickled her.

❧

A low chortle mocks the memory of my grandmother's playful laughter. It sounds like a throat full of broken glass. I picture the rows of sharp teeth in his sick, inhuman smile. A thin screech peals on the outside window. The nails of one hand run down the pane to test its merit.

What does he hold in his other hand? my mind asks madly. I know the answer. My stomach sickens once again. I try to block the image already forming in my mind's eye. It takes shape regardless: a rusty wire birdcage. Faded flecks of gold leaf fall from its frame.

And what does he cage there? my mind questions again. But no, I can't let that picture surface. Not yet. I have to remember the day first. I have to remember it all.

I struggle back inside my head, even as the tinkling music box song tries to burrow its dirge deeper into my mind.

❧

Grandma Hutson made us a couple of lunchmeat sandwiches before allowing us to go—pepper loaf and Swiss for me, hard salami and Colby-Jack for Terry, along with two ice-cold Cokes from her fridge. We kissed her goodbye. After a short sprint, we turned to the left at the VFW. A few more blocks and we arrived at our destination.

Jeff and Greg lived next door to Ross on Walnut Street.

They shared a driveway that held a basketball goal. I spent hours there practicing my three-point bank shots and free throws. We skirted into the gravel drive, and ran out into the empty lot to the left of Ross's house. Our cousins were already outside playing kickball. We joined right in.

Ross shot a screaming missile into the neighbor's siding. Loud curses bellowed from inside. We all got on our bikes and high-tailed it out to Sesser Lake where Aunt Judy, Uncle Jim, and Michael Man lived.

❧

We all called him Michael Man from the very beginning. It made us smile, calling the youngest and smallest of us cousins "man." It made him happy when we did.

The humor is long lost to me now. We got to grow up. He never had the chance. We didn't know that then. On that day, we were all innocent, and Michael the most. I can still see his face. Every time I close my eyes, I see my little tow-headed, blue-eyed cousin. God, I miss him so!

❧

Another chortle, thick and gravelly, like a spade to wet earth. The scratch of metal on the glass wrestles the image from me. And did I hear a faint squeak? He softly taps the birdcage against the window.

I almost turn, wanting to scream twenty-plus years of agony and self-loathing at him all at once. But I resist—somehow. I pull the sheet tighter around my head and shoulders like a small child frightened by the shadows of the night. I blame myself. Michael needed his oldest cousin to protect him. I did nothing.

Until now. Tonight, I will stare my misery in the eye. I will stand and face the Music Man. He tore Michael from us while the world slept and dreamed and woke to sunlight that has dimmed for me ever since.

I'm sorry to say that sometimes the boogeyman we see in the closet is all too real. And sometimes he plays his music box in the dark.

Remember.

◈

We climbed the huge hill that led to Michael Man's house. Aunt Judy had a beautiful place on the east side of Sesser Lake. We went there any chance we got.

We started the day by fishing with homemade cane poles off the spillway. Ross and Jeff took their fishing seriously. Each time we fished, they competed to see who could catch the most bluegill before sundown.

The scream of "Cannonball!" broke the silence. Greg jumped in the water in his skivvies. His splash soaked the studious fishermen. They hollered their heads off at him for scaring away the fish.

Terry and I were content to float leaves and empty Styrofoam worm containers down the slanted slope of the spillway to the stream below.

We came across a dinosaur of an alligator gar dead in the brush at the bottom of the spillway. The beast's length spanned four feet! We gaped at its pale flesh. One dark glassy eye gazed up into the trees above.

We yelled for our cousins to come check it out. They all took turns poking at it with sticks. Ross carefully pried open its mouth. We stared at the long dead teeth in its maw with wonder. We dared each other to touch them. No one did. I imagined it somehow coming to life and snapping off our fingers.

After the newness of this discovery wore off, we explored the woods behind Michael Man's house. We pretended to be cowboys and Indians, wilderness explorers, swordsmen, and superheroes. Our imagination had no end.

The sun dipped down across the lake. Aunt Judy hollered for us to come in for supper. It was hard to pull us away from our imaginings.

We ate the best spaghetti dinner I think I had in my entire life that night. I soaked up every drop of sauce with homemade garlic bread. And though we normally avoided vegetables like the plague, we even ate the salad. We had chocolate brownies that melted in our mouths for dessert. Everything tasted delicious.

Afterward, we went out into the front yard and caught lightning bugs in canning jars. We made glow rings out of the unfortunate ones' butts until called to come inside for the night. The day played out in the magnificent, slow speed of summer. Our childhood danced around us like heaven on earth.

If I had only known how dark the night could be.

Tap-tap-tap again on the window, a little more persistent now. He grows impatient with me—or the hour. I look at the digital alarm clock that I brought with me, complete with new batteries, to the old vacant house. No one has lived in it since Michael Man disappeared. The digits burn a steady 2:00 am.

I still have a little time. Enough, maybe, to remember the rest before I come to it. To what I came here for. The cage in his hand scratches a slow arch against the glass. The screech brings welcome pain to my ears.

I relish the dull ache over that sing-song tinkle that has echoed in my mind ever since that horrid night. It has jolted me awake, screaming, almost every night for the last month now. When I look at my bedroom clock, it always reads 3:30 a.m. My witching hour.

More squeaking from inside the cage. Another graveyard snicker.

I force myself back into my memories.

෴

We spent the night hours playing board games: Monopoly, Life, and Clue. We drank the generic cola Aunt Judy bought for our sleepovers like it was champagne, and ate bag after bag of potato chips and popcorn as if there was no tomorrow.

Around ten, we got out an old deck of cards and played rummy and the version of poker that only grade school boys understood. We laughed at the things young boys find hilarious: farts and belches, jokes about each other's moms, the "you should have seen your face when" memories of adventures past.

At midnight, we got out an Ouija board and played around with it. Every one of us accused each other of faking it. "You're making it move! Am not, I swear!" Inside, I think we secretly desired some supernatural cause for its movements. Our youth allowed us to still believe in things adults explained away.

I want to disbelieve, but I know things walk around unseen at the edges of reality. They hide in the corner shadows just out of sight.

I never shared this with anyone—not my brother, nor any of my cousins. After we grew bored of the Ouija board, we went into the living room to both watch and reenact wrestling on the television. I was pinned in my first match, so I went back into the kitchen. The game sat there on the table. Half-empty cola cans and ravaged potato chip bags surrounded it on all sides.

I looked at the board. The eye of the stylus stared back at me. My mouth felt dry. I took a sip of flat soda and washed the taste of fear down with a slow, solitary gulp. The stylus acknowledged my fear. The last question we asked left it pointed at the word "yes" next to the grinning sun in the top left corner.

For some reason, I put out my hand to touch the pointer. I felt a tingling sensation go up my arm. The thing jittered forward on its own, no joke. I jerked my hand back and returned to the living room where my cousins wrestled on the floor.

I joined the fray with a Macho Man elbow smash from the top ropes. Nine-year-olds have the unique ability to forget things that scare them. Some things, anyway.

A long, drawn-out hiss pierces its way through the window and into my spine. I chance a quick glance at the clock. 2:45 a.m. Not much time left for me or for him. He knows it, too. The Music Man's song will soon conclude for this night.

He yearns to take me before his appointed time. He longs to pull back the covers from around my head and pry open my eyelids. I feel the burn of his hell-fire eyes against them, lustful for a brief flutter to seal my doom.

The hour prevents him from acting, somehow. He is bound to the appointment as well. I have kept the arrangement I made last week. I did not call to cancel to avoid paying a fee. Oh, I will pay an awful price tonight. I just hope my soul can afford it.

I curl my fingers into my hair and pull hard. Tears well up in my eyes. I welcome the pain. Anything to get that cursed music out of my head. I can feel the weight behind my eyes dropping lower now, the strands of gore-covered twine snapping off one more thread.

Soon. We both know it will be soon.

We carried on laughing and shouting into the night. Uncle Jim came in to quiet us down. The man towered over us in the archway that divided the living room and kitchen. A coal miner by trade, he spent more time underground. He kept to himself.

We rarely saw him, to be honest, even though we lived at Michael Man's house nearly every weekend.

A memory of my uncle floats into my thoughts. I got a splinter in my finger while playing outside Michael Man's house. I came in looking for Aunt Judy to take care of me. Uncle Jim sat at the kitchen table. He sipped his coffee and eyed me over the brim of the cup.

"What's wrong with your finger?" Uncle Jim said in the deep voice I rarely heard.

"Just a splinter," I whispered.

"Come here," he said.

No one disobeyed that voice. I froze. He motioned me over with one large, calloused finger. I walked up to him.

Uncle Jim pulled a huge hunting knife from a case on his brown, leather belt. The blade looked a foot long to my young eyes. I felt the color drain from my face. My eyes grew wide. A tiny curl of a grin formed at the edge of my uncle's lips.

I closed my eyes as he worked the splinter out from underneath my skin. Later, I learned that he used a needle—the knife his jest. I did not learn this until I grew up. Until then, I thought he carved the splinter from my throbbing finger with the point of the hunting knife he used to skin deer.

Memories upon memories, and the ones I must remember now are black.

Uncle Jim. Yes. He came to calm us down for the night. Just his presence stopped our roughhousing in its tracks. We looked up forever at our larger-than-life uncle, Michael Man's dad.

"You better go to sleep before the Music Man gets you," Uncle Jim said in a low voice, that same hint of a grin on his lips.

"Who's the Music Man?" Ross asked. Ross beamed up at Uncle Jim. His curious smile stretched across his freckled face. Our uncle's stature had the least effect on him.

"Get in your sleeping bags, and I'll tell you. If you won't be too scared," he said. The grin broadened a little.

Calling nine-year-olds scaredy cats was tantamount to questioning one's manhood. We all scurried like moles into our sleeping bags spread out on Michael Man's bedroom floor. Michael Man himself had conked out a few hours before. He lay curled up on his bed like a caterpillar in a cocoon. The many clocks in Aunt Judy's house rang out the hour: 2:00 a.m.

Uncle Jim told us this tale—this awful, terrible tale no one ever needed to hear. But he told it anyway to a bunch of his wide-eyed nephews in his own home. He told it with his little boy asleep on his own bed.

He must have thought it was just a story. Why else would he tell it? Just a ghost story to frighten the wildness out of the boys and get them to sleep. He had to think that, right?

No one answers the questions asked in the dead of night.

"An old man lived across the lake many years ago, long before your great-grandparents lived. He led a simple life. He fixed things for a living: clocks, watches, music boxes, things like that.

"He had a small shop in town. If you wanted something worked on, you brought it to him there. At the end of each day, he loaded his wagon up with what needed repairing. Then, he returned to his shack to work his magic. People say he could fix just about anything.

"He lived in that small shack all alone. He had no wife or children. He did have pets, though. He had pet mice, a half dozen or so, which he kept in a gold birdcage. He brought them wherever he went. He talked to them, caring for them as his children. He fed them tiny bits of crackers or cheese through the bars of the cage.

"He came across a bit peculiar to the townspeople, but people minded their own business back then." Uncle Jim said this with a smirk, showing on his face what he thought of people these days.

"Hey, wouldn't mice just slip through the bars of a birdcage?" Ross questioned.

"The old man loved them. He took good care of them. They had no desire to run away," Uncle Jim countered. No one argued with him, not even Ross. He continued.

"One morning in the middle of winter, the old man left for town and forgot his pet mice. Maybe he feared getting them out in the winter air. Maybe he just forgot. Nobody knows for sure. But when he returned home late that night, he discovered his front door kicked in. Someone had broken into his shack. Vandals had ransacked the place." We barely breathed as he spun his tale.

"But his shock turned to horror when he closed the door and discovered his pet mice. He found their lifeless bodies nailed in a circle on the back of the door in a bloody wreath. The birdcage they called home lay on the floor next to the rickety table and stool where he ate his supper and fed them." Uncle Jim looked at us. He had us all hooked.

"The old man went crazy. He took their skewered bodies off the door and held them in his hands. He pressed them to his cheek, begging them to come back to life. Hours passed as he prayed for them, on his hands and knees. His tears wet the dirty floor. His prayers went unanswered. They were gone.

"The old man kissed each one on top of its furry head. Then, he noticed something on the floor, something that told him who had broken into his home and murdered his mice that winter night."

"What was it?" Jeff asked quietly. He scooted close to me.

"A music box," Uncle Jim answered. "He had fixed it just a week before for a young boy who lived across the lake. The boy carried it around like you guys lug your G.I. Joes.

"The mother of the boy and his three older brothers came by his shack to pick it up, instead of going all the way back to town to get it. Some people in town called those boys mischievous. Some might have even said cruel. The old man thought these boys had broken into the shack and killed his darlings."

"What did the old man do?" Greg asked as he pulled his cover up closer to his chin.

"He lit a lantern. Then, he put on his trench coat and tall, black top hat. Wiping the tears from his eyes, he opened his front door once again. With birdcage in one hand and music box in the other, the old man started walking across the frozen lake. They say you could hear him crying for his mice over the howling January wind. He headed for the home of those wretched boys to confront them."

Uncle Jim stole a glance at the digital clock on the nightstand. "He left for town at 3:30 in the morning."

"What happened to the old man?" I asked. I remember dreading the question even as it fell from my lips.

"The old man never made it to their house that night. No one ever saw him alive again," Uncle Jim said slowly, watching the color fall from our faces.

"But, one by one those boys disappeared. People say the ghost of the old man, the Music Man, came and got them." Each one of us barely breathed.

"They say the Music Man—whether a ghost or a demon—walks these very woods late at night. He holds a rusty birdcage in one crooked hand. A music box plays softly in the other. As the eerie song plays, the Music Man cries out for his pet mice." My little brother buried his head in his blanket.

"They say he looks in the windows of the houses around the lake for them still." Uncle Jim's voice lowered to a whisper. "And if he finds boys like you still awake at 3:30 in the morning—the time people say he died frozen in the woods—and he looks into your eyes, he turns you into mice to be his pets forever."

Uncle Jim paused then and looked around. Four of his nephews sat frozen to the floor in their sleeping bags. One—my brother Terry—had vanished completely beneath his covers. He glanced again at the clock.

"Better go to sleep. It's almost 3:00 a.m. now," he said. "And if you hear his music, keep your eyes shut." He closed the door and went into the living room to watch something raunchy on Showtime before going to bed.

We tried to laugh the story away, not wanting to look childish. But we all went straight to sleep as if someone had hit us on the head with a hammer. Everyone, that is, except me.

I couldn't get the story out of my head. I lay there with my eyes closed, picturing the Music Man walking through the woods, up towards the house. And then I heard it: that hellish tinkling sound of a music box just outside the window where we lay sleeping on Michael Man's floor.

At first, I thought I must be dreaming, or that maybe Uncle Jim was playing a trick on us, like he did me with the hunting knife. Surely that was it. But I didn't dare turn my eyes toward the window. The music grew louder.

I heard three light taps on the window. Tap-tap-tap. *(Again the image of the Billy Goats Gruff floats past my mind's eye. Who's that trip-trapping on my bridge?)* And then, a bump on the windowpane, and the shrill squeaking of mice. I cinched my eyes shut tight. My nine-year-old heart pounded in my chest.

Then, I heard a small voice join in harmony with the music of the night.

"Gotta go pee," Michael Man said sleepily. Through my peek hole in the covers, I saw his little body stir and stumble out of his bed, rubbing his eyes.

I watched him stagger from the bedroom. Then, he was out of sight, shuffling the short hallway to the bathroom. I lay there, frozen. The music grew louder, and something thumped against the side of the house by the window. I wanted to scream, but nothing came out.

The toilet flushed from across the house. Moments later, I heard the swish-swish sound of Michael Man's footed pajamas scooting across the living room carpet.

<hr>

I didn't know what to do! I was nine years old. Nine. A real boogeyman had appeared. Fear glued me to the floor. My screams to warn Michael and the rest of my cousins had died in my throat. And now he had Michael in his cage.

No one expects a child to face a monster. No one blames a child for fearing what lurks in the dark. My troubled heart whispers these words to comfort my aching soul. I listen to these pale excuses, trying to reason the guilt from underneath my blood-stained hands.

It never works. The oldest protects those younger than him. The night guard awake at his post does not fail to sound the alarm. I relive that night over and over, wishing for the courage to do something. Anything. But I did nothing. I lay there in terror and did nothing. Nothing at all.

☙❧

Michael Man walked slowly past me on his way back to bed. He stepped right past me, mere inches from my grasp. My fear paralyzed me. I watched him crawl back into bed, and in horror I heard him speak.

"Music," he spoke to the night. Then his voice caught in his throat, a choking sound. And still I couldn't move.

From the slit hole in my covers, I saw Michael Man frozen like a statue on his bed. His eyes bulged out of his head. A line of drool slid down his pale, white chin. His body jerked as if under some electric current.

On the wall above his head a gruesome shadow formed: a tall, slender figure in a top hat, holding a spider web-shaped shadow at the end of a nightmare arm. The rest of my cousins slept on, oblivious to the horror around them.

And then Michael Man just disappeared, his bed clothes crumpling down like a sheet from a clothesline onto the bed.

I stared in complete disbelief. My arms and legs ignored my brain's commands to run. My screams echoed only in my mind as the tinkling music played on around me.

Michael Man's bed clothes stirred. Above the music, I heard the squeaking—small frantic cries from within his pajamas. The whiskered face of a mouse peeked its head from the armhole of

Michael's pajama top. I bit my lip to keep from screaming out loud then, drawing blood that I barely felt.

Then, I witnessed through my somehow open eyes a horror to top all the others. The gangly arm of the Music Man, bony and white-fleshed, reached *through the closed window as if it was not there.* It opened one skeletal palm, and long, yellowing nails crusted with dirt tipped the fingers.

The mouse that had once been my little cousin crept from the pajamas. It sniffed the air and looked in my direction. It squeaked out one last cry for help before inching into that dead hand.

The arm retreated through the window pane as if through water. I watched his shadow turn away from the window while he put his new pet into the birdcage. That's when I noticed the music box.

A small, rectangular box of rich, red wood rested on the windowsill. Ornate feet set at each corner. An oval key of silver spun slowly towards the window on one side. The key was open in the center—an eye of silver looking out into the dark.

Edging framed the box about an inch from both the top and bottom. Between them lay a glass front. Miniature mechanical figures played out a scene behind the pane. Some meager light in the box shone behind them. I watched their tiny shadows move along the inside lip of the window.

A tall, gangly figure in front danced and twirled with one leg raised perpetually in the air. He wore a top hat and held a small stick up to his face.

The other figures were children who moved back and forth to mimic running. They followed behind the man in front. Tiny things ran in a circle around them all along some grooved line.

At first I struggled to make them out, they were so small. Then it came to me, and I gasped in horror. The tiny objects were mice or rats. An eternal scene from "The Pied Piper" played out behind the music box window.

The shadow turned back towards the window, and I snapped my eyes shut. If this nightmare man knew I was awake, he never let on. He paused for what seemed like an eternity. I felt his stare like crooked fingers wishing to pry my eyes open.

The music box played its funeral song for Michael. Then, the music faded into the night. When I could hear it no more, huge silent tears leaked from behind my closed eyes and down my face. I lay there in anguish, replaying every detail over and ever in my head.

Sometime much later, with the miracles that God reserves for children, I somehow fell asleep.

We woke up to the frantic scene of our aunt and uncle searching desperately for their little boy. Each time they called out his name, the word "guilty" resonated in my head.

I cried openly and loudly. Uncle Jim begged me to tell him if I knew anything that might help find Michael. Between deep sobs, I stammered out how Michael had gotten up to pee sometime in the night, and that I thought I heard something at the window. The unbelievable truth remained my burden, damning me behind my silent lips.

The mad search and rescue in the woods lasted for weeks afterward. Sesser volunteer police and firemen combed the woods day and night. My aunt and uncle were interrogated as prime suspects in their son's disappearance, heaping pain on their grief and weight to my guilt. Divers from the Search and Rescue Team searched the lake to no avail. No body rested at the bottom of that lake. Michael was gone.

Only I knew his demise. I alone carried that burden my entire life. My guilt takes shape as a music box hanging on a thin string. Its weight falls behind my eyes and sinks into my heart. Eventually, they pronounced Michael dead. His death was a tragedy shared by the entire town of Sesser.

I look at the alarm clock again. 3:10 a.m. Almost time. And as it should be, only a few memories remain. I think I have the resolve. I think I can go through with what I have planned. I made the contract. I signed my name to the bargain. My witching hour nears.

I can hear the nails on that skeletal hand scraping the window sill for purchase. He claws in to get me. The Music Man wants his pet. He will have me, but only at the appointed time.

I spent the last month catching live mice after work. Dead ones wouldn't work. I catch them at night in the storage room in the back of my store. I have remained wifeless and childless, and have lived alone my entire life. No one is there to question my behavior.

"Pete's Antiques and Pawn" sits on the edge of town past the fire station. We specialize in the location and restoration of items from the last century. I have restored just about everything: 1960s Shriner cars, 1940s bubble gum dispensers, 1930s and '40s radios, and once a 1954 Wurlitzer jukebox. I had it playing in the front of the store until the customer came from Evansville, Indiana, to pick it up.

My reputation for restoring antique clocks, old French mechanisms, English bell strike mechanisms, and mechanical clock towers brings me customers from across the country. I enjoy working on those clocks with animations—moving figurines.

I once labored on an antique Schneider eight-day chalet-style cuckoo clock. It had a spinning water wheel, dancing figurines, and lumbermen chopping and sawing wood on the full hour. I spent an entire night hand-laying the wooden shingles on that one. It played an enchanting version of "Edelweiss" in crisp music-box tones.

The mice seemed particularly active in the walls while it played.

I tell anyone who asks that my love of these types of clocks stems from spending so much time at my Aunt Judy's. She had a dozen or so lining her living room walls. But, the real reason is much darker. The movements of that music box have consumed my entire life.

I set up shop in an old building—previously an old IGA grocery—and the rodents love it. A field surrounds it on two sides. This allows the field mice easy access through the cracks and crevices of my 1950s grocery-turned-pawn shop.

Maybe they associate the building with a food source? Who knows? They come around, especially at night. I hear them scurrying about when I work late, even with all the lights on.

I thought about just buying them from a pet store, but when I went to do it, I got anxious. I shook so bad, I had to leave the store and walk around the block until I figured it out. It didn't fit the conditions, you see?

So, I put out little tidbits of meat and cheese, and caught them with a large mason jar. I have become quite good at it. I would boast about the skill, if it wasn't for such a grave purpose.

I tied the mice by their tails to a loop of wire and hung them in the window of Michael Man's old bedroom by the latch. I did this in the middle of the day. The room sat silent—stifling hot and dusty from years of being closed up. I didn't dare do it anywhere near night. I needed to build up my resolve to face this nightmare.

I hope my courage lasts.

⋙∘⋘

The deafening music pounds in my ears. The tinkling of broken glass plays like wind chimes on my tombstone. The notes trace my spine like the skeletal thrumming of broken guitar strings.

The Music Man's glowing eyes burn into the back of my skull. His ragged breath lands on my neck, although the window remains closed. The rotting odor of death permeates the room. I choke back my own vomit. The urge to end it prematurely deepens, but I hold on. For you, Michael Man. Only for you.

※

I cut my hand with a hunting knife much like the one Uncle Jim pretended to use on my finger years ago. I made one clean cut, a straight line up the palm and to the tip of my index finger on the left. It hurt like hell.

Relief and pain mingled together with that cut, like opening a festering wound to let the infection out. I let the blood trickle down my finger and watched it drip to the hardwood floor. Drip-drip-drip.

Who's that drip-dripping on my floor?

I bent down on my hands and knees and wrote my contract on the floor in my own blood. I wrote this:

Play your music, Music Man, and walk among the trees.
Sing to your pets, Music Man, as I now leave you these.
An offering, O Music Man, my life within your hand.
Return the child of innocence is but my sole demand.
Play your music, Music Man, and walk among the trees.
Sing to your pet, Music Man, my blood promise I leave.

I looked it over several times. Satisfied, I left the house, making sure to leave well before sunset. Then, I waited for the day. This day. The anniversary of Michael Man's kidnapping.

❧

I steal a glance at the clock. 3:29 a.m. My witching hour arrives at last. I rise up and let the sheet wrapped around me fall to the floor like a ghost. I stand with my back to the window.

His hunger rages like the heat from a furnace on a January night. The whole house shakes with the music from that damned box. I turn to face the window.

The air moves around my throat as the hands of the Music Man reach through the pane of glass. Deep, ragged breaths of corpse rot fill my nostrils. His dead laughter slices like a guillotine through my mind. I open my eyes to my fate, my release, my deliverance from this earth-bound hell of remorse.

I chance a quick glance at the music box on the window sill before I steel my eyes to his ravenous gaze. I watch the silver key spin away from the window. Satisfied, I surrender. The last thin string snaps at the weight of my guilt, and the music box falls, splattering the blood of innocence on the floor boards of my mind.

As my body shrivels and twists into its new form, I see the small towhead of Michael Man standing on his bed. He rubs his eyes with his tiny fists. He has slept for a long time. I think he recognizes his room, even though emptied of all his things, save his bed. Dawn will come. The sun will smile over the horizon.

Michael looks around, confused at his whereabouts. I pray he remembers nothing. "Mommy?" he cries out. I want to comfort him. I squeak my love for him as the Music Man places me in my new home.

I think I hear the faint warble of a police siren before we leave. I sent an anonymous letter to the Sesser police station earlier that week. It warned of the abandonment of a little boy at the old Laur house on the lake. I hope they did not dismiss the letter.

❦

My face peers between the rusty bars of my cage, my whiskers twitching in the dark. A small, white candle sheds its meager light across the ancient shack, its light flickering shadows around the top hat resting on the table. A withered, pale hand holds out a piece of cheese. I take a bite.

The other mice-children and I timidly nibble the treats he gives, and then scurry to the other side of the cage. We huddle together in terror. Soulless eyes stare at us through the tiny door. He closes it.

Then, his wraith-like form silently melts into the shadows at the other side of the shack. We can't see him, but we feel his presence all around us like a suffocating, cold fog.

Time has no meaning. No daylight shines here, only the light of the candle on the table and the death glow of the fireplace. It tricks the eyes, this dead light. Often the objects in the room around the cage—the hat on the table, the mantle over the hearth and the old rocking chair in front of it, the straw broom leaning like a hanged man against its side—take on a queer double exposure, as if they are both real and insubstantial at the same time. It made me sick to look out at the room, at first.

Only the music box stays in sharp focus. It sits centered on the mantle like a worshiped idol, next to an old bottle that flickers in and out of reality. We reside in a ghostly flux, some sort of purgatory between our world and whatever realm where souls reside. But the music box remains constant. It holds the key to our freedom, if I can figure out a way to get to it.

Ross had wondered about the mice squeezing between the bars. Our mice forms can easily slip through the space between the bars, with the smallest never touching them. That isn't the problem.

I tried the first night. As soon as the Music Man disappeared into the darkness, I squeezed my whiskered face between the bars. I barely got my pink nose outside the cage.

An ear-splitting wail emanated from every corner of the shack. The walls shook as if a tornado raged outside. The floor boards bounced up and down. Eerie blue flames flickered like fire glass in the cracks between them. The hearth roared to life with icy flames, casting pale light over the entire room.

The Music Man appeared in front of the cage, howling with rage. His eyes burned like red coals as he shrieked at us. He towered in front of us, growing to a terrible stature from floor to ceiling. His bony claws gripped the cage on both sides as he screamed out his fury, turning the metal white hot at his touch.

I fled to the back of the cage with the others and waited out his anger. It went on forever. After some time, the shack quit trembling and the screaming alarm ended. The Music Man retreated to the dark, but unlike before, his eyes burned like embers in our direction as a warning.

I learned a few things that first night. First, we had to escape through the birdcage door. Second, it only opened by one skeletal hand. The final revelation came as a complete surprise: I could communicate with my mice brethren.

As we cringed at the back of our cell, squeaking in terror, a strange thing occurred. An auditory version of our doubling vision began. I heard the squeaking mice sounds in my ears, but at the same time, I heard the cries and voices of the children echoing in my head. Their voices floated in and out of my mind: sometimes sharp and strong, sometimes muffled, as if spoken underwater. But I heard them, and they me. We could communicate. Through this strange telepathy, we planned our escape.

Every day—if you can call this endless shadow a day—a scene plays out in the shack. The day that started it all repeats like a black and white silent movie on a constant loop.

The door doubles in front of my eyes, remaining shut while a ghostly copy of it bursts inward. Three apparitions of young boys enter the room and begin tearing up the place. They smash an incorporeal copy of the rocking chair against the fireplace while the actual one remains where it always sits.

The tallest boy overturns the table, and we brace ourselves for the fall that never happens. We sit safe in our place while the doppelganger of the birdcage crashes to the floor without a sound. We watch as helpless viewers of this spiritual reenactment of violence and hatred.

Our squeak screams fill the shack. The ghost copies of the mice are crushed in the boy's hateful hands and nailed to the backside of the door in silent torture. When the carnage ends, the boys rush out of the open/shut door. The youngest one drops something: a pale version of the music box.

As I pray for this nightmare movie to end, the ghost door swings open again. The old man stands in the doorway. His eyes change from the joy of being home to the horror of being violated in an instant. I watch the tears well up in his eyes, and in that brief moment, I empathize with his terrible loss. Then, he transforms into the monster he has become.

The house erupts as it did when I tried to escape. Mind-shattering screams of fury bombard the previous silence. Flesh turns to bones. Elderly eyes filled with sorrow melt into glowing orbs of hell-fire. Wisps of shadow waft out from his skeleton in all directions. He hovers in front of the door and lets out a banshee wail at the ghost images of his dead pets.

Suddenly, his anger subsides and he turns towards the table. He floats before the birdcage, opening the door with his withered hand. One by one, he counts us with a bony finger, making sure we live. Then he fades into the shadows once again.

Does he hear our squeaking in that darkness? More importantly, does he hear our thoughts? Prayer affords me no answer.

I move towards a pile of straw I have claimed for my bedding. I scatter the other mice-children as I burrow in. At first I cannot find it, and my heart drops. Then I uncover it a few inches to the right of where I had left it. It lay hidden beneath the hay. The others must have moved it.

I take the shiny silver music box key—the one I hid in my mouth the night I exchanged my life for Michael Man's—between my mouse teeth, and practice turning it with my paws.

I never forgot that horrible night, not one second of it; Michael Man twitching and changing before the specter's ghastly shadow, his skeletal hand piercing the window like water—all of it. But mostly, I remember the music box and its hellish music. I held onto the image of that devilish box all of my life.

As owner of Pete's Antique and Pawn, I did just enough business to keep food on the table. I spent most of my time scouring the Internet for clues. I traveled to antique dealers and estate sales. I talked on the phone to historians and museum directors and anyone else I thought might have the answer. After years of searching, I finally found it.

It took me three days to open the package after it arrived at my shop. The UPS man practically had to shove it into my arms. It sat there on the grey table where I do my life's work: restoration. Restoring antiques was the façade. My true calling lay in restoring Michael's life.

When I finally opened it at arm's length with a razor knife, I screamed until I thought my lungs would burst. All the terror

I held in my entire life surfaced in one terrible cry. But once I stopped, I knew I had one more night of terror to face. There in front of me sat an exact replica of the Music Man's music box.

Even after all my planning, the doubts linger. In that brief glimpse, did I truly see what I thought I saw? What if I am wrong? What if it doesn't work the same way? But I have to try. One last turn of the key in the dark.

I look up at the mantle above the fireplace. There it sits. The music box takes center stage over the hearth, without the key. I figured he would keep it on him somewhere. I had planned for that. I feel my own key in my mouth with my small pink tongue. Will I have enough time?

As the gruesome scene plays itself out silently before us for the hundredth time, I put the plan into action. I gather the mice children together in the center of the cage. We stand in a circle of loss and pain. We take turns biting one another with our sharp, pointed teeth. As the blood flows and mats in our fur, we play dead and wait.

I fear one of us will lose our nerve before the door opens. I speak into the mice-children's minds. I beg them to stay strong and hide their fear as the screaming begins again. The Music Man has come home.

Déjà vu overtakes me as I squint to see his awful shadow mourning over the pale reflections of his dead pets. I return to that night, cringing on the bedroom floor and peeking through my sheets. I think of Michael and close my mouse eyes. It is now or never.

His wails intensify as he sees our bloody, lifeless bodies at the bottom of the cage. I hear the creak of the cage door opening. I scream "Now!" in my head with a loud squeak. We all leap to life and rush out to either freedom or death.

We scatter in every direction as we hit the table and bound to the floor. The Music Man's shrieks pierce my mind as he swipes after us. The table throws itself into the vibrating walls with such invisible force that it shatters into splinters. The birdcage floats up from the wreckage and into one of his dead hands.

I hear the children crying in terror in my head. The floor boards begin to pop to the ceiling one by one, revealing blue fire beneath. The world has gone mad. I rush towards the fireplace. Six feet.

The rocking chair in front of the fireplace bucks madly and then is flung into the fire. The flames explode outward, blinding me for an instant. My mind reels with screams for help as he captures one of the mice-children. I reach the broom and scurry up its length. Four feet.

The Music Man spins around like a demonic whirlwind, capturing another mouse-child in his clawed hand. A piece of the wall flies across and smashes into the other side. I can't help but look. Beyond the hole in the wall, I see darkness so deep that it defies description, a primordial place where light has never shone. I perch myself on the tip of the broom. I jump and the broom flies across the room and embeds itself in the door.

My claws almost lose their purchase on the lip of the mantle. I spin my hind legs frantically, scratching my way on. Two feet. I move the key to the front of my mouth and run.

The Music Man's rage shakes the shack to pieces. His screams tear through every cell in my body. He has captured most of the other mice-children. Their pitiful cries burrow into my skull.

An old bottle stands between me and the music box. I squeeze my body behind it and against the wall. I can see the key hole now. I shove myself through. The bottle teeters. One foot.

I reach the music box and spit out the key into my mouse fingers. It slips from my grasp with my spittle. I pick it back up with my teeth. The bottle topples over the mantle edge, shattering on the floor.

The Music Man spins in my direction. His eyes burn with pure hatred. His mouth gapes open, baring black razor teeth. He lunges across the shack. The flames from the fireplace reach up to lick at my fur. I am not going to make it.

I struggle, slipping the key into its slot. My mouse paws feel useless. I hold the key with my teeth and shove. The key slides in its groove. I turn the key backwards towards the wall, the way I saw it turning when he gave Michael back, the opposite direction of when he was taken.

The Music Man screams as he flies towards me with outstretched claws. I release the key as his hands crush me into the wall. I feel my small bones snap. I hear the tinkling notes of the music box begin to play. The world goes black.

Black. The room is black. I wonder if I am dead. Then I feel pain. My right arm and leg scream in agony. A sharp pain throbs in my side. Broken ribs, I think. I lay prone on the ground. My eyes begin to adjust to the gloom. I hold my hand, my human hand, in front of my face. I start to laugh. Then something touches my arm and I scream.

"Mister, where are we?" a child's voice asks. I turn to see five children huddled together across the room from me. The oldest one approaches me.

I realize we have returned to Michael's old house. Together. Resurrected. Restored.

"Free," I answer, and try to smile. I prop myself on my good arm and sit up.

A little red-haired girl in a Victorian dress walks up beside the older boy. She takes his hand and looks up at his face. He looks back at her.

"Is it really over?" she asks. The boy nods. Tears well up in her green eyes.

Suddenly she runs into my arms and gives me a bear hug. I wince in pain, but laugh anyway. I hug her back as best I can with my good arm.

"Thank you," she says, and I begin to cry.

One by one, the children come over and thank me. For a second, I fear they will disappear like the dust particles filtering through the rose-colored light in the window, returning to their proper times and places.

Minutes pass in silence as the children surround me in a

circle—another wreath. They all have the same look in their eyes; the watery gaze of relief and the wide-eyed stare of "what happens now?" The tears come in buckets. I cry for a long time.

With the children's help, I somehow limp my way back to where I had parked my car along one of the rutted roads that ring Sesser Lake. I had parked it there and walked the rest of the way to Michael's house to give my life up for his. It was a much shorter walk that night. I pile the children in the car and drive slowly back to my store. Thank God I don't own a stick shift.

After I make the children as safe and comfortable as possible, I tell them to wait for me there. Then, I take my cell, hobble outside, and dial 911. The ambulance driver shakes his head in disbelief.

"Running a man down on his morning walk and then driving away? There's a special place for people like that down below."

⁂

I hold my breath as a sharply dressed young social worker walks my little blonde-haired cousin into the conference room. I want to hobble over to him and hug him like there is no tomorrow. I lean on my crutch and wait. She closes the door softly and then kneels down in front of him.

"Michael, here is the man we've been talking about. The one who wants to take care of you. Would you like to meet him now?"

Michael says nothing but nods his head.

"I'll be right outside this door if you need me, okay?"

Again, Michael nods. The social worker stands up and gives me a smile before leaving.

I notice Michael staring at the cast on my arm and leg.

"I had a little accident, but I'm all right now," I tell him, knocking on the plaster leg sleeve with the tip of my crutch.

"Does it hurt?" Michael asks.

"A little, but it was worth it."

He finds that funny, and smiles. "My name's Michael. What's yours?"

"My name is Peter, Michael Man," I answer, and hold out my hand.

Michael gives it a hard shake. "My cousins used to call me that!" he exclaims, his smile now showing in his eyes.

"Is that so?" I reply, feigning surprise. "I would do anything for my cousins."

"Anything?" Michael asks, looking up at me.

"Yes. Anything at all."

And with that, we began to know each other again.

A year later, I find myself sitting on my back deck, watching Michael Man and his "cousins" play in the backyard in much the same way I did with mine growing up. Another circle in this merry-go-round we call life.

Allison brings me a tall glass of lemonade and sets it on the table. She leans over and gives me a kiss. She stands beside me, placing one hand on my shoulder. I reach over and brush my fingers across her bare leg. She may not be thankful for all those long days of social work in high heels, but I am.

I look up at her face and smile.

"I love you, Sugar Bear."

"I love you more," she answers. Her smile brightens my life like the summer sun.

I still don't understand why we had to endure such darkness. I did it for Michael, but maybe there was a bigger reason. It looks that way from where I sit. Life—like childhood—is both precious and brief. I hope our days in the sunlight last a long, long time.

Read more in *Shades and Shadows: A Paranormal Anthology* by Xchyler Publishing.

Xchyler
PUBLISHING